THE
FORESTWIFE
T R I L O G Y

THERESA TOMLINSON

CORGI BOOKS

for CLARE and ROSIE

4 6 8 10 9 7 5 3

A CORGI BOOK: 0552550345

The Forestwife first published in Great Britain by Julia MacRae 1993
(Part I The Green Lady originally published as The Forestwife)
Child of the May first published in Great Britain by Julia MacRae 1998
The Path of the She-Wolf first published by Red Fox 2000
Imprints of Random House Children's Books

This edition published 2003 by Corgi Books

Copyright © Theresa Tomlinson 2003

Papers used by Random House Children's Books are natural, recyclable products made
from wood grown in sustainable forests. The manufacturing processes conform to the
environmental regulations of the country of origin.

Corgi Books are published by Random House Children's Books
61-63 Uxbridge Road, London, W5 5SA,
a division of The Random House Group Ltd,
in Australia by Random House Australia (Pty) Ltd,
20 Alfred Street, Milsons Point, Sydney, NSW 2061, Australia
in New Zealand by Random House New Zealand Ltd,
18 Poland Road, Glenfield, Auckland 10, New Zealand
and in South Africa by Random House (Pty) Ltd,
Endulini, 5a Jubilee Road, Parktown 2193, South Africa

THE RANDOM HOUSE GROUP LIMITED REG. No 954009
www.kidsatrandomhouse.co.uk

A CIP catalogue record for this book
is available from the British Library

Printed and bound by
Cox and Wyman Ltd, Reading, Berkshire

CONTENTS

Part III: *THE PATH OF THE SHE-WOLF*

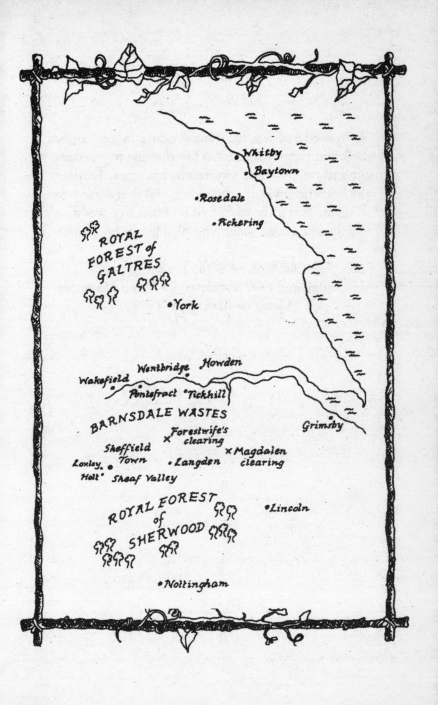

'She waited and waited, leaning against a tree, and as she stood there it seemed to her that the tree became soft and yielding, and lowered its branches. Suddenly the branches twined around her, and they were two arms. When she turned to look the tree was a handsome young man, who held her in his arms.'

From 'The Old Woman in the Forest', Grimms' Tales for Young and Old, translated by Ralph Manheim (Victor Gollancz Ltd. 1979)

Part I
THE GREEN LADY

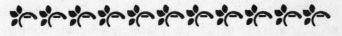

I

Ecclesall Woods

Mary stood before her uncle's chair on the raised dais at the end of the great hall. Her hands shook as she twisted the heavy garnet ring that she wore on her forefinger. It had belonged to her poor disgraced mother, Eleanor de Holt. It was all that Mary had left of her, and she wore it constantly, even though it was too big to stay in place on any of her other fingers. She worked it round and round frantically until she saw that her uncle was watching, irritated by the nervous, childish action.

The lord of Holt Manor tapped his fingers on the carved wooden armrests.

'Heaven knows, child, I have done my best by thee. I pray you'll not disgrace me.'

'But Uncle . . .' she whispered her protest.

'What? Speak up, child. Speak clear.'

Her uncle bent forward, frowning with the impatience that he clearly felt.

'Uncle, he is so . . . old.'

'No good fussing and fretting about that. 'Tis what a

girl child's reared for, marriage and breeding. Gerard de Broat is a grand match for a fatherless wench like thee. For my poor dead sister's sake tha must curb thy temper and accept my decision. I've more to worry about than maiden's fears, what with King Richard demanding high taxes for his crusade, and now Count John is wanting men and horses to strengthen his garrison at Tickhill Castle. I swear he's arming it against his brother's return, and here am I expected to deal out money to both these warring Plantagenets.'

Mary clenched her fists and her cheeks grew red with the helpless rage that rose in her.

Owen de Holt's patience was at an end. 'You are fifteen years old, girl. Many a maid is married at twelve. Go speak to thy aunt. 'Tis her job to calm thy fears, not mine.'

He rose from his chair, and strode out of the hall, calling for his groom.

It was early in the afternoon when Mary let herself out through the back porchway into the kitchen gardens. She carried her warmest cloak, though the month was June and the sun was hot on her head and cheeks. She pressed her elbow against her side to check that the loaf of bread was still there, covered by the cloak.

Despite the desperation that she felt, there came a twinge of excitement. She was doing her best to think clearly and act wisely. She had the fur-lined cloak for sleeping and bread so she'd not starve. Her stomach churned with fear, but she made herself walk slowly through the garden. She must give the appearance of a sad but resigned young woman, taking a stroll in the fresh air. There must be no outward sign of the rage that tightened her throat, threatening to choke her. She reached the end of the rows of beans and peas, close to the small lydgate, that led to wooded pasture land beyond.

Owen de Holt and his groom suddenly clattered out on horseback from the stable yard, and Mary froze. She bent down to the soil, as though examining the swelling pods with sudden interest. But she needn't have worried, her uncle glanced in her direction, shrugged his shoulders and trotted out through the main gateway, heading towards Sheffield Town.

Mary breathed her relief. She was close to the gate now. All she had to do was go through it. She lifted the iron sneck that held it, hesitating. The garden was quiet, her aunt, Dame Marjorie, would be dozing in her solar.

Still she paused. What of Agnes? How could she go without Agnes? Without even saying goodbye! She'd been in such a state that she hadn't stopped to think.

Agnes had come to Holt Manor to nurse Mary as a baby. Eleanor de Holt had died, far away in a convent, giving birth to her daughter. Owen de Holt told Mary how he had buried his sister with many a tear of shame, then brought her tiny child back to Holt Manor, to rear her as his own. He'd called for a wet nurse for the babe, and it was Agnes who'd come asking for the job. She'd been like a mother to Mary ever since.

A door opened and a chorus of joyful gruntings

3

greeted the kitchen maid as she scraped the vegetable peelings into the pig sty. If Mary went back now to speak to Agnes, this quiet moment would be gone. There might never be another chance so good. If she told Agnes she was running away, she'd only fret and grumble, and she'd probably insist on coming too. How would Agnes fare with her rheumaticky joints? Her nurse was not so very old, but lately she'd grown vague and forgetful. She'd even taken to wandering off for hours at a time, returning late and seeming puzzled at the darkness. No, taking Agnes could only bring them both to grief, and it would be kinder and safer not to tell her at all. If she knew nothing, she could say nothing.

Mary lifted the sneck of the gate and looked out through the orchard, and down the sloping wooden hillside that gave Holt Manor its name. The main track ran beside the river Sheaf, up past the cornmill, and on towards Beauchief Abbey. She daren't go that way, the track was always busy with pack horses and travellers; some who'd likely know her as Owen de Holt's niece.

Maud and Harry who worked the mill had known her since she was a baby. They'd help her now, she knew that, but her uncle could see them turned out of the mill should they be found to give her aid. It wouldn't be fair to go to them.

She'd have to go the other way, and take the small path that led to the wooded land to the south, belonging to Ecclesall manor. There was more hope of passing unseen in amongst the trees than on the open pathway.

Mary reminded herself of the reason for her flight and

shuddered – marriage to an elderly widower, who had rotten black stumps of teeth, and smelt of sour ale and saddle grease.

She slipped through the gate and ran.

Once she had started, she dared not stop. She dared not even look back over her shoulder, but hurtled down the smooth-trodden pathway, keeping to the trees and bushes wherever it was possible. Her soft leather slippers made no sound on the warm springy earth. There was an open patch of land just before the opening in the palings, the dividing line that marked the edge of her uncle's demesne. Mary crossed it with growing speed and panic, her cloak flapping heavily and awkwardly at her side.

Her footsteps slowed once she'd reached the shelter of the trees. This was Ralph de Ecclesall's land, and she was by no means safe on it. She'd have done better not to run down the hillside, a dignified walk would have been much less suspicious, but she'd done it now and no help could come from regrets. She made herself hurry along the path that they took when she came buying charcoal with Agnes.

Ecclesall Woods were not frightening like the thick, dark forests and wild wastes. They were networked with paths, and peopled with workers. Charcoal-burners lived in hovels that they raised in the clearings, close to where they fired their bell-shaped wood stacks. Families of coal-diggers, their skin grey with the dust, worked in small groups wherever the coal seams touched the surface. The clang and clatter of iron-workers rang through the trees. They made their bloom hearths close to the streams that they dammed and used as cooling ponds.

Mary hurried on, but whenever she heard voices or the clank and thud of folk at work she turned away and went in the opposite direction. Soon she'd strayed far from the main pathway. These folk who gleaned their living from the woods owed tithes and labour to the Ecclesall Manor. Yet they had a reputation for being awkward and independent. Mary could not know if they would betray her, should they glimpse her flight. They lived on the edge of starvation, she knew that well enough, and no doubt they'd earn themselves a rich gift from Owen de Holt for the return of his ungrateful niece. She managed to avoid meeting anyone face to face, but the feeling grew in her, that maybe she was being followed . . . the rustle of leaves, the crack of a twig.

Once she jumped and trembled at a sudden shaking of the undergrowth, but it was only one of the small pigs that roamed free in the woods. It ran away squealing and snorting in the grass, to root for acorns and beech-mast. They were tough scrawny things, those pigs, not like the fine fattened swine of Holt Manor, and they were harmless enough.

The going became more difficult, her feet ached, and her fine-stitched slippers did nothing to protect her from the fallen holly leaves or the sharp stones that rutted the paths. She was hot and tired and worried that she was stumbling around in circles, when she came upon the pool.

A stream tumbled white foaming water into a deep pool, surrounded by ferns, mosses and long grass. This was no iron-workers' dam, but clean fresh water. Just the sight of it made her realise how thirsty she was, and she threw herself down at the edge, cupping her hands to drink.

Her thirst satisfied, she spread her cloak and sat down, bathing her aching feet in the cool water. A slow feeling of contentment took the place of fear. The sun found its way through green willow branches, and warmed her head and hands. She tore at the loaf of bread and ate with relish. The long meals at her uncle's board had never tasted as good as this. Here she was, alone in the woods, but safe and warm, and dabbling her feet in a pool surrounded by plants, as pretty as any lady's bower.

What if she was lost? Didn't she want to be lost, lost from her uncle and the strict protection of Holt Manor? Though he and Dame Marjorie had never had children, Mary doubted that she'd really been raised as their own. She'd not been beaten, and she'd lived a comfortable life with good and dainty food, and fine clothes. Yet always there'd been the burden of disgrace. Her uncle never failed to remind her: she was baseborn. She must live in gratefulness and shame.

Mary sighed happily, and smiled. She was free of that for ever. She would protect herself now. She would be the lady of the woods.

Agnes had told her many stories when she was small. Her favourite story had been the tale of the green lady, the beautiful spirit of the woods, who walked through the forest, blessing the trees with fruitfulness, hand in hand with the green man.

Mary realised with a jolt that the sun had dropped to the horizon. She had no idea how long she'd been sitting dreaming and dabbling her feet in the pool. How could she have sat there so, letting her mind drift away with woodsprites and fairies? Her uncle or aunt might be discovering just now that their niece had vanished. Before long the light would fade. She must travel much further, and find somewhere safe to pass the night.

She pulled her feet up quickly, spraying water over her cloak. As she shifted, she caught a similar movement from the corner of her eye. Mary turned sharply towards the quivering branches. A face stared back at her, half-hidden by a leafy bush.

Mary jumped to her feet, snatching up her cloak.

'Who is it? Who is it that spies on me so?'

A young girl withdrew from the bush, pulling herself awkwardly to her feet. She couldn't have been older than Mary herself, and she looked terrified.

'I'm sorry, er . . . m'lady. I never meant you no harm.'

Mary hesitated. It was true that the girl looked harmless enough, but there'd be nothing to stop her telling what she'd seen. The girl backed away, frightened by Mary's fierce frown.

'Stop!' Mary bellowed. Then more gently, 'Stop for a moment, and let me think clear.'

The girl's cheeks were smeared with red strawberry juice, and she clutched a wicker basket, half-filled with the tiny woodland fruits. She was thin and pale, but Mary caught her breath as she saw and understood . . . the worn gown was pulled tight across the girl's stomach.

'With child?' she murmured.

'Aye,' she flinched as she answered.

Mary clicked her tongue, exasperated by the situation. Why did she have to be caught out by this pathetic creature? The sight of the swollen belly on the childlike frame brought echoes of her own fears. She stared down at the half-eaten loaf that had fallen to the grass when she got to her feet. She picked it up and handed it to the girl.

'Thanks,' she muttered, and fell to tearing at the bread with her teeth. Mary sighed, and wrapped her cloak around her shoulders.

The girl suddenly paused in her eating, looking down at the small basket of wild strawberries. She held them out, offering them to Mary.

'For thee. Aye . . . for thee.'

Mary tried to keep back the condescending smile that touched her lips. As if she, Mary de Holt, should have need of such a thing. Still, the gesture was kindly meant, and the quiet dignity with which the girl presented her gift hinted at friendship between equals, even loyalty. Mary remembered that she had great need of both those things. She took the basket and smiled her thanks.

'Do you know who I am?'

'Aye. I think I do.'

'Should Owen de Holt come looking for me, I pray you'll not tell.'

The girl's eyes opened wide.

'I will swear that I have never seen thee.'

'Will you tell me where this pathway leads?'

The girl didn't answer straight away, but continued to stare, then she walked slowly towards the earth-trodden track and Mary followed. At last she pointed ahead, and spoke.

'If thee follows this path, 'twill lead thee to a place where four ways meet. The uphill path will take thee to Ecclesall Manor. Straight on will lead to the bridge on the Totley brook. The downhill slope shall take thee towards the Abbey of Beauchief.'

Mary thanked her with growing respect. She wished she possessed such knowledge of the land.

'I go back to my home now,' said the girl. 'I shall never know which way tha went.'

She set off back along the path towards Holt Manor without ever glancing back.

Mary stared after her for a moment, then turned and hurried on to the meeting of the paths.

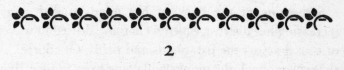

2

St Quentin's Well

Mary did not hesitate for long at the crossing. There would be no help at Ecclesall Manor and beyond the village of Totley lay the dangerous edges of Barnsdale Wastes, that vast and frightening wilderness that stretched for miles and miles. She took the path that led to Beauchief Abbey with the idea in her mind that a church might offer sanctuary.

The light was fading fast as the great soaring walls of the newly built abbey came into sight. Mary pulled up the fur-lined hood and gathered her cloak tightly around her. The summer evening had turned chill and she felt urgent need of a safe, warm place to sleep.

She crossed the wooden bridge over the River Sheaf and climbed the gentle slope towards the abbey, keeping close to the trees. The nearer she got, the more her doubts grew. How would they receive her, those austere white canons? She'd heard of folk accused of crime claiming the right to sanctuary, but they'd been men. Would the same apply to her?

Something at the back of her mind nagged away, increasing her distrust. Solemn chanting drifted in waves of sound across the fish ponds and fields. Of course . . . she remembered, the monks had come from France, they chanted in Latin and spoke the Norman tongue.

Mary moved along the edges of the wooded land, gratefully eating the tiny, sweet strawberries, watching the cloister doors. The candle glow in the stained-glass windows promised warmth and safety. There'd be guest rooms, a warm fire and good plain food. Her stomach told her that a handful of strawberries was not enough.

A fine carved statue stood in a niche beside the door. A Virgin and child, another Mary, one hand raised in blessing. Surely there was safety here. She took a step towards it, then she stopped, trembling. The carved stone face was blank. No blessing there at all – the hand was raised in warning. Stop! Go back! Run away!

With a fresh sense of fright, Mary gathered up her skirts and shrank backwards amongst the trees. Before she'd had a chance to move far into the shadows, the clattering of two horsemen made her turn in alarm. They rode at great speed, spurring their horses and shouting to each other, but drew to a sharp halt before the abbey door.

'Open up! Open up! A message from Owen de Holt.'

Mary knew the voices. They were her uncle's grooms. She did not stay to see how they fared with the canons, but turned and stumbled on through the surrounding woodland.

She ran wildly now, not thinking of the way, but going where the trees grew thickest. She did not stop, even though her legs banged against tree stumps and scraped on rocks. Fast uphill she went, borne onwards by the energy of fear. It was only as the trees grew taller and more spaced that she slowed her steps. She must stop at last, for her legs were growing numb. She staggered on, stiff-limbed, her head drooping in despair. What had she done? She could not go back, but dare she go on? She was heading towards the place she'd feared most to go. The wilderness of Barnsdale, beyond the reaches of the law.

There were others who'd been this way, that was well known. They took refuge here, those who'd killed, or robbed, or maimed. Why, even Agnes's nephew was one of them. Perhaps he hid here still.

Mary's knees gave way and she fell to the ground. Huge great sobs shook her body. She howled like a baby in the quiet woods, careless of the sounds, or of who might hear. At last, calm came from sheer exhaustion. As her sobs grew hushed and stillness returned, she began to hear other sounds . . . delicate sounds. The rustling of small bodies in the ferns, the screech of an owl, a faint trickle of water. Agnes had told her of St Quentin's Well and promised to take her there. Fresh, clean water that bubbled from the rocks. Folk made special journeys there. It promised a safer place in this fearful wilderness.

Mary pulled herself to her feet, and followed the gurgle and murmur of the stream. A bright moon came out from behind the thick clouds, and the chill wind dropped. She found the spring, sparkling and gleaming as it ran from the rocks. It was cold and reviving as she cupped her hands to drink. There in the moonlight was a fairyland of glittering water and fern. Her spirits rose. Perhaps there was still hope for her. She crawled beneath the thick drooping branches of a yew tree close to the water's source and fell asleep.

The familiar warbling sound of a low-pitched voice humming and singing woke Mary from her sleep. She smiled for a moment, thinking that she must have had a strange dream, but then her eyes flew open and she flinched, blinded by the beams of bright sunlight that picked their way through the branches of the yew tree.

Dark green patterns and sharp mottled light bobbed above her, and a soft, bitty mass of dried yew needles covered the palms of her hands. It was no dream – she lay beneath a tall tree, but still there was the singing. Agnes's deep croaky voice had woken her every morning since she was a child and now here it was, beside St Quentin's Well.

Mary sat up, scraping her head on the lowest sheltering branches. She rubbed her eyes to see clearer, for she could scarcely believe what she saw, and what she smelled made her dribble with hunger.

Agnes crouched before a fire of smoking beechwood, cooking big fat mushrooms threaded carefully onto sticks.

'Agnes!'

Mary crawled towards her bleary-eyed, her braided hair knotted up in tufts and spiked with yew needles and pink yew flowers.

'What!' cried Agnes. 'Is this a forest fairy, or a fierce wicked sprite?'

Mary smiled, and burst into tears.

'What a greeting,' said Agnes, pretending to grumble, 'and here's me tramping up hill and down dale to find thee, with a great bag of food and victuals on my back.'

Then, suddenly, the joy that had burst on Mary was gone in a flash of doubt. 'I'll not go back, whatever you say. I'd rather die.'

Agnes pulled a sour face and wagged her finger. 'Whatever art thou thinking, lass? Don't you know your old nurse better than that? I'd rather die than take thee back. Do you think I fed thee as a babe, and taught thee all I know, to provide a breeding sow for a rich old hog?'

Mary gasped. 'You think I've done right then?'

Agnes sighed, and flexed her stiff fingers.

'I was making my own plans. Perhaps I should have told thee. I never guessed tha'd go galloping off like a furious colt at the first sign of a bridle. Well now, let us eat these fine mushrooms that I've discovered. I shall be cursing thee if tha sits there arguing and lets them burn.'

Mary watched hungrily as Agnes drew a fresh-baked loaf from a great linen bundle and offered her golden singed mushrooms and a hunk of bread. She ate as though she'd never seen food before. It was only when she'd finished the last mushroom and drunk from St

Quentin's Well that she could manage to get out more of the questions that she needed to ask.

'But how did you find me, Agnes?'

'Huh. Tha's left a trail like a thousand snails. No, don't go alarming. Not a trail that Owen de Holt could follow, but clear enough to me and those that have eyes to see.'

'But . . . who else?'

'Oh . . . while your uncle went a-banging and a-bellowing round the manor, and a-calling out his grooms and horses, the kitchen maid set me on thy track. They think you're a silly spoilt brat – oh 'tis true, they do. No need to pull that face – but they've no love for their master and they wish you no harm. Then the charcoal-burner gave me the nod, though I had terrible trouble with that daft daughter of his. Not a word could I get from her.'

'Ah, that girl.'

'She'd tell me naught, though I could see she knew. So I puzzled a bit where the paths all meet, but I know my girl and I remembered how you wished to visit St Quentin's Well. So here we both are, but we cannot stay. We must be on our way.'

'Where?' begged Mary. ''Tis all very well to say go, but who will give us help and shelter? Everyone fears my uncle.'

'Aye, here they do, sure enough, but I know where to go, my lovey. Just trust me and follow me, and though we've a long way to go, we shall be safe by nightfall. Now, tha might help to share my burden, for I didn't leave in such a rush and thought well what might be needed.'

Mary opened her mouth to tell how she'd been careful to bring her cloak, but she closed it again and said nothing. Agnes rooted in the bundle and pulled out a strong pair of riding boots.

'I took these from the youngest groom. I guessed they'd fit thee well enough. He went tearing round in circles in his bare feet, cursing and swearing when the master ordered him out to search.'

Mary looked down at her slippers, they were in shreds. Torn ribbons of the soft leather trailed from her feet. She took the boots gladly and pulled them on. She'd never worn anything so heavy on her feet before and they felt strange and clumsy, but her toes grew warm.

A dark red kerchief, the colour of fallen leaves, came next from the bundle.

'Tie this around your head, like me. Aye, do it yourself . . . you must learn, for I've more to do now than act as a lady's maid.'

Mary flinched at the sharpness, but she did as she was told with a flush of shame. None of these things had entered her head.

'Kilt up thy gown, aye, that's right, like the maid that carries the slops. Now tha's more fit to go striding through the woods. Pack away that fine purple cloak, we shall have to change that. I've another good wool cloak in here to make up a bundle for thee. See what I've thought to bring. Two sharp knives, a bundle of the strongest twine, needles, best tallow candles and a tinderbox and flint.'

'All right, all right,' Mary gathered the goods into her bundle. 'Tha's wonderful, Agnes,' she said, a touch sour. 'I'd be lost without thee.'

They filled two flagons with the cool clear water from St Quentin's Well, and set off down the hillside.

The morning was bright and sunny. The woodland tracks were smooth and dry underfoot and edged with thigh-high grasses and ferns. Streams of running water criss-crossed the woods. Mary's spirits soared. The presence of Agnes brought a powerful feeling of safety and hope. The trees themselves seemed to echo her mood, for the far hillside made a gorgeous, abundant patchwork of lush green leaves at their fullest strength, with jewelled shades of emerald, olive and beryl. She'd never realised before how stale and dank was the air in Holt Manor from the rarely-changed rushes strewn on the floors. Here in the wilderness the air was clean and smelt of sap.

Agnes went before her, a dark-green felt hat pulled firmly down over her kerchief, her skirt kilted high, easing the great strides that she took. From behind, you could not tell whether Agnes was man or woman. Mary smiled at the thought. Perhaps that was just as well.

They passed through the woods of Chancet, and headed east towards Leeshall and Buck Wood, still keeping to the woodland paths. A few folk passed them with a brief nod, uninterested in the two women carrying rough bundles, too weary and harassed with their own concerns.

An old man approached with a mule piled high with coppiced wood. Agnes touched her hat to him and he nodded, but as he passed Mary he suddenly gave a growl, and snatched up her wrist. It was the silver and garnet ring on her forefinger that had caught his eye. Mary yanked hard.

'No-o-o . . .' she screamed.

He hung on tight, his face grown suddenly sly. He reached up, letting his mule go loose, and thrust back her kerchief, revealing her carefully braided hair.

Suddenly a flash of silver-grey gleamed between them. Agnes held her sharp meat knife to his throat.

The man laughed, but the laugh died in his throat as he saw the look on Agnes's face.

'Leave her be!' She spat it out.

Her face and her voice told him she'd use that knife. He threw off Mary's arm.

'Get on thy way,' Agnes snarled.

'I go . . . I go.'

His mule had set off without him, ambling along the path in search of freedom. Agnes kept the knife in her hand while she watched him go running after his beast.

'That damned ring of yours,' she muttered. 'Better to have thrown it into the stream.'

Mary pulled it from her shaking fingers. ''Tis my mother's ring, and I'll not be parted from it.'

'At least fasten it round tha neck with twine then.'

Mary, all flustered and upset, pulled out the twine,

and fixed the ring around her neck beneath her gown.

When at last they'd seen the man disappear into the far distance, Agnes sheathed her knife.

'Now we must go still faster. Get a move on, tha silly wench.'

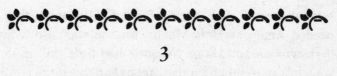

3

The Forestwife

Mary tried walking faster to keep up with Agnes, but she found it hard going. Her legs ached, and the soft skin on her feet was blistered with the rubbing of the boots. Still, she knew she'd never have got this far without them, for she was not used to walking beyond her uncle's demesne.

Agnes was angry with her, that was clear; the anger seethed in every stride she took and she'd give nothing but short replies. Mary followed her with growing uncertainty. Agnes's quick action with the meat knife had saved them from being robbed, no doubt of it, but the speed and fierceness with which she'd moved had shocked Mary. This was a strange, alarming woman, unlike her fussy old nurse, and she followed her warily.

Agnes had always been different from the other servants, something of a law unto herself. She'd insisted on tramping to Loxley valley every few months to visit her brother and nephew. Somehow Owen de Holt and Dame Marjorie had accepted it, though any other servant would have been whipped. Of course they'd needed Agnes at Holt Manor, for she was also a fine herbswoman and Dame Marjorie had little skill in that way. It was well known that Agnes had saved the reeve's life, when he was set upon and beaten about the head by robbers, and it was Agnes's special salves and potions that eased the aches and pains of all at the Manor House. For the first time it occurred to Mary that Agnes might be missed at Holt just as much, if not more, than her.

She broke away from her thoughts and saw with dismay that they seemed to be heading towards the thickest tangle of the wilderness. The grasses were tall and entwined with gnarled bushes and trees, and in the distance clumps of luxuriant green rushes showed the presence of marshland, and yet the path that they followed seemed firm and well trodden.

The midday sun was high in the sky when Mary saw ahead of them an ancient stone well. Agnes, who was a good way ahead, stooped to drink the water, then brought out the last of the bread from her baggage. She broke it in two, and held half of it out to Mary, who hobbled sore-footed towards the stopping place.

'And what well is this?' Mary asked, dreading the answer.

'Why, this is the Old Wife's Well, what else?'

Mary crumpled down beside the ancient carved stone trough, her baggage falling at her feet. 'Why have you brought me to this place? They say that those who pass this well are following the secret path. They go to seek the Forestwife deep in Barnsdale Forest.'

'Aye, they do say that, don't they.'

Mary rose to her feet again, angry now.

'How dare you bring me here? This is a place of evil. All decent folk who dwell in Sheaf Valley live in fear of the Forestwife. She's a witch of the worst kind. She blights the crops with curses and spells, and nobody is safe from her.'

Agnes chewed her bread, unperturbed.

''Tis true enough that they speak of her with fear, though I believe there's only one at Holt Manor who's ever set eyes on her. Look, my girl, Barnsdale Forest is the last place they'd wish to come looking for us, and so . . . 'tis straight to the Forestwife that we must go.'

'You must be mad.'

Agnes laughed, and struggled to her feet, picking up her bundle. 'Well, that is where I go. Thee must please theesen.'

'No . . . wait. Agnes! Come back!'

But Agnes strode away, following the narrower path that headed straight into the deepest darks of the dreaded forest that stretched for many miles at the heart of the wilderness.

Even though the great Roman road cut through Barnsdale Forest, everyone feared these woods and the wild bands of cut-throats who swooped out from its evil shade to prey on helpless travellers. Mary's uncle would not pass through that part of the country unless his journey was absolutely necessary, and only then if his guards were trebled and armed to the teeth.

After a moment or two of sheer, dithering panic, Mary picked up her bundle and followed Agnes, trembling with rage and fear. What else could she do? She could never find her way back by herself and Agnes, marching ahead without a backward glance, knew it.

Mary dared not let Agnes out of her sight, though she held back, refusing to walk companionably alongside her nurse. The afternoon light began to fade. Mary had passed so many trees that they merged into a scratchy green blur. Her shoulders were sore where the bundle rubbed, and her arms ached with the carrying. Every drop of that morning's joy of the woods had drained away. The forest was a cold, damp, frightening place. The tall thick trees blocked out the sun and made the barren ground beneath them smell of mould and death. Agnes, her saviour, had turned bitter and sharp.

Yes . . . she'd grown sharp. Mary brought herself to a sudden stop at the thought. Where had the vague, forgetful Agnes gone?

She forced herself to move onwards while she tried to puzzle it out. If she lost sight of Agnes now, she'd be lost indeed.

Agnes had not been her old busy efficient self for a while. Well, not at the manor anyway. Mary frowned, trying to remember.

It must have been a year since the terrible news was brought to Holt from Loxley. Agnes's brother had been found dead, out in the fields next to his plough. Robert had vanished, and he'd been named as his father's murderer. No wonder it was more than Agnes could bear.

She started to lose things and forget what she was doing. Sometimes she'd stop in the middle of speaking, as though her mind was on something else. She'd even go wandering off for a whole day at a time and come back saying nothing, not even seeming to know that she'd been gone.

Like so many odd things about Agnes, her wanderings had been tolerated. The servants whispered that the tragedy had turned her mind. No aunt could have been fonder of her nephew, that was clear for all to see, but then no sister could have been fonder of her brother, either.

Mary looked ahead through the leafy gloom, towards the small figure with its burden. Was it that same vicious Robert that she searched for now? Agnes had always claimed that Robert was innocent, but then, she would.

Now the older woman stopped where two paths met. She hesitated for a moment, but then turned decisively to the right. It was almost, Mary thought . . . almost as if she knew the paths. As if she'd been this way before.

At last Mary's anger gave way to cold and worry. She could not stop her shoulders from shivering and her teeth from chattering. They had covered miles of forest land, and there was no possible way back. She gritted her teeth against the rubbing of her feet and strode ahead to catch up. A bad-tempered friend who led you to murderers and witches still seemed better than no friend at all in this dark and frightening place. Soon she walked just behind Agnes as before.

They were still moving as it grew dark; such a thick, black, moonless darkness as Mary had never known. She walked into branches and rocks and groaned with pain and exhaustion. At last Agnes stopped and took her arm. She spoke kindly again.

'Not far now, my honey. Not far. 'Tis a hard long way to walk, I know, but I promise thee we shall be safe.'

'By nightfall you promised.'

'I know, my lovey. I misremembered how far.'

They stumbled on, though the path was invisible. But now they walked close, arms linked, each depending on the other not to fall. At last the trees grew thin and moonlight struggled through the branches. They came to a great oak tree that stood at the entrance to a clearing edged with yew trees. The moon showed just enough for them to see a small hut. There was no light within, but a tremendous din. Chickens clucking, goats bleating, and a great squawking and fluttering of wings.

Agnes hurried forward.

'What's to do? Where is she?'

Before the oak tree stood an ancient carved stone. A smaller, wedge-shaped stone was set into the curved top. It pointed towards the cottage door. Agnes touched the stone.

'She should be here.'

Mary dropped her baggage, and looked around. Three cats ran amok amongst the chickens and goats, jumping and nipping at the poor beasts' udders. Even in the dim light, it was clear that they desperately needed milking. It was not what she'd expected, this noisy domestic chaos.

Agnes pushed open the doorway and halloo'd inside the hut. There was no reply.

'Well, I don't know. I really don't.' She wandered round the side of the hovel.

Mary scooped up a small cat with white patches, just as it pounced on a screeching hen.

'Scat!' She dropped it down and clapped her hands in its face.

'Mary, come quick!' Agnes called from behind the hut. 'Fetch the candle and flint.'

Mary carried the tinderbox round to Agnes. Her hands shook as she struggled to drop a spark onto the tinder and make a flame.

'Hurry, child, hurry!'

At last she had the candle lit. She bent down towards Agnes with a sharp intake of breath.

A very old, wrinkled woman lay on the ground. She was quite still, her flesh gleamed yellow in the candlelight.

'Is she dead?' Mary whispered.

'Aye,' Agnes sighed. 'Dead at least a day and night I should say.'

'But . . . who is she?'

Agnes stood up, and Mary caught the glitter of a tear on her cheek. 'She is Selina . . . she is the Forestwife.'

'Nay,' Mary shook her head. 'She is just an old woman.'

'Just a woman,' said Agnes. 'Just a woman, like me and thee. Poor Selina, she has waited too long already. She can wait till daybreak, then we must bury her.'

They left her lying where she was, but Agnes covered her with her own cloak.

'Let's go inside and see what must be done.' She nodded towards the hut.

Mary carried the candle inside. A half sack of grain lay in the corner, the top fastened with twine, though one clever chicken pecked at a hole in the side.

'This is what's needed,' Agnes smiled. 'We'll get no peace here till these animals are dealt with. You take up that pot and feed the hens. That's it, fill it with grain from the sack, and throw it to the poor hungry things.'

She snatched up another pot herself, and set to milking the three goats. One of the cats leapt onto her shoulder. The others made her rock on her feet, so wildly did they purr and rub against her ankles, winding their tails around the goats' legs.

'I see the way of it,' she laughed. 'I see where the milk's supposed to go.'

Mary smiled too. It was comforting to hear Agnes laugh at so ordinary a thing. Though she was puzzled by the place, she was too exhausted to do much questioning.

'I thought perhaps you came here seeking your nephew?'

Agnes looked surprised for a moment, but then answered firmly, shaking her head. 'No need to seek for Robert. He shall come looking for me.'

At last the animals were quiet, and Mary and Agnes sank down gratefully to sleep on beds of dry bracken, in the home of the Forestwife.

Bright sun shone through the open doorway, lighting the small room. Mary was comfortable and warm, the black-and-white cat curled round her feet. She yawned, then groaned as she stirred. The cat stretched and yowled, complaining that its cushion would not keep still. Never before had Mary's legs and back been so sore and unwilling to move.

Yet the homely surroundings cheered her. The room was crammed with the basic utensils for living. Pots of different sizes, hempen bags of grains, stone jars and crocks, pestle and mortar, all a little dusty and jumbled. Great bunches of freshly-picked herbs slung from the ceiling to dry, wafting their sharp, astringent fragrance.

Another delicious smell came from a sizzling iron griddle that rested on the fire by the hearthstone. It was tended by Agnes.

'Ah ha, Sleeping Beauty has opened her eyes. There's cornmeal pancakes and cooked eggs for thee. The hens have paid thee back.'

Mary ate with relish, the feeling that all was well had returned.

'Is there water near?' she asked, thinking vaguely that she had heard the babble of a stream in the night.

'Go see for theesen,' said Agnes, and smiled.

Sleepy and bleary-eyed, Mary wandered from the hut, following the sounds. Willows drooped their branches over a small spring that bubbled up from the rocks. Mary stooped to splash her eyes, bracing herself for the chill. Her laughter rang out, so that Agnes could hear her from the cottage. She grinned hugely, knowing what the girl had found. The beautiful clear water was warm.

'This is a magical place,' Mary cried aloud to the willows, flinging the warm water into the air. 'This is a magical place that we have found.'

It was only when she returned to the cottage and Agnes pulled out a strong iron spade from behind the door, that Mary remembered with a shudder the sad, shrivelled thing behind the house.

'It must be good and deep,' Agnes insisted. She'd marked out a spot of soft earth where a golden-berried mountain ash grew close to the circling yew trees. Beyond it lay a stretch of humpy ground.

Mary groaned and rubbed her back.

'Work through it, that's how I keep my fingers moving.' Agnes flexed her rheumaticky fingers in proof. She swore that hard work was the best cure for aching legs and back.

She hovered on the edge, giving advice, for Mary had never before dug anything, let alone a grave.

It was noon, and the sun high in the sky, before Agnes was satisfied. She rolled Selina's body onto a woollen rug that they'd found in the cottage, and dragged it out to the hole. Mary was glad to leave that job to her. Then they both lowered her gently into the pit, and Agnes pulled the covering cloak away. Clasped between the clawlike hands was a fine woven girdle. Agnes loosened it from the clutching fingers and set it beside her on the ground. Then, to Mary's disgust, she pulled out the woven rug from beneath the frail body, and folded it carefully beside the girdle. 'We must not waste,' she said. 'Now take up tha shovel.'

They covered her with warm, foresty-smelling earth.

The solemn task was almost finished when the hens set up an anxious squawking. Mary and Agnes turned to see a young boy carrying a smaller child. He stood in the clearing in front of the cottage, looking fearfully from the stone pointer towards the doorway.

Agnes picked up Selina's woven girdle and the rug. She went over to the lad while Mary finished patting down the earth.

The boy was skinny but wiry, about ten years old. The small girl that fretted in his arms must have been two, and should have walked on her own, but it was clear that she was sickly and weak, her skin red with sores.

Agnes stood before them.

'Can I help thee, lad?'

'Art thou the Forestwife?'

Though the lad spoke up firmly, his face was white and his bare knees shook.

Agnes looked down at Selina's girdle. The intricately woven belt lay across the palms of her hands. She hesitated for a moment, but then she dropped the rug and cloak. Her face was solemn and pale as she fastened the girdle around her waist.

'Aye. I am the Forestwife. What is it that ails thee, child?'

4

In the Coal-digger's Hut

'My father has broken the Forest Laws.'

'Ah. Poor man.'

Agnes lifted the small girl out of the young boy's arms.

'Come, sit theesen down in the Forestwife's hut, and take some food and drink, then tha can tell us all about it. Mary, fetch them a bowl of milk, and can tha cook them both an egg?'

Mary struggled with the heavy iron griddle that was new to her, but Agnes had not let her grow up ignorant of boiling and baking and kitchen chores.

Agnes took the small girl to the spring and bathed her. The little one laughed with surprise and delight at the bubbling warm water. Then, after she'd patted her dry, Agnes gently rubbed salve from one of Selina's pots into the sore skin.

'I hope tha knows the right one,' Mary said, still fearing poisons and wicked sorcery.

'Pounded comfrey and camomile. I can tell by the smell, and so shall thee before long.'

While they ate, Agnes picked up the good rug that she'd taken from Selina's grave. She cut it into two strips, one larger than the other. Her sharp knife ripped a slit in the middle of each piece, and she slipped the soft warm wool over the head of each child, like a tunic. Then she fastened a short length of twine around each skinny belly. They both smiled at the comfort that it brought.

'A gift from Selina,' Agnes said. They giggled at that, not understanding what she meant.

'Now,' said Agnes. 'Tell us tha names, and tell us what tha can.'

'My name is Tom, and this is our little 'un, Nan. My father's a good man, but he's in trouble. He never beats us like most fathers do, and he worked right hard as a carpenter when we lived in Langden village. My father had an accident – he slipped and cut his hand with an axe. Well, he couldn't work for a while, and got no payment. He owed the Lord of Langden five days' work up at the manor and couldn't do it. We had to have some meat, for my mother is big with child, and she'd been sick and worn for lack of food, just like my little sister.

'Father went out a-hunting. He wandered away to the south from where we live, and he caught us a good pair of hares with a snare, but then the Foresters of Sherwood found him with them. They claimed 'twas royal hunting land that he took them from. Father swore 'twas Barnsdale, where any man may take the beasts . . . but he couldn't prove them wrong. It's six days now, since he was sent before the Forest Justices. He came back walking all hunched and moaning.'

'Tha's done the right thing, lad, to come looking for help.' Agnes stroked his head. 'What had they done to tha father?'

The boy tried to tell, but his eyes filled with tears, and his voice choked and would not make a sound.

He spread out his right hand before them, and brought his other hand down upon it with a quick chopping action across the forefinger and thumb.

'Ah!' Mary caught her breath. 'His bow fingers? For a pair of hares in a snare?'

'He could not pay the fine,' said Tom.

Agnes shook her head, unsurprised. ''Tis all the same to them. They make sure he'll not draw bow or pull a snare again. Do not expect fair treatment in the Forest Courts.'

'But I thought King Richard freed us from the Forest Laws,' said Mary.

Agnes shook her head, smiling sadly.

'Nay, lass. He emptied the prisons when he came to the throne. They all loved him for that, but now he's stripped the country bare with his crusaders tax. The prisons are full again . . . they groan with those who'd rather break the Forest Law than starve.

'Well? Did tha father recover, child?'

Tom shook his head.

'The lord of Langden Manor came by our cottage, and we dared to hope he'd give us aid. My father's been a loyal tenant all his life. The lord spoke kind enough, and rode away, but the next morning the bailiff came knocking on our door. His lordship would not keep a carpenter who could not hold a saw. He and his men, they turned us out . . . out of our cottage and away from Langden land.'

'You poor lad,' Mary said, taking his hand. 'What then?'

'We were desperate, wandering in the forest, my father sick and all of us hungry, but we found an old coaldigger's hut and thought ourselves lucky. At least we had shelter. 'Twas last night that it all turned bad. My father began to shake and shiver and we could not rouse him. He lies in the corner, he goes like this.'

Tom showed them how his father twitched and shuddered.

'And water, like a rain shower, comes out of his skin.'

Agnes got to her feet and began sniffing and sorting amongst Selina's pots and jars.

'A festering wound,' she muttered. 'Sage to cool the fever, then vervain and woundwort and comfrey leaves.'

'My mother,' Tom insisted. ''Tis my mother too. She was right bothered by the state of my father. Then this morning she started to moan and groan and clutch at her belly. Well, then . . . I picked up my sister, for I dare not leave her there, and I told my mother that I went to seek the Forestwife.'

'Is it far?' said Agnes.

'This side of Langden village. I set off when the sun was high in the sky, but my sister is heavy and the way was hard to find.'

'Tha mam and dad should be proud of thee,' said Mary. 'And tha carried this lass all the way.'

Within the hour, a strange procession set off for the coal-digger's hut. Tom led the way and Agnes followed, laden with cloaks and ointments and bundles of dried herbs. Mary followed leading two of the goats, steadying the little girl astride the biggest one. As they left the clearing Agnes stooped to swivel the pointer stone around.

It was late afternoon when they reached the hut. They heard the screams of the frantic woman before they reached the door. Tom ran ahead to his mother, while Agnes dropped her bundles and followed him. Mary found her on her knees beside the labouring woman, carefully pressing on her stomach. The poor mother groaned bitterly and rolled her eyes.

'The child wishes to come,' said Agnes, frowning anxiously, 'but it's turned itself the wrong way round.'

'Can you do aught?' Mary winced at the woman's pain.

'I can try.'

Agnes bent over to whisper in the woman's ear.

'Take heart,' she soothed, stroking her head. 'I shall be quick as I can.'

Then she pushed her fingers up inside the woman's body, reaching and twisting and grunting with the effort of it all. Tom's mother groaned and bit her lips, quietened by Agnes's calm assurance and faith in her own skill. The children watched in frightened silence. Then at last, with a sharp jerk that shocked the mother senseless, Agnes pulled free two kicking feet. A baby boy slithered out into the world, alive and shouting. His mother soon stirred again and blinked, then opened her eyes and set to grateful weeping at the sound the child's cries.

Agnes turned to the sick man who groaned quietly in the corner. 'He needs me now. Can tha see to the mother and babe?' she asked Mary. 'They will be fine, now that this bairn is free.'

'But, I've never . . .'

' 'Tis naught but common sense. Get them both clean and warm and comfortable. I must look to the father.'

It was thick dark by the time Mary settled down to try to sleep, curled up beside the little girl on a thin pile of ancient straw. She sighed with exhaustion, but also with satisfaction. She'd cleared up the bloody mess of birth, and seen the new baby washed and put to the breast, all the while receiving tearful thanks from his mother, whose name was Alice.

Agnes had made herself as comfortable as she could, propped up beside the wounded man, ready to tend him through the night. She'd cleansed and dressed his wound, and spoon-fed him with her simples. Now he slept, wrapped well in the cloaks and rugs that they'd brought, still twitching at times, but breathing calmly.

By the morning his fever had gone. He was very weak,

but calm and clear in his mind. Agnes milked the goats and saw the family well fed. Though there was much more that could be done, she insisted that they must return to the Forestwife's hut. The mother nodded her understanding and rose up shakily from her bed of straw to search out a small bag of dried beans. It was one of the few things they had managed to snatch as they left Langden village. She handed it to Mary.

' 'Tis all we have to pay thee with.'

Mary began to refuse. How could they take food from those who had nothing? But Agnes stepped in and took the beans.

'That pays us well enough,' she said. 'But there's something more I'd ask of thee. I've many tasks that I need a strong lad for. Will you send Tom to us, twice a week? I shall pay him with a good jug of goat's milk and a few fresh eggs.'

'Certainly he shall come,' Alice agreed. Tom looked well pleased at the plan.

Alice caught hold of Agnes by the hand, her face solemn. 'I am sad for the old wife, but glad of the new. We have great need of thee since the Sisters stopped their visiting.'

Agnes frowned. 'The sisters?'

'The Sisters of St Mary, from the convent in the woods.'

'You say they come no more?'

The woman shook her head. 'They were so good to us; to all around Langden. We wondered if we'd offended them?'

* * *

They left one of the goats behind to help the family through the first few days, with the agreement that Tom would bring it when he came to work for them.

As they wandered back through the forest, there was much on Mary's mind. Much that she wished to ask, but it was difficult to know where to start.

'Well . . . it seems that tha's taken Selina's place,' she began.

Agnes nodded, but she looked tired and sad.

'You knew her, didn't you?'

'Aye. I knew Selina. She helped me once, long ago. There's a great deal that you do not know about your old nurse, my lovey, and I shall tell it . . . but all in good time.'

It seemed that Mary would have to be satisfied with that for the moment, so she turned to more practical matters.

'Why did you take their beans, yet leave them with a goat? How do you know you'll ever see that beast again?'

'I took the beans in payment, which is only right . . . they have their pride. I left the goat for they need the milk, and it shows we have faith in them. We've taken upon ourselves a task that I do not think you rightly understand. Not yet.'

'What do you mean?'

Agnes fingered the woven girdle of the Forestwife. It was a beautiful thing, not like a wealthy lady's ornament, but intricately woven and rich with the forest dyes of madder, blackberry, sorrel and marigold. It was edged with finely plaited leather and fastened with a heavy metal clasp.

She sighed. 'It is an ancient and sacred pact, an agreement, between the forest folk. It will bring us safety, for none will know or even ask our names. The Forestwife may keep her mysteries. They will protect us, but there is our part of the bargain to be kept; always to be there, always to answer to those in need. It will be our refuge but, believe me, it will be hard work.'

'Do you mean that there was another Forestwife before Selina? That there's always a Forestwife?'

'Look beyond Selina's mound,' said Agnes, 'then count up the humps in the ground.'

'But . . . I have always feared the Forestwife. They call her evil and fearsome.'

Agnes laughed. 'An evil reputation has its uses. It keeps away unwelcome visitors, and those who dare to come are desperate.'

Mary remembered how poor Tom's knees had knocked when he first spoke up to the Forestwife. She wandered on in silence, thinking it all out.

At last she turned back to Agnes, grinning wickedly.

'So . . . you are the Forestwife, Agnes, and you *can* do the job, for I have always known you were a witch. But who am I? What part am I to play?'

Agnes looked thoughtful. 'That I don't know yet, my lovey, but you are most important, of that I am sure. I was not ready to leave Holt Manor, but you were. The time was right; you chose it, not me. I am quite sure there is a purpose that we cannot understand. A purpose that brought thee to these woods.'

They entered the clearing to a wild welcome from the fowls and cats and the lonesome goat. Agnes swivelled the stone around; the Forestwife was back. They laughed amidst the bleating and cackling. More of a joyful home-coming than ever Holt Manor had offered them.

They spent the rest of the day making order from the muddle that Selina's hut had become. Agnes sorted through the pots and potions, sniffing and tasting, throwing out any that were stale or sour.

Meanwhile, she sent Mary to pick great basketfuls of elder leaves and bracken tips. When she was satisfied with the amount, she set her to unpick the fur trimmings on the fine hooded purple cloak. Agnes boiled the leaves in the biggest pot and plunged the cloak into it, to pick up the woodland dyes.

When it was thoroughly drenched and dripping, they spread it out on the strong lower branches of a yew. It dripped and dribbled through the night, then dried and lightened in the midday sun. At dusk the following evening, they lifted it down all soft and warm.

Mary wrapped it around her shoulders. The soft, foresty green that the plants had given looked well with the healthy pink of her cheeks, and the dark gold of her hair.

Agnes smiled at her, hands on hips.

'You asked me yesterday what part you were to play,

honey. I could not tell you then, but I know the answer now. I shall give you a new name for a new life. You are Mary de Holt no longer. I shall call you Marian. You are the beautiful green lady of the woods.

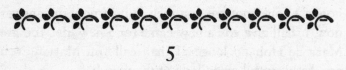

5

The Charcoal-burner's Daughter

Agnes's prediction of hard work was soon proved true. From early in the morning till late at night a constant trickle of miserable folk wandered into the clearing. Many, like Tom's father, had been punished by the Forest Courts. They came trudging through the wastes and forestland from outlying villages, with scratched and blistering feet, groaning and fevered with sickening wounds. Some brought dogs with festering paws, their toes brutally crushed by the warden's men, and so made useless for hunting.

But of all the many different forms that misery took, the most common sight was a weary woman, carrying a child and followed by a trail of hungry little ones, their father thrown into gaol, the family turned from their home. Few men survived to stand trial, so dreadful were the prisons.

There was little that Agnes could do for these desperate families, but she'd serve up warm pottage, and send Tom and Marian to help them build a shelter in the woods.

There were many more suffering from the small and dreary troubles of life: the lonely, the lovesick, the hungry, the mad . . . and all their ailing animals. Each one was listened to and offered help of some sort. Only once did Agnes refuse an angry, loud-mouthed woman, who sought a curse upon her mother-in-law.

'Tha must do thine own cursing,' she said. 'But best beware, for the curser may suffer the worst.'

The woman went off glowering, dragging her white-faced young son behind her.

Whenever there might have been a moment of peace or rest, Marian was sent out into the forest.

'No time to sit about, my girl. Tha must get to gathering.'

There were raspberries and bilberries, though honey was the sweetest treat. Wild thyme, rosemary, vervain and bitter rue were needed for Agnes's vital potions. Meadowsweet and lady's bedstraw flavoured their drinks and sweetened the rushes on the floor. Marian's eyes grew sharp at picking out the firm white shapes of mushrooms as she lifted the fallen leaves. Magical clumps of shaggy white fungus appeared overnight, but they must be picked and cooked before they turned black, or the taste grew foul.

Marian did as she was told, and gathered willingly enough, but she really couldn't see the need for it. Everyone paid them what they could, and they soon amassed a good store of grain. But Agnes would not touch it, swearing that it must be kept for winter.

'Well,' said Agnes watching Marian at her tasks, 'it

seems my girl's thriving as never before.'

She spoke with satisfaction, but still she fretted and worried, and built up her supplies.

'I don't know what tha's bothered about.'

'Tha shall see the need . . . before next spring.'

So Marian tramped the woods with Tom as her guide, carrying baskets and bags. Her legs grew sturdy, her hands like leather, her fingers quick and strong.

Barnsdale's vast tangles and swamps were no longer frightening; they hid a network of secret paths and signs. Marian soon discovered that the very perils of the wilderness became a source of protection to those who learned its dangers well. She grew to know each tree for miles around the clearing; to know each hovel and cottage, each warning smell and sound.

It was late in August, and a still evening when Marian returned laden with mushrooms and a few late raspberries and fat, dark bilberries.

A young girl stood hesitating by the pointer stone.

Though she had learnt to step silently, Marian purposely made a sound, not wishing to startle the girl. She was right to have done so, for the girl jumped nervously, and turned around. Marian gasped at the whiteness of her face in the gathering dusk. She knew this girl, and she knew her swollen belly.

Marian stepped forward holding out her hand, but there was no recognition in return. The girl was exhausted and ready to drop.

'Hungry?' Marian asked, offering the berries that

she'd gathered. She could not keep back a wry smile, remembering the strawberries she'd once scorned.

But the amusement vanished, for the girl put out a trembling hand and sank to the floor.

Marian caught her awkwardly, shouting out to Agnes, who came running from the cottage doorway. Between them they carried her inside.

'You see who it is?' Marian cried. 'She didn't know me.'

'I see her,' said Agnes. 'I hope we can trust her.'

'What ails her, do you think? Is she having the child?'

Agnes shook her head, puzzled for once.

They settled her on the bracken-filled sacks that were their beds. As they fed her with sips of warm goat's milk, she started to revive.

She sighed, staring surprised at Agnes. 'I know thee, but I came to see the Forestwife.'

'You have found her, honey,' Agnes laughed.

The girl stared, puzzled, for a moment, looking from one face to the other. Then her own distress came flooding back.

'I hope tha can help me, for I surely wish to die.'

They sat still on either side of her, listening to her sad story. Her name was Emma. The Ecclesall bailiff had caught her one day in the woods. He made her lie with him, threatening double land rent to her father if she told. She'd been terrified when she came to understand that she was with child. Her father had been angry, but he'd not turned her away. Then gradually, as the child had grown and moved inside her belly, she'd come to accept its presence, to wish to protect, and at last . . . almost to love. But suddenly, two days since, the child had ceased to kick or move at all. 'Then I came seeking the Forestwife, knowing my father would in truth be glad to see me and the child gone. It lies in my belly like a heavy stone. I know that it's dead, and I wish to die too.'

'No, you must not,' Marian snatched up her hand.

But Agnes shook her head. 'Let the girl rest,' she said. 'She cannot think straight after such a long hard walk in such a state. In the morning we'll talk again.'

Agnes brewed up a sleeping potion, while Marian fetched her own green cloak to cover the girl. Emma watched her warily, with just a spark of curiosity.

'Thou art . . . the lady,' she whispered. 'Thine uncle rages over thee still . . . but I never told.'

Marian bent over her, tucking the cloak snugly around.

'Aye. I know you did not.' She gave a low laugh. 'I call myself Marian. I am the green lady now.'

Once Emma had fallen into an exhausted sleep, Agnes and Marian sat whispering together by the door.

'Can you do aught to help her?'

Agnes sighed. 'There's little I can do, for she's right, that poor babe is quite dead inside her. All I can do is to bring it to birth. Then maybe she will recover and live – if she has the will for it.'

'She must find the will,' Marian said.

* * *

The next day was a hard one for all three.

Agnes nervously brewed up a potion from those herbs most dangerous in their uses. She fretted and fussed that the measures must be just right.

Marian sat by Emma the whole day through, helping and holding her hand. A birth took place, but a birth that lacked all joy.

In the late afternoon Marian was sent up to Selina's mound to dig a new and tiny grave. Then as the sun went down, Emma herself came walking slowly from the cottage, carrying a carefully wrapped bundle. Agnes supported her, her arms about the young girl's waist. Marian ran to take the bundle from Emma, but she shook her head.

'Let her see to it herself,' said Agnes, quite firm.

Marian backed away then, thinking Agnes hard and cruel, but as she saw the touching care with which the young girl buried her dead child, she understood that it was right.

She watched her old nurse guiding Emma through her miserable task. How was it that Agnes knew so much? For the first time the thought came to her that Agnes must herself have borne a child. Agnes had been her wet nurse, hired for her milk. She must have had a child to bring that milk. What had happened to it? Had she buried it herself like poor Emma did now? How stupid that she had never wondered before.

Marian sought around for some small token and gathered twigs of bright berries from the rowan tree.

Emma took them gratefully and set them in the small hump beside Selina's mound.

They both helped Emma back to bed, and Agnes brewed another sleeping drink.

Marian wandered outside, weighed down by the sadness of it all. She walked towards the strong green branches of the greatest spreading yew, and flopped down to lean against the trunk. Here in the forest she had never been so strong and free, and yet she felt that she might burst with sadness. There was hardship unlike anything she'd known.

She turned her face to the bole of the yew, sighing and wrapping her arms for comfort around its sturdy stem. As dusk crept through the forest Agnes came looking for her. She found her half asleep, still curled up there.

'Why, love, I couldn't see thee for a moment. What a sight tha makes. Has our green lady fallen in love with a tree?'

Though Marian shivered and rubbed her cheek, she could not help but smile. It was a reminder of one of the stories that Agnes used to tell when she was a child, about how a poor servant girl was lost in the woods and fell in love with a beautiful tree. The tree was really a handsome young man bewitched by a wicked old woman.

'I fear I'm not as clever a witch as that,' said Agnes, holding out her hand to pull Marian to her feet. 'And if I was, I'd turn the tree back into a fine young man for thee. Art thou sad and lonely, my lass?'

'Tha keeps me far too busy to be lonely, old witch.'
Marian grinned at her.

They both went back towards the cottage.

'There's one in there that needs a friend,' said Agnes.
'I can mend her body, if fortune smiles, but . . .'

'Aye,' Marian agreed. 'I shall be her friend.'

They went inside together, glad that the day had come
to its end.

Agnes was right, as usual. Emma's body mended fast,
but her spirits could not. Within a few days she was up
and walking easily, but she would sit for hours by the
small hump of freshly turned earth beside Selina's
mound. Marian worried and tried to distract her.

'Let her be,' Agnes said. 'Let her stay there as long as
she wishes, however long it may take.'

When Marian had finished her chores she would go
to sit with Emma. At first they sat in silence, just keeping company. Then gradually they began to talk quietly;
not of the lost child, but of their early lives in Sheaf
Valley, so close – yet so unlike.

Marian offered Emma the best fruits and cheese, but
she'd eat little. Tom did his best to gossip and smile, even
if he received nothing but a polite nod in return. Though
she was clearly strong enough in body, nobody suggested
that Emma might return to Ecclesall, and at least there
was no more talk of wishing to die. In the end it was the
charcoal-burning, and Marian's ignorance, that threw
Emma into the long haul back to life.

Agnes had been worried that the small supply of

charcoal in Selina's hut was almost done. In the long winter months to come, they'd have great need of slow-burning charcoal to keep the fire glowing through the nights.

Tom and Marian set to work to cut plenty of wood, and they could do that well enough. When they had a good pile ready they began to lay out a great stack in the middle of the clearing in front of the cottage.

Agnes watched, ready to call instructions from the cottage doorway, but then thought better of it, clamped her mouth shut, and went inside. Emma sat listlessly on the step, fitfully turning her head towards her baby's grave.

The stack began to grown in a wobbling, untidy way, with both builders shouting wild instructions to each other.

Emma became restless. She could not manage to sit still, and got to her feet. She firmly turned her back on them and sighed, then plodded off towards Selina's mound. But she could not quite ignore them, and turned to see again the toppling pile that grew from their hands. She could stand it no longer. Emma swung around and marched up to them, hands on hips.

'If tha builds the stack here, tha shall fill the cot with thick black smoke. And if tha sets it out like that, tha shall be burning half the clearing and the trees.'

Tom and Marian stared at her amazed. Emma licked her finger and held it up. 'The wind blows from beyond the cot. Tha must set the stack up there beside the stream. It must be built all neat and round, with a good space in the middle. I'd best show thee.'

A short while later Agnes looked out from the cottage door and smiled. All was well. There was busy building, and following of orders, and a deal of friendly chattering. The charcoal-burner's daughter was in charge.

6

The Blacksmith's Wife

Tom led his little sister, Nan, into the clearing. She was walking well now and growing strong, but Marian caught a hint of fear in the child's wide-eyed expression, and in the tense grip she kept on her brother's hand.

'Why, what ails thee little Nan?'

The child shook her head and hid her face in Tom's rump. He laughed and pushed her from him.

' 'Tis naught but the weeping in the forest that upsets her.'

Marian smiled, with a slight puzzled frown. 'And what weeping is that, Tom?'

'Has tha not heard it, lady? It often comes to me when I'm on my way to visit thee. I can't rightly say where it comes from. Some days it seems to come from all around.'

'Nay. I cannot say as I know what tha means. The forest is full of creaks and sighs, but most have a reason. 'Tis thee that's taught me so. If tha hears it again, come tell me quick, so that I can listen.'

But the strange wailing in the forest was soon forgotten, for Tom's mother, Alice, came following them through the forest to the clearing, carrying her new baby in her arms. She was out of breath with walking fast, and all upset at the news she'd heard from Langden village. Agnes and Emma appeared from inside the cottage, disturbed by the anger in her voice.

It seemed that a man who had worked the land for the manor had died of a fever, and no sooner was the man buried than the lord of Langden had turned his old demented mother from her home.

'As we know only too well,' Alice cried, 'there is no place at Langden for those who cannot work. He is a cruel master indeed. We found poor Sarah wandering in the forest three days since, half-frozen and hungry, quite out of her wits.'

Marian's eyes blazed with outrage. Agnes shook her head.

'I've known it happen before,' said Emma.

'But that is not all,' Alice insisted. 'We took Sarah into our hut and fed her, but not a word of sense could we get from her. So my husband went to Langden, as near as he dared to go. He's just come back with worse to tell.

'There is a woman who lives in Langden, she was my friend, Philippa, the blacksmith's wife. She was angry when we were turned from our home, but like them all she kept silent for fear. But she has not kept silent now. Old Sarah's treatment was too much for her. She led a gang of villagers up to the manor house and they marched into the great hall. Philippa shouted at William of Langden that Sarah should be brought back and cared for.'

Both Agnes and Emma gasped. 'What came of it?' asked Marian.

Alice bit at her lip. 'She is clapped into a scold's bridle, and fastened to the stocks. William of Langden has sent to the Sheriff to have her declared outlaw. They will brand her and chase her from Langden land.'

'Branded? Do you mean they'll burn her?' Marian demanded.

'Aye. Burn her with the outlaw's mark. 'Twill be there on her forehead for all to see.'

'What of the other villagers? What of her husband?'

'They say he sits and weeps in his forge. If he complains, he'll lose his living. Who shall feed their children then?'

They stood together in silence, their faces pale and tight. Only Marian could not keep still; she paced up and down clenching her fists.

'Come settle down, my lovey,' Agnes begged. ' 'Tis a harsh thing indeed to treat this poor woman so. But we must know when there is naught to be done.'

Suddenly Marian stopped her pacing.

'Nay, Agnes, there is something we may try. We cannot stop her being outlawed, but she shall not be branded. We must get her away from Langden tonight.'

Marian, Emma, Tom and his mother set out for the village as soon as dusk fell.

Agnes walked with them just to the edge of the

clearing, Alice's baby in her arms, for the Forestwife must stay behind. She caught at Marian's arm, her face drawn with worry.

'Must tha do this, lovey? We can be safe here in the heart of Barnsdale. Must tha go looking for trouble?'

For a moment they all hesitated, frightened of what they planned.

'I cannot leave Philippa to be burned and shamed,' said Alice. 'She was ever my good friend, but you owe her naught.'

' 'Tis not for your Philippa that I go,' said Marian. ' 'Tis for thee and thy man, and young Tom here. 'Tis for all the ills this lord of Langden did thee.'

'Bless you,' whispered Alice.

Agnes sighed, but she reached up to kiss Marian.

'Tha's a fierce rash little lass, but maybe I begin to see what part tha plays.'

Marian hugged her. 'We'll be back before tha knows.'

They moved off quietly, into the forest night.

Tom and Alice knew the way so well that the journey was not difficult. They moved stealthily, their cloaks wrapped close for warmth and disguise. Marian's fingers kept fastening around the handle of the sharp meat knife that she'd stuck into her belt; checking and touching, and wondering if she could use it should the need arise.

At last they came in sight of the stocks, set on the village common. The surrounding huts were quiet.

The blacksmith's wife stood tall and upright, her shape a dark shadow in the moonlight. She was unguarded, for who in that place would dare to rescue her? Marian looked up at that still figure. The heavy metal bridle stuck out around her head, ugly and humiliating. How could she stand so straight up there, alone and cold, yet refusing to sit or droop? A strong woman indeed. She began to understand why Alice cared so.

A bubble of hot anger burst over Marian, her doubts and fears fled. 'Look at that foul bridle,' she hissed to Emma. 'How can we get it off her?'

Emma shook her head hopelessly. 'Only they will have the key.'

'There is but one man who can cut it off,' said Alice. 'That man is her husband.'

'Will he risk it?' asked Emma.

'He'd better,' said Marian.

Tom was sent to the forge to warn the blacksmith and make sure that all was ready.

'Right,' said Marian gripping tightly onto the handle of her knife. 'Let us get her now.'

Once they had made their move they went fast, creeping swiftly towards the stocks.

'Hush Phil, 'tis Alice.' Tom's mother murmured low, so that Philippa would not be afraid, and know she was with friends.

Marian quickly cut through the rope that fastened the woman to the stocks, then, supporting her on either side, they made their way to the forge.

The blacksmith had candles lit, ready to set to work with his smallest knives and files.

It was clear the job could not be done instantly. Alice made Philippa sit. She stroked her hands and spoke soothing words. The blacksmith was smaller than his wife, but his muscles braided his arms like corded rope. He worked hard and fast, choking and weeping all the time. Emma kept a look-out by the outer door.

Marian lifted a curtain at the back of the forge. Six children slept soundly in pallets round a glowing fire. Philippa had much to leave.

'There's a barking dog, and light up on the common,' Emma cried out, before the work was done.

'No time left,' said Marian.

The blacksmith gave a powerful great rasp with his file, Philippa groaned and the metal snapped open. She was white-faced and staring as they lifted the burden from her head, and pulled the metal thong gently from her mouth. Dark blood trickled from her lips and fresh blood ran down her cheek. The last sharp effort had gashed her face.

Alice pulled her to her feet, and they were off, their cloaks whirling through the door.

'Do not leave me with this,' the blacksmith cried, picking up the hated bridle.

'I'll take it, sir,' said Tom.

'Phil . . . ippa!' the blacksmith's cry followed them out, into the cold dark night.

There was running and shouting and blazing torches coming closer as they headed for the forest. Several of the villagers saw them go, but the captain and his armed guards were bravely pointed in the wrong direction. The village was finding its courage once again.

They set off running through the forest, and at first all went well, but soon concern for Philippa slowed them down. She was a tall, well-built woman, but as they moved further from Langden and her ordeal, the stubborn pride that had kept her going began to drain away fast. She shivered and shook and made strange sounds.

' 'Tis all we can expect,' Alice cried out, frantic for her friend. 'Those wicked bridles mash the tongue. We must get her to the Forestwife.'

The last mile was a hard struggle, and they almost carried Philippa between them, but at last they reached the clearing and the blacksmith's wife was given into Agnes's tender care.

All through the nest day Philippa was nursed and tended. She was carefully spoon-fed, but slept heavily and made no sound. Alice watched her anxiously, and whispered her fears to Marian.

'I've known a scold's bridle so hurt the tongue that they never speak clear again.'

Marian had her own doubts. After the first wild pleasure of their success, she'd grown miserable at the sadness of Philippa's situation. The sleeping children by the fireside kept creeping into her mind.

Early that evening Philippa stirred and opened her eyes. She held her hand out to Alice, but stared with surprise at the tiny hut crowded with women. Tom squeezed in through the doorway, sensing that something was happening, followed by one of the goats and a clucking hen.

'We've little to welcome thee with,' said Marian. 'We took thee from the stocks to save thee from branding. I fear we've scarred tha face instead.'

Philippa put her fingertips to the cut, feeling gently and wincing, but then she pulled herself upwards until she sat. Much to their surprise, she would not rest with that, she pushed away Alice's supporting hand, and struggled to her feet. Then she stood tall and straight, as they'd seen her by the stocks, but now her eyes burned bright with triumph.

She moved her mouth awkwardly, as though chewing.

They all held their breath.

Then slowly but clearly she spoke. 'We have defied the manor.'

Tom raised both his arms and clapped and cheered. The goats and chickens squawked and bleated in reply, and the hut was filled with laughter and uproar.

The blacksmith's wife did not return to her bed, not that day nor any day. She took a quick look around the clearing and told Agnes that the Forestwife was in need of more shelter. Everyone was quick to agree, and the following days were full of cutting and sawing and hammering. Tom's father came to give his advice, though he could not do much of the work. It was Philippa who did the heavy lifting and sawing, throwing herself into it with relish, speaking steadily and with good humour, though slowly.

Alice came through the woods every day, to give help and see her friend. She brought old Sarah with her, who wandered round the clearing happy as a child and got in everyone's way. Once the alarm was raised when Alice noticed that the old woman was missing and work had to be stopped while they searched and brought her back.

Marian blinked back tears when she saw Philippa quietly stroke the cheek of Alice's baby, or stoop to pat little Nan's head.

Gradually a lean-to grew on the side of the hut, making twice as much room as before. It was sturdily built and smelt of fresh oak, so that those who slept beneath the Forestwife's roof slept safe and warm and dry.

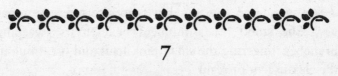

7

The Green Man

It was an early evening in late September, with a cool wind blowing through the yew trees, when Marian heard the wailing once more.

The clearing was quiet, for Philippa had gone to take Sarah back to the coal-digger's hut, saying she'd stay with Alice for the night. They had found the old woman wandering, lost in the forest again. Poor Sarah had been quite distressed.

'The trees are crying,' she insisted. 'They lose their leaves and they moan and weep.'

The others had smiled kindly, but Marian had set to wondering, remembering the wailing that Tom and little Nan had heard.

Agnes and Emma were busy in the new lean-to, crumbling dried herbs into pots to keep for winter use, when Marian thought that she could hear crying herself. She said nothing, but wandered out into the clearing, holding up her licked fingertip as Emma did. The wind could carry sounds a long way, she'd learnt that much.

She wandered towards her favourite tree, the great yew. She stood for a moment beneath its sweeping branches, fingering the small pink fruit and breathing in the clean scent of resin.

It was only as she turned to go, glancing down to where a bramble caught her foot, that she saw it. Her stomach leapt – a hand, sticking out from beneath the curling bracken. The skin was the same gingery brown as the dried bracken fronds, making it hard to see. Her heart thumped and her throat went tight as she bent down and carefully pulled away the leaves. Close by the yew, well hidden amongst the undergrowth, a man lay fast asleep.

He was young and thin-cheeked, with a dark growth of beard. He was dressed in a grey hog-skin jerkin, worn silver in patches like the yew tree's bark, and dark ginger leggings that blended with the colour of his hand and the drying bracken. His cloak was a deep foresty green, like her own. Marian stared down at him, then up into the branches of the yew, her mind drifting into a dream of the green lady and her forest lover. It seemed he was part of the woodland itself; grown from the trees, the bracken and the rich dark earth. He was a very beautiful young man.

Suddenly he groaned in his sleep and muttered, twitching restlessly. She bent close, wrinkling her nose at the rank smell of sweat and sickness, and saw that his face was bruised. His cloak was good homespun, but ragged and torn. How stupid she'd been. This was no fairy lover. He was not asleep, but ill. The skin on his cheeks was white beneath smudged dirt and glistened with moisture. He was real enough – he stank – and he was somehow familiar. Yes . . . her hands shook at the thought. She knew him; she had seen him once before, though only from a distance, when he'd stayed with Maud and Harry at the mill. He was Agnes's nephew, Robert, the fierce wolfshead, the wicked one.

He cried out, a low, growling sound like a wounded boar.

'Mother,' he seemed to cry, then he rolled to the side. His hand and stomach were caked in dried blood.

Marian turned and ran, shouting for Agnes.

'Why, what is it, lass?' Agnes came to the doorway, a bunch of lavender in her hand.

'Agnes. He is here beneath the great tree. It is Robert. He is hurt, and he cries out for . . . his mother?'

'Show me,' Agnes dropped the flowers and ran.

She bent down beneath the branches, then fell to her knees beside the lad. She touched his head, and caught hold of his hand.

'Mother,' the beastlike growl came again.

Agnes looked up into Marian's puzzled face. 'He has found his mother,' she said. 'For Robert is not my nephew, he is my son.'

Marian stared open-mouthed, but Robert groaned again and Agnes turned quickly back to him.

'No time to stand there gaping, girl. Take up his legs, while I lift him round the shoulders. Ah, he's no weight! What has the lad been doing these months?'

They carried him carefully into the cottage and settled

him on the bedding. Emma came forward to help, supposing him just another unfortunate lad who'd come seeking the Forestwife.

There was dark dried blood on his hand and shirt. Agnes pulled open his jerkin, clicking her tongue at all the clotting blood. Then she turned his head to the side, tenderly feeling at the temples. He had a black eye and yellow and grey bruising above.

Agnes clicked her tongue again.

'Clout on the head, and a sword cut. Marian! Fetch water! Quick, lass!'

Marian picked up the bucket and ran.

She dipped the bucket into the clean warm water as quickly as she could, though her hands would not stop shaking. Then she set to frowning as Agnes's words sank in.

'What has he been doing, these months?' As far as she knew, Agnes had not seen Robert for a year at least, and what had she called him? Her son?

Marian shook her head, she could not understand at all, but there was not time to stop and think.

When she returned, Agnes and Emma knelt over Robert, their heads bent together, carefully cutting away the shreds of bloodsoaked homespun from his shirt that had dried around the wound. Emma glanced anxiously across at Agnes, then down at Robert. Something had been said between them . . . Emma knew.

Without waiting to be told, Marian squeezed out a cloth in clean warm water and began the job of washing him. Robert still muttered and rolled his head, the words making no sense, his mind still far away. She bent over him, gently cleaning the dust and mud from his face. There was broken skin beneath his matted hair. She wrinkled her nostrils as she wiped dried vomit from his cheek. What a fool she had been! How ever could she have thought him so beautiful . . . the magical green man?

Despite the offers of help that came, Agnes insisted on sitting up all night with the wounded lad, and in the morning her devotion was rewarded. Robert was calm and quiet, smiling up at his mother with recognition. Marian carried in a bowl of bread soaked in fresh warm goat's milk. She knelt at his side. He smiled at her and whispered his thanks, then turned to his mother.

'Where is the fancy m'lady then?'

Marian froze, and Agnes pressed her lips tight together.

Robert looked from one to the other, his mouth falling open.

'She is not the one?' He laughed low and winced. 'My lady of Holt, with a freckled nose and dirty face?'

'I would clout thee good and hard,' said Agnes, 'if someone had not already done it for me.'

Marian's hands started to shake, so that the milk looked like to spill. 'I am Marian,' she said. 'I am Mary de Holt no longer.'

Robert said nothing, he would not look at her, but smirked down at his feet. Marian was clearly beneath his contempt, though she could not see why.

'Give me the bowl,' said Agnes, taking it from her. 'Take no notice, my lovey, he knows nowt, and believe me, when this head of his is mended he will think a different way.'

She spoke sharply over Robert's head, trying to catch Marian's eye, and make her smile.

But Marian could not. She knelt there for a moment, staring down at the trodden earth floor, her fists clenched, fighting to hold back tears. Then suddenly she leapt to her feet and ran outside into the cold clean air. She hated this sick man, with his sneering mouth, hated the very smell of him. And besides all this, was he not a murderer?

She strode across the clearing, taking her usual path to the great yew, but as she lifted her hands to its soft, sweeping branches she stopped, remembering how she had found him there. She turned away, her anger stronger than ever. He had somehow defiled the beautiful yew. She could never turn to it again without thinking of him.

Then, as she shifted, she caught another movement from the corner of her eye. She whipped her head round quickly, catching only the sense of a dark shadow slipping away, and the faint crackle of dry leaves. Branches of the further, smaller yew trembled, but when she caught hold of them, there was nothing there. They were thick, sturdy boughs, and the wind had dropped.

Agnes came from the cottage, calling her name. Marian did not move. She thought of hiding, punishing her.

Her old nurse saw her standing amongst the yews and called again. Marian still would not turn towards her, but she waited, her face turned away. She stood there while Agnes came to take her hand.

'Tha must let me explain it all to thee, lovey. You owe me that. I left him with my brother when he were less than two years old. I left him when I went to be your nurse.'

'Aye.' Marian sighed. 'I suppose I can but hear thee out.'

Agnes led her back to the hut, but turned her away from the old room where Robert lay. They went and sat together in the new lean-to. Marian paused at the door, glancing quickly round the clearing.

'I thought I saw someone just now out there, hiding amongst the trees. I thought I heard a voice.'

Agnes joined her, but there was no sound or movement.

'Maybe you did see something,' she whispered. 'There's others, and they'll come for him.'

Agnes settled herself in the corner, by the pots of herbs. Instinctively she took up the work she'd dropped in haste the night before, crumbling dried comfrey leaves into pots. Marian picked a bunch of crisp, dark-golden tansy flowers, and joined her in the task.

'His father,' she began, nodding her head towards the old room, 'his father, my husband, was Adam Fitzooth, a yeoman farmer and a freeman. We had a bit of land over Wakefield way, that we rented from the Lord of Oldcotes, for payment and fieldwork at ploughing and harvest.'

'What?' said Marian, staring in surprise. 'I cannot see thee as a married woman.'

Agnes laughed. 'Well I was, and for many a year. I was happy with him too, though we wished for children, and they never came.'

'But?'

'Don't rush me, girl, I must tell it my way. We had a good life together . . . but then it all went wrong. It was the year of the great rebellion. The northern lords cut themselves off from King Henry, and there was a great call to arms. Adam was the best bowman in the county, he went to fight for the King. The Lord of Oldcotes sent him in his place, and promised us gold and gifts. But Adam didn't go for what he'd earn, he went to fight for the King – the fool.'

'You didn't want him to go?'

'No. King Henry cared naught for England, and his son is even worse. 'Twas yet another stupid quarrel, amongst those you'd think had power enough. I could not care who won or lost. But Adam would not listen to me, and well . . . he went . . . and there's not a lot more to tell. He was killed, and when we got the news the Lord of Oldcotes turned me from our land. I was with child you see, and not young. It was clear I couldn't do the work that was owed. I'd had my wish for a child come true, but it came too late.'

Marian dropped the herbs, and took Agnes's hands in her own. 'All these years, I've known so little. What became of you?'

'I found Selina, that's what became of me. I wandered

miserable, hungry and sick for days, no . . . for weeks, but at last I walked into this clearing. I'd heard wild tales of the Forestwife, but I was desperate, much like poor Emma. Selina took me in.'

Marian sat silently, listening with growing sadness.

Agnes smiled, though she blinked back tears.

'I was luckier than Emma, for my babe was born alive and strong. We lived here with Selina for more than a year. Perhaps we should have stayed, but . . . perhaps what happened was meant to be.' She squeezed Marian's arm.

'My brother lived in Loxley valley, and worked a small piece of land. I was strong again and wished to show him my son; so I went to find him. He made us both welcome, and begged us to stay. It was when we were there that we heard from Maud and Harry of tha mother's death, and how the lord of Holt needed a wet nurse for his sister's child. I thought to offer myself.'

'But what of Robert?'

'He was almost two years old and he was strong, and ready to be weaned. A wet nurse earns as good a wage as any woman can hope for. I only meant to stay with thee for a year or so. I told them that my child had died. That's what they wanted to hear. They wouldn't want a nurse as might have put her own bairn first. My brother loved Robert and swore that he'd care for him as though he were his own. He kept his word, right to the end. I left them together, as well set up as any father and son. I thought I could save a bit of money and then go back to them.'

'Well? What happened? Why did tha stay so long?'

Agnes shrugged her shoulders and sighed. 'I could not leave thee, when the time came.'

Marian smiled. 'Was I such a sweet child then?'

'Nay. Tha were a poor, thin, grumpy little thing. 'Twas only I that loved thee. I could not leave thee to Dame Marjorie's tender care.'

'Huh.' Marian twisted a lock of her hair between her fingers, then tugged at it. 'So . . . he is angry that you stayed with me?'

Agnes frowned. 'Yes, he is, though he knows well enough that I loved him. How often did I go walking over the hills to be with him. I took him food and clothing, the best Holt Manor had. And when my brother was killed and Robert blamed, he came to hide in Beauchief Woods.'

'But . . . ?'

'No. He did not kill my brother, though there's many a wild and stupid thing he has done. They were truly like father and son, and they had been quarrelling. Their neighbours knew it, and it looked bad for Robert. But he loved my brother, and could not have killed him.'

'Even in rage?'

'No. He could not,' Agnes snapped. 'So he hid in the woods, and Maud and Harry's son brought me messages. Where do you think I wandered off to all those times? I knew they all thought my wits were fading, up at Holt Manor. I let them think it. Meanwhile I took him food and clothes and all he needed.'

Marian's mouth dropped open. 'So when I ran away, and you followed me, he was left alone?'

'Nay, nay. He'd been gone a while then. He had heard that the Sheriff was arming Nottingham Castle, and not too fussy who he took so long as they could draw a bow and not run from a fight. He's a fine archer, Robert, just like his father, and ripe with anger. He craved a fight, so off he went, taking Harry and Maud's son with him.'

'Do you mean Muchlyn, the small one?'

'Aye. He were always daft with Robert. Would do aught he told him. Maud and Harry were wild with worry, and I was vexed with him, but neither lad would listen, and they went.'

'How is he hurt then?'

Agnes shook her head. 'I've not got it quite clear yet, but there has been trouble amongst the men-at-arms. He's like his father, is Robert, in his passionate support for the King, and naught I can say will make him see sense. He found out that the Sheriff was really arming the castle for Count John, against the return of Richard. It's ended in a quarrel, and they had to fight their way out and run ... right through Sherwood Forest he's come.'

They sat in silence for a moment, Marian finding it hard to take in all she had heard.

Agnes sighed. 'So that is what he is like, my lovey. Do not take what he says to heart. Though he's my son, he is a wild and reckless lad. I fear for him.'

8

Muchlyn and John

Laughter and shouted greetings could be heard out in the clearing. Philippa was returning with Tom, and it sounded as though Alice and her husband were with them.

Agnes got to her feet, and rolled up her sleeves ready to return to her work. 'Now tha knows the truth, lovey. Right or wrong, 'tis what happened, and cannot be undone. Can tha try to understand his ignorant way?'

Marian frowned and nodded. 'Aye, maybe I can.'

There was a great deal of noise and chatter and explaining to be done. None of the other women was surprised that Agnes should have a son, and Robert was clucked and fussed over to his heart's content.

He said no more to Marian – indeed, he ignored her – and she kept out of his way, quietly getting on with the dreary chores, fetching the water, gathering wood, and feeding the animals.

Two days passed, and Robert looked much better. He

still winced and groaned when he moved or twisted; but his colour returned, and he did much chattering with Emma and Philippa. He told them tales of the short time he'd spent in the Sheriff's pay; the mischief he and his friends had revelled in, and the chaos they'd caused. Emma listened shyly, smiling and hesitant. Philippa pinched his cheeks and slapped his leg. She said he was a grand lad, for the Sheriff of Nottinghamshire was known even in Langden for his meanness and cruelty.

Once Marian carried a pitcher of water into the hut when they were talking. She felt a sudden hush as she entered, and noticed the tailing off of Philippa's voice. '. . . without her I'd have been branded, you see.'

There was an awkward silence as Marian poured the water into a bowl. Then, as she turned, Philippa spoke up with her usual openness. 'We've been telling Robert how you stole me away from Langden stocks.'

Robert grinned shamefaced, and looked away.

'Oh . . . have you now,' said Marian, and went outside as quickly as she could.

It was on the third day that Marian again had the feeling that they were being watched. The same low murmur of voices, and slipping away of shadows amongst the trees. She went about her tasks as usual, ignoring her suspicions, but when the first glooms of evening fell, she set off as though leaving the clearing, wrapped in her green cloak and hood. She hadn't gone far before she turned round, kicked off her boots, and tucked them under her arm.

She had learned to move through the forest like a lithe green ghost, treading soundlessly through the undergrowth, her long dark cloak echoing the shapes and shades of the woodland. Stealthily she returned to the clearing, moving towards the great yew. Such a tree offered shelter from wind and rain, and a soft matting of dried leaves beneath.

There they were, just where she thought they'd be, a big man with wide shoulders, sitting with his back against the trunk of the yew, and a smaller man hunched beside him on the ground. Marian smiled, she thought she knew the small man . . . and she certainly had no fear of him.

Closer she moved, and closer still; then silently sat down between them.

The big man leapt to his feet, light and quick as a wild cat. He whipped a knife from his belt.

'Nay,' she screamed, terrified by her stupidity. 'I know thee. 'Tis Robert of Loxley tha seeks. I've news of him.'

'What news?' The big man caught her round the back of the neck, his great height lifting her from her feet, his breath stale in her face. The sharp blade of the knife pressed against her throat.

'He is there in the cottage, with his mother. And I know you,' she grabbed at the small man's knife. 'You are from Holt Cornmill. They call you Muchlyn, Maud and Harry's son.'

'Aye . . . tha knows me right enough,' his voice faltered with surprise, 'but who are you? Leave her be, John, and let her speak.' Muchlyn pushed back the steady clenched hand that held the knife at her throat.

'I am Marian, I live with the Forestwife.'

'Th'art . . . the lady. John . . . she is the one, the one that ran away from Holt.'

John laughed and set her on her feet again. He sheathed his knife. 'Tha'art a fool, m'lady, to creep up so on John of Harthersage – but tha's a fearless fool, I'll say that for thee.'

Marian breathed out and rubbed her throat, trying to snatch back a bit of dignity. 'I came to say . . . to tell thee both, that there's shelter and food in the cottage of the Forestwife.'

The two men followed her out of the undergrowth, and warily went with her to the cottage door. The big man towered above her, but Marian could see when the candlelight caught his face that he was nothing but a great, strong, overgrown lad. As soon as they saw Robert looking well and comfortable, they set their suspicions aside.

'We lost thee, Rob,' cried Muchlyn. 'We saw thee jump from the steps, and we took our chance to run, while they followed thee. We knew tha'd seek the Forestwife – if tha lived.'

Both lads had suffered a battering and bruising in the fight that had ended their service with the Sheriff of Nottinghamshire. Muchlyn limped and groaned as he set his foot to the ground. Agnes was soon mashing a comfrey poultice and wrapping up his leg.

'Why, lad, how has tha managed to walk so far on that?'

Muchlyn laughed, and thumped the big man's thigh. 'I had a great ox to carry me. I call him Little'un for he's so tall. He calls me Big'un.'

John laughed and thumped him back, making Much's eyes water, so that they all had to smile and shake their heads.

Robert struggled to his feet, though he winced with the pain. He made play of grabbing John by the neck, grinning into his face.

'Want some fight, big man . . . pick on me.'

'Be still,' said Agnes, 'or I cannot mend this lad's leg . . . sparring like young wolves.' She clicked her tongue.

Marian backed away, crouching in the shadowy corner.

'Tha'd best show Rob what else I carried,' said John, his face bright with excitement. 'I swore and blasted at him that he was so heavy for such a little 'un. Show him, Much.'

Muchlyn's eyes shone, and his dirty face cracked into a great grin. Slowly, from inside his kirtle he drew out a glinting silver cup, and then a platter, and then another cup, and more plates, all wrought in the finest chastened silver.

The whole company drew breath as each piece was revealed.

Robert put out his hand to touch and take one cup. He gave a cruel laugh. Marian shivered at the sound of it.

'Now Much, tha's made theesen into a thief. Tha's wolf indeed. Wolfshead now, the same as me.'

'Aye.' Muchlyn grinned, pleased at that.

Agnes found ale that she'd brewed from a gift of grain, and there was gossip and laughing and storytelling till late into the night.

They stayed in the Forestwife's clearing for two days. Robert was on his feet and walking well, and Much hobbled nimbly, supported on a stick that John shaped into a crutch. At first they were busy cutting great staves for longbows from the straightest branches of the yews, and ash staves for their arrows. They gathered up the feathers from the hens and geese, shouting with pleasure at the fine fletchings they'd make.

But on the second day they gathered by the doorstep, cuffing each other and sparring restlessly and getting in the way. They ate as though they thought they'd never see another meal, shouting foul oaths at each other all the while, hopeless and uncomfortable at the sight of the miserable procession of those who sought the Forestwife.

Tom hovered around them, listening to their yarns, copying their oaths, refusing his work, and leaving Marian to do the chores. John would follow Emma in her round of tasks, attempting to help her stack the wood that she tirelessly replaced when each slow charcoal burning was done. He did not tease her or touch her, but it was plain to see that she shrank away from him.

Agnes watched them all anxiously, rubbing her stiff fingers, and shaking her head and clicking her tongue. Suddenly it was clear that they could not go on as they were.

Agnes caught hold of Philippa's arm. ''Tis no good,' she said. 'We must be rid of them.'

'Aye.'

Philippa firmly took John aside, and Agnes called Robert into the lean-to.

Marian watched from the cottage doorway as Philippa wagged her head and folded her arms, speaking solemnly to John. She could not hear what was said, but the big lad listened well, his face serious. Philippa pointed to the tiny grave beside Selina's.

Then Agnes called Marian inside. Mother and son sat close together, Robert looking none too pleased. 'These lads are on their way,' said Agnes. 'They are well enough to fend for themselves. Well enough to be looking to cause trouble here.'

Marian said nothing, though she was glad enough to hear it.

Agnes got up, and Robert awkwardly followed her.

'Come here, both.'

Agnes stood between them, taking each one by the hand. She spoke slowly and seriously. 'You two are the ones that I love best in all the world. T'would be a blessing on me, if you could manage to agree.'

They stood in silence for a moment, Robert and Marian both red-faced and staring at the ground.

'Well?'

'Aye,' they both muttered and nodded their heads. Then, very stiff and formal, Robert bowed to Marian, and just as stiffly she dropped a curtsy to him.

All the women gathered to see them go.

'Where will you be heading?' asked Agnes, anxious again.

'South,' said Robert. 'South, to where the great road passes through the forests. Full of rich travellers it is, yet close to Sherwood bounds, so that we may not starve for lack of venison.'

'Aye,' said John. 'We shall do well enough there for a while.'

Agnes sighed. 'I do not wish to nurse thee for a severed hand, or hear tha's died in Nottingham gaol.'

Robert hugged her and laughed.

'They'd have to catch us first, Mother. We are too fast and fine for them. And we have other plans that might find us a shelter and food for the winter.'

'Oh aye, and where might that shelter be?'

'We think of going north to Howden Manor, for we hear the Bishop of Durham is gathering fighting men there. Old though he is, he's loyal to Richard still, and he's making ready to take Tickhill Castle from Count John.'

'Can tha find naught to do but fight, lads?' Philippa shook her head.

'Nay,' they laughed. 'What else is there for such as us?'

John bowed to Agnes. 'I thank thee for our rest and food. We will not linger here, for you have strange sad ghosts that cry and moan about your forest. Isn't that right, Much?'

'Aye. John fears nowt, but he got the shivers when he heard the weeping that's carried in the wind. It came to us beneath the branches of your great yew.'

With much waving and calling the three lads went on their way, but Marian turned away from the others as they saw them off. She went back into the clearing, heading straight towards the tallest tree, her eyes sharp for every movement, listening for the slightest sound.

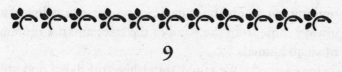

9

The Heretics

The clearing seeming strangely quiet after Robert and his friends had gone, though Marian had little time to notice it. The autumn gathering was in full swing, and Agnes fretted about her stocks more than ever.

Marian and Emma tramped the woods with Tom, seeking out blackberries and crab apples for pasties and pies, elderberries for wine, and hips and haws for Agnes's remedies. Then for the winter stocks they must gather and store chestnuts, hazel nuts, beech mast and acorns.

Marian and Tom stood beneath the yew tree in the dusk, though they were weary from their hard day's work.

'I can't hear it,' said Tom. 'Anyways . . . it don't come every night.'

Marian put her finger to her lips to silence him. She was determined that once and for all she would hear the weeping in the woods.

They stood there still and listening, though there was

nothing but an owl hooting, and the distant rustling that always came from the wind in the trees and the running of small animals.

Tom sighed. 'We could stand here till dawn and still not hear it.'

'You go then,' Marian snapped. 'I'll see to it myself.'

Tom shrugged his shoulders and turned towards the cottage as though he might well take her at her word, but as he bent down to pick up their heavy baskets . . . it came. Just a faint eerie sound, so indistinct that it could have been imagined. Tom stopped and turned to Marian.

'You heard it too?' she whispered.

He nodded. 'I think I did.'

They both stood in silence, until once more the faint cry reached them.

'Wolves?'

Tom shook his head. 'I've heard wolves afore.'

Marian nodded. 'There . . . it comes from beyond the stream, that way. Will you come with me, Tom?'

'Aye.'

It was hard to follow at first, for the cries came in faltering, fitful bursts. Sometimes they'd miss them for the crack of a twig, or mistake them for a wild cat's howl.

At last, as the glooms of evening thickened around them, the cries became louder and more distinct.

Tom stopped and scratched his head. 'We go towards Langden village. I swear this is the way.'

The cry came again, and Tom turned his head. 'No . . . not Langden. Over there, towards . . .'

'Where?' cried Marian. 'What is it?'

Tom suddenly ran ahead in the direction of the sounds. Marian chased after him, and caught him by the arm. He stopped and turned to her, frowning.

'This is close to where the Sisters live.'

'You mean . . . the convent? The Sisters who have vanished from the woods?'

'Aye.'

Once he'd got the convent in his mind, Tom went fast, Marian striding along beside him. There was no doubt about it, the crying came from that direction. The night grew darker and the miserable wailing loud and fearful. Tom reached the top of a grassy bank and stopped. They looked down the hillside to where the trees had been cleared for the small convent buildings and kitchen gardens. A strongly built wooden fence protected it all. A low light showed at one end of the building. To Marian it all looked peaceful and organised. The gentle clucking of fowls and the grunt of pigs rose from the sheds.

'What is it, Tom? It seems to me that all is well.'

Tom shook his head. 'The Sisters never built that great stockade. 'Twas open for all to come and go.'

Suddenly the sobbing came again, not from the convent, but from further up the ravine, where the sloping hillside was wooded. Cries of such despair that they flooded the valley with sadness. A shiver ran down Marian's spine, lifting the hairs on her neck.

Tom clutched her hand and trembled, pointing up the valley.

' 'Tis the Seeress,' he whispered.

As Marian turned off towards the source of such misery, hoofbeats rang out below. A rider was fast heading in the same direction. Marian grabbed Tom's hand and pulled him after her. They stumbled down the hillside as quickly as they could in the dark.

Then came the harsh shouting of a man's voice, and loud banging.

Marian ran fast, but she could not see clearly what was ahead. It looked to her almost as if the man on horseback attacked a tiny chicken hut. There was the clatter of wood on wood, and angry bellowing, then the clang of metal, and more shouting. The wailing ceased and the horseman whirled around, his horse braying loud in protest. He headed back towards the convent at a good speed. Marian crouched with Tom behind the gorse scrub, as he galloped past.

The crying had ceased, but in its place there came a small pathetic whimpering that Marian found even more distressing. It seemed to come from the chicken hut.

Marian got up to approach it, but Tom held her back.

'No,' he whispered, more scared than ever. ' 'Tis her. 'Tis the Seeress.'

'But who is she? Have they locked her in there?'

'No,' Tom shook his head frantically. 'Don't you understand? She has locked herself in there. She is not like the other nuns. She never comes out.'

'Ah,' said Marian. 'An anchorite. I have heard of such women, but never—'

'I have not seen her,' Tom interrupted, 'but I know all about her. She is strange and frightening, some say she is mad – more of a witch than the . . . the . . .'

Marian smiled. 'More of a witch than the Forestwife?'

She could not see his face clearly, but she knew that Tom smiled back at her.

'Aye. But then the Forestwife is just . . . Agnes.'

'Yes,' said Marian. 'This Seeress is but a woman too. And though I cannot see why, someone is treating her very ill.'

Tom followed her then, though he was still fearful. They crept down towards the dark hump of the hut, half buried in earth. A stale smell of decay seemed to emanate from the tiny dwelling, and hover in the damp shrouding mists that surrounded it. There came again the sound of low whimpering, and the rustle of long robes.

There was silence, and then a shaky, frightened voice. 'Who is't?'

'I am Marian. I live with the Forestwife and help her.'

There was silence for a moment and then another shuffle. A patch of white moved, indistinct in the darkness of a small window, barred from the outside and covered with a fine metal mesh. The quavering voice came again.

'Then I saw true. Selina's dead.'

'Aye, I fear she is, but I have come to see what ails thee. Why does tha weep and wail so? We have heard thee from afar.'

'I weep because I must. I give utterance to their misery. They weep in silence, so I must cry out for them.'

The voice rose in a wild passion. Tom clutched tight to Marian's sleeve.

'Men of God they call themselves, but 'tis no god of mine that starves little children of the sun. And so you see, I must weep. I weep for myself and them.'

Marian sighed. It was hard to understand what it all meant, and the thought came that maybe Tom had been right when he spoke of madness.

But it was Tom himself who answered now.

'She is the Seeress.' He spoke with conviction. 'What she sees is the truth.'

Marian shook her head. 'But . . .'

'You never knew 'em,' he insisted, nodding back over his shoulder towards the convent. 'Something is wrong down there. The Sisters lived there, quiet-like and good, but they were busy as bees in a hive, digging their gardens, scrubbing and cleaning and tending the beasts. They came to our village twice a week with food and medicines. They brewed a good ale. And – and Mother Veronica, she was fat, and she laughed, and she brought the two little lasses with her. Naught but bairns they were, carrying their own small baskets.'

Marian frowned, but the Seeress spoke calmly. 'The lad speaks truth. He understands.'

'Who was that man,' Marian asked, 'and has he hurt thee?'

'Nay.' The Seeress answered now with quiet strength. 'He bangs on this grille and shouts to shut me up. But I shall not be silenced. He is one of the white monks, Cistercians from the great abbey. You see, we are Cistercian nuns, and by right they may rule us, but though we've been here fifteen years, they have never interested themselves in us. Then three months since, six of them came, and with them the Lay Brothers.'

Marian and Tom listened as she told them in quiet, sensible tones, how the Lay Brothers had built a stockade around the convent. Then the monks insisted that the nuns be locked up in their cells, even the two children. There they were to spend their time in prayer, and contemplate their wickedness. Dreadful rumours of heresy had reached the Abbot. Nuns had no business to go wandering about all over the countryside, as they had done, meddling in things that did not concern them. Worst of all, they'd allowed their lazy chaplain, Brother James, to roam the forest with his dog, while they – the nuns – took their own services, preached their own sermons, held their chapters and meetings without the advice of a priest.

Tom listened wide-eyed and open-mouthed.

'Why, 'tis true enough, they did all that, but they brought comfort to our village, and life has been hard since they've gone.'

The Seeress went on speaking, clear and firm.

'The Lay Brothers have returned to the abbey, but the white monks stay. That one you saw, he brings a little bread and water each day. I see no other but Brother James. He wanders about the woods with his dog in a miserable drunken state, but he is still my friend. The

Sisters and even the little girls, they weep within their cells.'

'But how . . . ?'

Tom's pressure on her arm answered. 'Ah yes. The Seeress knows.'

'I chose this life,' she went on. 'It was a hard life, but not miserable. The Sisters consulted me, they brought me their worries and their joys. Sister Catherine looked after me well. These monks,' she shuddered, 'they will not even bring me water to . . . cleanse myself.' Her voice shook.

Marian could bear no more.

'I can bring thee water. I could fetch it from the stream, if I had something to carry it in.'

The Seeress was eager. 'I have a wooden bucket, and I would be glad of help.'

There came the squeak of a rusting bolt, and then a sudden clap of wood on wood. A small hatch flopped open beside the window grille. A pair of startlingly white hands held out a bucket. Marian wrinkled her nose at the smell that issued through the opening.

'Do not look at me,' the Seeress cried. 'I am banished from the world. None may see my face.'

Though Marian wished very much to peer inside, she kept her glance down. She could not bear to be the cause of more distress.

She filled the bucket from the stream, and handed it carefully back.

'We will come again,' she promised, 'and though I cannot think how, I swear that you shall have help. We have friends who once lived at Langden. They will stand by you, and the Sisters.'

'Aye, that we will,' said Tom.

Marian stood up to go, but through the darkness she saw the faint, thin shape of a hand come stretching and beseeching through a small space at the bottom of the grille. Marian clasped it in her own, though it was damp from the water, and carried with it a sour smell. She could have wept to feel the frail bones beneath the cold white skin.

The Seeress clung to her for a moment, then she whispered, 'My heart leaps up to find such a friend. You shall bring us all joy, I see that clear enough.'

They set off back through the forest. Both Tom and Marian were quiet and shaken by what they'd found. It was when they reached the top of the hill above the convent that Tom almost fell over a dark shape, curled up in a dip. A growl and flash of white teeth warned them to step backwards fast. Then a man's deep voice fell to cursing, and there came the strong smell of ale.

'Watch out. 'Tis him.' Tom pulled Marian away. 'All right, all right, boy,' he soothed. 'No harm, no harm.'

'What was that?' Marian whispered, once they seemed far enough away. She'd been glad enough to do as Tom had told her.

'That were the one she spoke of. That were Brother James. He's a big fat fellow and he likes his ale, though he's kind enough when sober. That hound of his never leaves his side. Once it belonged to the lord of Langden. 'Twas his best hunting dog, but it was found in Sherwood by the regarders and they lamed it.'

'Poor thing, no wonder it growls and snarls.'

'Well, that is their right. But they hadn't realised who it belonged to. There was trouble, and William of Langden went into one of his rages. He swore he'd cut the beast's throat now that it was useless for hunting.'

'I don't like the sound of that man,' said Marian. 'The more I hear of him, the more I dread him. Well, how did that drunken monk get the dog?'

'He marched into the great hall at Langden Manor, red-faced and full of ale, and asked for it. First the lord said no, but the monk lifted up his great staff and said he'd fight any man William chose, to get the dog.'

'So did he fight?'

'Nay. Brother James is a big strong feller. William of Langden kicked the dog, and said he might have the useless cur, if he was so bothered about it. Though he's nasty and mean, he wouldn't want to lose one of his best fighting men, not for a dog.'

'So Brother James took it?'

'Aye. And though it's not much of a hunter, it defends its new master as you saw, and it's learnt a trick or two that might surprise its old master.'

Marian walked on deep in thought, then she turned again to Tom.

'You say he's kind enough when sober, this Brother James. Did he care for the nuns do you think?'

Tom laughed. 'Aye, he cared for them. Specially Mother Veronica.'

'I shall have to go seek him, in the daylight. Though I think I might take Philippa along.'

10

The Sisters of St Mary

Marian was surprised, for Philippa hesitated when she asked her to go looking for Brother James.

'I never thought tha'd have a doubt. Not for a moment. I cannot bear to leave them there so miserable and imprisoned.'

Agnes pushed her down onto the stool, and set a bowl of steaming porridge in her lap.

'Calm theesen. Tha's fair done in, tramping through the forest all night, and me worrying and wondering what tha's up to. We cannot go rushing into this, there's much to think about. The Sisters chose to make their vows. That's no light matter, and disobedience in the Church may be called heresy.'

Emma caught her breath. 'You mean, they could—'

'Aye,' Agnes was stern. 'They could burn, by right of the Church's law, should they disobey the Abbot.'

Philippa sighed. 'Agnes is right. 'Tis not the law of the manor, or even the law of the King. This is a matter for the Church and maybe even for the Pope. More powerful than the King, he is. I will not turn my back on it, Marian. I owe the Sisters much, and I will come with thee, but we must tread carefully.

'And there is something else, that I . . .' Philippa's voice tailed off, so unlike her usual firm way of speaking.

They all looked up at her.

'It is this. That we must go close by Langden, and I . . . well, I have been thinking lately that I must go back. Not to stay. I know that cannot be, but . . . it comes into my mind that William of Langden may treat my little ones ill, to punish me. So you see . . .'

There was quiet for a moment, then Emma spoke.

'I'll go with thee to Langden. Tha must be certain that the little 'uns are safe.'

'Let us all three go,' said Marian, 'and we may meet the drunken monk upon our way.'

The three women set off, well wrapped and Marian with her meat knife in her belt. Tom ran at their heels like a hound, he would not be left at home, and they were soon glad of him, for none of them knew the woods as well as he.

Brother James was not difficult to find, for they saw his great dog resting, but still alert, beside an ivy-covered fallen tree. The monk snored loudly, in a pile of beech leaves, sheltered in the bowl of earth that the torn-up roots had left. Beside him was a pile of chicken bones, a fallen stoneware flagon by his feet.

The dog leaped up, growling at their approach, but the monk snored on.

They moved forward warily.

'Brother James, Brother James ... shift theesen,' Marian called, pulling her knife from her belt.

The dog crouched, preparing to spring.

'Wake up, tha great fat fool,' Philippa bellowed.

'What? What?' Brother James, snorted and jumped to his feet. The dog snarled and leapt at Marian, a flying shadow of black fur. She screamed with fright and staggered backwards, angry and shocked.

'Pax, Snap!' the monk shouted.

Though Marian was shaken, she realised that she was unharmed. The knife had gone from her hand; it glinted from the corner of the dog's mouth, as he dropped down onto his haunches, obedient and watchful now.

Brother James blinked round at them, fuddled and muzzy in the morning sun.

The dog growled again, and dropped the knife. His master stared and rubbed his eyes, puzzled by what he saw. Three women, steadfastly placing themselves to surround him. There was the crack of a twig behind, and he turned to see a young lad.

Two of the women were only girls, one frightened but determined, the other red-faced and angry at the loss of her knife. The third, who stood before him, was big and strong, and he knew her well, just as he knew the lad.

'Peace, Snap,' he soothed the dog again.

He staggered forward, holding out his hand to Philippa.

'What the devil . . . ? Haul me out of this hole.'

He laughed as she heaved him up.

'Tha's not lost thy strong arm nor thine impudence, since tha became a wicked outlaw woman. I wondered what had become of thee.'

'From what we've been hearing, tha's become a bit of an outlaw theesen.' Philippa grinned. 'But 'tis Mother Veronica and the Sisters that we're fearful for.'

Brother James sat down amongst them, rubbing at his dirty stubbly chin and pulling his mud-stained habit straight. What he told them proved the Seeress true. He swore that he'd been threatened with expulsion from the Church. The monks had turned him out of the convent, into the woods, as punishment for neglecting his work and allowing the nuns the freedom they'd enjoyed. He'd had it in mind to go off to the Abbot and plead for them, but not much faith in the reception that he'd get. He couldn't quite bring himself to desert the Sisters with whom he'd lived so comfortably. Since then, he'd hung around the stockade, stealing ale and food whenever he got the chance.

He wept as he spoke, and heaved great sighs. Emma listened with sympathy, but Marian and Philippa fidgeted and shook their heads.

'So tha can get inside the convent, when tha wants?' Philippa demanded.

He grinned then. 'I know that building better than those prating monks. I creep inside while they chant their offices. They don't even know I've been or what I've taken. I carried a sup of ale to the Seeress, but she'll do naught but whine and wail.'

' 'Tis her cries that have told us that there's trouble,' Marian snapped, exasperated by him. 'You could have let the Sisters out. You must know where to find the keys. You could have done something for them!'

He stared up at her, puzzled at her rage. Who was this furious young girl in a good green cloak?

He turned to Philippa for some sense. 'I could maybe let them out, but where would they go? They're vowed to obedience. Dear God! 'Tis heresy indeed that tha suggests.'

Philippa sighed. ''Tis their wishes that we need to understand. Instead of filching ale, can tha not search out Mother Veronica and offer her our help?'

He scratched his head, where stubble grew on the old tonsured patch. 'I can try. Aye, I can do that.'

'If they wish it,' said Marian, 'we shall help them build some shelter in the forest. There are more of us . . . friends that we may call to aid us.'

He scrambled to his feet, clicking his fingers to Snap, who leapt at once to his command.

'Mother Veronica always did things her own way. I shall do what you ask, young woman. No need to look so fierce at me. Tha may take tha knife back from Snap. I shall meet thee here tomorrow at dusk.'

'Aye, we've other errands.' Philippa was restless to be off to Langden.

Marian took her knife back, still frowning, but as they walked away, she turned to see Brother James filling the flagon with water from the stream. She could not help but smile as he poured it over his head, snorting and shuddering, while the great black shadow beside him danced and barked.

Emma and Marian approached the blacksmith's cottage by the forge, leaving Philippa hidden in the gorse scrub at the edge of the woods. It was a quiet midmorning, most of the village folk busy at their chores. The blacksmith recognised Marian, and welcomed them inside. As they stood by the warm fire's glow and looked around the small neat home, they could see that all was well. The children were strong, and all had good warm clothes and clean faces.

'Tha's been looking after them well,' said Marian, impressed and pleased for Philippa's sake.'

'Aye, but I've had help,' her husband told them, though there was something of a puzzle in his face.

'From thy neighbours?'

'My neighbours have been grand, that's true. But we have had better help than they could have given.'

'What then?'

He shrugged his shoulders. 'Presents. Presents of good food and clothing, brought in secret in the night.'

'And you do not know who sends them?' Marian's eyes were wide with interest.

The blacksmith shook his head. 'No one in Langden could give such presents. No one but the lord.'

He laughed, though there was no joy in the sound.

'We can be sure it is not him. The only one we can think of is his wife, the Lady Matilda, but she is a poor sick woman, rarely seen. Some say that William beats her.'

'Why should he do that?' Marian demanded.

'She's given him but one daughter. William wants a son as his heir. There are many who would say that that is reason enough.'

Marian shook her head at the injustice of it all.

'She's a kindly woman though,' the blacksmith spoke softly, 'and I swear these presents come from her.'

The children were wild with excitement at the thought of seeing their mother, and yet they fell obediently quiet when they were told. Used to living in fear, thought Marian.

Emma took three of the children straight off with her to see their mother, each carrying log baskets, as though they were going to search out firewood. Marian waited until they returned and then gathered up the others, insisting that there must be no fuss or commotion.

'Will tha come too and bring the bairn?' she asked the blacksmith.

He hesitated and turned towards the forge. 'I have much work in hand . . .' His voice trailed off, and Marian frowned.

'I daresay Philippa will wish to see you too.'

The man sighed, then turned back to her.

'Aye, surely I shall come, and bring the bairn, but I fear it will not please Philippa.'

The man took the smallest boy from the crib where he slept, and wrapped him well in a warm, soft woven blanket, one of the mysterious gifts. Then he set off with Marian and the two other children.

* * *

Philippa rushed forward to hug her children, but then she moved slowly towards her husband and suddenly slapped his face sharply. Marian flinched and backed away from them; the blacksmith had been right.

'That is for this scar.' Philippa touched the long red weal that still showed on her cheek, flaming livid with her anger. Then suddenly her face changed. She flung her arms around the man and child, hugging them both and planting a kiss upon her husband's mouth.

'That is for keeping my little 'uns so well. Now give me that bairn.'

She gathered the baby into her arms and settled back against a tree stump, rocking the child, her cheek against his head.

'Rowlie, my little Rowland,' she crooned.

Marian smiled with relief, but saw that the man still looked troubled.

Philippa's smile faded. Slowly the rocking stopped; she looked down at her child, then up at her husband.

'How long have I been gone from Langden?'

He sighed and sat down beside her, putting out his strong, work-marked hand to touch the baby's head. ' 'Tis all but six weeks, my love.'

Philippa's voice shook. 'And this bairn has not grown a jot.' She unwrapped the small body. 'His little arms and legs are like sticks.'

The blacksmith shook his head. 'I swear that I have done my best, and others have tried too, but we cannot get him to feed. He should be trying his feet by now, but he frets and will not take milk or sops.'

Philippa's face crumpled. 'Mother's milk is what he needs, and I have none for him.'

Marian sat down beside them, understanding their concern now. The two older children stood still and quiet, watching.

'We have good fresh goats' milk in the clearing,' Marian spoke gently. 'And the Forestwife to give advice. Best of all, we have his mam.'

'Aye,' Philippa picked up the idea and smiled. 'I shall take him back with me.'

'I think it's maybe best,' her husband agreed.

'Will William of Langden see that he's gone?' Marian asked.

The blacksmith laughed. 'Do you think he knows or cares how many children we have? And no one else will point it out to him.'

'Does he treat you ill because of me?' Philippa asked.

He shook his head. 'He needs his horses shod, and his guards well armed.'

Once the decision was made, Philippa was keen to be on her way, and get the baby back to Agnes. One of the other children was sent to tell Emma, and to fetch the good wrappings and baby clothes that had appeared with the other gifts.

Goodbyes were said, and soon Philippa was striding smiling through the forest with her little lad strapped to her front. Marian and Emma struggled to keep up with her. Emma had gone very quiet.

They were close to the clearing when Philippa slowed

her pace at last. She had begun to see and understand Emma's silent pain. She stopped by the pointer stone and caught hold of her hand.

'I never thought,' she said. 'Seeing me with this little 'un must hurt thee sore.'

Emma's eyes filled with tears, but she lifted her hand and gently stroked the fine hair on Rowland's head.

'Your Rowlie is a sweet child,' she whispered.

'He is that, and I must try my best to save him. I'll never do it on my own. I'll need a deal of help.'

'Aye,' said Emma shyly. 'I'd be glad to do what I can.'

'Might tha take him in for me, while I sort out these wrappings?'

'May I?' Emma held out her arms, her chin trembling.

Agnes came to greet them, surprised to see Marian and Tom carrying rugs and blankets, Philippa grinning and satisfied, and Emma with a baby in her arms.

11

Bunches of Rosemary

Agnes examined the small child carefully, pressing gently on his legs and arms, and at last lifting him up to try his feet. Philippa and Emma both watched anxiously. At first the two poor, thin legs trailed, and the child stared blankly into Agnes's face, but then he drew up his knees and kicked his feet down weakly.

'Boo!' Agnes shouted suddenly.

The child jumped in her arms, and then, slowly, a delightful one-toothed smile brightened his face.

'There's naught wrong with this little chap,' Agnes turned to Philippa. 'Naught wrong that good goats' milk, fresh air and mother's love won't cure.'

Philippa snatched up her child, laughing with relief, and Emma went to fetch a cup of milk, still warm from the beast.

All the next day Philippa fussed and fretted over little Rowland, and Emma ran round in circles, fetching and carrying for the child.

Late in the afternoon Marian brought out her cloak, and fastened on her boots. Philippa stared at her, puzzled, for a moment, then suddenly got to her feet, the child crying out at the sharp movement.

'Brother James! I forget.'

Marian laughed.

'Settle theesen down again. I shall take Tom with me. I do not need thee, nor Emma. There's nothing to fear from him, I know that now.'

Brother James was waiting as he'd promised, leaning against a sturdy oak, Snap sitting quietly beside him. The monk lumbered to his feet at their approach.

'Well?' Marian demanded at once. 'What of the Sisters? Has tha spoken with them?'

He bowed deeply, chuckling and ignoring her questions. 'Greetings to you, my wild lady of the woods.'

Marian sighed with impatience and Tom grinned at the monk. Then Brother James's face grew solemn. 'Indeed, I've news for you. Mother Veronica and the Sisters are longing for the freedom of the woods. I can let them out. Can you build shelter for them?'

Marian's face lit up. 'We shall do our very best.'

'We'll do that all right,' Tom agreed.

'Can they really burn for this?' Marian asked, suddenly frightened by the plan.

The fat monk's cheeks trembled. 'By right and by the Church's law they could. But then they would have to be hunted and discovered, and carried off for judgement. These bishops are too busy fighting amongst themselves.

I hear that Geoffrey of York has excommunicated Hugh of Durham yet again, and even sent his men to smash Hugh's altars. Still the old man laughs in his face, and gathers his army about him. In truth, I cannot see even the most vindictive churchman paying men to search these vast and desolate wastes for six poor old women and two dowerless girls.

' 'Tis the two lasses, Anna and Margaret, that are the greatest worry for Veronica. They were given into her care as babes. Unmarriageable daughters! Young Margaret's face is scarred by the hare lip, and Anna born with a crooked back. How can Veronica set such children outside the Church's law?'

'But should they then spend their lives like prisoners, locked away in cells?' Marian insisted.

'Nay,' he shook his head. 'And that is why she will bring them with her. You know these Sisters set themselves up as working nuns. They never claimed to lead the solitary life of contemplation . . . only the Seeress aspires to that. Oh no, Veronica and the Sisters never wished to be saints, just decent women leading safe and useful lives. That's why they were so happy with their special saint.'

'What? The Blessed Virgin?'

'Nay!' He laughed. 'They are the Sisters of St Mary Magdalen.'

As Marian turned to go, Tom caught her arm.

'Will the Sisters bring their beasts?'

Marian looked surprised.

'Oh yes, they must bring their beasts.' Brother James

agreed. 'How should they get through the winter without them?'

Brother James paused and sighed. 'There's one who'll not come. The Seeress will never leave her cell. I spoke with her last night, and though I talked till dawn, I could not win her over. All she cares is that the nuns go free. She will not break her vow.'

Marian remembered the childlike hand in hers. 'We'll see. I'll speak to her.'

Brother James shrugged his shoulders. He touched her head. 'A heretic's blessing,' he whispered.

Marian stood quietly with Tom, watching him stride purposefully away through the crackling leaves, Snap bounding after with his awkward gait.

It took many days and a great deal of help searching through miles of forest, wild wastes and marshes, before a site for the new forest convent was found. It had to be far from Langden Manor and the old convent, but it had to have a good supply of strong straight timber for building and, most important of all, clean running water that would not fail.

At last such a site was found, far south towards Sherwood, yet still within the thickest tangle of Barnsdale. A marsh lay to the north-eastern side. Dangerous marshland would offer protection. They chose a patch of level ground, sheltered by a sloping bank of beech and holly trees.

Philippa sent Tom to Langden to beg axes and saws from her husband. Tom's father, his damaged hand healing well, went around the chosen clearing, marking the trees to be felled.

Tom returned with a great sack of tools. But the blacksmith regretted that he was short of nails, and could not spare the few he'd got.

'Of course he's short, for 'twas me that made his nails,' said Philippa. 'If only I had iron to melt down, I could make all the nails we need and more for him.'

Tom looked at her and bit his lip. 'I know where there's iron,' he said. 'But I fear tha might not like it, Philippa.'

'What can tha mean?'

Tom ran to the side of the clearing and dived into one of the smaller yews, where thick green branches swept the ground. There was a clanking sound, then he emerged, his forehead wrinkled with worry, dragging the rusting scold's bridle by the chain.

Philippa's face fell. The busy work and chatter around them ceased.

Tom stopped, dismayed. 'I feared tha'd not like it. I carried it that night, and I knew how tha must sicken at the sight of it, so I hid it. Shall I drag it away and you'll see it no more?'

Philippa stared white-faced at him. For a moment she seemed unable to answer, but then she spoke up, her voice stern.

'Nay. Bring it to me.'

He dragged it on, till it rolled clattering before her feet. She suddenly laughed, and bent to kiss him.

'Tha's a good lad. 'Twill make a thousand nails, and I shall beat it and hammer it and thrust it into the fire.'

She fetched the stout sweeping brush that stood at the cottage door, and whacked the hated thing across the grass. Everyone clapped and cheered to see her treat it so.

Later that afternoon, Marian set off alone, laden with freshly-picked bunches of rosemary. As darkness came, a bright moon sailed above the leaflorn branches of the trees. She clambered down the bank near the convent of St Mary, heading for the lonely cell of the Seeress.

The woodlands were quiet and still, though the air was damp and chilly. Moonshine threw graceful waving shadows across the ground, creating constantly changing patterns of dark and light. Marian moved slowly towards the hump of earth that covered the small cell, with a growing sense of intrusion. A low clicking came from the hut, and, as she moved closer, Marian realised that the sounds came from the Seeress. She stood still for a moment, recalling those desperate cries that had brought her here before. These sounds, strange though they were, held no misery.

Marian saw a startling and lovely sight. A young dog fox sat by the Seeress's grille, twitching his ears and making small growling yaps in response to the eerie clicking song. Marian froze, mouth open, scarcely breathing. The magic held only for a moment. Some other sense told of her presence. The creature turned towards her, and in that instant she glimpsed the deep yellow fire that burned in his eyes. Then he was off, leaping into the undergrowth, leaving only the rank smell of fox to tell of his presence there.

The Seeress caught her breath, and Marian hastily stepped forward to explain.

' 'Tis I, Marian, the Forestwife's girl.'

The Seeress's voice was calm. 'I knew 'twas not one of the monks. They have left me much alone of late. I weep no longer, now that Brother James has told me of thy plans.'

'Aye. We make a hiding place in the forest. I swear we shall do all we can to keep the Sisters safe. But you must come too. The Brothers are bound to be angry. They may harm you, or even leave you to starve.'

'I stay here,' she insisted. There was no waver in her voice.

'By why?' Marian was almost angry.

'I made my vow, and I keep it. I am not like the others. Mother Veronica and Catherine were always decent, religious women. I am here for my sin.'

Marian sighed. 'What sin? Whatever could you be guilty of that demands this of you?'

The white face shimmered behind the grille and vanished.

'Do not go!' Marian pleaded.

Once more the indistinct, white, moonlike oval moved towards the grille, and the childlike hand came creeping through the space beneath. Marian caught it up, frightened by its coldness, rubbing it between her own warm palms.

'It was a great sin,' the Seeress's voice shook. 'Nobody

knows . . . only my brother, and one other. 'Twas my brother built this place for me, and sent me here. I must bear this life with patience, and hope for salvation through my suffering.'

Marian let go of the hand. She raked her fingers through her hair in frustration. What could she say? What could she do to shake this blind belief?

Then the Seeress spoke again, her voice warm and loving.

'I am not unhappy. I have great faith in you. I cannot always see, as they think I can, and I cannot see clear what lies ahead, but this I know . . . in your presence, I feel that there is hope for us all. There is even hope for me.'

Marian sighed. 'I almost forgot. I have brought thee a good supply of the cleansing herb, rosemary. At least you may keep your cell all clean and sweet.'

'You see,' the Seeress's voice was deep with pleasure, 'tha knows full well what I desire most. Brother James brings me ale, but he would never think of rosemary.'

Marian did not stay till dawn as Brother James had done. She returned to the Forestwife's cottage before the candles had guttered for the night. There was no hope of changing the Seeress's mind. Marian was sure of it, and must content herself with promises that she should be watched and cared for, even when the other nuns were gone.

Over the next few days, those who'd pledged themselves to help were thrown into a wild fury of work and preparation.

Marian rushed about shouting and begging and worrying. She was all in a spin with excitement and fear at what they were daring to do. Philippa's skills and strong arms were much in demand. She strode through the clearing with her little lad strapped to her chest. Whenever she had a dangerous job to do, Emma stood by with willing arms, ready to cuddle and fuss him. Despite the hard work that surrounded him, the child was clearly thriving. Tom insisted that they change his name from Rowland to Rowan, for the fine red cheeks that he'd gained.

The frame of a small building was raised with strong beechwood planks and Philippa's good nails. Everyone was needed to slap wet mud onto the wattle panels, woven about with moss and twigs. There were no thatching materials close by, so great bundles of rushes and heather were dragged through the forest tracks. The clearing that they'd created soon became known as the Magdalen Assart. Even the smallest children worked till the wintery sun sank behind the hill.

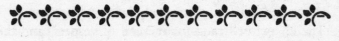

12

The Magdalen Assart

All too soon, the appointed evening came when Brother James would free the Sisters. Marian, Alice, Philippa and Emma crept up to the hill above the convent. Brother James was waiting there with Tom and Snap.

'Is the potion ready?' he asked. He was sweating and anxious, his fat cheeks shook with concern.

'Aye.' Marian took a small phial from her belt. ' 'Twas not easy to persuade her though. Agnes swears that they will sleep till midday, though the taste may be bitter.'

'I shall see it goes in the richest dark red wine.'

Brother James held Marian's hand for just a moment. 'I pray we do right, my bold lady.'

Then he set off through the thickening twilight, faithful Snap limping at his heels.

The four women and Tom settled down to wait. There'd been others willing to come, but they feared large numbers might draw attention and spoil the plan. In the end it came back to just the four.

All was quiet in the convent buildings beneath the hill.

They waited, tense and strained, barely whispering.

The chapel bell rang for the end of vespers, and the monks filed out. There were quickening footsteps below them as the Brothers moved in line to the refectory. Candles flickered through the small windows, and the faint chink of cups and platters could be heard. The meal began.

Up on the hillside Marian and her friends grew hungry and anxious. The darkness gathered around them.

'What now?' whispered Emma. 'How will we know?'

'We must listen for the compline bell,' said Marian. 'If it rings, we have failed to drug them, and must wait till they go to their beds.'

'But how will we know when compline time comes?'

Marian frowned. 'Brother James will give us some sign.'

Never had time dragged so. A bright moon drifted from the clouds and lit the woodland hillside so that they shrank into the bushes, worried that they'd be seen.

The lights still glimmered in the refectory, but it seemed the distant sounds of chatter had ceased. Still there was no bell.

'The time for praying must be past,' said Emma.

'I doubt they take their prayers so seriously,' said Philippa. 'They break what other rules they wish.'

Marian stood up. 'I think we should go down, but quiet and careful, mind.'

'Aye.' They all agreed. They'd waited long enough.

All stealthily and slow, they crept down the bank

towards the convent. Still there was no sound nor sign of movement from inside. Then as they gathered at the bottom of the hill a man's voice suddenly rose, chanting the prayers of the night.

They all stood frozen together, listening and scared.

The singing did not come from the chapel. All at once the lone voice was answered by a chorus of female voices, some deep and sweet, some childlike in their tones. The nuns were singing compline with Brother James.

Relief spread from Marian to the others. They smiled at each other, though they stood with itching feet beside the door, wishing to be on their way.

At last the singing stopped, and suddenly there was wild bustle and chaos. The door was flung open and six nuns poured out, each loaded with bags and sacks so that they could scarcely move.

'Do the brothers sleep?' Marian asked.

'They snore like pigs, my darling,' said a fat nun, her arms wrapped tightly around two frightened little girls.

'Sister Catherine is henwife,' said Brother James. 'Go with her and catch the fowls.'

'I have bags for them,' said Emma, rushing off after the flustered nun.

'I'm pigwife,' said a tall young nun. 'Sister Rosamund. Who'll help me with the swine?'

'You go, Tom,' said Brother James, 'and Snap. Go fetch the pigs!'

Marian reeled amongst the turmoil, wondering where to help next. A nervous young nun clutched the arm of one who was old and stooped.

'Sister Christina, she cannot walk well,' she cried.

'We'll make a chair with our arms and carry her,' said Marian, snatching up the young nun's hands, and bending down to pick the old woman bodily from the ground.

Then all at once they were off, in a noisy, bustling gang. Pushing and shoving and tripping over each other's feet, they went off into the chilly forest night. Soon the pushing stopped and turned to puffing, as women and animals set themselves to climb the hill.

'Ooh dear, you should leave me, such a nuisance I am!' Sister Christina trembled and cried.

'Hush now,' said Marian. 'You're no weight at all.' And that was true enough, for the old nun was frail and light.

Mother Veronica went ahead with the two little girls, talking calmly to them all the while.

'What an adventure, my darlings.'

As they reached the top of the hill, Sister Christina continued to whittle and whine so that Marian was tempted to take her at her word and leave her there, but she caught the eye of the young nun who helped her with the carrying, and they both giggled instead. Sister Christina looked suspiciously from one to the other and fell silent.

Once they had gained the top of the hill they felt that they could slow down a little, and make some sort of order. Emma and the henwife were the last to reach the top. They set the others smiling, for they both carried angry squawking hens in bags, and more tucked beneath each arm. The cockerel rode precariously upon the old nun's head, flapping his clipped wings and crowing frantically.

They moved on through the forest, vowing their thanks to Agnes's potion, for they made enough noise to wake the dead. It was slow progress, for one way and another they had to keep stopping. The hens squawked and complained, and fluttered away whenever they got the chance. The pigs were puzzled that they could not root and snuffle wherever fine acorns could be found. Snap earned his keep, and more, by chasing runaways and fetching them back with gentle nips. Sister Christina began her whimpering once again, till Mother Veronica said she wished they'd left her behind, making the two pale children giggle.

With all the fuss and stopping, it was almost dawn as they neared the Magdalen clearing. They were joined and greeted along the way by forest folk, for the nuns were widely known for their kindness. By the time they reached the assart, faint gleams of morning light came through the stark branches of the beech trees. The carrying was shared about, and all the nuns walked free of their burdens.

'Why, child,' Sister Catherine put up a wrinkled hand to touch Marian's cheek, 'I feel I know thee, now I see thy face clear in the light.'

Marian shook her head and smiled at the old nun's vagueness. She looked around for Tom, but could not see him. She wondered where he was, but could not go hunting for him. He knew the woods better than any, she told herself. As they reached the top of the wooded slope and looked down upon the clearing, a quietness fell. Marian lowered Sister Christina gently to her feet. There was a moment of anxiety amongst the forest folk. The hut they'd raised was rough and small compared to the sturdy convent buildings.

'Someone has made us a fire,' said Mother Veronica.

Smoke trickled out of a hole in the roof. Agnes appeared at the open doorway with mugs of ale on a long wooden platter. Little Rowan staggered out behind her, clutching at her skirt. Two black-and-white kittens jumped at his wobbling ankles – they'd been brought to keep the building clear of mice.

The two novices left Mother Veronica's side and crept towards the kittens, laughing with delight and clicking their fingers.

Mother Veronica took hold of Brother James's hand. She turned to Marian, smiling. 'This is a blessed spot you've brought us to. I thank you with all my heart.'

It was late next evening when Tom came running up to the newly-built convent hut.

'They rage,' he cried, laughing and excited. 'They rage and curse and run round in circles. Never have you heard such oaths.'

'Do you mean the monks?' Marian asked.

'Aye. I crept back to the convent, and I sat with the Seeress till morning. Then I hid amongst the bushes, high up on the hill.'

'What happened?'

'Agnes's potion worked true. There was no sight nor sound of them till the sun was high. Then they came stumbling from the great hall, angry and white-faced and bleary-eyed, rubbing their heads and groaning.'

'Have they harmed the Seeress?'

'Nay. I think they've forgotten her in their anger. They blunder around the building, still searching for hidden nuns and food. All they can find is a sack of oatmeal and plenty of drink. The last I saw they set to broaching a cask to quench their fury. I guess they'll sleep again.'

The next few days were spent helping the Sisters to settle into their new home. Although the oldest nun was frail, Marian saw that the others were strong and capable, and used to working together. Sister Catherine was old but spry, she soon had a gang of willing workers building winter shelter for her hens.

Sister Rosamund had been the cellaress, but she'd declined to bring away the stocks of wine and ale. Instead she'd brought sacks of grain, beans and peas. Good stocks for the coming winter, Marian pointed out to Agnes. It was Sister Rosamund who'd calmly served the monks their pitcher of drugged red wine, for they unlocked her cell each evening to cook and wait on them.

Mother Veronica was delighted with all the help they received. Though there were tears and worries and adjustments to be made, she kept things calm and good-natured throughout. Her greatest pleasure was in watching the two girls, Margaret and Anna, exploring their new world.

'See them run!' Mother Veronica caught Marian's arm. 'That is how children should be.'

Margaret, the oldest, was lithe and slim; she ran and jumped around the clearing like the young hare that her misshapen lip was named for. Anna was a year younger, and she loped after Margaret, determined to follow wherever she went, and not be left behind.

'Sisters is the right name for them,' said Mother Veronica. 'They have shared their lives, and are inseparable.'

Marian smiled. 'And Mother is the right name for you,' she said.

Though the nuns welcomed him, Brother James would not stay in the building.

' 'Twould not be right,' he said, 'now that you all sleep in one room. Besides, Snap and I have got used to the woods. We shall never be far away.'

Mother Veronica fretted that he might get sick, or chilled. 'And who shall take our services?' she begged.

Brother James smiled. 'We are true heretics now, so take your own services. You were always better than me . . . ready to mouth the words, when I forgot the chant. Take care.' He hugged her. 'I go to see the Seeress, and carry her a good meal.'

Agnes and Marian watched him take his leave and go.

'I wondered,' said Marian, speaking softly. 'I wondered about those two. I thought perhaps they were more like . . . well, husband and wife.'

Agnes smiled and shook her head. 'There are many ways of loving,' she said.

As the days grew short and cold, the Sisters withdrew into a hard-working routine. A period of heavy rain turned the forest tracks to thick mud. There was less coming and going between the Magdalen Assart and the Forestwife's clearing, each group of women turning inward to their homes, their energy spent on the hard work of providing food, keeping themselves and their animals alive through the grim winter months.

Brother James and Snap were the only ones who travelled back and forth through the woods, whatever the weather. He carried news and gossip and food to the Seeress. Two weeks before Christmas he arrived at the Forestwife's hut with news that pleased them all. The monks had left the old convent. They'd finished all the ale and wine, and gone. They'd boarded up the doors with planks of wood and notices of excommunication from the Bishop.

'Could the Sisters return?' Marian asked.

He shook his head. 'We must wait. A change of abbot or bishop might see them safe. We must wait awhile and see how the wind blows.'

'Is the Seeress safe?'

'Aye, safe and glad for the Sisters. They have not harmed her but, as we thought, the monks would have left her to starve. Still, Snap and I see her well fed, and she has another visitor,' he smiled.

Marian frowned.

'Aye. Old Sarah spends much time with her. But now I have an invitation for you. Mother Veronica begs that you visit them for Christmas. The Sisters wish to make a feast for all who've given help.'

There were smiles and excitement at that, for their hard-won supplies were going fast with the great numbers of hungry folk that came each day.

'Tell them we'll come with pleasure,' Marian said.

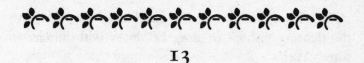

13

The Storyteller

Christmas was a glad time. The Sisters prepared a feast for all the hungry folk who found their way to the Magdalen Assart. There was singing and storytelling and much anxious wondering about King Richard, who had left the Holy Land to return to England. The other ships that sailed with him had come safely to harbour months ago. There was general consternation. What had happened? The King had not come back to England! Was he shipwrecked, drowned, or worse?

Marian sat by Agnes under the strong hide shelters that the nuns had raised in their clearing. The Sisters had been busy providing rough-cut trestle tables to seat their guests.

'Why so sad?' she asked Agnes, who sat quietly amongst the singing and laughing. 'Are we not having a fine celebration?'

Agnes shrugged her shoulders. 'A great feast indeed, but the worst is till to come, and I wonder about . . .'

'Ah! You wonder about that wicked lad of yours?'

'Yes, I do. Does he dine in comfort at Howden with the fighting bishop, or does he shiver with hunger in some cave?'

'Do you not think that he'd find his way to the Forestwife if he was in trouble?'

Agnes smiled. 'Aye. You are right.'

Marian could not stop her own mind wandering to the strange woman in the woods, who chose to be alone. She had been to visit the Seeress twice since the Sisters had left, and found her well fed by Brother James. Marian had taken her one of Selina's old cloaks to fight the winter cold.

Marian smiled as a group of young girls snatched up the hands of the two young novices and pulled them into a twirling dance, but she rose from the table, and picked up her own warm cloak. Then she gathered a fine collection of wholesome pastries that the nuns had made, and packed them carefully into a clean cloth. It was bad enough to be alone all year, but much worse to be alone at Christmastide.

'Brother James,' she bent to touch his arm. He sat beside Mother Veronica looking contented and sleepy, with a mug of ale in one hand and a pastry in the other. 'Brother James, may I take Snap? I go to see the Seeress, and take her Christmas fare.'

'I should go too,' he struggled to his feet.

'You shall not,' Mother Veronica spoke firmly. 'You're in no fit state to stand.'

Brother James wearily did as he was told, and called up Snap. 'Guard Marian!' he ordered.

* * *

The old convent stood dark and deserted as Marian passed it by. Just as once before, she heard a voice as she approached the Seeress's cell. She put out her hand to hold Snap back, thinking that the Seeress entertained her foxy friend. But as she grew closer, Marian realised the voice did not belong to the Seeress. It was older, yet somehow familiar. It rose and fell dramatically. A story was being told.

'And Lancelot escorted Guinevere through the tracks and forests of Cornwall. It was springtime. The air was full of sweet smells and blossoms. Guinevere was so beautiful that he could not help but fall in love . . .'

Marian crept close, not wishing to interrupt the speaker. She'd rather wrap her cloak close and sit down to listen, but the heavy panting of Snap could not be silenced.

The voice changed, it took on a frightened, querulous note. 'The trees, the trees are listening . . .'

Marian knew it at once. It was old Sarah.

The Seeress spoke soothingly. 'It's all right, Sarah. 'Tis only Marian. I knew she'd come.'

The Seeress welcomed her special meal, but she begged Marian to take Sarah back with her.

'Take her to the feast, for they should love to hear her tales.'

Marian stared at the old woman, though she could not see her face clearly in the forest gloom. She could not believe that those beautiful words had come from the crazed old woman's lips. How had they overlooked such a thing?

'We never knew you had such fine tales as those locked up in your head,' said Marian.

Sarah did not answer, but poked vacantly at the spikes of a holly leaf.

''Tis stories her grandfather told,' the Seeress explained. 'Each word falls perfect from her tongue . . . once started. Take her back, sit her down comfortably with food and drink, and ask her to "tell of the ancient time, when good King Arthur ruled this land."'

'And she will tell it?'

'Oh yes. Her voice will grow strong with her memory.'

So, reluctantly, Marian and Snap guided Sarah back through the woods. Marian doubted still, as Sarah muttered nonsense most of the way. But the Seeress had spoken true. For late the next evening, when the fires were burning low and all had feasted well, they sat Sarah down by the fireside.

'Can you tell us about good King Arthur?' Mother Veronica spoke gently to her.

For a moment Sarah stared blankly. 'That is not how it must begin.'

'Then tell us, dear Sarah. How should it begin?'

'Merlin . . . it begins with Merlin,' Sarah spoke indignantly. 'Merlin was the greatest magician in the land . . .' Her voice grew in strength. 'And it was Merlin who raised the young Arthur, in his secret cave.'

There were gasps of wonder and surprise, then they settled to listen. Sarah held them enthralled. Her stories told them of a long time gone, a time when hopes of justice had prevailed.

Sarah's stories were remembered and retold around the hearths long after the Christmas celebrations were done.

January was the harshest month. The forest clearings were thick with snow. There was nothing to do but shiver by the fires and eke out the food. Still Marian tramped and slithered through the forest tracks, wrapped in her green cloak, to carry food and beg the Seeress to leave her frozen cell. She begged in vain.

Though early February brought a thaw, it was then that the greatest hardship began. They came trudging and slipping through thick muddy tracks . . . whole families of them, the folk who sheltered in the forest, desperate for food. They set up camp in the clearing of the Forestwife, huddled beneath thin hides, or in the shelter of the yew trees. Crying babies, hollow-cheeked children and despairing mothers, begging for nourishment.

Agnes took it calmly for a while. She had prepared for this and hoarded her stocks. Marian was shaken as the numbers grew, and spoke of visiting the nuns to ask their help.

The chickens were slaughtered one by one, leaving only the cockerel and two skinny hens that must be guarded for safety. Then Agnes insisted that one of the goats that had ceased to give milk was killed. Marian found that hard, for goats and people must huddle beneath the same roof for warmth, and the poor ailing beast had curled on Marian's feet each night. She worked her fingers raw chopping holly leaves, in hopes of feeding the remaining pair. Agnes insisted there was goodness in the spiky leaves, if they could but be chopped fine enough.

The numbers of the hungry grew and the stocks of peas and beans dwindled, till Agnes turned fearful. There were but two sacks of meal and barley left.

'Was it like this in Selina's day?' Marian asked.

Agnes sighed. ''Twas bad, but ne'er as bad as this. I swear this is Richard's doing. He drained the manor lords of funds for his fighting crusades. Now the lords drain their villains and serfs, and refuse to feed any extra mouths.'

'We shall go to the Sisters and beg their help,' said Marian.

So Philippa and Emma went with her, and they took Tom and a few of the strongest older children, hoping they'd be able to carry back sacks of grain.

The forest tracks were foul with slush and mud, and the going was difficult. Their despair was absolute when they reached the Magdalen Assart. The Sisters were surrounded by more hungry folk.

'I should have held back from the Christmas feast,' Mother Veronica cried. It was strange to see how lean she'd grown, and even Brother James gaunt-cheeked. It was clear they'd both denied themselves.

'There is but one way left to us,' Philippa said.

Marian looked at her. 'What?'

'A deer stalk. Sherwood is full of them.'

Marian shivered. 'The King's deer? Break the forest laws?'

Philippa shrugged her shoulders. 'What else?'

They all stood silent, frightened by the thought. Then Mother Veronica spoke in her firm, decided way.

'We have no choice. We have good knives that we brought with us, and Sister Catherine has twine to make us nets.'

Marian gasped. 'We will do it. You Sisters should not come. It is a hanging offence.'

Mother Veronica laughed and hugged her. 'Why, when I might burn for heresy, should I fear to hang?'

It was early morning when they set off, for with the thick mud they must walk through it would take them the best part of a day to reach Sherwood. They hoped to make their kill at dusk, and carry their quarry home secretly through the darkness.

Mother Veronica and strong Sister Rosamund went with them, leaving the other nuns to manage as best they could. Tom went, for a fast runner would be needed. Brother James would not be left behind, though he would not risk Snap in Sherwood again, and left him in Sister Catherine's care.

'What we really need is a fine archer like Agnes's lad,' said Philippa.

Marian frowned.

'Can we really get a deer with knives and nets?' Emma asked.

Philippa nodded. 'We can, if we are not fussy which

we take. There is always some poor beast that's lamed or wounded, or sick.'

'Must we look for that?'

'The meat will taste as sweet. We do not hunt for sport.'

14

Those Who Break the Forest Law

The light was failing as they crossed the ancient road made by the Romans, and found their way into the Royal Hunting Forest of Sherwood. With thundering hearts they strode onwards through the stark woodland of leaflorn oaks, that gave little cover. Though there was no immediate sighting of deer, it was clear enough they'd passed that way by the fresh hoof marks in the mud and trees stripped of green bark.

Tom was sent ahead. At last he came haring back, waving his arms wildly.

'I've seen 'em. Hundreds of 'em, drinking at a stream, down beyond the rocks.'

Marian grabbed the handle of her knife and caught up her skirt to follow him.

'Nay,' Philippa hissed. 'We must use stealth, and we must stay upwind.'

They gathered together, whispering and making their plans, then, quietly and carefully, they crept up onto the rocks, stretching their necks to see the deer. At least there was more shelter down by the river, with shady yews and holly trees.

The fallow deer were a fine sight indeed. The vast herd drank and moved in rushes and flurries, so that they joined together as a great swirling mass. It was hard to pick out one poor beast for their victim.

Sister Rosamund pointed and gestured towards the stream. They all screwed up their eyes and tried to follow her directions.

'There,' Tom whispered to Marian. 'Can tha see it? A young stag, with antlers half grown . . . yes, see there, he limps. I think he's been gashed on the shoulder.'

Marian saw the beast at last. Then Philippa was pointing, not at the deer but at a place beyond the stream where two great yew trees stood, then further on towards a rocky outcrop that curved around to form a bowl.

'We must chase him towards those rocks, and trap him there.'

What she meant was clear enough. There amongst the rocks they might make their kill.

Rosamund and Mother Veronica nodded. They all got to their feet carefully. The two nuns carried one net between them, and Emma and Philippa another. Marian drew her knife, Brother James clutched the strong ash stave that he'd sharpened at one end.

They crept towards the beasts, slowly at first, but when the first scent of panic hit the deer, they had to run. Tom hurtled fast and furious towards the nervous, startled beasts, his arms stretched wide. Suddenly their intended victim was lost amongst the many. 'Where is it?'

' 'Tis gone! 'Tis lost!'

'There,' shouted Tom, 'there he goes.'

They saw him again, but wounded or not, the stag had plenty of fight and energy. Twice he broke through the half circle that they tried to form, but such was his fright that he turned and ran towards the rocks.

Tom cheered, and the two nuns ran at the deer, managing to tangle his antlers in their net, but he tore it from their hands. Though his antlers were but half grown, he managed to wrench Mother Veronica's arm so sharply as he twisted, that she could not help but cry out. Brother James dropped his ash stave and ran to her.

Again the wild-eyed stag dodged Tom's waving arms, dragging the net behind him. Then once again he headed straight back into the circling rocks. Marian followed fast behind, gripping her knife tightly, but suddenly a huge figure rose up growling from behind the rocks, and the whistle of an arrow sang past her ear and landed with a great thwang in the deer's neck.

Marian turned her head, stunned by the shock of the arrow. She was puzzled and dazed by the suddenness with which the shaft had sung through the air. She could not clearly understand what had happened, but outrage and anger burnt through the surprise. All she could see was that someone else was claiming their deer ... snatching it from under their very noses.

The hungry children of Barnsdale flashed before her eyes. The deer was theirs and no other had the right to claim it. She was the nearest . . . she must be the one to make the kill and claim it for the Forestwife.

The wounded beast staggered towards her. It dropped to its haunches, trembling and bellowing through its open mouth, its eyes rolling wildly. Yet still it struggled to get up. The fine dappled hairs on its hide smelt of musk and fear. Marian gripped her knife, eyes blind to all else around her. She calmly knelt down and cut its throat.

'Nay,' a man's voice cried out in rage. 'No blood!'

Marian staggered backwards. Warm blood spurted out across her arms and face. The deer fell dead at her feet.

Marian stared stupidly up at the big man who'd shouted at her, faintly recognising him. There was a distant thud as another man dropped out of the yew tree. Then Philippa shouted and ran towards him. It was Robert; he carried a bow on his shoulder. The big man standing on the rocks was John.

As Robert bent to look at the deer, Marian shouted crazily up at him, ' 'Tis ours . . . 'tis for the children!'

'Fool!'

Robert spat it out. But then he stared at her in silence, shaken at what he saw.

She crouched in the forest mud, her face white with anger, though splashed with blood. More blood ran down from her wrist and the hand that still gripped the knife. Her hair was wild and tangled, her long skirt hitched up almost to her knees, showing worn riding-boots, bare legs white and trembling and spattered with more blood.

He turned to look round at the others. Two dishevelled nuns clutched knives, unsure who these intruders might be. A grizzled monk crouched before them, his staff at the ready. Tom and Philippa looked defiantly at him.

'As you see,' said Philippa. 'We will fight to claim our kill.'

Robert turned to John and spoke quietly. 'Look at the state of them! This deer is theirs!'

John nodded his head, and pointed at Marian.

'"No blood," I told her. "No blood to taint the ground and prove us guilty."'

Marian blinked at Robert uncertainly. 'You agree then, this deer is ours?'

'Aye. 'Tis yours.'

From far away there came the faint sound of a hunting horn. Robert glanced at John.

''Twas Muchlyn giving warning, I think.'

'Aye. There's foresters on the prowl, we must go.'

Robert kicked the deer's hindquarters. 'Tha must move this beast fast.'

Marian stared at him, still dazed, though her heart thudded. The two lads turned to go, and Sister Rosamund pulled a ball of twine from her pocket. 'Lash the legs together,' she said.

John leapt up onto the rocks, ready to run in the direction they'd come from, but then he turned to watch their efforts to tie up the deer.

'They'll be caught,' he said.

Robert hesitated, ready to spring up and join him.

'Aye. Caught for sure. A sled might help . . . do you think?'

'Aye.' John leapt back down, and ran to the lowest branches of the nearest oak. He worked a strong, straight branch back and forth, then suddenly broke it from the tree. He threw it to Robert and set about another branch.

'Here,' Robert shouted to Sister Rosamund. 'Fetch that twine, and fasten it tight round here.'

She hurried to follow his instructions. Within a very short time a rough sled had been lashed together, and the deer lifted onto it. Robert swung his cloak from his back and laid it over the deer. The antlers and head stuck out.

He turned to look round at the women and pointed to Marian's green cloak. She did not stop to answer, but tore it from her shoulders, covering the beast's horns, tucking it neatly all about.

Robert pointed to the pool of blood, where the deer had fallen.

'Cover it,' he said. 'Leaves, earth, anything.'

Tom ran to do it, scooping up armfuls of rotting oak leaves.

John bent and touched Emma gently on the arm.

'You must ride,' he said. 'Sit thee down on there.'

Emma hesitated, but Philippa pushed her into place on the sled, on top of the warm deer carcass.

'Yes . . . he's right,' she encouraged. 'Cover it with tha skirt.'

Robert caught Marian roughly by the arm.

'Go wash in the stream, quick! Shift that blood!'

She obeyed without a word, though she could not stop shaking.

John lifted the makeshift yoke of oak over his shoulders, ready to drag the burden, and before long they were off, moving quickly through the thickening darkness.

'This way,' Robert pointed, kicking earth over the first deep sled marks in the mud.

' 'Tis not the way we came,' said Marian.

'Nay, but it will lead us away from the foresters' paths.'

Again the sound of a hunting horn in the distance made them run. John led the way and the others followed. Marian and Robert came last, with many an anxious backwards glance.

It was all the more shocking when a sharp animal cry and sudden metal clang came from the far bushes in front of them.

Marian caught her breath.

' 'Naught but a hare?' She turned to Robert for reassurance.

He stopped. Though she could not see his face clearly in the darkness, still she sensed his disquiet.

He spoke softly. ' 'Twas the clang of a mantrap, I fear.'

John and the others were well ahead now, and it was clear that they'd not heard the cry.

'A mantrap you say?' Marian darted off towards the dark undergrowth from which the sound had seemed to come.

'Nay!' Robert grabbed her arm again. 'There may be more. They set them up in twos and threes.'

'I must be sure 'tis an animal and not . . .'

'Aye, come then. A step at a time, and careful like.'

Deep in the bushes a dark shadow moved and groaned, hunched upright over the cruel iron jaws of the mantrap.

Robert crouched beside the dark shape.

Marian put out her hand to touch the familiar head and shoulders. Her belly lurched with horror.

' 'Tis Tom,' she whispered.

Robert bent over the wicked iron trap. He pressed gently, so that Tom moaned. The sharp metal teeth of the trap had cut into his thigh.

'He's bleeding fast. But the trap is not quite closed. 'Tis a strong stave of wood that's holding it apart. Why, look! The lad still clasps it in his hand.'

Marian peered into the darkness. 'I swear 'tis Brother James's staff,' she cried. ''Twas meant for killing deer, though Tom has found a better use for it,' she gabbled on, almost laughing with relief. Then suddenly the danger of it all came back to her. 'We must get him out of it.'

'Nay . . . we cannot. 'Twould take four strong men to open it.'

'Then run and fetch them back.'

Robert put his lips close to her face.

' 'Twill risk us all. Is that what you want?'

Marian leant against the cold, rusting iron of the trap. She wrapped her arms about Tom's shoulders and stroked his clammy head.

' 'Tis the best lad in Barnsdale, and I'll not leave him.'

Robert cursed, but he turned and ran ahead.

The trap was awkward to open, and it took the full strength of John, Robert, Brother James, Philippa and Sister Rosamund to lever it apart. Though Tom was nearly senseless with the fright and pain, he groaned as they worked to set him free. They used their knives and John's oak staff, and at last the cruel trap creaked open. Tom slumped backwards into Marian's arms.

The sound of the hunting horn came again.

'We must go now – and fast,' Robert whispered urgently.

'This leg must be bound up, or he'll die from all the bleeding,' Mother Veronica spoke firmly.

Marian cut a strip from the hem of her kirtle, and set to binding up the wound as best she could in the darkness.

'I fear the bone is smashed,' she said through gritted teeth, her hands shaking wildly now.

'No time to tell,' Philippa cried, as they heard the sound of hooves in the distance.

Tom was placed hurriedly onto the sled, and cloaks thrown over him. John once again set his shoulders to drag the burden, while Philippa and Marian snatched up the ropes that they'd used to lash the sled together. They ran on either side, heaving on the ropes, helping to speed their precious load over the rough and muddy ground.

It was clear that Robert and John knew the forest well, and soon they were leaving Sherwood behind them. It was difficult going, moving with such urgency through the dark.

John plodded steadily onwards, patiently dragging the heavy sled like a great ox. Robert walked beside Marian in awkward silence, though once he caught her arm with clumsy courtesy when she tripped over a rock, and blundered into him. Later, when they left the shelter of the trees, he asked if she was cold without her cloak.

'Nay,' she answered him shortly. But she lied, for as they moved towards the safety of Barnsdale, and the worst fears faded, Marian found herself in the grip of a shaking fit that she could not control. Her skin turned icy cold, and her legs trembled so that it was all she could do to put one foot before the other.

Darkness began to lift as they reached the outskirts of Barnsdale Forest. Robert, who'd fallen into halting conversation with the nuns and Brother James, walked ahead. He suddenly stopped, and turned to John.

'I dare say they may be safe enough here.'

John halted, unsure.

'Aye,' Marian said. 'We're glad of thy help, but we can manage now.'

John turned to look at Emma who lay shivering, half asleep on the sled, her arms cradling the still, white shape of Tom.

'I'm for seeing them safe back, Rob. Maybe we shall have ourselves a leg of roasted venison.'

Robert laughed, and agreed.

Marian wondered if they'd laugh when they saw how many the deer must feed.

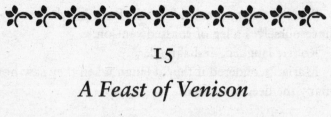

15

A Feast of Venison

The sun was high in the sky as they drew close to the Magdalen Assart. Mist rose from the frosted tips of dark piles of bracken. Sharp pointers of sunlight cut down through the trees to touch them. They walked between tall columns of magical twirling mist that curled upwards from the ground, then vanished high above them in the branches of the trees. Emma sat back on the sled, wide awake now, stroking Tom's hair, and watching John's plodding back with an expression of bewilderment.

Marian's spirits soared with the curls of mist. Despite her misery at Tom's plight, they carried back fresh hopes of life for him and for the hungry ones. And Robert . . . ? She looked ahead to where he smiled and nodded at Mother Veronica. Since they'd hastened from Sherwood, and struggled to free Tom, and walked through the night, there'd been no more sneering, no more calling her fool. He was almost . . . almost courteous. Of course she did not care what he thought of her, but ... it was more pleasant to have him courteous.

As they clambered down the hill above the convent clearing, they were met by hordes of quiet children, who gathered around them, staring wide-eyed at Tom, and whimpering with joy as the deer was revealed. Robert and John were baffled by the throng. Then as they came in sight of the camp of shelters, and understood, they fell silent.

John lifted the yoke of the sled from his shoulders and turned to Robert.

'This deer must feed them all?'

Robert shrugged his shoulders, and Mother Veronica answered for him.

'It must feed them all and more. We shall butcher the beast and send half to your mother, the Forestwife. Just as many poor souls shelter by her cottage.'

'This beast cannot make good roast meat to feed all of these.'

'Nay,' the nun smiled sadly. 'We must be careful. These folk could not eat roast meat, 'twould sicken them. We must make first a thin gruel, and hold back the meat for a day or two. Then we may try a richer venison stew, and hope to strengthen them.'

'What then?' John asked.

Mother Veronica shook her head.

Tom was awake, though his face was ashen. They lifted him gently from the sled, and carried him inside. While he groaned through gritted teeth, Marian and Mother Veronica examined him carefully.

' 'Tis a sickening wound,' the old nun said. 'But I do not believe the bone is snapped. I thank the Lord for Brother James's staff.'

'What can we do to help him mend?' Marian begged.

Mother Veronica shook her head. 'That wound needs searing, and the sooner it's done, the better.'

Marian nodded, though she hated the thought of it.

Mother Veronica heated up one of the knives, while Marian patiently fed the last drops of the nuns' elder-berry wine to Tom, hoping that it would help with the pain.

Brother James came to help Marian hold the lad still, while Mother Veronica pressed the burning flat of the knife to the wound. Marian gritted her teeth against the smell of burning flesh, and the fierce cries that she dreaded to hear. But Tom was as brave as he'd always been, and though he gave one deep angry growl of pain, he quickly fell into a merciful faint again.

Out in the clearing, Sister Catherine sharpened her knives and quickly set to work on the carcass of the deer. John offered to help, frowning as guts and innards spattered onto the old nun's homespun apron.

'Nay,' she waved him away. 'I have hacked up more beasts than ever tha's seen, lad.'

Philippa hovered at her shoulder. 'Will tha keep the antlers and the skull, Sister? For we must dance for the deer when spring comes.'

Sister Catherine wagged a bloody knife. 'Brother James and Veronica do not hold with that. Heathen rites they call it.'

Philippa nodded. 'Aye, 'tis called heathen, I know. But Sister, when I saw that great herd, drinking from the river, I swore to myself that at least we should dance for them, come spring. They are such beautiful beasts.'

The nun paused in her work, and smiled. 'Beautiful indeed. I shall keep the antlers and the skull. I know how to cut the hide just so. I was once a butcher's wife.'

Robert and John went on with Marian and her friends who carried the wounded boy and half of the deer's carcass to Agnes. This time they were prepared for the hunger that they'd find, but Marian was saddened to see more humps of freshly-dug earth beside Selina's mound.

Agnes was glad to have her son safe and well, though she could not help but chide him. 'Where has tha been, lad? I hoped thee safe at the board of Bishop Hugh.'

'Aye. And so we were. We feasted well at Christmas-tide, but then we thought it best to disappear.'

'Why so?' Marian asked.

'A man arrived at Howden. One we'd seen before. He came from Nottingham.'

'Ah,' Agnes began to understand, but she frowned. 'The Sheriff's man, at Howden? I thought the Bishop had quarrelled with Count John and his Nottingham friends.'

Robert's laugh held no joy. 'This man bears loyalty to none. He may be in the Sheriff's pay for now, but he works for himself. They call him wolf-hunter, but 'tis human wolves he stalks. He kills for money, serving whoever will pay the most. They say he is relentless in his pursuit, and we know that the Sheriff has put a price upon our heads.'

Marian shivered. 'Who is he, this man-hunter?'

'His name is Gisburn.'

'So that is why you left the Bishop?'

Robert shrugged his shoulders. 'We though it best not to wait and see if we were the wolves that he sought. We shall return to Howden in the spring. When the Bishop moves on Tickhill Castle, we shall be sure to go to fight with him. The Bishop needs every man that's loyal to Richard.'

Agnes did not like it. 'Look, Rob . . . see the state of these forest folk. Why does not tha wonderful Richard come back and see justice done for them?'

Robert shook his head, stubbornly hunching his shoulders. 'You do not see it right, Mother. 'Tis Count John and all the warring priests and barons, not Richard, that's to blame for this suffering.'

Agnes muttered angrily. 'None of them care.'

Tom was put into Agnes's own bed and his mother was sent for. His wound was cleansed and wrapped around with a plaster of pounded bayberry bark and oatmeal, to draw off the poisons. Marian and Emma sat on either side of him, feeding him strengthening wood sage tea, and the thin venison broth.

Robert and John stayed only to make a small meal.

'Will you go so soon?' Agnes's voice was full of regret.

The two lads laughed. 'Last time we came,' said Robert, 'you could not wait to see us gone.'

'Aye, tha were a nuisance then, but now tha's been a help.'

Robert looked around the clearing, at the misery there. He spoke softly and awkwardly.

'We can be more help to thee in Sherwood, Mother. We shall be back within a se'enight with more venison.'

They kept their word and when six days had passed they marched into the clearing, dragging a sled with a fresh-killed deer and a wild boar. They'd carried a pair of deer to the Magdalen Assart first and brought Brother James along with them, and better news from the nuns. Muchlyn came too, and another lad, named Will Stoutley. They were welcomed with wild rejoicing, and a feast was called for. Agnes agreed to it, for the first thin venison stews had done much to revive the sick, and there'd been no more deaths. Tom was recovering faster than any of them could have hoped, and it was all that Alice and Marian could do to keep him from leaving his pallet to try his leg.

At last Marian persuaded him to rest by fetching John and Robert to sit by his side. They told him tales of their escapes from the foresters and wardens as they whittled the new bow staves that they'd cut from the great yew.

Late in the evening, after they'd eaten, and sat around contented and chattering, wondering if they had the strength for a song, Robert picked his way through the gathering until he stood before Marian.

'Will tha stand up?' he asked.

Marian was puzzled, but she could see no reason to disagree. She got to her feet, and frowned as he set a strong yew stave beside her. Then he notched it where it reached her shoulder.

'If tha must go a-hunting, I'd best teach thee to shoot,' he said. Then he walked away.

Early next morning he came looking for her. He'd strung the bow, and carried a quiver full of arrows.

'Does tha wish to shoot?' he asked.

She stared at him, still surprised, but she answered, 'Aye. I do wish it.'

He turned and walked out of the clearing; she followed him. They didn't go far before he stopped.

'This'll do . . . space enough. Now see, I shall set up a willow wand.'

Marian did as he told her, trying to follow his instructions. He showed her how to take her stance and how to hold the bow. She was awkward and clumsy, with half a mind to tell him not to waste his time. But he was patient enough, and cut a broader wand, moving it closer.

He stood by her shoulder, pointing out the flaws in her aim without the hint of a sneer.

'That's it, pull back till tha thumb touches thine ear. Then close one eye, and so . . . let it go.'

They worked together until the sun stood high in the sky. Though the wand was brought closer and closer . . .

still she could not hit it. At last she threw down her bow in frustration. 'I cannot do it,' she shouted. 'Surely 'tis something that must be learned as a bairn. 'Tis too late for me.'

Then Robert laughed. 'Too late? Was I wrong then? I felt sure 'twould be the right thing for thee. When I saw thee kill that deer with a meat knife, I thought . . .'

'You thought me a fool. That's what you called me.'

'Aye, and tha were a fool, to let the blood spill so. But then I thought different. I thought, a lass like that, so fierce and stubborn . . . well, she should learn to shoot.'

She stared back at him for a moment, her mouth dropping open. Was he sneering again? Or was it perhaps as close to a compliment as he could manage?

Silently she raised the bow once more and took aim. He touched her hand where she gripped the bow, raising it, just the slightest hint. Then she let the arrow fly, and nicked the willow wand.

When Marian and Robert returned to the clearing they found Emma and John sitting happily together weaving osier strips into baskets. John was clumsy, his big fingers would not bend to the delicate work, but they laughed together, and Emma reached over to set his work to rights.

Marian and Robert watched them uneasily, both unsure whether they liked what they saw.

'We'd best be off to Sherwood, John,' Robert spoke sharply.

John looked up at Robert, surprised. Then he glanced at Marian.

'Aye, we'll soon be off,' he agreed unhurriedly. 'Tha'd been gone so long, I thought perhaps . . .'

'We'll be off at dawn,' Robert insisted. He turned to Marian. 'We shall fetch thee more venison.'

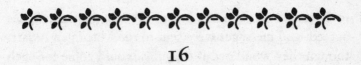

16

To Honour the Deer

The young men returned to the clearing twice more before spring came. Each time they dragged a good supply of fresh game with them. John's friendship with Emma grew, and the brawny, quietly spoken lad spent many an evening sitting beneath the great oak with the charcoal-burner's daughter at his side. Marian teased them both by calling it the trysting tree.

Tom's wounds healed steadily with Agnes's firm care, and warnings that it would turn bad if he tried it too soon. Though the angry blue-red scars would never fade, by the end of March he was hobbling about the clearing propped on stout crutches that his father and Philippa had made.

One warm spring afternoon, the sound of a hunting horn sent Emma running outside, pink-cheeked and flustered, to find a bigger gang of lads than ever marching into the clearing. She flung herself up into the arms of the tallest one.

Philippa insisted that there should be dancing, not yet

to celebrate the summer, but to honour the deer. Agnes agreed, and messages were sent to the Magdalen Assart, though they wondered if the nuns would come for such ancient and pagan rites.

'Will tha stay to celebrate with us?' Agnes begged Robert.

John looked pleased, though Robert frowned.

'We were but passing by, on our way to join Bishop Hugh. There's rumours that the King is captured, and prisoner in a foreign land.'

'Never!'

'Aye. 'Tis not clear yet, but it seems there's talk of a ransom. Count John will think it his chance to take the throne for himself. We shall attack Tickhill, and hold it for Richard.'

'Might we not stay for the feast?' said John. 'Then we shall go.'

Robert agreed, though grudgingly.

Only Sister Christina disapproved. The other nuns came walking through the woods and settled cheerfully to the feast. Mother Veronica and Brother James declared themselves happy enough, as heretics.

'We still give praise to our God,' they said. 'But we shall give the deer their due. They got us through the winter.'

They feasted in the early evening, so they might dance as darkness fell. It was Muchlyn who was chosen to fasten the antlers to his head, for Sister Catherine had preserved them well.

As they lit the candles, the strange horned figure circled the clearing, the tanned deerhide floating down his back. Philippa took up a tabor that she'd made with deerskin stretched on a wooden frame. John put to his lips a pipe that he'd whittled from a branch of deer's horn. It had but five notes, yet the simplicity of the tune he got matched well with the steady thud of the tabor.

Though Muchlyn was small, they had chosen rightly, for he could leap and prance, copying faithfully the delicate moments of the deer.

Little Margaret sat at the feet of Mother Veronica, holding up one hand to cover her hare lip. As Much began to dance, she watched him with wonder, and her hand fell from her face. She reached out to him, twisting and turning her fingers, following every move that he made. Much smiled at the delight in her eyes. He beckoned to her, inviting her to join him. She hesitated for a flustered moment, but Mother Veronica nodded her approval. The young girl rose to her feet and followed Much into the dance. She imitated his swift leaps and bounds with such grace and nimbleness that the whole company watched them spellbound. As the pure pipe music rose and fell, she lost all sense of bashfulness, seeing only the prancing figure of Much, and the magic of the deer's dance.

At last the music ceased. Margaret blinked, suddenly anxious as Much smiled down at her. Her hand flew up to cover her mouth.

'Do not cover theesen,' said Much, gently pulling her

hand away. 'Tha face puts me in mind of the beautiful deer that we dance for.'

Mother Veronica watched it all with sudden anxiety, but Brother James put his arm around her. 'Don't worry,' he said. 'We make our own rules now.'

Later in the evening they all joined in the singing and dancing. John would not leave Emma's side, and Much danced with little Margaret. Marian jigged and twirled in the middle of the throng, until she found herself face to face with Robert. He was laughing and merry from the ale. He wrapped his arms around her waist, and swung her round fast and furiously. She grinned back at him, though she could hardly catch her breath. When at last they were both worn out, and the dancing was coming to an end, he turned awkward again, dropping his hands to his sides.

'You go at dawn,' she said.

'Aye. I must get some sleep.' It was true that his face had gone suddenly white.

'We shall dance again for May Day. Will you dance with me then?'

'Aye.' He nodded his head, then he turned and walked away.

When they'd gone, there followed days of steady drizzling rain that turned the forest into a mire.

' 'Tis not the best weather for besieging,' said Agnes. 'Those inside fare dry and warm compared to those without.'

Sparse news came to them from Tickhill, but the

whole country was spinning with news of the King. It seemed that he was certainly captured by the Duke of Austria, and seventy thousand marks must be paid before he'd be released. Queen Eleanor had come to England to raise the money for her son, and harsh taxes and demands were made on landowners, manor lords, churches and abbeys.

'Thank goodness 'tis not the serfs and villagers that must pay,' said Marian.

Agnes shrugged her shoulders. ''Tis them as shall pay in the end, you'll see.'

Life in the forest clearing went on at the usual busy pace. Agnes taught Marian and Emma much of her knowledge of herbs and healing, and there was the endless gathering to be done. As the weather grew warmer they had to search out watercress from the streams, pick tender green angelica stems, and also comfrey for healing poultices.

Agnes worked to build up the strength of her few fowls and goats. Soon the clearing ran with cheeping chicks and two wobbly-legged kids.

May Day came and they set a tall pole in front of the giant oak that they'd come to call the trysting tree. Philippa skipped happily with little Rowan, who was growing strong now and walked sturdily. Emma was sad, for there was no sign of John or Robert. Marian was simply annoyed.

'He said he'd be here for May Day.'

'Who?' Emma asked.

'That Robert,' she snapped.

'Ah,' Emma sighed, and nodded her head.

The dancing was well under way when John came alone down the track. He hugged Emma, and told them his news. They had nearly taken Tickhill Castle for the Bishop, but then ruling had come from the great council that the castle was to stay with John, in return for him handing over Windsor. Bishop Hugh had been furious, but he could not disobey. Disappointed though they were, John and Robert had set themselves to help to raise King Richard's ransom, though they did it in their own wicked way.

'We hide out down by Wentbridge, near the great road,' John laughed, 'inviting travellers to dine with us. Then . . . we make 'em pay.'

'What if the poor folk cannot pay?' demanded Emma.

'Why, then we wish them well and send them on their way.'

'Does Robert not come for May Day?' asked Marian.

John shook his head. 'He's mad for his King's return. Naught else will move him.'

Late that night, Marian lay restless on her pallet, though all about her snored. She rolled over, stretching out her arm to Emma. Suddenly she opened her eyes and sat up. Where Emma should have been sleeping beside her there was nothing but a cold space.

'The silly wench,' she muttered. 'I hope she knows what she does.'

John had gone when morning dawned. Emma came

creeping into the hut with grass stuck in her hair. Marian pretended to be asleep.

The summer months were kinder to the forest folk. Though there were still the sick to tend, at least the forest was blessed with fruitfulness and teemed with rabbits and pheasants and hares. Bellies were filled, and it was warm enough to sleep beneath the stars.

It was early in August when Tom's mother, Alice, brought the message that old Sarah had wandered off as she always did, but this time she'd not returned.

'I fear I lose my patience with her,' Alice's voice shook with weariness.

'So do we all,' Marian answered her.

Agnes looked worried when she heard the news. They searched the woods close to the coal-digger's hut, calling out her name, but there was no sign of the old woman.

Three days passed and still Sarah did not return. 'We'll gather a gang of lads and lasses to hunt for her,' said Marian. 'And we'll send to the Magdalen Assart, so that the Sisters may seek her too.'

Agnes shook her head. 'I fear they'll not discover her.'

'What troubles thee so?' Marian asked. 'I swear we'll find her wandering as usual.'

'Aye. 'Tis naught but a foolish fear.'

'Don't fret,' Marian told her. 'I'll get Emma, and we'll go seeking the old nuisance once more.'

Marian found Emma pale and watery-eyed, still curled on her pallet, though the sun was high in the sky.

'Why, Emma . . . are you sick?'

'Nay,' Emma smiled weakly, 'I feel sick, but I am not really sick.'

'What then?'

Emma smiled. 'I am with child.'

Marian's mouth dropped open with horror. 'Are you sure?'

But Emma would not let her be angry or fearful.

'Aye . . . you forget, I know how it feels. Do not look like that, for I am glad. I have chosen to have this child. I have chosen the man. I pray that it lives.'

Marian shook her head, exasperated. 'I fear we're in for a bout of trouble. You with child and Sarah lost. Agnes wishes us to search for her, but you cannot go now.'

'Here, pull me up,' Emma insisted, holding out her hand. 'A good walk through the forest shall suit me well. Come on, we shall find the old woman and bring her back.'

But though they searched for three more days and nights Sarah could not be found. Brother James came with messages from the Magdalen Assart. The nuns could find no sign of her. The Seeress was greatly distressed at the old woman's disappearance and she swore that sorrow would come of it.

At last Agnes admitted her fears.

'I think we should send a message to Philippa's husband at Langden.'

Marian stared at her, realising only dimly what that might mean.

Philippa, who was usually so brave, turned pale. 'You think she might have wandered back to her old home? Aye, such a thing can happen with one like Sarah, whose memories come and go.'

'What if she did?' asked Marian. 'What would William of Langden do? Could she betray us, do you think?'

Agnes shook her head. 'How can we know?'

'I shall take Snap, and go to Langden,' said Brother James. 'For none of us are safe until we know.'

Can This be the Sea?

Brother James returned the next day. Marian and Philippa were up to their elbows in the dye tub, though they left it at once when they saw the monk stride into the clearing.

'Have you news?' Marian cried.

'Aye. 'Tis not good . . . though it could be worse.'

Agnes and Emma came running to hear what was said.

Brother James had hidden in the thicket close to Langden village, for he'd found that Snap would not stop growling once he'd scented Langden land.

He'd stayed hidden until at last he spied one of Philippa's sons. The lad had told him all he needed to know. Sarah had indeed returned to Langden. She had marched up to her own old cottage and demanded of the new tenants what right they had to be in her home. Fortunately, the young wife remembered Sarah well and the harsh way she'd been treated. She made no fuss, but took poor Sarah in and settled her by the hearth, and there she'd been ever since. The villagers were all doing their best to help. So far, they'd kept the old woman quiet and safe, but no one could tell what William of Langden might do if he saw her.

'Any attempt to persuade her to leave her old fireside sends her into a screaming fit of rage,' Brother James told them. 'But there is more that the lad told me, Philippa.'

'What?' Philippa looked fearful.

'William of Langden has had angry taunting messages from Nottingham's Sheriff. It seems that foresters found bloodied cloth upon a mantrap, and small footprints in the mud around. They say the cloth was torn from the habit of a nun. The Sheriff believes that the wicked heretic nuns have organised a gang of ruffian children to steal the King's deer from Sherwood.'

'Ah . . . 'twould almost be laughable,' said Philippa, 'though I'm fearful of what they'll do.'

'Aye. The Sheriff says that the nuns came from Langden land. He says 'tis William's job to catch them, and he jeers and makes great ridicule – William of Langden bested by a pack of children and chanting women!'

Marian's eyes were wide with fear. 'And old Sarah could give us away to him, any day.'

Brother James shrugged his shoulders and shook his head.

The dye had dried bright green on Marian's arms while they were talking. Once they'd heard the news they could not settle back to their work again. They made Brother James sit down to eat with them, while they went over the problem once more. It was while they were still eating that they heard the sound of hooves.

Marian jumped to her feet. 'William of Langden?' she cried.

'Nay 'tis but one horse,' said Philippa. 'He would only come with all his guards.'

Emma suddenly let out a cry of joy and ran forwards, for a bay stallion trotted into the clearing with John in the saddle.

He flung himself down, and hugged her, though it was clear his face was drawn with worry.

'Something's wrong?' Marian cried.

'Aye. Something wrong indeed,' said John.

He looked to where Agnes stood behind Marian. He walked slowly towards her, pulling Emma gently along with him.

'Bad news of tha son, I fear.'

'Is he dead?' Agnes asked, her voice calm.

'No . . . but I fear he may be wounded unto death.'

'How then?' Agnes stumbled forward and they made her sit down upon the doorstep.

John crouched at her side. 'That foul man-hunter we told thee of . . . Gisburn. He came upon us down Wentbridge way; he and a gang of Nottingham's best armed fighters. We split up and ran our different ways, as we had always planned we should. Much and Stoutley followed Robert. I wish I'd gone with them, but I went flying off towards Wakefield. 'Twas just three days ago that Stoutley found me and told what happened. Robert headed north towards the River Humber, and . . .' The big man paused, sighing.

'And what?' Marian asked. 'Did Gisburn follow him?'

'Aye. Nottingham's men dropped back and gave up the chase . . . but not Gisburn, he clung to their trail like a rabid dog. That man! Still, he's dead now. Gisburn is dead at last, killed by Robert. He'll hunt no more, but they made a bitter fight of it. Stoutley had gone to Howden for help. He fetched three brave fellows with him, friends we'd made at Tickhill, from amongst the Bishop's men. They were too late.'

'So Robert was alone when Gisburn came upon him?' Marian clenched her hands.

'He and Much. Poor Muchlyn hid in fright. I'm glad he did or he'd be dead for certain.'

'Where is my son now?' Agnes asked.

'In the north, safe in a cottage close by the sea. They'd travelled far with Gisburn on their tails, up through the Forest of Galtres. 'Twas close to Pickering Castle that Robert turned and fought. Bishop Hugh's men carried him across the heather moors, to Baytown, not far from Whitby Abbey. They've friends there who'll protect him. Much is with him, and does his best to nurse him, but Rob has fallen into a sleeping sickness from his wounds.'

John caught Agnes by the hand. 'I have this fine horse from the Bishop's stable, 'twill carry thee and me. We might be there tomorrow if we rode through the night.'

Agnes shook her head.

'I should take good care of thee,' John begged.

Agnes smiled sadly. 'I do not fear to ride with thee, John. 'Tis simply that I am the Forestwife; I stay here.'

John looked to the other women for help, but they shook their heads. There would be no moving Agnes, they knew that. Then Agnes looked up abruptly, biting at her lips.

'Another could go in my place. Both Emma and Marian know enough of healing.'

The two girls looked at each other.

'Will tha come with me, Emma?' John smiled.

Emma suddenly flooded with tears. Marian threw her arm around her shoulders, 'Emma must not go. It shall be me. I'll come with thee, John.'

John looked puzzled and hurt, but he nodded. 'I think there is no time to lose.'

Marian got to her feet, and pulled Agnes up. 'Tell me what herbs to taken and what to do. John, tha must find the time to talk to Emma before we go.'

The women rushed madly about, helping Marian to make herself ready for the journey, William of Langden forgotten for more urgent fears. John and Emma wandered hand in hand towards Selina's mound. When they came back, Marian was ready, wrapped in her cloak and loaded with bundles of herbs, cordials, and two warm rugs.

John kissed Emma, and hugged her. 'I shall come straight back to thee,' he promised.

Marian climbed up behind John, and Agnes fussed and fretted.

'Take care of theesen, my honey. Make a hot poultice of comfrey. It must be kept hot and freely changed. Has tha heard me right? And you must keep his body warm, though he sweats and sweats. 'Tis the sweating that brings the fever out.'

Marian nodded and smiled, her stomach tight with excitement.

'What of old Sarah?' she said.

Agnes shook her head. 'There's naught we can do. Just wait and hope she comes quietly back to us.'

'Tell the Seeress where I've gone,' Marian begged them.

John blew a last kiss to Emma, then he turned the stallion and they were off, cantering through the woods.

There was plenty of room for two in the saddle. It had been shaped for a knight in chain mail with room to carry weapons. Marian soon grew used to the rocking motion of the horse's stride. The best memories she had of Holt Manor were of riding pillion behind one of her uncle's grooms.

'Does the Bishop send his horse willingly?' Marian asked.

John laughed. 'The Bishop does not know he's harboured outlaws. 'Twould seem discourteous to let him know. So, better not to ask. The Bishop shall have his stallion back, and he'll not complain, so long as we answer his call to arms.'

'Aye!' Marian sighed. Nothing had changed.

They headed north towards Pontefract, close to where

the great road ran. They dared not travel on the road in daylight, but kept to the forest tracks that ran close by. At dusk they stopped to eat the bread and goats' cheese that Agnes had packed for them. Marian's back ached, and she staggered around stiff-legged.

Revived by the food and fresh water from a stream, they returned to their journey. As darkness fell, they clattered out onto the wide Roman road. The horse made better progress then, and soon they passed York in the far distance. They left the road, heading east through the Forest of Galtres in the dawn light.

They stopped to eat again, sitting up on a high wooded hillside above an abbey. Below them the bell rang for prime, and an orderly line of nuns filed into the church.

'Could that be Whitby Abbey?' Marian asked.

'I think not,' John shook his head.

'Where are we now?'

John hesitated. 'I've not travelled this way before.'

'Do you mean we're lost?'

'Nay. Not lost, exactly. I know from the stars and the sun that we turned east, and must keep going east, until we reach the sea.'

'I've never seen the sea,' Marian was eager for it.

John scratched his head. 'Nor I.'

Marian frowned. 'How shall we know it then?'

'I do not think we shall mistake it. They say it is like a great lake, that spreads and spreads.'

Marian nodded. 'We'd best get on.'

They rode down the sloping hillside into the valley, and stopped a man with a mule to ask the way.

'Why, this is Rosedale Abbey,' he answered, surprised they should not know. 'For Whitby, tha must head up the valley, then on to High Moor. Follow the beck through Glaisdale till it joins the River Esk. Tha'll see Whitby town ahead, though the land juts out into the sea, so Whitby faces north.'

'And shall we see the sea then?'

'Oh aye,' he grinned. 'Tha'll see the sea.'

They journeyed onwards through banks and hills of bright-flowering purple heather that stretched as far as the eye could see. The sun was sinking behind them when the river widened, sharply dividing two steep cliffs on either side. Clusters of small dwellings clung precipitously to the crags.

'Can they live safe up there?' Marian asked.

John whistled in amazement. 'I swear this must be Whitby town.'

He dismounted, leading Marian upon the horse, openmouthed, and staring about her at great white birds that swooped and cried.

'See,' John pointed to the eastern side. 'there is the Abbey.' Marian craned her neck to see, but as they walked on she clutched suddenly at the horse's mane. While she rode and John walked, she could see further ahead than he. The cliffs had fallen away, so that the river swelled to spread itself across the wide horizon. Swelled till it seemed to touch the sky. The sight of it made her giddy.

'John,' she whispered. 'Can this be the sea?'

'Aye, for sure it must be.'

They moved slowly onwards, till the horse's hooves sunk into softest silvery sand. Then they paused, staring at the wonder of it. Marian's head turned this way and that.

'I never guessed that it would move so. Like a great lapping beast it is. Do you hear its gentle roar?'

'Aye,' said John. 'And how it taints the wind, with such a smell of fish and salt.'

They stood for a long while, just watching the waves as they crept towards the shingle. At last John dragged his gaze away, to realise with a jolt that they were a growing cause of interest. A group of ragged children had slowly and quietly gathered about them. They stared at Marian with her green cloak and her bright green arms.

'She's the Green Lady,' they whispered.

'Marian laughed. 'Nay, just a girl like any other! 'Tis just that I've had my hands in the dye tub. 'Tis forest dyes that make this fine strong green.'

'We travel on to Baytown,' said John. 'Can tha show us the way? We must try to reach it before the light has gone.'

They were set well on their way, up the steep horse road that took them past the Abbey. Up onto the highest cliff tops, where Baytown could be seen in the distance.

'There's men round here who're loyal to Bishop Hugh,' John told her. 'You shall be safe here.'

As they rode towards the first straggling cottages of Baytown, a joyful shout rang out. Muchlyn came hurtling towards them through the falling gloom.

'Thank God,' he cried. 'Thank God that you've come.'

'Does he live?' John asked.

Much's face fell. 'He breathes, but he does little else. I cannot make him eat. I fear he's going fast.'

Marian struggled down from the horse. Much stared at her, puzzled that it was not Agnes who had come. He did not stop to question it, for he was anxious that they should see Robert. Marian followed him into a small thatched hut.

A single candle sent flickering shadows jumping up the walls. A dark shape lay still upon a pile of straw beside a meagre fire that smoked and spluttered on the hearth. The hut was filled with the stench of sickness.

'Light,' said Marian urgently. 'I must have light.'

Much pulled two more candles from the pile by the hearthstone. Marian snatched one from his hand and lit it. She bent down to Robert holding up the candle to see his face. It was grey and bruised, but the skin seemed unbroken. He shivered and muttered nonsense, rolling his eyes but seeing nothing.

Marian put out her hand to touch his forehead. She found it cold and clammy, and he jumped away from her touch, turning his head towards the wall. Then she saw it; a great jagged, festering gash that cut into his skull from his cheekbone to the back of his ear. It stank, and oozed thick pus stained with dark blood. Marian clapped her hand to her mouth. She ran outside to vomit by the snorting horse.

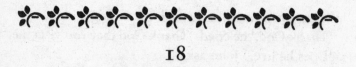

18

The Green Lady

Marian straightened herself, and wiped her mouth,
putting up one hand to steady herself against the steaming flanks of the horse. She closed her eyes and took
great gulps of salty air into her lungs. The gentle swish
and lap of the sea below the cliffs soothed the throbbing
of her head.

'I must think clear,' she told herself. 'Warm poultices
and a good fire.'

She turned and went into the hut.

'Build up the fire for me, Much.'

'But, lady,' Much hesitated, ''tis hard to make a good
fire. It is a strange place. They give us all we want of eggs
and milk and fish, but they burn this powdery coal upon
their fires. It glows slow and steady. 'Twill not burn
fierce.'

Marian stared at him, close to panic.

'I must have a blazing fire of wood,' she barked.
'John, you heard what Agnes said.'

'True enough,' John soothed her. 'We shall find wood.'

'And water,' she demanded.

'Here! 'Tis good and fresh from the stream.' Much brought a bucket from the cottage doorstep.

'Bring wood then, quick!' Marian gave her orders.

She swallowed hard to quell her lurching stomach and set to cleaning Robert's wound. It was difficult to see clearly in the flickering candlelight and it took a long time to boil water on the fire, but at last she had a comfrey poultice mashed and ready. Robert groaned and shouted when she tried to put it to the wound. Marian clenched her teeth, and tears welled up into her eyes.

'Forgive me, love,' she whispered, and pressed it firmly into place, despite the way he thrashed and growled.

John came rushing in, with his arms full of wood.

'What ails thee?' he cried, seeing her tears.

'Naught,' said Marian. 'Can tha please build up the fire?'

They'd found dry wood down on the beach, above the level of the tide, and soon they had a roaring fire.

Marian set Much to hold the poultice steady, while she washed the sick man, wincing at the stink of him. Then she spoon-fed him with Agnes's sleeping draught, and wrapped him in the rugs.

John and Much snatched a little sleep, but though Marian's head twitched with weariness, she sat up all night, changing the comfrey dressings, keeping them warm and fresh. At last Robert sweated, as Agnes had said he must.

*　*　*

In the morning, Much brought eggs and milk from the village, but none of them could eat. John paced about, until at last he spoke.

'I do not like to leave thee, but . . .'

Marian nodded her head. 'You must go, John. Emma has need of thee, and whether tha goes or stays will make no difference here. I am doing all that Agnes told me, and I cannot do more.'

John nodded. 'Much will do anything you want.'

'I know he will.'

John rode away.

Despite her words, and Muchlyn's willingness, Marian was afraid.

All through the next day they kept the fire blazing, and Marian settled to a short sleep in the afternoon while Much sat by Robert, holding the poultice in place. Marian kept watch beside him through the night.

Though Robert's skin ran with sweat and his body shrank to skin and bones, still the fever raged. Sometimes for a moment she thought he stared at her with recognition, but then he'd shout for his mother . . . or sometimes for his King.

'Is he any better, do you think?' she'd ask of Much.

He'd frown, and scratch his head and say, 'He is no worse, lady.'

As the light began to fade on her third evening in that place, Marian went outside for air. Much had said she should rest, but she could not sleep.

'A breath of fresh sea air will help me more,' she told him.

She wandered from the cottage, over the sloping clifftop, and down a winding pathway to the beach. She sat down on a rock, and hugged her knees. Despair and panic had been growing in her through the day. The comfrey that Agnes had sent was almost used and done. The fever should have broken, if it was ever going to. She stared out at the heaving sea, her eyes stinging with bitter tears.

An old woman came wandering along the beach, picking up driftwood and filling a small sack with the black powdered coal that was washed up on the sand. As she came close by, Marian wiped her eyes and stared down at the ground, not wishing to be disturbed. The old woman looked at her, and paused, then she came towards her. Marian gave an angry cluck, but the woman ignored her rudeness, and sat down beside her. The smell of fish was strong upon her hands and clothes.

'I heard tell that a strange lady in green had come to nurse a poor wounded man.'

Marian made no answer, but gave a sniff.

'I heard tell that this poor man's wound has turned foul and festering,' the woman continued. 'And that maybe he is close to death.'

At last Marian managed a reluctant response.

'I fear 'tis true. The wound is foul, and will not mend.'

The woman got up, and Marian thought she was going away, but she walked only a few paces, and pulled up from the sand a mass of dark tumbled weeds. She came back to Marian, dragging it beside her. Then she sat down again.

'Hereabouts,' she said, 'we cure our wounds with seaweed.' She pulled out a handful of the faintly shining strands.

'This? It looks foul and slimy,' Marian touched it. 'Oh . . . surely it would poison a wound even worse.'

The old woman laughed.

'Now . . . if it were my son, all sick and wounded, this is what I'd do. I'd wash this seaweed clean, then chop it fine, and shape it to a plaster.'

'You'd set it to the wound?' Marian asked, hope suddenly flickering in her mind. Dare she put her trust in this woman?

'That's what I'd do, my honey,' she answered, putting Marian sharply in mind of Agnes.

She did not stop to thank the old woman, but snatched up the seaweed and ran.

That night Marian sat up late, holding the seaweed poultice in place, Robert still shook and shivered, but he was quieter. At least it seemed there was no poison in the weed. She thought the wound looked cleaner.

The night was bitterly cold. A strong wind blew from the sea, lashing the waves so that they crashed and roared like devouring beasts. The fire blazed fiercely. She could not make the sick man any warmer . . . could she?

She crouched beside him, though her arm ached and her head dropped from weariness. She glanced at Much, who slept soundly in the far corner on a pile of straw, then looked back with pity at Robert's thin face.

Marian carefully pulled back the covering rugs, and crept in to lie beside him. She lifted his head so that he rested on her arm, and she could hold the poultice in place. She wrapped her legs around his twitching body, and closed her eyes.

When Much awoke next morning he could not see Marian for a moment, and he got up, puzzled, from his pile of straw. Then he saw her, fast asleep beside Robert. He shrugged his shoulders and grinned.

'A fine way to heal a man,' he chuckled. Then as he bent close above them, his face turned solemn with relief. Robert slept calmly. His cheeks were pale and gaunt, but he had ceased all muttering and shivering.

The small man scratched his head, and smiled, 'It seems it's worked,' he whispered.

Much went out for eggs and milk, and when he returned Marian was up and mixing soothing herbs for a drink.

'Have you seen him?' she cried. 'He has not spoken, but he sleeps peaceful. If we can build up his strength now, I am sure he'll live.'

Much nodded, but he hesitated.

'Thanks to thee, lady, tha's saved him for sure. I am that glad he's better, but I hate myself for running from the fight. What will he say to me? I turned sick with fear and hid from that beast of a man. Leaving Robert to face him . . . alone.'

Marian went to Much and hugged him. 'How can you say that? If you'd not hidden, you'd both be dead. You were there to pick him up, and carry him here. You saved him just as much as me.'

Later in the day, when Much was out collecting wood, Robert stirred and opened his eyes. Marian was standing by the window with her back to him.

She froze, not daring to turn as she heard his voice. It was faint and croaky. 'Mother . . . I had a dream,' he murmured. 'I dreamed that a great stretch of wild water roared below me. A wonderful dream . . . for the green lady slept beside me.'

Marian turned from the window, and went to kneel by his bed. The light fell on her from the window, making Robert gasp. 'Marian,' he whispered.

That night he ate a little coddled egg, spoon-fed by Marian as though he were a child. He was very weak and could do no more than lie there, watching them as they stoked the fire and prepared him tempting food. Marian slept on her own small pile of straw.

Muchlyn brought fresh cod from the village. Marian had never seen anything but salted or fresh-water fish and didn't know what to do with it. She snatched it up and ran over the clifftops, until she could see the beach. The old woman was there, just as before. It seemed she spent her whole life gathering wood and coal. Marian ran down the pathway, waving and calling to her.

'The seaweed poultice worked,' she told her.

'Well, I said it would.'

Marian clutched one silver-skinned fish to her chest. 'Shall I give him this to eat?'

'Aye. That should strengthen him.'

'What shall I do with it?'

The woman laughed. 'Give me that sharp knife from tha belt. See . . . like this. Cut off its head, then slit along its belly to clean the innards. Now poach it in a bit of milk. 'Twill be the best thing in the world for him.'

So Robert was fed on eggs and poached cod and he grew slowly stronger every day.

There was much to tell him and he lay there happily listening, though she thought he looked a little uncertain when he heard that Emma was with child.

Marian had such faith in seaweed now that she continued to treat the wound with it, and gradually the flesh knit itself together. The side of his face would be scarred, no helping that, and he'd a fine slit ear.

Though he could hear it in his waking and his dreams, Robert had not yet set eyes upon the sea, and he was curious. One sunny afternoon in late October Marian allowed him to get up from his pallet. She supported him to the doorway, where he stood, breathing in the salty air.

Winter approached and the wind grew colder. As the days passed, Robert grew stronger, to Marian's delight, and he begged her to walk with him over the cliffs to glimpse the sea. She agreed at last, insisting that he wrapped a rug about his shoulders. Then she took his arm, and led him outside, turning anxiously to see him blinking in the daylight by the doorway. It hurt her so to see the pallor of his cheeks, and his scar stood out red and livid in the sharp glare of the sun.

'Wait,' she told him, darting back inside, leaving him clinging weakly to the door post.

She took up her green cloak and pulled the knife from her belt. Carefully she cut the strong woven hood free of the mantle, then came back to him triumphantly. Gently she fastened the green hood around his head.

'There, that shall protect thee.'

He smiled, and winced at the pain that came.

'You should not have done that,' he said.

'I can stitch up my cloak, and make a fine mantle of it. Now, lean on me.'

He did as he was told, and they walked towards the sea.

Robert stared, just as Marian and John had done when they first saw it.

'It fills me with terror,' he whispered.

She nodded her understanding. 'I thought so too. But I have grown used to it, and now I love its roaring voice. 'Twas seaweed that brought healing to your wound, and I do believe the fresh salt air brings strength with it.'

They paced along the clifftops, with Much watching them anxiously from the cottage door. Marian moved ahead and Robert hesitated.

'Are you weary then?' she asked.

'Nay,' Robert rubbed his stomach. 'I am hungry.'

They both laughed and turned back to the cottage, walking close together.

'That night . . .' said Robert. 'That night I dreamed the green lady slept beside me . . .'

Marian stopped, her cheeks flamed suddenly red.

Robert pulled her to him. 'Well, it is just that I have often wished she'd creep into my bed again.'

That night Marian fell asleep wrapped in Robert's arms. In the morning Much went off for eggs, as usual, but when he came back, he led a sturdy black-and-white pony.

They both looked up at him in surprise.

'One of Bishop Hugh's men has lent him to me. I may ride him to Howden, and stable him there. Winter comes on fast, and I should go to seek out John.'

Robert struggled to his feet. 'I shall come too.'

Much grinned at him as he tottered and fell foolishly back upon the pile of bedding.

'I think not, dear Rob. You must both winter here. You shall be safe and well fed with fish; the villagers shall see to that. But . . . 'twill be a harsh winter in the forest.'

They nodded, remembering the deer hunts.

'Agnes says 'twill be even worse this time,' Marian agreed. 'She swears the poorest folk shall pay the ransom in the end.'

'I'm angry that I cannot come with thee, Much.' Robert put his head in his hands.

Muchlyn squeezed Robert's arm. 'I vow that we shall keep the Forestwife in venison.'

Robert rose again, carefully, and they went to set Muchlyn on his way.

19

The Lone Wolf

Marian and Robert lived together in peace and safety through the winter months. The little sea-battered town stayed free from frost and snow, though the wind was bitterly cold. They made good friends amongst the folk who lived in that isolated place and celebrated Christmas at Whitby Abbey. Marian learned much of seashore plants and healing lore from her new wood-gathering friend.

It was the end of February when news came to them that King Richard's ransom was paid. Count John had fled to France, fearing his brother's return.

Robert was strong and well, though scarred like a fighting dog. Marian watched him sadly from the clifftops as he paced along the beach with his bow, sending arrows whizzing over the rocks. Since they'd heard of Richard's hoped-for return, Robert had done nothing but practise his shooting to strengthen his drawing arm.

She sighed. 'He's like a restless wolf,' she muttered to herself. 'Who could hope to tame such a one?'

She could not hold him there much longer, that was clear enough, and at the same time a picture of Agnes and the Forestwife's clearing came into her mind, and then followed a picture of the Seeress's lonely cell. A strong surge of longing made her smile to herself.

'And I must go too, for I know now where I belong.'

She turned back to the cottage with a sigh, and began to pack their small possessions into bundles.

'What do you do?' he asked, when he returned.

' 'Tis time to go,' she told him.

He did not deny it, but stood in silence watching her. Then at last he caught hold of her and hugged her.

'I have been happy here,' he whispered. 'Happier than ever before. But my King has need of me.'

Robert begged a good strong horse that would carry them both, with the same agreement that Muchlyn had made. They'd leave it safe in the Bishop's stable at Howden.

Marian took charge of their directions, for Robert had no memory of how he'd reached Baytown. They turned reluctantly away from the sea at Whitby, and crossed another heather sea – the moors – still rich with amber and purple hues. Then they travelled on to the Forest of Galtres, and there they made their camp.

They built a good fire, and sat beside it late into the night. A lone wolf howled out in the shadows and Robert leapt to his feet, an arrow gleaming in his bow. He took aim and bent his bow. The grey wolf could be seen clearly, its yellow eyes glinting in the firelight.

Marian braced herself to hear its death cry, but it did not come. Robert lowered the bow. The wolf sat down in the distance, still watching them.

'Why?' she asked.

Robert sat down beside her. He shook his head, miserably scratching at the ground with the arrow. 'I shall watch him, as he watches me. I doubt he'll come closer. I know . . . what it is to be hunted. I have more in common with yon grey beast than I do with most of my own kind.'

His words made Marian shiver. She stared across the fire at him. He'd taken to wearing her hood almost all the time. His face was still lean, his eyes glittered hard and clear in the reflected firelight.

'And now,' he whispered, 'I know what it is to take a man's life.'

Marian stared at him. 'Gisburn?'

'Aye.'

'Was he the first?'

He smiled bitterly at her. 'Did you think I killed my uncle, then?'

She hung her head.

He reached across and took up her hand. 'Believe me, Gisburn was the first, and I would wish him the last.'

Marian clung tightly to his fingers. 'You had no choice. 'Twas kill or be killed.'

He nodded. 'No choice indeed.'

'Can you not give up this fighting, then? Must you still fight with Bishop Hugh?'

He shrugged his shoulders.

' 'Tis all that I can do.'

Later Marian lay awake beneath their blanket, her arms wrapped tightly about him. She was filled with sadness. There would never be another night like this, alone together in the woods.

They wandered a little from their pathway, and went to the west of Howden.

'I shall take thee to Barnsdale first,' said Robert. 'Then ride back to Howden.'

With relief they entered the rough shelter and safety of the great wastes of Barnsdale. They were close to the Forestwife's clearing when Tom spied them from the branch of a tree.

Marian waved and called to him, but he dropped down to the ground, and hobbled away towards the cottage.

Robert slowed the horse to a walk and turned to Marian with a puzzled frown. 'Something is wrong,' she whispered.

Then John came striding towards them from the clearing. The grim set of his face did nothing to calm their fears.

Robert climbed down from the horse and waited till his friend came close.

'What is it, John?'

The big man shook his head. 'I don't know how to tell. 'Twas a se'enight since. I was making ready to travel north to find thee both.'

Marian sat still upon the horse, her stomach heavy as lead.

'Is it Emma?' she asked.

John shook his head. 'Nay. 'Tis Agnes.'

'What?' They both cried out at once.

'She is dead.'

Marian bowed her head, and covered her face with her hands.

Robert stood stiff and pale, blinking at John.

' 'Twas William of Langden.'

'How?' demanded Robert.

John sighed. ''Twill take a bit of telling. Philippa's oldest lad came with an urgent message from Langden, but I fear we had gone to the Magdalen Assart to help them build more shelter for the sick. Only Tom and Agnes were here.'

'What message?' Marian knew the answer.

'The one we'd all dreaded,' said John. 'William of Langden had discovered old Sarah when she wandered from the shelter of her cottage into the spring sunlight. He had her set in the ducking stool, demanding that she tell him where the wicked nuns and the outlaw Philippa were hiding. The villagers were terrified at what he'd do so they sent the lad to find us.'

The big man paused, and dropped his head into his hands, close to tears.

'We were not there.'

'What happened?' Robert demanded, his voice quiet and cold.

'Tom set off to the Magdalen Assart to find us, as fast as he could, but Agnes . . . Agnes broke her rule. She left the clearing and went straight to Langden with Philippa's boy.'

Marian's lips moved slowly. 'She . . . left the forest?'

'Aye. The villagers say that poor Sarah would tell him naught, though he ducked her again and again. It was too much for her, I fear she's dead too. But they say her mind was clear enough at the end. She swore that William would be cursed by the Forestwife. That made him more furious than ever. He had Philippa's husband thrown into the lock-up, and her children dragged from their home. He had them roped together on the village green, threatening to duck them next if nobody would tell him where to find the wild women of the woods. The villagers were horrified, but then came Agnes, all alone. She marched straight up to William of Langden, and she did curse him. They say that he turned white with fear and rage, and had his men throw Agnes into the pond.'

'He drowned my mother?' Robert spoke low, his hands shaking.

'He tried to.'

'Did none go to her aid?'

'Yes, someone did. The villagers were astonished. Lady Matilda came all weak and shivering from her sick bed, led by her daughter. She faced up to her husband and quietly demanded that he cease his cruelty and let the women and children go free. They say that Lady Matilda's daughter took a knife from her belt and calmly cut the children's bonds. Then the villagers grew bold with the lady's presence, and pulled Agnes from the pond, but I fear 'twas too late.'

Robert's fist clenched around his bow. 'I shall kill that man.'

'No need, he's dead. As soon as Tom found us, I set off for Langden, with Philippa and Brother James. We ran as fast as we could, and Brother James set Snap to go racing ahead. Snap reached the village before us. He flew at his old master and tore his throat. Most of his men-at-arms stood by, unwilling to go to his aid. The others fled. I think that even they had little stomach for their work. The villagers carried Agnes up to the Manor, and set her in Lady Matilda's bed. She lived for two days, and Mother Veronica went to nurse her, but she had taken a lung fever and she died.'

Marian keeled forward in the saddle, and John caught her. Robert stared blankly at them both.

Reluctantly they entered the clearing. They went . . . not to the cottage, but to stand by the newly-turned earth beside Selina's mound that was Agnes's grave.

Emma came slowly to them from the house, her stomach swollen with the child. Philippa followed, and then came Tom, pale and hesitating. Marian turned to her friends, wishing to hurl herself into their arms, but there was something solemn in the formal way that they approached her. Then she saw that Emma carried the girdle of the Forestwife. She held it out towards Marian, offering it.

Marian shuddered and stepped back.

'No,' she cried. ' 'Tis not for me.'

John put his arm about Emma's shoulders. 'Marian . . . it is for thee. Agnes spoke to us, before she died.'

Marian shook her head, she could not bear to hear.

'What?' said Robert. 'What was it that she said?'

Philippa answered him. 'She said that she understood it all at last. That we must not grieve, for 'tis all come about as fate would have it. Marian was ever meant to be the Forestwife.'

Marian stared white-faced at Philippa. 'I cannot. Philippa, it should be you.'

But Philippa shook her head. 'I have waited for your return, but I must go back to Langden and all my little ones now that William is dead.'

Emma offered the girdle again. 'Do not be afraid. I will be here to help you,' she promised.

Marian lifted the beautiful thing from Emma's hands. She could not look at Robert. Tears poured down her cheeks as she fastened it around her waist. Emma and Philippa wrapped their arms around her on either side, and led her to the cottage door.

Later, they all sat talking quietly. There was a great deal more to tell. The Langden reeve and bailiff had sworn loyalty to Lady Matilda and her daughter, and though the woman was not strong, she'd already made great changes on the Manor. She'd invited the nuns back and begged their help and advice. Mother Veronica had taken courage from the protection that Lady Matilda offered them and gone back to their convent. They'd left two Sisters at the Magdalen Assart, opening it up to any who needed a home.

'They know they may hide in the woods again at the first sign of trouble,' said John. 'Miserable though we are, it seems there's something good come out of this. But Brother James feared for Snap, and he's taken his dog and gone off with Muchlyn and Stoutley to see if they may serve Bishop Hugh.'

Marian stared about her in distress. How could she be the Forestwife? She felt the loss of Agnes bitterly. How could she manage without her? Who would tell her what to do?

'What of the Seeress?' she asked.

'She is safe in her cell,' Emma told her.

'I must go to see her,' Marian said.

20

The Lost Child

Marian threw herself into the work of the Forestwife. It stopped her thinking. It blotted out her sorrow for a while, as she wracked her brains to think what Agnes would have done for every little hurt and pain that the forest folk brought to her. While she worked, she could not feel the bleak and empty space that Agnes left.

Robert stayed there in the clearing, awkward and quiet and ill at ease. Though they clung together through the nights, they had little to say. It seemed they could not share their misery.

When Emma went into labour, Marian was filled with dread, and a desolate yearning for Agnes's presence. She need not have feared, for as the birth progressed, it was almost as though Agnes whispered in her ear, calmly telling her what to do, step by step.

A girl was born, big and strong and kicking. Marian sat back, satisfied with her work. Emma leaned on John, weak with the effort. They both smiled down with pleasure at their child. Even Robert came in to share a little of their joy.

'You two should get wed,' said Marian.

They both laughed. 'We were wed last Michaelmas,' John told her. 'As soon as I returned from Baytown.'

'Who wed thee? Brother James?'

'Nay.' Emma grinned. 'We were wed in a circle of nuns. Brother James said he'd forgotten how, and that six nuns were much better.'

'Six nuns? Is that truly wed then?'

'True enough for us,' said John.

At sunset Robert sought her out.

'Shall you and I be wed?' he asked. 'Shall we stand together in a circle of nuns.'

Marian clenched her hands with sorrow, till the nails bit into her knuckles. She wished very much that they might belong together like Emma and John. It was clear enough that he had feared to be tied to a woman . . . and yet now he begged it of her. She answered him as she must, but gently.

'I can be no man's wife. I am the Forestwife. For me that must suffice.'

He sat beside her in silent misery.

Marian pulled out the length of twine that fastened her mother's garnet ring about her neck. She clasped the ring in her hand, wanting to give it to him, wishing to find some way of comforting. And yet she could not quite bring herself to part with it. She let it drop back into place. They sat there side by side until the sun had gone.

Next morning he took the horse, and left for Howden.

Philippa went back to Langden with Tom and Alice's family. John and Emma were besotted with their child. Marian thought she'd die from loneliness. There was but one person who would always listen, who would weep with her, as she spilled her sadness out into the blossoming spring woods. She took her cloak and set off through the forest for the tiny cell.

The Seeress had little comfort to offer, but her presence and concern always helped. When Marian returned through the forest, she'd gathered strength, enough to go on.

News of King Richard came in March. He'd landed in the south and made his way to London, then headed north to Nottingham. John went marching off to join Robert, besieging Tickhill Castle once again. Emma was sad, but accepting.

They heard that Tickhill Castle had at last been taken, to Bishop Hugh's great delight, with a great army of fighting men who'd come down from the north. Then, later, they heard that the King had marched with a gathering army to Nottingham Castle, where Count John's garrison still held out against him.

Marian came more and more to rely upon the Seeress. Emma was always kind, but wrapped up in her lovely child. Marian remembered the first birth, and did not begrudge her such happiness. The Seeress would listen endlessly, always with sympathy, but also with firm good sense. Marian made many journeys through the wood.

Often she begged the Seeress to leave her cell.

'We could build a new small hut for thee, close to my clearing. I have such need of thee, for there are so many folk who want naught but someone to listen to them.'

But the Seeress would not have it.

' 'Tis a lovely picture you hold out to me, and I long for such a life. But . . . you do not understand. 'Tis for my sin, for my penance that I must stay here.'

Frustrated and despairing, Marian went to visit Mother Veronica, safely settled once more in her old convent home. They sat in the stone-flagged kitchen by a good fire.

'At least we may see the Seeress well comforted and fed, now that we're back,' Veronica tried to soothe Marian's worries. 'Here, sit thee down and take a cup of ale, for we worry about thee. 'Twas clear to us all that you were the chosen one, but you are young indeed, dear Marian, to take up the burden of the Forestwife.'

Marian sighed and sat down to her cup of ale. Sister Catherine brought in a tiny piglet runt, wrapped in a cloth. She set about warming it some milk. Marian smiled at the pink snuffling creature, but still her thoughts were pulled back to the Seeress. She turned to Mother Veronica.

'I have begged the Seeress to come to live near me. Do you think it wrong of me? I swear she would be happy, and I need her so, now that Agnes is gone. You would not think it wrong, would you?'

Mother Veronica laughed. 'I would not. I have long since given up judging others.'

'All she will say is that 'tis her great sin that prevents it. What terrible thing could she have done?'

'I've never known,' Mother Veronica shook her head. 'The Seeress was here before we came, enclosed in her little hut – by her brother, it was said. The Bishop sent us here to guard her, and to take the name of Mary Magdalen's nuns. I believe the Seeress chose the name.' The fat nun shrugged her shoulders. 'That's all I know. She does not wish to tell us more, and I have respected that.'

Marian sat in silence, watching the piglet snuffing up milk from the old nun's fingers, though her mind was still on the strange lonely woman in her cell.

'Though I have never seen her face, I swear she is not an old woman,' she spoke her thoughts out loud.

'No,' said Sister Catherine, who'd been quietly listening to them both while she fed her tiny charge. 'She is not an old woman. And I have seen her face.'

Marian and Mother Veronica both looked sharply across at her.

Sister Catherine blushed. 'I have seen and heard what I should not.' She laughed and gently scratched the piglet's head. 'But then I am a wicked nun.'

'Whatever do you mean, Catherine?' Mother Veronica demanded. 'Most would say that we are all wicked nuns.'

'Yes,' said Sister Catherine, 'but I was wicked long before you. Do you remember that the Seeress was sick? It must be three years since?'

'Yes . . .' Mother Veronica and Marian turned to her, listening intently.

'Well,' Sister Catherine went on, 'I took her food and drink as was my job to do. But the Seeress was so sick that she couldn't even open her hatch.'

'What did you do?'

'I broke all the rules. I opened it myself and I climbed inside – 'tis easy enough to do. The Seeress was shouting out in her sleep. It did not all make sense, but it was clear she sorrowed and cried for a lost child.'

'Ah,' Mother Veronica nodded. 'A child, you say?'

The old nun nodded. 'A child called Mary,' she said, shooting a quick nervous glance across at Marian.

Marian went very quiet.

'What happened then?' Mother Veronica asked.

'I woke her, and I fed her. She was distressed and we talked. 'Twas all against the rules, I know.'

'Drat the rules,' said Mother Veronica. ' 'Twas a good and Christian thing to do.'

'Well,' the old nun continued, 'she was sad and sick, and just for a while all her iron resolution had faded. She told me all about herself. How she'd given birth to a child, a daughter. The father was a sweet-faced minstrel, who'd come to sing to the ladies in her home. The Seeress's brother was beside himself with rage when he discovered their love. He'd planned to marry his sister to a powerful and wealthy man. The minstrel was found poisoned in a ditch. Once she'd given birth to a bastard child, her brother's ambitions to marry her well were over. He'd persuaded her that she must be dead to the world, and lock herself inside that cell to pay for her sin.'

Marian stood up suddenly, sending her stool clattering to the floor.

'What was his name?'

Sister Catherine stared up at her, frightened by the anger in her voice.

'What was his name? Her brother?'

'It was something like a name of a woodland, or a wood.'

'Holt,' thundered Marian. 'Was it Holt?'

'Yes,' the old nun said, dropping the squealing piglet to the floor. 'Yes, that was it, for sure . . . de Holt. The Seeress's name is Eleanor.'

'What can it mean?' Mother Veronica was white with worry.

Marian shook from head to toe. 'It means . . . it means that . . . she is my mother. I am Mary. I am that child.'

Marian ran out of the convent building, heading straight for the Seeress's little wood.

'Can this be true?' Mother Veronica cried.

'Yes,' said Sister Catherine, wiping her eyes. The old nun was pale and shaken, but she spoke with determination. 'Remember, I have seen her face.'

'Did you know?'

'I did not know, but I guessed. They are so alike. I pray that I have done right to speak up.'

Marian ran up to the Seeress's cell. 'I know your sin,' she shouted as she ran. 'I know your sin.'

There was silence from the hut.

Marian pressed her hands against the window grille. 'It is no sin at all,' she whispered.

'Marian?' The Seeress spoke low. 'Is it you?'

'Yes . . . I am Marian. I am the Forestwife . . . but I am Mary, too. I am your daughter.'

There was silence once more. A thick heavy silence and then a small, heartrending cry.

Marian suddenly snatched at her own throat, snapping the silver ring from the thong around her neck. She held the garnet in her hand. The Seeress's fingers came snaking through the gap, and took the ring. She held it cupped in both of her trembling palms.

'Yes,' she breathed, her voice faint and shocked, 'you are my child.'

'Then will you not come out of this damned hole and see me?' Marian cried.

'I cannot! I have sinned against . . . you!' she broke down, sobbing.

'You have not,' cried Marian. 'You gave me life! I am strong and free!' Then her voice dropped, suddenly soft with longing. 'But you know more than any. The one who mothered me is gone and the man I love thinks more of his King than me. I need my mother now.'

Marian scratched frantically at the grille as Mother Veronica and the nuns came rushing into the glade.

Mother Veronica put her hand on Marian's shoulder.

'Marian, stand back,' she ordered.

Sister Catherine carried her meat cleaver. She gripped it tightly in both hands.

'My dear Eleanor,' she shouted, 'do you wish to be free?'

Then the Seeress's voice came clearly through the rustling trees.

'Yes, yes. I beg you, set me free.'

Mother Veronica held tight to Marian, whispering comfort into her ear.

Sister Catherine gave three great chops with her cleaver, and broke a hole through the top of the thatch. It was not difficult, the cell was rickety with age. Then the nuns all set about the hut with a good will. They ripped it apart with their bare hands.

A small, trembling woman stood amongst the rubble, her bed and bucket covered with dust. Marian rushed forward, arms outstretched; she hugged her mother, and rocked her in her arms.

It was May Day, and Philippa had brought her family to the Forestwife's clearing to celebrate. They raised a maypole on the grass before the trysting tree. Emma carried flowers to decorate the pole, her fine daughter strapped to her chest.

Philippa's children ran to Marian, who sat by the cottage door. They presented bunches of flowers to the Forestwife, and to the older woman who sat at her side.

The Seeress smiled, and lifted the flowers to her face. She turned to Marian. 'I never thought to see a day like this.'

In the distance there came the sound of heavy hooves, and the creak of wagon wheels going at a good pace through the forest tracks. Marian got to her feet, fearing trouble.

At last a great ox-cart rumbled into the clearing. Emma cried out with pleasure, for John held the reins. Robert rode astride the ox, his head wrapped still in the green hood.

Marian stared and went over to them, puzzled.

Robert jumped down, smiling.

'We've brought a real ox for you this time.'

'What can this be?' she asked.

He bowed, with a flourish. ''Tis peas and barley and cornmeal and grain, all for the Forestwife.'

She shook her head in amazement.

''Tis a long story,' Robert shifted uncomfortably. 'But I fear I can have no more to do with King Richard.'

Marian stared at him in disbelief. She reached up and took his arm.

They went slowly hand in hand to stand by Agnes's grave. Robert spoke with quiet despair. Marian found his broken spirit harder to bear than recklessness.

He told her how they'd helped Bishop Hugh to take Tickhill Castle, and how they'd then marched with him to Nottingham to support the King. Nottingham Castle had been taken, but they'd had to fight for it.

'Then the King called for a great council,' Robert waved his arms dramatically at the yew trees. 'I thought 'twould be the longed-for day of justice, the day we've waited for. Richard sacked the sheriffs – and how we all cheered. I thought 'twas good King Arthur come back to us.'

'What then?' Marian asked.

Robert frowned, and shook his head. 'Why then . . . he roared and ranted that we'd had it easy. We'd been safe at home while he went fighting wars. We'd been mean and slow to raise his ransom. Now we must find more money, so that he may got to fight for his lands in France.'

'Nay!'

'True enough,' Robert's face was pale with anger.

' 'Tis just as Agnes said.'

'Aye.' He sighed and shook his head again. 'I rage against myself that I would not listen. Now the King has sold the sheriffs back their jobs.'

'What?'

Robert laughed with bitterness. 'Aye, Nottingham-shire has bought his way back into power again, and we may whistle for our pardons.'

'What will you do?'

Robert took her hand, and suddenly the old fire flashed in his eyes. 'I cannot serve my King – I shall serve thee instead. I know you cannot wed, but I shall be the Knight of the Forestwife, devoted to the Sisters of the Magdalen.'

Her mouth parted in a wondering smile. His wild zeal had taken a new and hopeful turn. He spoke with excite-ment of his plans. 'If I can raise money for a king's ransom, then I can raise money to buy grain. Fat bishops and rich lords who travel the great road shall all make a contribution. Next winter will be harsh indeed, but those who seek the Forestwife – they shall be fed.'

He knelt down before her, wrapping his arms around her waist, hiding his face against her stomach.

Tears poured from Marian's eyes as she bent down, over his hooded head. 'Come, get up, dear Rob,' she whispered, 'for I, too, have much to tell, and someone for you to meet.' She wiped her eyes and smiled at him. 'Look, they have set the maypole by the trysting tree. And though the Forestwife may not be wed, each May Day she shall dance with the green man.'

Part II

CHILD OF THE MAY

21

The Green Man

It was autumn. The paths were slushy with mud and falling leaves. Robert and John travelled steadily through the russet and golden woodland of Barnsdale, their faces grim.

Robert walked beside the horse. His scarred face was pale with the silent anger that burnt within, yet he led his friend's steed with great care. John hunched forward in the saddle, carrying his little daughter in his arms. They slowed their horses almost to stopping as they approached the clearing of the Forestwife.

Marian was chopping wood vigorously in front of the cottage. The goats and chickens ignored the regular thumping of her axe in their hunt for food, while the cats dozed in patches of sharp sunlight. Tom stacked the wood carefully ready for the slow burning that would turn it into charcoal. He still dragged his leg from the time he'd been caught in the mantrap. Suddenly Marian threw down the heavy axe and stretched her back.

'That's enough,' she cried. 'I'm fair worn out.'

'Aye,' Tom was quick to agree. 'Shall I fetch ale?'

But before she could answer, she looked up and saw the two men who'd entered the clearing without a sound. They stood by the great oak, still as statues.

Marian ran to them, but slowed her steps as she saw their solemn grey faces and the small struggling burden that they bore.

'What has happened? Where is Emma? What of Bishop Hugh?'

Robert stepped forwards and took hold of her by the shoulders. His voice was harsh and his head dropped with weariness. 'I'm sorry Marian. The fighting bishop is dead. Poisoned we swear.'

'But where is Emma? John . . . where is she?'

The big man sat astride his horse, clutching the child. He looked away shamefaced, then put his head down and wept quietly into the child's soft brown thatch of hair.

'Count John sent his mercenaries to Howden Manor, as soon as his brother left for France,' Robert told her. 'They were there the moment the old man died. They took his house, his servants, his horses and his fighting men. We were surrounded in the great hall while we sat at table. We were named as WOLVESHEADS and ordered into the dungeon. Emma could not bear it. She ran to us, the little one in her arms. A vicious fellow, one of their captains, aimed his crossbow and shot her. Shot her in the back, there in the hall.'

'No!' Marian cried.

'Aye,' he nodded. 'There was outrage in the place even amongst the mercenaries, and our friends rushed to our aid. We got out and found horses, hoping that we'd reach you in time, but . . .' He shook his head.

'She's dead?' Marian whispered.

Robert nodded.

'Where is she?'

'Much and Will Stoutley follow. They carry her in a litter, but what can we do? We bring you the child!'

Marian stepped back. 'I told you not to go,' she shouted. 'I told you, all of you! How could you be such stupid fools to think that the bishop could get you pardoned?'

'You were right,' Robert spoke with quiet anger. 'Does it give you pleasure?'

Marian shook her head, dumb with misery.

'The child?' Robert spoke more gently. 'We cannot care for her. The frosts will be on us soon.'

'Take her away!' Marian cried. 'I do not want the child. I want Emma.'

They stood beside the fresh-piled earth of Emma's grave as the sun sank and darkness fell. Still they stood there, though the evening grew cold and the stars began to show. Then the child began to cry in her father's arms. John seemed to start as though waking from a dream. He turned towards the cottage but Marian followed him and reached up to touch his shoulder. He turned to her, surprised.

'For me,' she said, holding out her arms. 'The little

one is for me. You said that I should have her.'

John dropped a kiss on the small head and gave her the child without a word.

'Magda, little Magdalen,' she whispered. 'Let us find thee some nice warm bread and milk.'

'Help them! Help them! They shall burn!'

Magda was dragged from her peaceful dream. She rubbed her eyes and shuddered as she heard the cries. Eleanor, the old one, was having one of her terrible dreams again.

'Hunger . . . bitter hunger!' The old woman's voice rose. 'They bring hunger, fire and sword to the forest.'

Magda rolled over on her straw pallet and sat up. A dark shape moved across the small sleeping space, cutting out the fire's glow for a moment. Then she heard Marian's tired voice, speaking with patience.

'Wake, Mother. 'Tis but a dream. Come, Mother, wake up and take a sip of ale.'

The terror subsided to gentle sobs. Magda heaved a great sigh and settled down once more, pity turning to irritation as Marian's murmuring voice continued low and soothing. Why couldn't they let her get to sleep, she'd worked hard all day. They'd made her dig up the last of the grain from the keeping pit, then made her grind the stuff into flour. Her arms still ached from it.

She had now lived in the Forestwife's cottage with

these two strange women, for fifteen years and didn't see why she should stay longer. Neither of them was her real mother. Just because she was tall and strong like her father, they gave her the vilest jobs of digging latrine pits, and even worse, filling them in. She longed to leave the wilderness of Barnsdale and see the world beyond.

Still, she thought with a faint smile, tomorrow there'd be fresh bread and best ale and May Day dancing. They'd raised a maypole by the trysting tree and her father and Robert would come. Maybe they'd bring Tom with them. That thought cheered her. The Forestwife's clearing would be spinning with folk, bent on welcoming the summer and having a wild time while they were about it.

She snuggled down beneath her rug. Yes, she'd stay for the May Day dancing, but then persuade her father to take her off adventuring with him. She'd leave the forest – but a small wisp of doubt seemed to drift through her mind. What if Eleanor's dream should have special meaning? What had she cried out? *Hunger*, *fire* and *sword*. Many believed that what the old one saw and dreamed was the truth.

Magda could not settle properly to sleep again.

All three were up early and on the move. Eleanor seemed her usual calm self once more. Even before the sun was up they heard shouts and giggles from outside, then came a knocking on the door.

'Where's the lady?'

'Is she ready?'

'Where's our May Day Queen?'

Though she was pale and tired, Marian laughed. 'They must have been up all night!' she cried. She took up her faded green cloak. 'I'm getting far too old for this.'

'Nay.' Eleanor shook her head. 'You are not too old my daughter, but I must warn you! Maybe . . . the Green Man shall miss his May Day dancing.'

'What do you mean?' asked Marian.

Eleanor shook her head again. 'I cannot see clear.'

'Are you ready?' Magda asked. 'I cannot hold them back much longer. It'll soon be sun-up.'

Marian nodded and Magda threw open the door.

At once the small hut swarmed with skinny excited children, dressed in rags but with flowers in their hair. They bore thin starlike rush lights and a beautiful wreath of hawthorn with its creamy pink-tipped may blossom.

'Crown the Queen! Crown the Queen!' they chanted. Marian bowed her head to be crowned.

The clearing was lit with flickering candles and lanterns. Marian went to stand before the maypole, while the children rushed off into the forest. The gathering turned quiet, waiting in tense silence. Magda stood beside Marian, her heart beating fast. This was the moment that she'd always loved, ever since she was a tiny child. Her hand crept into Marian's and squeezed it hard. Then they heard it, gentle at first, faint sounds of chanting.

'Summer is a-coming in! Summer is a-coming in!'

It grew steadily louder, until streams of children broke from the cover of the trees, dragging ropes of plaited ivy.

They hauled on their ropes as the sun came up, dragging a dark figure from the depth of the forest. It was hard to see him clearly at first, for like the very trees he was covered in leaves and blossom.

Marian turned to the old one. 'He comes, after all thy fears.'

Eleanor smiled and nodded.

At last he strode from the shade out into the growing sunlight: the frightening, wonderful, magical Green Man.

Magda stared at him. This was not Robert! Ever since she could remember, Robert had been the Green Man. He'd come each May Day to dance with the Forestwife. This man was huge but he leapt across the clearing with the grace of a deer. His thick beard was as green as his skin. Magda's heart thumped faster than ever as he came towards them. Could this truly be the spirit of the forest, the guardian of the plants and trees?

'It's really him!' she whispered and clutched at Marian's cloak.

A fleeting moment of disappointment touched the older woman's face. Then quickly Marian smiled. She reached up to her crown of may blossom and swiftly placed it on Magda's head.

'You shall be Green Lady today,' she whispered.

'Nay,' Magda cried out.

'Oh yes,' Marian insisted, laughing now. 'Go greet the Green Man.'

Magda turned fearfully towards the terrifying figure that danced towards her. Then suddenly she was laughing too and racing to him, her arms outstretched.

'My father, my father,' she shouted. 'My father is the Green Man.'

22

A Place of Ancient Magic

The day was filled with wild laughter and dancing, but in the evening the clearing quietened as young men and women slipped off in pairs into the forest. As dusk fell, Marian found Magda and dragged her back into the hut.

'But I want to dance with Tom,' Magda complained.

'Tom can come inside too,' Marian insisted. 'Your father sits by our fireside and there's much to talk about.'

'You're angry because Robert's not here,' Magda snapped. 'If *you* can't have any fun, then neither can I!'

Marian did not deny it, just shrugged her shoulders and sighed. Then Magda wished that she had kept silent as she glimpsed the shadow of sadness that crossed Marian's face. Couldn't she keep her mouth shut? Was it not hurtful enough that Robert was not there to dance with the Forestwife? Magda quietly did as she was told, contenting herself with sitting down beside Tom and leaning with pleasure against his strong back.

'Well?' Marian looked across at John as he sprawled

beside the hearthstone, still wiping traces of green dye from his cheeks. 'What is it now that keeps him?'

John sighed. 'He travels through Sherwood into Nottingham Town.'

'What? Is he gone completely mad?'

John shook his head. 'Aye, maybe so! But I must follow him in the morning and when you hear it all you'll see that something had to be done. Your friend Philippa will go with us.'

'Philippa?' cried Marian. 'I was surprised that she didn't come today. Tell me quickly!'

'It was only yesterday that we discovered it,' said John. 'We stopped by Langden village on our way to you. Lady Matilda was worried sick and all the villagers rushing about the place. Matilda and her daughter Isabel have been summoned to Nottingham by King John.'

'What? The King's in Nottingham too?'

'Aye. He celebrates May Day with the Sheriff and we've heard that he has sold the man the shrievalties of Derbyshire and Yorkshire!'

'Oh no!' Marian gasped. 'So Gilbert de Gore is Sheriff of all three counties? That puts paid to Robert's trick of crossing the borders for safety.'

'It does,' John agreed. 'We'd have far to go to be free of his bullying laws.'

'I begin to worry,' said Marian grimly. 'What do they want with Matilda?'

John shook his head. 'It seems the King wants Isabel to marry one of his men. Langden lands shall be used as a reward. Isabel has made the lands rich and fertile. You could feed an army from them.'

'But that's not right,' Marian cried. 'Matilda raised every penny she could and bought permission to marry her daughter where she wished.'

'Aye,' Tom butted in. 'They stripped Langden of everything of value to pay his price and never regretted it, for Isabel has more than repaid the villagers with her kindness.'

John shrugged his shoulders. 'When was anything ever fair? This King's as greedy for money as his brother was and he's slippery as an eel. Now he says that Isabel is well past the age when she should marry, and she must marry the man of his choosing or pay the freedom tax once more.'

'He can't do that!' Marian was outraged.

John laughed bitterly. 'He does what he wants. Even the barons are growing to hate him. He invents his own taxes all the time. But this cruelty to Isabel will hurt all of us. Some manor lords would have bled their own peasants dry to build up their funds, but not Lady Matilda. She and Isabel have nothing but the house and the land they own.'

'What will happen now?' Magda asked anxiously.

John stroked his beard thoughtfully. 'The King demands that they present themselves at Nottingham Castle, so off they've gone. They cannot refuse, even though Lady Matilda's so frail.'

'And so,' Marian said with resignation, 'Robert has gone with them?'

'Not exactly with them,' said John. 'There's Brother James and Much and Will Stoutley too, all going into Nottingham by their own secret ways. Philippa insists on coming as well. We shall stick close to our two Langden ladies, doing our best to keep them from harm. Now do you see why Tom and I must follow tomorrow?'

'Yes,' said Marian, turning to Eleanor who sat very still beside her, looking troubled. 'Do you see aught to fear, Mother?'

'Nothing clear,' she said, shivering a little. 'Just cold and hunger, cold and hunger and thirst.'

Marian sighed. 'I am weary of this struggle,' she said. 'For eight years we have fought against King John, I swear he is even worse than his brother. We can never win.'

'We must rise early in the morning,' said Tom, yawning. 'We need as many pairs of ears and eyes as we can get.'

'Right,' said Magda. 'Then I shall go too.'

'You will not,' said Marian.

Magda jumped to her feet and stamped out of the hut, banging the door hard behind her. She marched off towards the edge of the stream, kicked off her boots and slipped her feet into the water. The comforting warm spring bubbled up from deep inside the earth, soothing her a little. Hot tears of anger filled her eyes, blurring the moonlit woodland.

They treated her like a child, like a prisoner almost.

Faint rustling came to her as she looked into the darkness beyond the babbling water. Bushes twitched and she heard the sounds of low laughter. This night was supposed to be special for young girls and their sweethearts. Others had built bowers for their courting, filled with scented herbs and flowers. There'd be babies born from this night's loving. Was she not such a one herself? Child of the May, her father called her.

The door of the hut opened again and she heard her father calling her name. She got up and went slowly towards him.

'Come here, sweetheart,' he begged.

John went to sit on the doorstep, pulling Magda down beside him. He put his arms about her, hugging her tightly.

'You are the most precious thing in the world to me,' he said.

Magda sighed. She loved her father dearly but she'd heard it all before. 'I know,' she said. 'I am all that's left to you of your beloved Emma.'

'You do not know how cruel this world is!' he told her. 'Here in this clearing, you are safe. There's ancient magic in the place.'

'Safe! Safe!' Magda exploded. 'But, Father, I do not want to be safe!'

She pushed John away and strode back into the cottage. Marian looked up as the girl stormed in, angry and tear-stained.

'Don't look at me like that,' Magda cried. 'I will go, whatever you say. This place may be enough for you, but it is not enough for me!'

She threw herself down onto her pallet, turning her face away from her friends.

'Leave her! Let her stew!' said Marian, but Eleanor went quietly to sit beside her, stroking Magda's hair in silence. Tom looked uncomfortable.

Marian stared angrily into the fire until John came back inside. 'Come sit beside me, John,' she said, holding out her hand to him. 'You and I must take council over this unruly child of yours.'

John and Marian whispered together late into the night, while the others slept.

23

The Young Vixen

Magda was woken early by the sharp bang of wood on wood. Marian had built up the fire so that it flared and crackled. A fine smell came from freshly-made oatcakes sizzling on the flat iron griddle that hung over the hearthstone. Magda sat up and watched, bleary-eyed, as Marian rummaged purposefully in the wooden box that contained the few worn scraps of clothing they possessed.

Magda groaned and pushed her warm rug away, swinging her long legs to the side. 'What are you doing?' she asked. 'It's not even sun-up! You look as though you've been awake all night.'

'I have,' said Marian.

Magda frowned. 'Can't you let decent folk sleep?'

The older woman pulled out a worn pair of breeches that had once belonged to Tom. 'These will do,' she cried. 'And a cloak and hood. That's what's needed.'

Magda got up and stretched. She stood there, hands on hips, watching with irritation. Suddenly Marian swung round and held the breeches up in front of Magda, as though measuring them against her.

'What are you doing? I'm not wearing them!'

'You are,' said Marian. 'You'll wear these breeches if you're going to Nottingham with the men. And keep that sullen look upon thy face – sharp as arrowheads, that look is. It will protect thee well!'

Magda's mouth dropped open, her hands fell to her sides.

'Don't stand and gawp!' Marian snapped. 'John and I've agreed. You can go if you dress as a lad and if you stay close to him or Philippa.'

Magda was amazed. 'Or Robert,' she said.

'He'll get you into trouble worse than any,' Marian replied sharply. Then she sighed. 'Or Robert,' she agreed.

'I'm going to Nottingham! I'm going to Nottingham!' Magda cried.

All at once the snappiness drained from Marian's voice. 'Truth is,' she said, 'you are not growing up much like Emma. Last night you put me more in mind of someone else. Someone I remembered from long ago.'

Magda frowned, puzzled by her words. 'What do you mean?'

Marian shook her head. Then she laughed, though the sound she made was harsh. 'Myself,' she said. 'You put me in mind of the girl that I once was. I fear it's more like me that you grow, not your gentle mother. Believe me, Magda, there are times when I wish myself far away from this place. I may not go, but you can. It seems the time has come.'

Magda blinked hard. Her eyes brimmed with tears and her heart filled up with a sudden fierce love. She flung her arms around Marian. 'I am happy if I grow like you,' she said.

'Aye, well,' said Marian, smiling and pushing her gently away. 'Let's hope tha's learnt enough to keep thee safe. Now there's no time for worrying, we must sort things out. There's much to do.'

'Must I really wear Tom's old breeches?' Magda sniffed at them suspiciously.

Marian nodded firmly. She pulled out the sharp meat knife that she always carried tucked into her girdle.

'You must wear breeches, cloak and hood, and that shiny chestnut mane must go. A tall, handsome lass like you with all that lovely hair will cause a stir. Your father has trouble enough keeping himself from being noticed.'

'Aye,' Magda agreed. 'Not like Robert.'

Marian smiled wryly. These days Robert came and went mysteriously like a flying shadow. He robbed rich bishops in Yorkshire one day and fooled the Sheriff's guard in Nottingham the next. The Hooded One was what they called him and ridiculous stories of his doings had spread throughout the north of England. Rich rewards had been offered for his capture, alive or dead. Certainly he had become the most wanted man in the north.

'Aye,' said Marian sadly. 'He keeps his secrets, does Robert.'

* * *

The sharp blade swished and Magda clenched her knuckles tightly till they turned white. Dark chestnut locks fell all about her feet like autumn leaves. She watched through a watery mist, her eyes still blurry with tears.

At last Marian stood back. 'It's done,' she said.

Magda brushed the itchy coating of cut hairs from around her neck and tossed her head from side to side.

'Feels funny,' she muttered.

'Does it feel bad?'

'Nay,' said Magda, flicking her hands through the short strands that now swung neatly just beneath her ears. 'Nay, it feels fine. It feels free.'

'Good,' said Marian, smiling with relief. 'Now take up these oatcakes and carry them round to thy father. See if he knows thee!'

When the girl had gone, Marian's smile faded. Wearily she gathered up the dark locks of hair, stuffing them into a basket. But when the job was done and the basket set aside, she turned impulsively back to it and snatched up a small handful of the soft curls. She went to the salt crock and took up a pinch of the precious stuff, then sprinkled hair and salt together in a circle above the fire. The hair and salt flared with a swift blue flame. Marian spat into the fire and as it hissed she murmured,

> 'Water, earth, air and fire right,
> Keep my girl safe, both day and night.'

They left soon after sunrise. Magda strode ahead,

delighting in the new freedom that Tom's breeches brought. She was filled with excitement and energy for the journey ahead. John and Tom followed more slowly, with many a backward glance at the small figure of Marian. She stood by the ancient turning stone watching till they had vanished from sight.

They went to the south and reached Langden village when the sun was high in the sky. The manor house stood proud on a mound with a deep ditch all around. It was well cared for and surrounded by orchards, pigs and good-sized vegetable strips all fenced in with low palings. At times the villagers complained that the manor had no defences, but Isabel insisted that she was a farmer, not a fighter. She ignored the villagers' fears and fed them well.

The small cots that surrounded the manor were built close to the main cart track; Magda thought that Langden seemed unusually quiet. Philippa was waiting by the forge in her best gown and cloak, with her husband. She kissed Tom and tugged at his beard.

'Tha's more of a man than ever,' she said. 'When are you coming back to Langden? We miss you here – this was once your home!'

Tom shook his head. 'I can't come back,' he said. 'Not since Mam died.'

Philippa nodded her understanding. 'But who's this young lad?' she asked, glancing at Magda and winking at John.

'A lad I'd rather see safe at home,' John told her. 'But he's promised to stay close by us, has this lad.'

'Right enough,' Philippa agreed. 'The time comes for each young vixen to creep from her den.'

'Aye,' said John. 'She may creep from her den, but can she hunt?'

Philippa hugged her husband and Rowan, who was now a fair-haired lad, of seventeen.

'I think I should be going with you,' said Rowan teasingly. 'If Magda's going, so should I.'

Philippa gave him a playful punch on the cheek. 'You've to stay here and take care of our guest from Mansfield,' she told him, glancing back to where a man stood half-hidden in the dark thatched entrance to the forge.

Magda looked at him and gasped. Just for one moment she thought that it was Robert. Was that not Robert's cloak and hood? She knew it well. Then he moved forward into the light and she saw that his face was strange to her. The man glared angrily at them, then turned back to the warm fire inside the forge.

'Who is he?' Magda asked.

Philippa snorted with raucous laughter and took Magda by the arm. 'He's a guest,' she said. 'Unwilling, but still a guest. Come, let's get on our way, for we must reach Sherwood before nightfall. At once. For Langden shall see no peace or thriving until Matilda and Isabel have returned.'

24

The Wolfpack

The wastes and woodlands were lush with springing grass and yellow-green bursting buds; the undergrowth, alive with young hares and waddling partridges. The scent of sap and blossom hung in the air.

'Maytime! Maytime! Best time of all the year,' Magda cried.

'Not bad,' Philippa admitted. 'A good dry time for taking to the road. At least we shan't be shivering in a ditch tonight.'

'I wish your Rowan could have come,' Magda sighed, seeing again his handsome face and teasing smile.

'Eh lass! Isn't one strong lad enough company for you?' Philippa lowered her voice, nodding behind them at Tom.

'Huh! Tom's fine and I love him,' said Magda. 'But he does drag his leg so. Besides, he's more of a brother to me.'

'You weren't there when Tom near snapped that leg in a mantrap,' said Philippa darkly. 'I was. I tell you this for nothing: though Rowan is the apple of my eye, you'll never find a braver lad than Tom – not in the whole of Yorkshire.'

'Well,' said Magda cheekily, 'aren't we in Nottingham-shire now?'

She ducked fast as Philippa's hand swung close to her cheek.

They reached the edge of Sherwood as the sun began to sink. Tom led them through secret paths to a small cave mouth.

'They were here,' he said, dropping to his knees to sniff at a light patch of wood ash that lay within a darkened circle of burnt earth. 'Yes, Robert and Muchlyn. Two days ahead.'

Magda stared at him. 'Daft lad,' she muttered.

'If Tom tells thee so, tha'd best believe it,' John told her.

'How?' Magda still doubted.

'A faint smell of burning.' Tom held a pinch of ash to her nose. 'That will be gone by sunrise, and see how it's raked out in a circle with one stone dropped into the centre here – that's Robert. And the small white pebble – that's Much. The circle is broken here; they've travelled on to the south.'

'Hugh,' said Magda. 'And I suppose you'll be telling me what they ate for their supper?'

'Venison,' said Tom. 'Smoked venison.'

'How can you tell that?'

Tom gave a wicked laugh. 'Because I smoked the meat

for him myself and wrapped it up in burdock leaves. Anyway, it's what the Hooded One always eats when he's journeying and there's no time to make a fresh kill.'

They quickly got a fire kindled and settled to eat Marian's bread and goat's cheese.

'I thought you'd snare us a hare or shoot a fat partridge,' said Magda, disappointed.

'Nay,' said John. 'We must leave them to raise their young in spring, then we shall eat well of them when winter comes. Besides, who'd want burnt meat when they can have fresh bread?'

They slept in the sheltering cave wrapped in their cloaks with sweet-smelling rushes piled beneath them. In the morning they woke with the sun and ate the rest of their food. They were on the road to Nottingham by the time the sun was high in the sky.

As the great city rose in the distance before them, the road became thronged with rumbling carts, packhorses and dust-stained travellers heading for the main northern gate.

Magda grabbed Philippa by the arm. 'Look there!' she yelled, her cheeks pink with the excitement of it all. 'See the towers that soar high into the sky? Is that Nottingham Castle? How does it float up there above us? But look . . . in that fine wagon. A lady dressed in scarlet with gold on her head! Is she the Queen? She must be the Queen!'

Philippa could only laugh. She turned to John. 'Look at this lad of yours. His eyes are fair popping at the sights.'

John could not smile. He put his hand on Magda's shoulder. 'Look and stare as much as you wish but stay close, I beg.'

'Don't fret so.' Magda waggled her shoulders impatiently, moving away from his protective touch.

A horn sounded three times behind them. 'Wolfpack! Wolfpack!' The cry rose all about.

There came the sound of galloping hooves and panic spread as folk dragged their wagons and mules to the side of the road. Philippa grabbed Magda and pulled her through the scrambling crowd. The horses were moving fast. Stragglers threw themselves into the ditches as a large party of armed soldiers galloped by on huge snorting horses. They sped along the road, regardless of people still struggling to get out of their way. There were cries and screams and everyone was spattered with mud and filth.

'Christ have mercy!' shrieked a woman who landed almost on top of Magda, leaping into the ditch just as the soldiers passed. 'They've crushed my toe!' she yelled.

Magda rolled over and turned to her with concern. 'Let me see.' She was used to treating crushed toes and feet.

The woman ignored the young person trying to help her and continued to yell after the gang of soldiers fast disappearing into the distance in a cloud of dust. She screamed and held up two fingers. 'Hell and damnation take them!' she cried. 'The Witch of Barnsdale curse them!'

'Witch of Barnsdale?' said Magda, puzzled, carefully

taking the woman's foot into her hands to massage the toes.

'Aye,' said the woman, turning to her at last. 'You must have heard of her, lad – the evil Witch of Barnsdale? The one they call the Forestwife? They say she's enchanted the Hooded One and keeps him from the gallows with her spells!'

'Why, of course!' said Philippa hastily. 'Of course he's heard such tales, but I dare say they're all rubbish.'

'Oh . . . yes!' said Magda quickly.

Now the woman was staring down at her foot as Magda worked her fingers gently up and down. 'Why, that feels better lad!' she cried, soldiers and witches all forgotten. 'Good as new! I thought they'd crippled me. Thank you – tha's an angel sent from heaven. Where did tha learn to do that?'

Philippa took hold of Magda by the arm, hurrying her away to where John and Tom waited anxiously. 'He's a grand lad,' she called back, 'but we must be getting on or we'll be late.'

The woman stared after them. 'Bless you both!' she cried.

'Walk on, walk fast!' Philippa muttered. 'Try not to cause a stir.'

Magda obeyed, but as soon as they were on their way, she had to satisfy her curiosity. 'Wicked Witch of Barnsdale?' she spluttered. 'And who were those men? The ones they called the wolfpack?'

'The King's special guard,' John told her through gritted teeth. 'Mercenaries every one; more feared than any. They're no dutiful feudal gathering, but trained fighters who kill for money. They'll do any filthy deed the King wishes so long as he pays enough.'

Magda shivered and moved closer to her father.

It was after noon when they passed over the deep ditch and in through the northern gate of Nottingham Town. They walked past the Butter Cross and through the market place. The market was in full swing, rowdy with the shouts of pedlars and stallholders, but above all the bustle loomed the great stone towers of the castle, built upon a high rock.

Magda was distracted by the market sights and sounds, her head muddled with the clamour and her nose twitching at the strange mixture of smells.

'Spices from Araby! Cinnamon and ginger!' A woman wafted a pinch of sharp-smelling brown powder beneath her nose.

'Fresh pies,' another shouted.

'Sweet honey cakes!'

'Fine roast pork! Fill your belly! Salted crackling!'

Philippa grabbed Magda's arm and led her boldly on towards the castle. 'Not here,' she insisted. 'Look out for a potter's stall.'

Magda wondered what on earth they could want with pots when Lady Matilda and Isabel were in danger, but she was so amazed by what she saw that she didn't argue. John and Tom followed as she and Philippa went on through the stone-built gateway and into the castle's outer bailey.

Here there were more stalls and bustle, but Philippa took a quick look around and marched on over the next bridge and into the middle bailey.

'There,' Tom spoke quietly. 'I see him.'

John swore under his breath. 'Damn the man. Can he get no closer? Must he sit under the Sheriff's nose? If he got any closer he'd be in the Sheriff's kitchens.'

Philippa shrugged her shoulders. 'Best place to see what's going on.'

The middle bailey was alive with soldiers and horses and kitchen maids buying produce from stalls and pedlars. Magda looked about for Robert, but she could see no sign of him. There were just two pottery stalls and a loud-mouthed fellow in a straw hat, grabbing all the customers with his shouting of wares and low prices. Then all at once she saw Brother James, handing out benedictions to the castle guards, and collecting pennies in a bowl, a saintly look upon his face. John went to him and knelt down.

Brother James made the sign of the cross and whispered in his ear. John answered and Brother James looked piously up to heaven and spoke again as though chanting.

'A long blessing this is going to be!' Philippa folded her arms and tapped her foot.

When at last John returned, they clustered about him. 'Well?'

'What's up?'

John sighed and wouldn't be rushed. 'Robert's worried about Isabel. King John has told Matilda that she must pay him another four hundred pounds or marry her daughter to some murderous soldier captain. Robert and James want us to find a horse and have it ready up by the northern gate. They've seen that the wolfpack has arrived. Brother James has his eye on their steeds – trust him.'

'Nay!' Philippa swore quietly. 'Does he think we're tired of living?'

'Just one,' said John. 'One good fast horse to hitch to the wagon. Lady Matilda cannot ride.'

'We could maybe manage to steal just one of their mounts,' said Tom. 'There's plenty of us to distract them while it's taken.'

'Not Magda,' said John. 'I'll not have my lass at risk. This is what I feared.'

'Leave her with Robert,' said Philippa. 'He's only watching, isn't he?'

John looked anxious. 'When did he ever just watch?'

Magda stared about her, puzzled. 'Robert? He's not even here.'

Her friends laughed quietly and John relented. He put his arm round his daughter's shoulder and gently turned her towards the noisy potter's stall. 'Our Robert is here all right, my darling. Go up to yon fellow with the plates. Stand behind the trestle as though you were the potter's lad and do not move from the man's side.'

Magda took a few hesitant steps towards the busy stall and then stopped. There, chalked at the top of the wooden frame for all to see was a circle, with one white shape in the middle.

'Ahh!' She caught her breath. 'Robert's sign!' She turned quickly then to look at the man who stood shouting and bawling in the centre of the crowd. His face was turned away from her and she could not see him clearly as the crowds pressed so close.

'Best Mansfield earthenware!' he sang out. 'Goodwives, you'll never find better! Plates and bowls, fine enough for the Sheriff's own table!'

Magda stared at the back of the potter's neck. How could it be him? This was not Robert's quiet, angry way of speaking. The hat he wore was covered with fine spatters of dried clay. Magda moved closer. Even the hair at the back of his neck was clay-streaked. Then he turned and she saw at once the ugly scar that marred his cheek. It *was* Robert. Ever since she'd been tiny she'd shuddered at the sight of that scar. But where had all these pots come from? All at once she understood; she remembered the angry face of the man who sheltered in Langden forge. An unwilling guest from Mansfield, Philippa had said.

Suddenly Magda's stomach lurched, for Robert had seen her. He looked directly at her through the shoving crowd. Would he know her, looking like this? Just for one brief moment he frowned and hesitated, but then quickly he shouted at her.

'So there you are, you rascal! Where have you been? Pass me those platters! I can't keep pace, they're so greedy for pots in Nottingham today!'

Magda blinked and swallowed hard, then dived behind the stall to do as he asked. As soon as she had time to pause, she glanced back at her father. Tom and Philippa strode off towards the castle stables. John followed them slowly.

The potter of Mansfield and his lad worked hard. Never at any time did Robert speak to her as anything other than his apprentice, but at one point when she turned to pick up a fine set of platters from the back of the trestle, he told her to let them be.

'Not those,' he hissed. 'I'm hoping that I'll get a special customers for those, what with the wolfpack arriving unexpectedly and the castle full of guests.'

Magda did not understand what he meant, but she was distracted by the loud complaints that came from the man on the next stall.

'No profit at those prices,' he grumbled to his boy. 'Might as well pack up – the light is fading fast. Set about it and don't tha drop aught this time.'

The other potter's lad looked utterly miserable. Magda could not help but feel a touch sorry and bent close to whisper in his ear. 'We'll not be here next week.'

The boy glowered and showed her his fist and Magda remembered that he must suppose her to be a lad. She had a job not to giggle, but stood back and tried again in a deep gruff voice.

'My master may be selling plates like hot cakes today,' she said, 'but he'll be off to another town next week. Then your master shall have his custom back.'

The boy pulled a face. 'Mind your own business,' he said, again making fists of both his hands and throwing a punch close to Magda's face.

'Watch out!' he warned her. 'I'm training to be a squire.' He pulled a cheaply-made dagger from his belt and swung it close to her cheek.

Magda was not John's daughter for nothing. She closed her right fist hard and hit him smartly on the chin. The lad went down, sprawling at her feet, the dagger clattering on the cobbles. His jerkin slipped open revealing a strange red patch beneath his collarbone.

Magda stared and the lad covered himself quickly.

'Does that pain thee?' Magda asked.

'Nay.' The boy spoke sharply. 'Not at all.'

Magda took the boy's hand and pulled him to his feet. 'You're hot,' she said. 'Feverish?'

'No,' he insisted, sticking the dagger back into his belt.

So many years spent in the Forestwife's clearing brought Marian's wisdom flooding into Magda's head. 'Has tha tried a lavender brew?'

'To drink?' The boy's eyes showed reluctant interest.

'Nay. Brew it up, then let it cool and dab it on those sore patches.'

All at once, the boy's hands were shaking. He pulled two pennies from his pouch and without another word was off, running between the stalls to where the herbwives sold their wares.

Magda turned back to the Mansfield potter's stall, a little shaken. Truth was she'd never seen sores quite like those strange patches.

'Shall we pack up?' she asked Robert. 'You've nothing left to sell, only your special pots. Everyone else is going.'

'Hush!' Robert smiled, as a sudden flurry of noise and movement started up in the entrance to the castle kitchens. 'I believe my special customer arrives.'

An angry maid and a young kitchen lad ran out from the castle kitchens. Their aprons were smeared with fat and flour, sleeves rolled up, faces pink and sweating.

'See! It's too late, they're all going,' the maid cried.

'Nay, here's one.' The lad caught her arm and pointed to the Mansfield potter's stall. 'And look – a pile of decent platters left. Will you wait a moment, good potter?'

'I'll go and fetch my lady,' said the maid.

Magda felt her heart thudding fast. Whatever was Robert up to now?

' 'Tis like hell in that kitchen,' the lad complained. 'You'd think we'd got enough to do finding food and drink for the King and his court, without the wolfpack arriving as well! Drink like fishes they do, and now we've run out of platters!' The lad pulled a fearful face and crossed himself. 'Sheriff's lady is right put out! She don't like to spend her pennies needlessly.'

Robert shook his head wisely. 'Doesn't do to offend those fellows.'

'You're right,' the lad answered with feeling.

'Don't fret,' said Robert. 'The potter of Mansfield shall come to thy mistress's aid.'

The maid appeared again, with an older woman whose silver ladle thrust through her belt marked her as cook. A young page in smart velvet livery burst from the kitchen behind them, and after him followed the grandest woman that Magda had ever set eyes on.

The Sheriff's lady was plump and at least fifty. She was dressed in crimson velvet with gold trimmings. The high waist of her gown unfortunately made her large stomach appear even rounder. A horned headress wreathed in veils had slipped slightly to the side, giving her the look of a disgruntled cow. Her fingers were covered in rings, her long nails rouged. Just like her servants she was pink and sweating, and she rubbed her jewelled hands together anxiously.

'You'd better be right,' she snapped at the cook. 'Have you got my purse?' She slapped the small page on the head.

'Yes, madam,' he squeaked, holding up a leathern drawstring pouch.

'Fancy having to buy earthenware,' she muttered.

'Better than no platters at all,' the cook told her firmly.

By now she was standing before the stall and Robert bowed low to her. Magda almost curtseyed, but remembered in time and copied his deep bow.

'I hear my lady is short of platters for her guests,' Robert said. With one swift movement he gathered up the pile of good earthenware that he'd saved and spread it across the stall.

'Hmm! Not bad!' the woman cried. 'Though I dare say this will cost me a pretty penny.'

'Ah no, lady.' Robert spoke quickly. A certain flinty glance at Magda warned her to say nothing, whatever came next. He gave a great sigh and smiled boldly at the Sheriff's wife. 'For such a lovely lady the price is . . . nothing at all. It is an honour to serve such beauty. A gift from the potter of Mansfield.'

All the servants gaped and Magda had great trouble keeping still and quiet, but the Sheriff's wife went pinker still and giggled. She flapped her pink bejewelled hand at Robert.

'Why, Sir Potter,' she said, 'I fear you are a very wicked fellow. I accept your gift and . . . you shall dine with us tonight.'

'Ah no!' Robert was all modesty and hesitation.

'Yes, you shall – you and your lad! Come pack up your stall and fetch in these pots. I shall make space for you amongst my guests.'

And with those words she swept away, leaving her servants open-mouthed. But Robert was not for wasting time; he clapped his hands, smiling wickedly at Magda. 'Come on, boy! We're dining at the castle.'

The kitchen lad had spoken truly, for the castle kitchens were indeed like hell. Cauldrons bubbled over fires, suspended from great chains hooked on to wooden beams. Huge spit roasts of meat flamed and spluttered on the hearths. The place was crammed with servants squabbling and shouting and getting in each other's way.

Torches were fixed to brackets on the walls, but they gave off little light and a lot of smoke. A young servant girl heaved a steaming bucket of water past Magda, slopping it on her arm and making her gasp.

'Sorry, sir,' she cried. 'But it's no good you standing there, I shall be back for another in a moment. 'Tis for the King's bath tub. Terrible clean and fussy, he is. Says he must bathe before he eats. Have you ever heard of such a thing?'

'Come,' said Robert taking hold of Magda's arm. 'Come stand at the end of the great hall and see if our grand lady remembers to give us a place.'

He led Magda through the madness of the kitchens and up the steps into the enormous hall. Already people were gathering for the evening meal. Set upon a raised platform at the far end, the high table was empty. Six long trestles laid out in rows were filling up with soldiers, ladies in waiting and guests of lesser importance.

'Where shall we sit?' Magda asked, half-fascinated, half-alarmed by the excitement of it all.

'Just stand and watch,' said Robert. 'That suits me well for the moment. Ah yes . . . as I hoped.'

Magda followed his gaze and saw a young woman in a homespun gown leading a frail old lady. Isabel and Matilda, their poverty more apparent than ever in such gaudy surroundings.

'Watch them closely,' said Robert. 'Ah, I see that help arrives.'

Magda could not stop herself from smiling at the sight

of Brother James slowly parading up and down the hall, still handing out blessings in a most condescending manner.

'Who could have invited him?' she wondered.

Robert snorted and grimaced. 'Nobody,' he said. 'Priest's garb and knowledge of the Mass will take the man anywhere.'

'Where is Much?' Magda asked.

'Guarding my potter's wagon, up by the northern gate, I hope.'

Trumpets sounded and everyone rushed to take their seats at the trestle tables. Robert pushed Magda towards the long bench set opposite Langden's ladies. There was a scramble to sit down, and, for a moment Magda and Isabel looked straight at each other. Just the slight raising of an eyebrow told them that Isabel recognised her fellow guests.

The trumpet sounded again and everyone struggled to their feet as the King and his queen arrived and took their seats. The Sheriff and his wife bowed and curtseyed profusely, fussing nervously as King John sat down. Magda strained her neck to stare at the man whose cruelty was feared throughout the land.

'He's thin and small,' she whispered. 'And look at the Queen. She's nowt but a lass!'

Before Robert could reply, Magda felt a heavy hand upon her shoulder.

'Out of my way, lad. How dare you sit before My Lady!'

Magda yelped as she was cuffed over the ear and

thrust aside. A powerfully built, heavy-jowled man with a close-shaved chin bent across the table and snatched up Isabel's reluctant hand to kiss.

'Get out,' Robert whispered, pulling Magda along behind him towards the bottom of the next table where Brother James sat.

'He hit me,' Magda cried out, red-faced and rubbing her hurt. 'Aren't you going to stand up for me?'

Robert's face had gone white. His voice hissed with anger as he spoke. 'I promise you this, my child: death shall be too good for that one. But now is not the time.'

'Who is he?' Magda demanded.

'Hugh FitzRanulf,' he told her. 'Leader of the wolf-pack. Dealer in misery!'

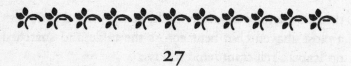

27

To Dine with the Sheriff's Wife

Brother James quickly made room for them on the bench beside him and the meal began. Though the table was groaning with food, Magda could not eat. Her head thudded and her stomach heaved. Excitement had turned to fear.

'Can we not slip away now?' she whispered, suddenly longing for the wildness and safety of the Forestwife's clearing.

Brother James seemed to be calmly eating up everything within reach, but Robert spoke low and answered her. 'We've not done what we came for yet. You'd do best to eat. Who knows when we'll eat again! Here, share my trencher and cup.'

Reluctantly seeing the sense in his words, Magda took a sip of heady spiced wine and began picking at a leg of roast guinea fowl. She tried not to look at Robert's scarred cheek and slit ear. In the rush to find a seat, she'd sat down on his right-hand side, something she usually avoided. The meal continued and the servants were in and out of the kitchen, bringing platters piled high with roast swan and heron. Gentle strumming of lutes from the musicians up in the gallery soothed her a little, as did the sweet scent of violets and green herbs strewn on the floor. Her spirits lifted at the delicious sight of rose-scented confits stuffed with candied orange peel, rich creamy frumenty porridge, and hazelnuts in marzipan with honeyed dates.

Though Robert had told her to eat, he seemed distracted and ate little himself. Magda sensed a tension in the man. He looked up towards the top table and silently reached out to touch Brother James. Though the fat monk did not move a muscle, Magda saw that he was instantly alert, all pleasure in food forgotten.

'A messenger!' Robert told him. 'Could it be they have discovered John and the stolen horse?'

Suddenly the King was on his feet and flinging his wine cup across the table so that the strong red liquid splashed across the fine gowns of the ladies in waiting.

'Matilda! Damn the woman!' he screamed. 'I'll have her now!'

Magda gasped, but Robert pressed her arm. 'Hush,' he whispered. 'Not our Matilda, surely.'

'FitzRanulf!' the King screamed. 'Leave thy food, man! Get your fellows up to the Scottish border. I have her at last – my Lady de Braose.'

'See,' Robert soothed. 'Not our lady. It's Matilda de Braose, wife to William. Powerful Marcher Lord, he is . . . or was.'

'Brave woman,' growled Brother James. 'I sorrow to

hear her captured. His wolves have chased her through half the kingdom!'

There was no time for Magda to ask more; the great hall was in uproar. The wolfpack rose quickly from their seats at the King's command. Wine spilled, kitchen lads and lasses were shoved aside, bread and sweetmeats rolled to the floor.

'Look sharp,' hissed Robert, 'this may be our moment. Make for Isabel.'

Caught in the chaos, Isabel looked wildly about her, sure that she'd had a glimpse of Brother James. 'Thank God,' she cried at the sight of him battling sturdily through the crowd towards her, two familiar figures behind him.

'Come, dear lady,' James cried, gently lifting Matilda of Langden into his arms. 'We think it time to go.'

Robert took Isabel's arm and steered her towards the kitchens. 'Let's leave,' he whispered. 'None shall think of you at this moment.'

Magda followed them as best she could, but Robert had been wrong. The Sheriff's wife stood just inside the kitchen, marshalling her servants to save what food they could.

'I want no waste!' she shrieked, her face red and sweaty. 'And where do *you* go, my Lady of Langden?' she demanded.

For just one terrible moment Robert seemed to hesitate, Magda shivered, despite the heat and fuss that surrounded them.

'Why, to their home, fair lady.' Robert was quickly

silken-tongued and confident again. 'The potter of Mansfield shall see them safely to Langden.'

'Oh would you indeed, Sir Potter?' The Sheriff's wife twitched with surprise at such boldness. 'But you would pass through Sherwood and Barnsdale! How can you and your young lad protect these ladies from murderous thieves?'

'Ah, we can outwit the Hooded One,' Robert winked. 'We potters have our own safe and secret byways. Besides, 'twill save you the expense of keeping these ladies here.'

The woman still doubted. 'Isabel?' she said. 'Would you go off with these men? You were told to marry or pay the fine.'

'I cannot think of marriage when my mother is sick,' Isabel answered firmly. 'She craves the comfort of her own hearth. I know this man and I trust him.'

The Sheriff's wife folded her arms and pursed her lips. Robert delved into the money bag that hung at his belt. He brought out his day's takings at the pottery stall and more. 'There's forty pounds here,' he said. 'Take this as surety. We shall send the rest of the money as the King demands.'

The Sheriff's wife gaped open-mouthed at the cheek of this man, but as she looked at the worn ashen face of Lady Matilda, a touch of pity turned her flushed face kind. Jewelled fingers closed around the money that Robert held out. 'Go Isabel. Take your mother home,' she said quietly. 'No more money will be required.'

Brother James quickly carried the old woman through

the noisy kitchens, Isabel pushing at his side. Robert snatched up the plump hand of the Sheriff's lady and kissed it. 'This kindness shall be remembered,' he whispered.

In spite of the noise and confusion that surrounded her, the Sheriff's wife stared, puzzled, after the retreating backs of the potter and his lad.

They ran down Houndsgate and past the Butter Cross until a series of familiar whistles and the bellow of a snorting horse led them to Muchlyn, John and the others with the potter's cart, now hidden in a blacksmith's forge close to the northern gate.

'About time!' John cried. 'Can't keep this damned animal still.'

Philippa ran to take Lady Matilda into her care. 'Whatever have they done to thee!' she cried, concerned at the old lady's frailty.

Brother James swore quietly when he saw the stamping, powerful beast that they'd taken from the castle stables. 'When John steals a horse, he don't muck about,' he said. 'We'd best be away before this beast wakes the whole of Nottingham.'

'But if we go now, we'll meet the wolfpack on the road!' cried Magda. 'Isn't that right? They're heading north?'

'Yes,' said Robert, with a sharp crack of laughter. 'But at least they're one horse short! That'll slow them up a bit. John, you must go at once with James and Philippa. Take the ladies in the cart, and make a dash for

Sherwood. Hide in Bestwood Dell till they've passed. We'll catch you up.'

'Aye,' said John, helping to lift Matilda into the wagon. 'Come ladies. We've cloaks and straw. I hope the journey won't be too rough.'

'Never mind comfort,' Isabel told him, leaping up after her mother. 'Just get us out of here!'

'Magda?' said John. 'She should come too!'

'Nay,' Robert replied, 'you've got a wagonful. She'll be just as safe following with me and Tom. She can ride the potter's old nag.'

John looked as though he wanted to argue, but Isabel was clearly desperate to be out of Nottingham Town.

'You take good care of my lass,' said John as he snatched the reins of the wolfpack's steed and steered the wagon towards the northern gate.

28

A Bundle of Rags

Robert and Magda emerged from the narrow close near
the forge. Tom followed them, leading the potter's worn
old horse, but the sound of shouting in the distance and
the faint clatter of hooves made them shrink back
into the darkest shadows.

Robert's arm pressed Magda against the lumpy stone
walls of the blacksmith's home as the pounding of
hooves and snorting of powerful horses came close.
Suddenly the wolfpack was upon them . . . and passing.
The streets were filled with the sound of angry voices
swearing and the clink and scrape of weaponry. The
wolfpack headed out of the city gate and into the night,
the clamour fading until only the grumbling of the gate-
men was left.

Robert relaxed. 'Our turn,' he said. 'Get up and ride!'

'Who's this?' the guard called.

'Potter o' Mansfield and his 'prentices,' Robert told
him, leading the bony grey mare with Magda astride.

'Where's your wagon, then?'

'Stolen! Some great oaf! Giant of a fellow!'

The man grinned and scratched his head. 'It's a bad night, right enough. Half o' Nottingham's setting out for Sherwood. I saw a wagon go tearing past a while back, pulled by some devil horse. I thought to myself that's no potter's nag! But then the King's wolfhounds followed fast. Tha wants no trouble with them!' The man hurriedly crossed himself.

'I'll get the thieving swine,' Robert spat.

'Mind the Hooded One!' the man called out, laughing. 'Watch out, or he'll be getting thee.'

By the time they reached the first sheltering trees, Magda was bitterly cold and weary of the jolting. The old mare stumbled through thick darkness.

'Why could I not go ahead in the wagon?' she moaned.

Robert ignored her bleating, walking in silence ahead.

Tom who led the horse, turned to her patiently. 'He has his reasons for not sending you ahead. Good reasons, I believe.'

'My father wanted me to go in the wagon.' Magda could hear the whine in her voice and hated it, but she was too cold and tired to stop it.

'Shall I tell her?' Tom called out to Robert.

'If you wish.' Robert's uninterested voice floated back to them from the darkness ahead.

'Tell me what?' demanded Magda, suddenly warmed a little, curiosity arousing her.

'Well,' said Tom. 'We had to get John out of

Nottingham fast, before he saw the wolfpack's leader.'

'That FitzRanulf man? The one who hit me? Why should my father not see him?'

Tom went on in silence for a moment, and Robert spoke again. 'She'll find out soon, anyway . . . best tell her.'

With a nasty lurch of her stomach, Magda knew that she would not like what she was about to hear. 'Tell me,' she hissed, the jolting of the horse forgotten.

'That man, Hugh FitzRanulf,' said Tom plainly. 'It was he who killed your mother. We could not let John know he was there.'

The shock of hearing it numbed her; she strode on in silence, suddenly shivering, though the night was not cold.

'Magda?' Tom was anxious. 'Are you all right? Did you hear me?'

'Aye.' She spoke with quiet certainty. 'I heard, and you were right. My father would have gone for him with his bare hands. He'd have killed him.'

'Yes,' Tom agreed. 'Then his wolfhounds would have killed John. And if we had made a move, we'd all have been taken.'

Again Robert's voice came back to them out of the darkness, oddly gentle this time. 'Do you remember what I promised you, little one? There in the hall?'

'Yes,' she whispered between gritted teeth. 'You said that death should not be good enough for FitzRanulf.'

They travelled on through the darkness, for Robert

insisted that they were not safe on the outskirts of the forest.

Magda rode in thoughtful silence for a while, but weariness caught up with her. 'We're miles from Nottingham now,' she complained. 'How does Robert know where we're safe and where we are not?'

'He knows,' said Tom. 'Eyes like a fox, he has, and ears too.'

At last Robert turned about. 'This'll do. Sleep now,' he said. 'We'll wake at dawn and go to find John.'

'Can we make a fire?' Magda asked.

'No,' Robert told her. 'We're not far enough from town for that.'

'But I'm cold,' she whispered.

'Here's a fine patch of dry springy moss,' said Robert, kicking around in the undergrowth. 'Come wrap that cloak around and snuggle down between the two of us. Not every little lass has two fine fellows like us to keep her warm! 'Eh Tom?'

'Aye.' She could hear the answering laughter in Tom's voice.

'I'm not a little lass,' she said, wishing Robert would go away and leave her there beside Tom. But she did as she was told, making sure that she settled down on Robert's left side.

'There. Warm and safe?' Robert asked.

'Yes,' she answered, grudgingly comforted by the warmth of two strong male bodies and the familiar woodland sounds.

* * *

It was not the morning light that wakened them but the faint creak and rumble of a cart. Robert and Tom were at once alert and ready to jump. A low bellow in the distance was answered by a whicker from the potter's horse, then came a small thud.

'What is it?' Magda whispered.

'Hush!' Robert hissed. 'Be still. An oxen and cart, I think . . . but it's moving away.'

They crouched in silence, peering through dim light that showed them the muzzy shapes of trees, but nothing moved.

'You sleep again,' Robert told them. 'I'll watch.'

'I can't,' said Magda. 'I'm wide awake now.'

'They dropped something,' Tom insisted. 'I want to know what.'

Magda watched him tread soundlessly through the grass and then crouch to peer close at a bush. Suddenly sharp clattering arose, sending rooks screeching from the trees. Tom leapt backwards. Robert and Magda were both ready to run, but Tom quickly recovered and called to them.

'Nowt to fear. Come here!'

Magda went cautiously towards him but all she could see through the gloom was a bundle of rags, dumped beneath the bush. As she stepped closer, the bundle moved and a thin white hand wagged a noisy wooden clapper in the air, making her cry out in alarm.

Robert grabbed Magda by the arm and pulled her back. 'Tom!' he cried. 'Keep away! A leper!'

Magda's heart thudded with fear at his words. Was

that the meaning of the harsh clapper? She'd never come across the disease, not in all her years with the Forestwife, though she'd heard enough about it to dread it.

'Get back, Tom,' she yelled.

But Tom did not retreat again. He bent down towards the bundled rags. ''Tis but a child,' he cried.

'Do not touch! Do not touch!' Magda screamed it frantically at him. She went slowly to see for herself, then caught her breath. She looked down though the faint dawning light on the pinched face of the Nottingham potter's boy, a dark bruise showing on his chin where she had hit him.

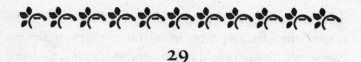

Magda remembered the strange red patches on the boy's throat and his frantic search for herbs.

'Look!' she told Robert. 'See who it is! His father sold pots on the next stall.'

Robert scratched his head. 'The lad you sent flying? Aye, so it is. What are you doing here, boy?' he asked.

The boy sat mute and still as a statue, staring blankly; he would not look at them. When Tom held out his hand, he quickly snatched up the clapper and set it snapping its harsh rhythm through the quiet trees.

'Stop it!' Magda cried, covering her ears with her hands. 'I hate it.'

There was silence again until Tom spoke. 'But you are no leper,' he said. 'Surely?'

Then in a small shaky whisper, the boy answered. 'Father says I am.'

'Why?' Magda cried. 'Why should he think it so?'

'My mother was stricken soon after my birth,' the boy whispered.

Magda shivered.

'Where is your mother? Does she live?' Tom asked.

'Stoned.' The lad spoke without emotion. 'The villagers stoned her. Father says it is best that I go, seek out my own kind. Better than suffer my mother's fate.'

'Your father!' Robert almost spat it out. 'Was that he?' he asked, pointing after the cart.

The boy nodded.

'I cannot believe it,' Tom cried. 'You are no leper! Magda, tell him so!'

But Magda could not forget the sight of the patched red skin. She shook her head. 'I don't know,' she said. 'His skin is marked.'

Tom stood up. 'We must give him food and let him have the horse,' he said.

'That was for me.' Magda heard her own voice sounding pettish.

Robert shook his head, uncertain for once. 'Give him the horse, but he'd best keep his distance from us. I'm sorry for the lad, but we've troubles enough of our own. We must eat and find ourselves water and be on our way.' Suddenly his expression was lighter. With a flourish he brought out a loaf of fine white bread from his potter's sack. 'A gift from our Sheriff's lady.'

'It cheers you to think you've cheated anyone,' Magda cried.

'Only rich fools,' Robert laughed.

They divided up the loaf and Tom carried a good hunk over to the potter's boy. His hands closed about the soft white bread that was such a treat, but he seemed unable to eat. Tom crouched down, full of comforting words, but Magda was quickly on her feet and shouting furiously again. 'Do not touch him!'

When at last they were ready to go, Tom held the bridle and soothed the horse, while the lad obediently struggled to mount. He accepted the reins without thanks. Tom slapped the bony flank and the horse set off north towards Barnsdale, the boy sitting stiffly astride like a straw-stuffed doll.

Tom watched him go, a troubled expression on his face.

'There's nowt we can do,' Robert told him, shaking his head.

'He says his name is Alan, same as my grandfather,' Tom said.

When at last the potter's son was out of sight, Robert made them walk north-east, along one of his secret paths, heading for Bestwood Dell.

There was no sign of the wagon at the Dell, just Brother James settled on a rock and John striding back and forth, crushing a pathway of thick green bracken beneath his feet, his face like thunder.

As soon as the big man heard their approach, he leapt across the small clearing, whipping his meat knife from his belt. 'You crafty whippet, you lying hound,' he growled, grabbing a fistful of jerkin and thrusting the knife at Robert's throat. Brother James hurriedly got up from his rock.

For a moment Magda was frightened, but Robert's silence was reassuring. He stood there white-faced, blinking up at his friend, but he would not give ground.

'You kept the bastard from me,' John spat at him. 'You took my daughter in there! You sat my child down before her mother's murderer!'

Magda kept still and quiet, but remembered with resentment. Aye, and he let him hit me about the head, she thought.

Even though John prodded at his neck with the sharp point of his knife till a trickle of blood ran, Robert did not speak. 'I could have killed the man!' John spat furiously. 'I could have torn him apart!'

Still Robert said nothing, but Tom went slowly to stand at his side and face John. 'We don't doubt that you would have killed him,' he said. 'But then what! I think Robert did right to keep you in ignorance.'

Magda lurched towards her father, but she daren't grab his arm. Though she knew he loved her dearly, he was still a huge and very angry man.

'Robert has promised—' she said, swallowing hard to stop her voice shaking, 'Robert has promised me this FitzRanulf shall be punished. Look at me, Father! Did you want to lose me too?'

John turned to her and his face crumpled. He swung round and threw down the knife with so much force that it buried itself up to the hilt in the grassy earth. He crouched down amongst the bracken, covering his face with his hands. Magda went to him and wrapped her arms about his shoulders.

The others watched solemnly.

'Leave them,' said Brother James. 'Let them grieve. Old wounds bleed afresh.'

'Come here! I've something to show you.'

James waved Robert and Tom over to the rock that he'd been sitting on.

'Where's the wagon?' Robert asked. 'And Lady Matilda?'

'Philippa insisted on taking Isabel and Matilda straight home,' James told him. 'Muchlyn and Stoutly went with them. Matilda looks poorly. A frail old woman should not be dragged away from her hearthside like that. Our King would steal the gold from a dying man if he thought he could get but a pennyworth. The thought of Isabel wed to that wolfhound of his makes me shiver.'

'Yes,' said Robert thoughtfully. 'We've bought the girl a bit of time, but we shall have to think long and hard about it. Even if we can manage to raise the money he demands, the man never keeps to his word. Once John has dealt with my Lady de Braose, he'll remember this other Matilda and he's in such a rage, God knows what he'll do.'

The fat face of Brother James lit up with excitement.

'Matilda . . . de . . . Braose.' He said the words slowly and with pleasure. 'I have a wild idea that might teach the King what true rage is!'

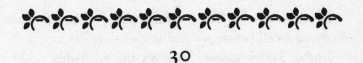

30

The Bravest Woman in the Land

Robert was instantly excited and smiling hugely. 'Why, damn it, James!' he cried. 'Is this one of your crazy plans? I need something mad and risky to cheer me.'

'What's this?' Tom frowned down at a muddle of scratched lines and marks upon the rock.

'It's a map,' James told them. 'Though only clever learned folk like me can read it.'

Robert threw a mock punch at his face. 'All right, all right! Explain it to us poor fools.'

James pointed with a dirty finger. 'Now see this line here, the Great North Road, and this patch here, Barnsdale Waste, and here that dip in the land where the River Went runs.'

'Our favourite spot for bishop-baiting,' cried Tom.

John and Magda came slowly to join them, calmed a little and intrigued by Brother James's excitement.

'What's this you're plotting now?' John asked.

'A rescue.' Brother James spoke so fast that tiny beads of spit flew from his lips. 'A rescue that will stagger the King.'

'Steady on,' said Tom, wiping his eye. 'You'll have drowned us all before we're done.'

Brother James ignored him, waving his hands wildly. 'Don't you see? We have a bit of time to make a plan, for it will take those foul wolfhounds a se'nnight to reach the Scottish borders and then start back again.'

'What?' Robert cried. 'He'd have us set about the Wolfpack?'

'Wherever they are taking my Lady de Braose, they shall have to travel the Great North Road and pass through Barnsdale.' Brother James wagged a finger in Robert's face. 'That is where they are weak and we are strong.'

'I'm for it,' cried John at once. 'It'll give me a chance to get my hands on FitzRanulf.'

'It's the woman I'm after,' said Brother James.

'What do you want with her?' Robert asked, amazed. 'When have we bothered with mighty lords and their wives!'

James's face was red with concern. 'She's the bravest woman in the land.'

It was dusk when they began crossing the wilder scrub land at the edge of the Waste, and Magda was exhausted. Robert and Brother James marched steadily ahead of them, discussing their plans with wild enthusiasm. The truth was that Magda longed for the comfort of her sweet-smelling straw pallet, and Marian's glowing fire. A faint clop, clop of horses hooves made Tom whistle a quick warning and without further fuss, they all melted into the ditch.

John gently pushed Magda's head down beneath the cover of a holly bush, but then she felt her father relax. 'Just one horse,' he whispered, 'and nowt but a stringy bairn.'

Magda got up and recognised at once the pathetic rider. 'Oh no,' she sighed, somehow irritated. 'Not him again. We gave him the horse! Isn't that enough?'

Robert, Tom and James climbed out of the ditch and joined them. Tom went forward to meet the boy, but though he stood there staring up into Alan's face, the lad made no attempt to halt. Tom dived to the side, to avoid the horse's trampling hooves, then quickly recovered and ran after it, snatching at its bridle. 'Whoa!' he shouted.

The old nag stopped willingly enough when bidden, but Magda warned the others off. 'Leper!' she cried. 'Beware!'

Quietly they gathered about the rider, keeping a good arm's distance. The boy's face was white and blank, his eyes focused far beyond them on the road ahead. 'Alan,' Tom spoke gently. 'Where have you been? You set off far ahead of us.'

No answer came. No response of any kind.

'He set off north,' Tom told them. 'How has he taken so long? What is wrong!'

They all looked up again at the small figure. Magda thought him as lifeless as a statue she'd seen in the great hall of Nottingham Castle. If it was not that he sat so straight and still clutched the reins, he might be dead.

Brother James patted the steaming rump of the potter's mare. 'I think this old lass has been in charge,' he said. 'I dare say she's been taking her chance to feed on marsh-watered grass, but now she wants warm stabling so she heads for her home in Mansfield.'

'Aye,' Robert smiled. 'The lad has sat like a moppet, and never taken charge.'

Brother James shook his head sadly. 'I fear that this poor lad can take charge of naught.'

31

None Shall Be Turned Away

'We should take him to Marian,' said Tom.

'What?' Magda cried. 'And risk ourselves?'

Robert and John were both silent, worried by Tom's suggestion.

Brother James shook his head. 'I know naught of leprosy,' he said. 'But Mother Veronica does.'

They all turned to stare at him, surprised.

'The nuns have never had lepers in their care,' said Magda.

'No, not here in the wastes.' Brother James smiled with amusement. 'But Veronica was not always a nun. She's travelled widely! Why, when she was just a young lass she was maid to King John's mother. Eleanor of Aquitaine went off over sea and land to Outremer with her first husband, the young French king. Veronica went with them.'

'You mean Mother Veronica went to Jerusalem? Following the crusaders?' Robert was amazed.

'You sound a touch envious!' said John.

'I thought they'd always been there in the woods,' said Magda. It was very hard to see fat, bossy Veronica as an adventurous young woman travelling with foreign kings and the famous Queen Eleanor.

'There's much you do not know about Veronica.' Brother James chuckled. 'She was once betrothed to a brave knight, but she never married him. Veronica refused to follow her mistress back home to France, so they parted company. Veronica stayed out there in those strange heathen lands for many years, helping to set up a hospital for lepers.'

There was a moment of silence while they struggled to fix this new picture of the nun in their minds.

'So, what of this lad?' Tom was determined to make them think of the present. 'We're not far from Langden now.'

'There are leper hospitals here,' said James. 'I believe there's one at York.'

'He looks half dead, anyway,' Magda muttered.

James turned to her and spoke rather sternly for him. 'I think it only Christian and decent that at least we take him with us to the Forestwife.'

Magda frowned and felt mean. Truth was, she was desperate to get home now.

'Aye,' Robert agreed. 'We can all keep our distance from him. Let the poor fellow follow behind us. We'd best not call in at Langden – they've trouble enough.'

'You go on ahead,' Tom insisted. 'I'll lead Alan's horse. I swear he knows nowt of what's going on.'

They set off again as fast as they could, hoping to

reach the Forestwife's clearing before the light went. As they trudged through the gloom Magda longed to be home. Her feet were sore, but she knew that each step brought her closer to her familiar woodland. She had had enough of adventuring for the moment. Even the muddy, sappy smell comforted her.

'Not far now,' her father soothed. 'Shall I carry thee?'

Magda shook her head. It would be shameful to arrive back from her first outing into the world beyond Barnsdale, carried; especially in front of Tom. She turned to look for him as they reached the secret maze of paths that protected the Forestwife's clearing. She stared, puzzled, though it was hard to see in the failing light. The horse ploughed on with the silhouette of the lad above. Magda could see no sign of Tom.

'Tom! Where is he?' she cried.

John turned round, screwing up his eyes to see better. Then as the horse plodded towards them, they saw the dark shape of Tom riding behind the leper boy. He was supporting him; arms around the lad's waist, the reins in his hands. Magda was so shocked she could not speak. Blood drained from her face. She and John stared, horrified.

As the horse came close Magda could only whisper, 'Why, Tom? Why? You have put us all at risk!'

'He has given up all hope,' Tom told her. 'I came to the Forestwife like him, my life in tatters. Though I was only a child, and it was long ago, I can't forget it!'

'Thank goodness, you're back.' Marian's voice rang out

clear and a flickering light showed through the dark trees. She strode towards them from the shadows, carrying a lantern high.

'Aye,' Robert answered her. 'We're all back safe, but I fear we've brought more worries with us. See what this mad fellow has done.' Robert pointed to Tom.

Marian shielded her eyes to see better. 'Is that Tom?'

'Aye,' said Robert. 'And we believe the lad to be leprous.'

'He's gone mad,' cried Magda. 'It's bad enough that Tom insists we bring the boy here, but then he goes and climbs up on the horse with him. He'll make lepers of us all!'

Marian frowned and moved closer as the horse snickered and stopped. 'I know Tom,' she said. 'He does naught without good reason.'

Tom's face was pale in the lantern's light. He shrugged his shoulders. Brother James went to put his arm round Marian. 'Veronica knows much of the disease,' he said. 'I thought perhaps she could help.'

'It seemed hard to leave the lad,' John agreed. 'He's nowt but a bairn. It seems his father carried him out to the woods and left him outcast. I know the man's right by law, but it's a bitter decree that makes a father throw out his child.'

Marian lifted the lantern until it lit Alan's blank, still face.

'What is your name?' she asked.

There was no reply.

'He is called Alan,' said Tom. 'He's too fearful even to speak.'

Marian gave a great sigh, but then she spoke solemnly. 'Of those who seek the Forestwife, none shall be turned away.'

'I hope you know what you do,' said Robert thoughtfully. 'Does not the law say lepers must be cast out?'

'And does that trouble thee?' Marian feigned astonishment.

Robert suddenly laughed and kissed her. 'You are right, sweetheart. He's one of us! We might as well add another small crime to our great list!'

'Aye,' Marian sighed. 'Tom, will you take Alan and the horse round to the shelter at the back. There's straw to make a bed and I shall bring round rugs and food. And Tom, I fear . . .'

'Aye,' said Tom. 'I know. I'll stay there with him.'

Marian nodded. 'We'll send for Veronica at dawn.'

There was a great to-do getting everyone fed and warm inside the small hut, but the old one had the fire built up and a great pot of mutton stew bubbling above it.

It was only when they had eaten their fill and wiped their bowls with fresh-baked bread that they began to tell what had happened in Nottingham.

'So, do you think Matilda and Isabel are safe?' Marian asked.

'Safe for a time,' Robert told her. 'The King has a greater Matilda to worry about now, and James has a wild idea of rescue in his head. So crazy a plan that I warm to the thought of it.'

Marian smiled. 'I thought I knew that gleam in your eye.'

'If we could succeed it would delight all of England,' said James. 'It would make the King a laughing stock.'

Marian listened well as they told her how the King had sent the wolfpack off to the Scottish borders to take captive the Lady de Braose.

'Aye,' Marian agreed. 'Though she was once rich and powerful, I do honour her actions. She's lost all she had by defying the King, and she's done it in defence of her children. She is a good mother – I'll give her that.'

Magda went to her straw pallet and snuggled beneath her goatskin rug. Even Marian seemed keen for this new scheme of theirs. Magda could not share their interest; she was still angry with Tom, though she could not quite work out why.

As the fire died down, one by one the company fell asleep until, besides Magda, only Robert and Marian remained awake. At last they went to Marian's straw pallet and settled down together for the night. Magda could hear Marian laughing softly. She turned over so that she could not see them any more. Marian had not laughed like that for a long time. I suppose she'll be singing in the morning, Magda thought.

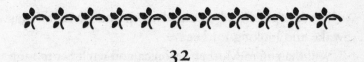

32

An Awkward Man

Magda did not sleep well and crept out of the hut at the first touch of dawn. She stumbled round to the spring behind the cottage as darkness slowly lifted from the sheltering yew trees, but someone was there at the spring before her.

'Tom?' she called.

'Aye.' He dipped a wooden bowl into the clean warm spring water.

Magda crouched beside him and splashed water into her face, then as Tom stepped back towards the shelter with a full bowl she remembered Alan.

Her stomach tightened with fear. 'Don't you let him touch this water!' she cried. 'He might foul it all up with his disease.'

Tom nodded. 'That's why I carry water to him.'

Magda watched as he carefully carried water into the lean-to and listened as he woke the boy, speaking gently to him. Then she heard a faint and husky reply.

Magda sighed and returned to the hut. Marian was awake and looking for her.

'Will tha run to Mother Veronica and fetch her to look at that poor lad?'

Magda pulled a face. 'Can't Tom go?'

'I think it best Tom stay by Alan's side until we hear what Veronica has to say. Besides,' said Marian, touching Magda's cheek, 'there's none that can run as fast through the secret tracks as you, and the sooner we know how to care for the boy the better, don't you think?'

Magda had to agree. The sooner they were rid of him the happier she would be, so she pulled on Tom's breeches again and laced on her strong boots. 'I think I like men's clothes,' she said more cheerfully. 'Better for running in.'

The sun gave sharp light and good warmth as Magda went through the woods. Her spirits soared as she ran like a hare through dew-laden grass, past branches of trembling hazel catkins. As she neared the forest convent of the Magdalen, she found that a fine carpet of blue-bells covered the ground. She drew in deep lungfuls of scented air. The rich sights and smells of Nottingham Town had nothing to equal this.

Magda arrived at the convent breathless and hungry. Sister Rosamund took one look at her and quickly served up warm fresh bread and goat's milk cheese with a mug of the nuns' thin ale.

Mother Veronica sat at the table and listened as Magda gasped out the story of Alan.

The old nun shook her head. 'Poor boy, poor boy!' she said.

'But he'll make us all sick like him!' Magda cried. 'Even the law says it . . . lepers must live apart from healthy folk.'

Mother Veronica shook her head. 'Aye, but there's much within the law that is unjust. Believe me, child,' she said, taking Magda's hand, 'there is no need for all this fear. I spent seven years living with lepers and caring for them. I did not catch the disease, nor any who worked alongside of me. We must be careful not to touch leprous sores or share food and eat from their bowls, but that is all.'

'I hit him with my fist,' Magda cried, clenching her fist again.

'Poor boy,' repeated Veronica.

'But will I get leprosy?'

The nun smiled and shook her head.

Magda had a sudden picture of Tom carrying the bowl of water to Alan. 'Eat from their bowls? Drink from their bowls? But what if Tom—?'

'Stop it,' said Veronica firmly. 'We will go straight to see this fellow, then I can tell you more.'

Alan meekly allowed Veronica to examine his face and limbs. All the company waited anxiously outside the lean-to shelter.

'Fetch me a needle!' Veronica demanded.

Marian brought a rusty iron needle from the hut. Veronica cleaned the point and lightly pricked the red patches of skin. The boy did not flinch.

'Ah,' said Veronica. 'Yes. I fear it is leprosy, but the disease is young. There is no contagion as yet from these patches of skin. Tom, you are quite safe.'

'Thank goodness,' said Marian.

But Magda was not so easily satisfied. 'Did you eat or drink from his bowl?' she cried.

Tom shook his head.

Magda's eyes suddenly filled with tears of relief; she dashed them hurriedly away.

Veronica took off her cloak and wrapped it around Alan's shoulders. 'With good feeding and care we may hold the sickness back and keep him strong. There is an oil – a precious oil that we used in the lands of Outremer. It came from far away to the east, beyond Jerusalem, but we cannot get it here.'

'Does it cure?' asked Marian, interested as ever in healing skills.

Veronica shook her head. 'No, but it seemed to help. If he'll come, I shall take the child back with me to the sisters. We will do all we can for him.'

Alan looked worried. 'Will you come too?' he begged Tom.

'Of course,' Tom nodded.

Magda was relieved, though she wished Tom didn't have to go off with them. Alan seemed to watch him like a faithful puppy dog. Marian agreed to the arrangement, for the Forestwife had misery and sickness enough to deal with in the secret clearing in Barnsdale Woods.

* * *

Magda stood with Marian by the turnstone, waving them off. 'I hope Veronica is right,' she said. 'I hope we are all safe from contagion!'

'Veronica is always right,' Marian told her sharply.

Magda looked surprised at such sharpness. 'What are you angry about?' she asked. 'We are saved from leprosy and I thought you'd be happy, now that he's back.' She nodded towards the hut where she supposed Robert still slept.

'He?' Marian said. 'Have you not noticed? He's taken that horse and gone.'

'So soon? Where?'

Marian shrugged her shoulders. 'Who knows? I have no time to worry over him. There's herbs to brew for a woman with dropsy and a lad with a poisoned wound to clean. You should do your shooting practice. Who knows what may come next! Don't let your visit to Nottingham make you grow slack!'

'Is my father . . . ?'

'Aye, don't fret. Your father cuts yew staves round by the shelter.'

Magda went gladly to help John with the task he'd set for himself.

'Just what I need,' said John. 'A fine strapping lad to help me!'

She smiled at his teasing for, beneath his jokes, she knew that he was proud of her strength and skill with a knife.

'Marian insists on shooting practice,' Magda complained.

'She's right,' John told her. 'Shooting practice could save your life, honey. Come help me with these staves, then I'll fetch my own bow and go along with you.'

'Why does Robert make Marian so miserable?' Magda asked. 'I swear I would not take up with a man like him. He blows hot and cold all the time.'

John put his arm around his daughter's shoulders and sighed. 'It is not just Marian on whom he blows hot and cold. The man is that way and he cannot change himself. I think the bitterness of this world hangs very heavy on him. When we are out in the woods and wastes he will often slip into a foul mood and never speak to us for days. Then he'll go off alone and believe me, we are glad to see the back of him.'

'Where does he go?'

John shook his head. 'Derbyshire, Loxley, Sheaf Valley . . . who knows? Sometimes he comes back smelling of salt, with a sack full of seaweed for Marian.'

'I wondered how she kept her supplies so well stocked. But how does he find you again?'

John laughed. 'We leave our secret signs: knots in branches, pebbles on the ground. He tracks us through the woods and catches up with us when it suits him. He'll suddenly turn up, wild with plans for some reckless scheme and full of love for us.'

'He's such an awkward man!' said Magda. 'How can you be his friend?'

'When he is happy, he is the best fellow in the world,' said John. 'There is nothing he will not attempt, nothing he will not dare. I love him like a brother.'

Magda sighed for she could not understand, but she worked on with her father until the sun was high in the sky. After they'd eaten they took their bows and enjoyed a shooting match that Magda won, though she suspected that John let her.

When they wandered back to the hut, they found Marian scraping fresh-cut herbs from a wooden bowl on to the hearthstone to dry, her knife rattling fast and angry.

'No sign of him, I suppose?'

John touched her shoulder. 'You chose the wrong man if you wanted a tame house cat.'

'Aye,' said Marian, wiping her hands and her knife. 'I chose the wrong man! I chose the wrong place! I chose the wrong life!'

The old one came into the hut, her arms full of elder flowers. She gasped as she heard her daughter's words.

Marian dropped her knife and ran to hug her, crushing the flowers. 'No, Mother! I am sorry. It is just that man! I would not change *you* for the world.'

'Good to see someone pleased with life!' said Robert, ducking his head and stepping in across the doorstep. He was rid of the clay-spattered clothes and wore his own faded cloak and close-fitting hood.

'Where have you been?' Marian demanded.

'To Langden, of course. I thought the potter deserved to get his horse back and I wanted to speak to Philippa's husband. We shall need a good blacksmith if we are to rescue this poor Lady de Braose. We shall need swords, knives, arrowheads. And Philippa's man's the best I know!'

He grabbed Marian round the waist and kissed her cheek. 'What do you think, sweetheart?'

'I wish you would tell me where you go,' she said.

33

A Defiant Company

Over the next few days, the clearing was filled with activity. Much, James and Will Stoutley went off with messages to hamlets and villages where they knew they had friends. Robert and John marched back and forth through the woods to Langden, carrying weapons and new-made arrow tips from Philippa's blacksmith husband.

'There shall be many to feed,' the old one said, and she worked hard producing oatcakes and stews of peas and beans, spiced with garlic and a little venison.

Slowly a great company gathered. Dusty-skinned coal diggers left their shallow bell pits and soot-blackened charcoal burners set their stacks aside. Shepherds and swineherds left their flocks with their children, and strong-built woodlanders left their coppicing, for they'd many grievances against the King and the defiance of the de Braose family was admired.

'What is it that this woman has done?' Magda asked as she pounded grain with Marian and Eleanor.

'William de Braose was the King's friend,' Eleanor told her. 'So close a friend, it seems he knows too much. He owed the King money so, as usual, King John demanded the family send their sons to him as hostages. Well, Matilda de Braose refused.'

'She did more than that,' said Marian. 'She declared to all who'd listen that she'd not let her sons suffer the same fate as Arthur of Brittany!'

'Arthur?' said Magda. 'Do you mean King John's nephew?'

'That's the one,' Marian agreed. 'You know what happened to him?'

Magda was puzzled. 'Did he die?'

Marian shook her head sadly. 'Rumour has it that the King strangled the boy with his own hands.'

Magda stopped her pounding. 'Do you think that true?'

'If anyone knows the truth it is Matilda de Braose. Her husband was there in the castle in France when Arthur disappeared.'

'But isn't William de Braose a powerful lord?'

'He *was*,' said Eleanor. 'He's a fugitive now – as much as any of these lads here in the wastes.'

'Do you think they *can* rescue the lady? Can you see what will be, old one?'

Eleanor shook her head and smiled. 'I can't see that, honey. But whether they succeed or not, at least they are strong and defiant while they try.'

Magda begged her father to take her with them, but John would not hear of it. 'This is the most dangerous task we've taken upon ourselves,' he said. 'And I am going to get FitzRanulf? I cannot be worrying about my child.'

'But Philippa and Mother Veronica go with you!'

'Aye, for we must have someone the lady will trust.'

The afternoon that they went, they packed up bundles of smoked venison and dried oatcakes, for they'd need their strength. The company left at dusk so that they could move through the woodlands under the protection of darkness. Then they'd set up camp within view of the Great North Road.

Tom, back from the convent, packed his food, then told Robert that he would not be going with them.

Robert looked surprised but listened carefully to what Tom had to say.

'Mother Veronica believes there may be a source of that rare oil Alan needs.'

'Where?' Magda asked.

'Up beyond Doncaster, not far from Wakefield, there is a place called Temple Newhouse.'

'Do you mean the preceptory?'

Tom nodded. 'That's the place.'

'The Templar Knights? You'd go calling on them?'

Marian frowned. 'I begin to see,' she said. 'If anyone has brought back medicines from those distant lands, it would be the strange fighting monks.'

Robert drew in his breath sharply. 'Be careful, Tom. Those men are fierce fighters and a law unto themselves; even the King cannot control them.'

'Sounds just like us,' said John.

'Don't go,' cried Magda. 'Why risk yourself?'

'Everything we do is a risk.' Tom shrugged his shoulders.

'Robert goes chasing off to risk himself for a brave lady. I go for Alan. Besides . . .' he smiled, 'Mother Veronica has given me a letter that she swears will keep me safe. Walter of Stainthorpe is a powerful Templar Knight, and he is the man she was once to marry.'

'Ah!' Marian understood.

'They may not have the oil,' Tom insisted, 'but I must try.'

'Fair enough,' said Robert. 'I wish you well.'

When they had gone, the clearing seemed quiet and dreary. Though the usual procession of sick people and animals came and went, Magda was restless and dull. She went about her chores, fetching wood, picking berries and herbs, cutting rushes and digging latrines.

One afternoon, as she set out laden with baskets and sacks, she caught a glimpse of a small figure dashing behind a tree. Magda dropped her bags and ran lightly towards the place. Behind a thick elder bush she found a young girl with mud smudged cheeks and a blood stained skirt. She clutched a dead-looking grey dog in her arms.

Magda sighed. This was a common sight in the clearing. She bent down and lightly touched the dog's dangling right paw that was wrapped in a dirty rag.

'Regarders caught our Fetcher . . . chasing deer,' the

girl whispered. 'They came and lamed him.' She shook so much that she could hardly be heard.

'What?' said Magda. 'Speak up!'

'The Forestwife. I seek the wise woman's help.'

'Too late,' Magda spoke without mercy. 'I think your Fetcher's dead.'

She pushed her fingers into the rough fur of the dog's neck and felt a faint pulse beat.

'Oh well,' she said. 'You'd best come with me. Where have you come from?'

'Clipstone, within the bounds of Sherwood.' The girl struggled to her feet and Magda took the dog from her.

'He's a weight, all right,' she said more kindly. 'How have you managed him? How old are you?'

'Twelve last birthday.'

'You've come a long way and he's lost a lot of blood. I don't know that we can save him. What's your name?'

'Joanna.'

'Are you hungry?'

The girl nodded, but suddenly stopped.

'What's wrong?'

'I'm feared. Feared of the Forestwife and the man, the Hooded One.'

Magda could not help but smile, remembering what she'd heard in Nottingham of the fearful Witch of Barnsdale.

'Come with me and don't be feared. The Forestwife is my mother ... well, she's all the mother I've got. She lives here with Eleanor, the old one. And as for the Hooded One, he's away from here just now.'

A touch of curiosity showed on Joanna's face and she allowed herself to be led into the clearing. She stared quietly up at the tall woman in the worn homespun gown with the beautiful woven girdle, while Magda told her story. Marian made them put Fetcher by the hearthstone, and sent them to bring water from the spring to wash his wound.

'He's very weak,' she said, 'but some scraps of meat and our good spring water can sometimes work wonders.'

34

The Return

Joanna would not leave Fetcher's side; she brought him water and fed him scraps of meat by hand. It was slow work, but the big rough dog did not die in the night as they'd feared. On the third day he looked much better and though he still could not get to his feet, he whimpered and licked Joanna's hand.

'Take the little lass out for a walk,' Eleanor told Magda. 'She's sat by that beast too long.'

'Yes,' said Marian. 'Take her and go to visit the sisters. Ask if they've heard aught of Robert's gang.'

It took a bit of persuading, but once the two girls were out in the sunshine, striding through the bluebells, Joanna began to look happier.

'Won't be long now,' said Magda. 'Then you can take him home.'

'I'm not sure I can find the way again,' Joanna said. 'Maybe I can stay here with you?'

'But what of your parents?' asked Magda. 'Are they kind to you?'

'Mother shouts and Father sends me out in the cold for firewood,' said Joanna.

'Huh!' cried Magda. 'That's what Marian does to me! Will they be worried?'

The girl looked thoughtful. 'Aye, they will. Mother will cry and Father will be looking for me.'

'Then I think you should go back,' said Magda. 'My father will take you. He'll take you as soon as he comes back.'

Sister Rosamund welcomed them to the convent kitchen and brought them bread and small ale. She shook her head and looked worried when they asked for news of Robert. 'Veronica should never have gone,' she said. 'She's getting too old to go rushing around the country-side with a great gang of outcast fellows.'

'I suppose you think you should have gone instead,' said Magda cheekily.

Sister Rosamund laughed and nodded her head.

As they left, Magda noticed a small hut set a little apart from the main convent building, new-thatched and panelled, surrounded by bluebells.

'What have you made there?' Magda asked.

Sister Rosamund sighed. 'Alan,' she said. 'The poor leper lad. We've set him up there amongst the bluebells to cheer him, but he waits like a little lost dog for Tom's return.'

Joanna shuddered at the mention of the disease.

Magda sighed. 'Come on,' she said. 'I suppose we'd better go and see him.' She grabbed Joanna's arm and walked over to the hut.

Alan was staring into the distance, his thin arms folded still in his lap. At last he looked up at his visitors and suddenly recognition showed in his face.

'I thought you were a lad,' he said to Magda.

'Aye,' said Magda. 'I can fight you!'

Alan stroked his chin. All bruising had gone. 'Yes, you can,' he agreed. ''S'pose I'll never be a squire now.'

Magda sat down in front of the hut. 'No,' she said. 'But if it's possible to get this special oil, Tom will find it for you.'

The two girls walked back through the woods, both quiet and deep in thought, but as they neared the Forestwife's clearing something made Magda feel uneasy.

She stopped and grabbed Joanna's hand.

'What is it?' she whispered.

Magda shook her head. 'Too still, too quiet,' she said. 'No birds, no squirrels, and look at the path.'

Though the earth was dry there were footprints and scuff marks on it as though an army had passed that way.

Joanna picked up a piece of brown blood-soaked rag.

'Was that from your Fetcher?' Magda asked.

Joanna shook her head, then they heard the sound of men's voices and the clink of weapons.

'Careful,' Magda warned. 'Get off the path!'

The two girls crept away from the open space and hid for a moment in the undergrowth. Nobody came along the path, but they could clearly hear the sounds of voices.

'They're in the clearing,' said Magda. She put her finger to her lips.

Joanna followed her along a deep and secret path that brought them up beside the sweeping branches of the great yews. It was men's voices that they'd heard, but pitifully groaning and whimpering. Then Magda heard Marian calling for food and water.

They pushed the branches aside and saw the most dreadful sight. The soft green turf was littered with wounded men. Marian and Eleanor strode back and forth amongst them with water, clean rags and ointments. Veronica was there, her habit dirty and torn. She saw the two girls and beckoned them through.

'What is it?' Magda asked, her voice shaking with fear. 'Is my father . . . ?'

'He's got a clout and a wounded leg,' Veronica told her quickly. 'But he'll be fine. Now come, we need your help! They've struggled back without food or water. Can you run to the convent and get the sisters to come? Ask Sister Rosamund to bring her bundles and potions. We need food and ale and clean rags!'

Magda sighed at the thought of the journey she'd just made, but she nodded. 'Is the lady saved?' she asked.

Robert's bitter voice answered her. 'She is not!'

Magda ran back faster than ever and brought the nuns and their supplies. Isabel had been visiting Sister Rosamund and she insisted that she came along with the nuns to help. They worked hard through the rest of the day and at last by nightfall the men were all fed and made as comfortable as possible, their wounds cleaned and bandaged and wrapped in warm rags.

'It's a good thing we're not caught like this in freezing winter weather,' Eleanor said, building up her fire.

Robert sat hunched and gloomy by the hearthside, refusing to lie down and rest though he'd a long sword cut on his good cheek and painful smashed ribs.

'What's this mutt?' he asked, pointing at Fetcher, who'd crept quietly into the shadows and was watching the activity with new fear.

Brother James turned to look into the darkness at the edges of the hut.

'That's my dog Fetcher.' Joanna spoke out fearlessly. 'Who are you?'

Robert answered through gritted jaws. 'I am . . . I was the Hooded One.'

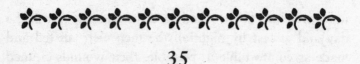

35

The Knights of Saint Lazarus

Slowly, bit by bit the story was told. The men had made camp by the Great North Road and set a lookout for the closed wagon that would carry Matilda de Braose and her son. They'd just begun to run out of food when three closed wagons, escorted by the wolfpack, were spied. They'd hesitated, but only for a moment. Though the King's mercenaries were heavily armed, Robert's lads were fired up and they guessed they could outnumber them.

Robert led a fierce attack, but while the first wagon was hurried on, the second two proved to be packed with armed footsoldiers who leapt out onto the outlaws. They had made a bitter fight of it, but the rebels had not had a chance against so many. FitzRanulf had ridden away fast with the leading wagon. John had found himself in the middle of thick fighting, unable to leave his friends to pursue his own quarrel. Fifteen lads had been killed outright and every one of the others carried some hurt. Though the women worked hard to save them, five more died in the night. One of them was Muchlyn.

John sat by the fire with Robert, growling out his anger.

'The blasted coward! Could not stay and fight but runs off, leaving his men to do his dirty work.'

Robert's face was grey, only his scar standing out livid, and streaked with fresh cuts. Somehow John knew that his friend needed comfort more than he.

'We made ourselves felt!' he said. 'Much would be proud to go in such a fight. We cut that gang of mercenaries down to half!'

Robert would not answer or allow himself to be tended.

Marian walked back and forth with a face like stone. She worked all day and most of the night, feeding, cleaning, making up simples and poultices. Magda and Joanna did all they could to help; the miserable plight of the men gave them the energy to carry on with little food or sleep. Magda did not even complain at the hated job of digging latrines; it was better than digging graves!

Three more died, though at least their pain was soothed by Marian's sleeping draughts. At last, when six days had passed, those who could walk began to leave the clearing and Eleanor insisted that Marian sleep. When she woke Robert was gone, his place by the hearth taken by Fetcher. Magda and Joanna sat beside him gloomily, pulling at his ears.

'Now *he's* gone ... she'll be miserable for days,' Magda whispered, nodding her head in Marian's direction.

'Shall I follow and track him down?' John asked.

But Marian shook her head. 'It will take time for us all to struggle through this disaster.'

James came and settled himself beside the two girls. 'Now the lads are mending, let's have a look at this dog of yours.'

He gently pressed his fingers into Fetcher's mutilated paw while Joanna watched anxiously.

'It's healing well,' he murmured.

'Will he walk again, do you think?'

'Oh aye, he'll walk. He'll do more than that, with the right training. He'll make as fine a bodyguard as any lass could want.'

'Would you help me, sir?' Joanna begged.

'Certainly I will. We'll have him lolloping about in no time.'

Marian smiled across at them, remembering Brother James' old dog, Snap, who'd died many years ago.

In the weeks that followed, James set to training Fetcher as though his life depended on it. Each day he went out into the woods with the two girls, tempting the dog on to his feet with meat scraps, till at last Fetcher could run from one to the other with a strange lopsided gait. His muscles grew hard and strong, his coat glossy, and they progressed to slinging bones and straw-stuffed sacks for him to fetch.

John stayed in the clearing and Magda was pleased to have her father by her side.

On a hot afternoon towards the end of August they

were lazily sitting in the sun outside the hut when they heard the sound of hooves. As always they sprang to their feet and melted into the lower branches of the yew trees.

'One horse,' whispered John, 'though a big 'un, I'd guess. Seems to stamp four times, then stops.' Suddenly John was laughing. 'Tom! That's his signal, though I've never heard it done on horseback.'

They came out from their hiding places wondering how Tom had got himself a horse. There was only a moment to wait before he came trotting into the clearing astride a fine grey stallion.

'I have the oil,' he shouted. 'I have the oil and more besides.'

'Well!' John laughed. 'At least one of us has done summat right.'

Everyone cheered and gathered round, patting the horse and touching its good halter and bridle with amazement.

'Good quality gear, is this,' said James. 'The best.'

'You've taken so long,' Magda cried. 'I thought you were dead in some ditch.'

'Not me.' Tom laughed, sliding down from the saddle and kissing her. 'Walter of Stainthorpe was not with the Templars at Newhouse. I had to travel on to the wastes of Bitterwood.'

'Where's this marvellous oil!' Marian asked.

Tom patted a strong leather pouch fastened to his waist.

He ate and drank with them, and was saddened to

hear of Much. But despite this, he was also eager to be off to the Magdalen convent with his precious oil. 'I've much to tell Mother Veronica,' he said. 'I've done myself a lot of good, but I've sorry news for her.'

'Oh dear,' said James. 'Shall I come with you? Is her man dead?'

'No,' said Tom. 'Not dead, but maybe he wishes he was. He's taken the leprosy himself. He grows aged and weak and his face is fearfully marked. He came back from Outremer with the seeds of sickness in him. That's why he was not at the Temple Newhouse. He's gone to live in a wild and lonely place with five other fighting monks, all suffering like himself.'

'Now then,' Brother James sighed. 'I believe I have heard of some such men. Do they call themselves the Knights of Saint Lazarus?'

'That's it,' said Tom. 'They still endeavour to live by the Templars' strict rules. They pray and keep their fighting skills sharp, but they live in the wilderness as outcast as we.'

'As hard a life as ours, and worse,' John agreed.

'But Walter Stainthorpe has given me this fine grey stallion,' cried Tom. 'He's grown too old and weak to manage such a spirited steed, and their rule states that they must give away all they cannot use. The knight has found himself a quieter mount and Rambler is mine!'

They all admired the powerful beast.

'Can you manage him?' asked John with a touch of envy.

'Certainly I can. He's trained to obey every small

command. Didn't you hear? I can get him to stamp out my signal!'

John laughed and slapped the horse's rump. Tom galloped off to visit the convent, returning in the morning, still pleased with himself.

Weeks went by and there was still no word from Robert. As autumn approached, Marian made them all set about the yearly gathering. Everything possible must be garnered from the woods and stored before the first frosts.

Nuts, berries, mushrooms, ladies' bedstraw and meadow-sweet all had their uses; dried poppy heads, hard-skinned sloes and sour-tasting juniper berries were carefully collected and carried back to the clearing. The work was a little less arduous this year as John, Tom and James all stayed to help. No message or sign came from Robert.

Fetcher's training went better than ever and though he still limped, James taught him a few good tricks, just like Snap. He could snatch away a weapon with his jaws, disarming a man before he knew what came at him. And catching flying arrows in his mouth was Fetcher's favourite sport.

October was the pannage month, when pigs were herded into the woods to search for acorns. One afternoon early in the month, Marian stirred dark red elderberries in a tub of dye, while Tom and Fetcher brought sticks for Joanna and Magda's charcoal stack.

John and James sat by the doorsill in the sharp autumn sun.

Marian turned to them. 'That lass and her dog should be returned home,' she said. 'Somehow we've forgotten, what with all the trouble and hurts. I dare say she thinks she belongs here, but she should be back with her parents before winter comes.'

John nodded and scratched his beard. 'Shall we take her home?' he asked James.

The monk nodded. 'We grow too safe and fat sitting here,' he agreed. 'A little outing to Clipstone would do us fine.'

'Take her now, while the pannage lasts,' said Marian. 'Travelling will be at its safest, with the woods full of pigs and children.'

Though Magda cried when they left, Marian insisted. 'Her parents will have given up hope,' she said and Joanna agreed that she could not leave them in distress. She hugged Magda fiercely.

'One day I'll come back,' she said.

36

Bad News Travels Fast

The men were gone for four days, but then they came hurrying back into the clearing with glum faces and the dog still at their heels.

'Why have you brought Fetcher back?' Magda cried.

'He would not leave James's side,' John told her hurriedly. 'But we have more to bother us than Fetcher, sweetheart.'

Marian put down the pot she pounded roots in. 'What is it now?' she demanded.

'The King has been at Clipstone hunting lodge with the Sheriff.'

'What of that? He hunts while the weather's warm.'

John shook his head. '*He's* gone on to Nottingham now, but he's left the Sheriff and that damned FitzRanulf at Clipstone. There's the remains of the wolfpack and, with them, a great gang of new hired mercenaries.'

A shiver crept up Magda's back when she heard her father's words.

'We don't like the look of it.' James' face was grim.

'That's no jolly hunting party gathering there – they've got three blacksmiths hard at work fettling up their weapons. We did not hang around to be recognised. We came at close quarters to some of them, up at Wentbridge.'

Marian frowned and looked round at her mother. 'Is this it?' she asked. 'Is this the great fear that haunts tha dreams?'

Eleanor had gone very white. 'I think so,' she whispered.

Magda dug her fingers deep into Fetcher's warm rough coat for comfort.

'What do they plan? Can you tell us, old one?' James begged, but Eleanor shook her head.

'Fire and sword,' she said. 'Fire, sword and hunger in the forest . . . nay, in Langden. I cannot see more.'

'Damn it! I wish Robert was here,' John said. 'Should I go off hunting for him?'

'Aye, maybe the time is right that you should,' Marian agreed.

The following morning John set out to track his friend down. Tom and James went snaring hares for the pot and those left in the clearing went about their tasks with an air of foreboding. Their fears were heightened when Philippa arrived, breathless and angry, just before midday.

'What is it?' Marian cried, running to her friend. 'Bad news?'

'Aye,' Philippa gasped. 'Bad news for Langden. It's the

wolfpack, all the lot of them. They've marched in and taken over the manor house. They're bristling with weapons and foul mouthed as sin.'

'What of Isabel and Matilda? Have they been turned out?'

'Nay. Not so bad if they had. At least we could give them shelter then. No one has seen them – the wolfpack will let nobody in or out.'

'What does it mean?' Marian demanded.

Magda's heart thumped fast as she watched the two women striding up and down the clearing. They were unaware of the goats, chickens and cats who scattered in their path, so deep was their concern. Magda's safe existence in Barnsdale seemed badly threatened. The old one watched anxiously from the doorsill.

When Tom and James returned with a pair of hares, they all sat down and talked again.

'What can we do against so many?'

'There's no way that we can raise more men, not after our last defeat!'

Brother James shook his head despairingly. Then suddenly he got up. 'One thing I do know – I'd rather die than cower here in the woods.'

'Me too,' cried Marian. 'But what shall we do?'

James shrugged his shoulders. 'Bow practice,' he said. 'Come on, every one of us. Don't sit here worrying, let's fettle our bows and be ready to make our move when we may.'

They all jumped up at his suggestion. Anything was better than sitting there in gloom. They worked all afternoon, fitting new shafts for their arrows. They were grimly letting their arrows fly at a swaying willow wand when Sister Rosamund came tramping through the woods with worse news.

'It's Mother Veronica,' she told them. 'She went visiting the Langden ladies yesterday and she's not returned. I've been to the manor to ask after her, but there's soldiers at every door and they won't let me in. The little windows up in Matilda's solar are boarded up, though I thought I could hear a scraping sound from within. I fear they've all been taken prisoner.'

'This gets worse and worse,' Marian cried.

'I must go to Langden,' James insisted.

Tom looked thoughtful. 'No, wait a while,' he said. 'They may have made a great mistake when they imprisoned Veronica. Walter of Stainthorpe may be old and sick, but he still leads a band of fierce fighting men.'

James looked suddenly interested. 'You mean the leper knights? They're not exactly an army, but you are right, Tom; they're trained as sharp as any fighting men and fiercely disciplined. I've heard it said that once they move to fight they will never turn back, even though they face certain death.'

'But would such men give us aid?' asked Marian.

'I believe so,' said Tom. 'Though they've both devoted their lives to God, Walter of Stainthorpe is still Veronica's man and would do anything for her.'

Philippa was puzzled by mention of the leper knights, but Marian was eager now. 'What have we to lose?'

* * *

Tom led out Rambler, the stallion, from the lean-to where they'd stabled him and climbed into the saddle.

'Come on, fellow,' he murmured. 'I bet you never thought to see your old master so soon.'

Magda could not stop herself from running to Tom and grabbing his leg. 'Take care!' she cried. 'Please come safe back! We are all depending on you!'

Tom looked surprised but pleased and stooped from the saddle to kiss her. 'I'll be back as fast as you can blink,' he cried.

The ones that were left sat whispering together round the fire that night, then slept badly once they had settled to rest. Two more days passed in constant fear and anxiety. Plans were made, only to be discarded as hopeless and ridiculous. Then early one morning they were surprised by the sound of voices calling out their names.

Magda lifted up the skins and stepped over the doorsill, thinking that she recognised the voice. And she was right. Joanna stood before her with an older man and a lad.

Magda went to hug her, filled with surprise. 'What's brought you back so soon?'

'We've walked all through the night, me and Father and Jamie, for Jamie has heard some terrible things that we think you should know.'

Marian came up behind Magda, also amazed to see Joanna back again. 'What is it?' she asked.

'Our Jamie is apprenticed to Clipstone's blacksmith,' Joanna told them. 'And while he was stoking the fires he heard two soldiers from the wolfpack boasting of what they did. He didn't like the sound of it. You tell them, Jamie!'

Everyone gathered around the doorway, looking expectantly at the young lad.

'They said,' he muttered nervously, 'they said that Matilda and Isabel of Langden were to get the same as the great Matilda.'

'You know who they mean,' Joanna cried. 'That brave lady, the one you tried to rescue.'

'Yes,' Marian agreed. 'We do fear greatly that the wolfpack have imprisoned Langden's ladies in their own home, along with Veronica. And that is what we suppose has happened to the great Matilda de Braose.'

' 'Tis worse than that,' Joanna cried. 'Go on, Jamie! Tell them what else you heard.'

'Well,' said Jamie hesitantly, 'I can't be certain that I understood their meaning right, but they said that the great Matilda and her son have gone without their dinner and Langden's ladies shall do the same!'

They all frowned at that, unsure what it might mean.

Then Jamie spoke up again. 'They began laughing in the most horrible way and . . . I'm not sure, but I fear that it may mean . . .'

The whole company stood horrified as his thought sank in.

'Can it really mean . . . they would starve them?' Philippa cried. 'Imprison them and starve them to death?'

Suddenly the old one was shaking; her eyes ran with

tears. 'Yes, they would,' she whispered. 'This is it! This is my dream. I have no doubt. Sword and fire and hunger!'

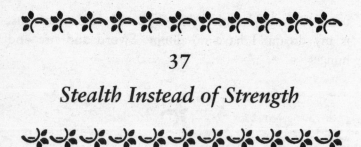

37

Stealth Instead of Strength

A dreadful silence followed, so that the bleating of goats and soft clucking of fowls was all that could be heard. Then Marian whispered, 'No. No, surely. They have Mother Veronica there too. They would not dare to starve a nun!'

James laughed bitterly at that. 'Would they not? Since the King still quarrels with the pope, the church gets no protection at all. I heard just last month that a party of nuns were stoned outside Nottingham. The Sheriff's men stood by giving encouragement. Indeed, King John would probably pay his mercenaries double for ridding him of a troublesome nun as well as two defiant women.'

'The wolfpack would do anything,' said Philippa with certainty. 'You cannot believe the foulness of their mood. I fear they do not forget the outlaws' attack at Wentbridge.'

'But they don't know that Matilda and Isabel have anything to do with us,' said Magda. 'Do they?'

James shrugged his shoulders. 'They'd pay well for such information and if the King is in a temper, anyone can come off the worse. There is no fairness or sense about it.'

There was another moment of quiet while they thought, then Marian's hand went slowly to the meat knife that she always carried tucked into her belt.

'We must *do* something,' she said. 'Anything. We cannot wait for Tom or John or Robert, or leper knights who may never come.'

'Yes,' James agreed. 'But we must not go rushing up there without any kind of plan; they'd kill us quick as a flash. No . . . we must work out the best way to use our small strength.'

'That's right,' Philippa agreed. 'How many have we got on our side to start with?'

James patted her shoulder. 'You've a fat monk who's handy with a quarterstaff and a well-trained dog.' Then he turned to Marian. 'You've a woman who's fast with a knife and a fine archer.'

'Two,' shouted Magda. 'I am as good a shot as any.'

Marian looked unhappy at that, but Philippa nodded her head. 'We need every scrap of help we can gather,' she said. 'All who live at Langden will support us, though they've few weapons or fighting skills, and we have a convent full of angry nuns.'

They smiled at that thought, but then Philippa shook her head at Marian. 'It's *you* that should not come. The Forestwife should not leave Barnsdale Woods.'

Marian folded her arms stubbornly. 'I'll not be left behind.'

'I can help,' said Eleanor, and she pointed to Marian's beautiful woven girdle, the symbol of her work as Forestwife. 'Take it off, daughter!' she said. 'Give it to me. There shall be a Forestwife here for those in need, however long you are gone and whatever becomes of thee. I will use my small skills and do the best I can.'

Marian did not hesitate. 'Thank you, Mother,' she said, unfastening the belt and giving it to the old one with a kiss.

'Now,' said James, 'we must make our plans and act together. We need stealth instead of strength. In place of swords we'll carry food and water flasks, as we fear starvation. In place of slingshot, we'll carry wood and kindling and tinder, for they may need warmth.'

Most looked puzzled at that, but Marian picked up the way his mind worked. 'Aye,' she said. 'I like your way of thinking, James. Instead of lances and pikes, we shall need hammers, chisels and nails. For we must get inside with the prisoners and barricade ourselves in with them.'

James nodded. 'I fear we must settle for a siege!'

'Ah, James,' Marian said, her eyes glittering. 'I have a wicked idea. Use what strengths we've got, you said. I've been drying my special herbs for many years – now I know what I saved them for.'

She went into the hut and carefully reached up to the high shelf, bringing down an earthenware pot.

Magda caught her breath. 'The forbidden herbs,' she whispered.

Marian's smile made her shiver. 'That's right, child. A healer can turn poisoner, easy as that,' and she clicked her fingers. 'What did Robert tell you? Death shall not be good enough for FitzRanulf. Now I begin to see how.'

Magda had never seen Marian so determined. She rushed about the clearing giving orders and instructions. Her furious energy raised their spirits and catapulted them into action. Though for Magda, the change in Marian brought a touch of fear. She could not believe this was the calm, steadfast woman who'd mothered her so long.

By dusk they'd made themselves ready and packed their weapons and bags. Magda was exhausted from running backwards and forwards through the forest tracks, carrying messages to the nuns and to Langden Forge.

They tried to settle to sleep, but it was difficult. Each time Magda opened her eyes, she saw the dark shape of Marian still moving about. Before dawn Marian woke them all and handed out rush lights.

'The time has come,' she whispered. They obeyed without a sound.

They reached the outskirts of Langden before dawn, their bows and quivers strapped to their backs along with sacks of grain and lentils. Magda looked anxiously up at the dark shape of Langden Manor on its low mound. The ditch that surrounded the thatched stone-built house, with its courtyard and barns, had only a trickle of water in it. The low stockade that surrounded the garden was just high enough to keep in pigs and fowl. Magda remembered the great stone turrets of Nottingham Castle, beside it Langden seemed so homely.

'What does FitzRanulf want with marrying Isabel?' she asked. 'Langden's nowt but barns and kitchen gardens.'

'He doesn't really want Isabel,' Marian told her. 'He wants the land. I dare say he has plans to tear down this old house and build a grand hunting lodge in its place.'

'How can he treat her so badly, if he hopes to marry her?'

Marian looked grim. 'I fear this is punishment for refusal. He does not care whether Isabel lives or dies.'

They crept past the church and met Philippa's husband, behind the forge.

'Why must we be stumbling about so early in the dark?' Magda asked.

'To catch them unawares,' Philippa told her. 'They have their weaknesses. They are all drunken sots and will be snoring in their straw.'

It was not long before Magda turned and saw faint lights moving deep in the woods.

'Here they come,' she whispered to Marian.

As the lights came nearer they smelt the smoky scent of incense and saw a solemn chanting procession winding its way towards Langden. Each light was carried by one of the Magdalen nuns. Sister Rosamund was in front, Alan at her side.

'Time for me to join them,' said James. 'I'll go to rally help as soon as I know that you are inside.'

He kissed them solemnly and then went to head the procession with Sister Rosamund and Joanna's family. The three women with their bows watched from behind the forge as Philippa's husband strode from hut to hut, whispering low. The villagers came quietly from their hovels to swell the ranks of the strange procession. The singing grew louder and some of the wolfpack who'd been sleeping out in the courtyard leapt, puzzled, to their feet. They pulled out their swords and started shouting at each other. Brother James marched up to the open outer gate.

'We demand to see Lady Matilda!' he bellowed.

'We must speak with our prioress,' cried Sister Rosamund.

FitzRanulf himself came yawning from the hall with straw in his hair. He drew his sword and thrust it towards James' throat.

'Who dares to ask?' he growled.

Magda caught her breath in fear, but Marian whispered: 'Trust in James! Now's our moment.'

Though her legs shook and her stomach heaved, Magda clutched her bow tightly and followed Marian and Philippa as they ran quietly round the stockade and in at the small back gate to the kitchen gardens. They jumped the ditch and crept past the grunting pigs, past Isabel's neat rows of beans and onions, making for the kitchen door. They paused for a moment, not knowing what they would find on the other side.

' 'Tis now or never,' Philippa hissed.

Marian turned to Magda. 'Brave lass,' she whispered. 'Are you ready?'

'Aye,' Magda nodded.

Philippa tried the heavy wooden latch and gave a good push, almost falling in as the door swung open. A frightened kitchen maid turned to see them.

'Don't fear, Margery,' Philippa whispered. ' 'Tis us, come to help. Where are Matilda and Isabel?'

Margery pointed up the narrow stairs to the solar and burst into tears.

'Are they locked in?' Marian asked.

' 'Tis worse, far worse.' Margery swallowed hard and tears spilled down her cheeks.

Marian pulled her bundles of herbs from her pack and pushed them into Margery's hand.

'Here – put this in their food or drink, this first and then the other. Only the wolfpack, mind – only them!'

Margery took the bundles with shaking hands as the three intruders dashed up the narrow wooden stairs.

Philippa pulled back the rich tapestry curtain that covered the doorway and stared at the solid blank stones that formed a new-made wall.

'Dear God!' she cried. 'It's true.'

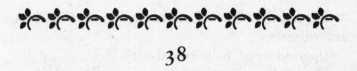

38

Water Has Never Tasted so Sweet

The clatter of swords and heavy boots came from below, then men's voices bellowing in a foreign tongue. Marian pulled her bow from her back and notched an arrow, covering the narrow way up the stairs. Philippa pulled hammer and chisel from her bag and set to work to loosen the stones.

'If we could shift just one,' she said, 'then the others would come easy.'

Magda pulled the meat knife from Marian's belt and began to work at the stone with her. A grumpy yawning soldier appeared at the bottom of the stairs.

'Stupid hags,' he snarled, lunging towards Marian with his sword. He soon fell back, cursing, as Marian's arrow pierced his hand. His sword clattered to the floor and fast as a whip she notched another arrow. She let fly again, wounding a second fellow in the shoulder. Much cursing followed, then sudden quiet.

FitzRanulf appeared at the bottom of the stairs, furious that he'd been rushed back into the house when he was trying to deal with the strange deputation of nuns and villagers.

'Damned fools!' he bellowed at his men.

'There's three ragged forest women up there!'

'The hell cats . . . they've split my thumb.'

'They're raining down arrows like needles! We can't reach up to spit them.'

'So what?' FitzRanulf gave a chilling laugh. 'Where do you think they are going? Now we have six witches to starve instead of three. Just guard the stairs, damn you, and don't let any of them down.'

Philippa sighed, then grunted with effort. 'It gives!'

Marian turned to Magda. 'Can you cover the stairs!'

'Aye.'

The two older women worked at the stone with their chisels and knives, and at last a definite grating movement rewarded them. Magda stood at the top of the stairs with arrow notched and bow bent. It was very uncomfortable; the sharp straw of the thatch came down low and stuck into her head. Her arms ached with the tension of the ready bow. One of the men looked up again through the narrow stairwell.

'I zee nozzink but a stupid chilt,' he sneered.

'But I can shoot,' Magda answered and loosed an arrow that landed with a thwack in the wooden beam just by his ear. The fellow withdrew fast, swearing furiously, though Magda could not understand the words he used. Her hands shook and she felt sick, but she whipped out another arrow.

'It's sliding away,' Philippa hissed. 'Push, push . . . someone is helping from the other side.'

Then with one great heave, the stone slithered away and landed with a thump.

'Help us! Oh, help us!' a faint voice cried.

Philippa opened her tinder box and struck the flint sharply while Marian held a rush light to pick up the tiny flames. As soon as it was burning steadily they thrust the small wand into the hole. It was snatched at by blood-stained fingers with ripped dirty nails. Then they saw the shadowy top of Isabel's head, covered in dust.

'Water! Water, for the love of God!' Isabel choked out the words.

Marian pulled a small waterskin from her belt.

'Quick! Quick!' Isabel sobbed. 'Veronica will not leave Mother's side. I fear she is dying.'

'Hush, sweetheart,' soothed Marian. 'We have good food and drink with us.'

Isabel's poor torn hands came stretching through the gap. Greedy fingers closed about the waterskin and vanished.

'Listen, Isabel,' Marian put her mouth to the dusty hole. 'You must give them just a small sip each, then wait a while, or they'll die for sure with bloated stomachs.'

'Yes.' Her voice floated back to them. 'I understand.'

'Are they strong enough to hold back, do you think?' Philippa asked anxiously.

'We are,' came a sharp reply.

'That was Veronica.' Philippa smiled to hear her voice so firm.

So they set about moving more stones with renewed energy. They worked steadily and soon Isabel came back to help from the other side.

'Bless you! Bless you!' she murmured. 'Water has never tasted so sweet.'

They worked on and Isabel tore at the stones from her side. At last Marian spoke to Magda without turning. 'Are you still taking aim, my brave lass?'

'Aye,' she answered through gritted teeth. 'But I can't keep it up much longer!'

'I think you can let up,' said Philippa. 'This is wide enough for a little 'un and that's you, my girl.'

'Come, Magda,' said Marian. 'Climb through this hole and I shall take your place again!'

Magda lowered her aim and waggled her aching shoulders with relief. Marian snatched up the bow.

'I'll heave,' said Philippa, bending to cup her hands like a stirrup.

Magda stuck her head through the hole into the shadowy room.

'It smells bad in here,' she said.

'Aye, love, it will,' Philippa told her. 'Murder always smells foul. But don't be afraid. 'Tis only the odours of our friends' poor bodies, struggling to stay alive.'

Isabel took hold of Magda's shoulders to pull her through. They both fell into the darkness together and it was only when Veronica came over with the rush light that Magda saw the terrible state of Isabel. Exhaustion was clear on her thin dusty face, her clothes torn, her feet and fingers bleeding.

'Oh, Isabel,' Magda cried with pity, hugging her tight.

'Bless you,' Isabel sobbed. 'I could not see how anyone could help us.'

'I'm not so sure that we are such a wonderful help.' Philippa's down-to-earth tones came to them through the hole. 'I fear we've come to share this cruel imprisonment with you.'

Bread and goat's milk were handed through the hole. 'Just a small sop each,' Marian warned.

Magda tore the fresh bread into tiny pieces and dribbled the milk on to them in her cupped hand. She'd fed folk close to starvation before, though never had she cared so much that they should be revived. When all three had taken their small portion of food, Magda and Isabel set about working more stones loose, and at last the hole was big enough for Philippa and Marian to scramble through.

'But can't they come up here and get us now?' Magda cried.

'Quick,' Marian told her. 'Fit these stones back into the wall. Their cruel intentions shall provide us with some safety, at least for a little while.'

Once the hole was filled again, they began to take stock of their situation. Marian took a small axe from her pack.

'At least we can get a bit more daylight in here.' She began to hack at the shutters.

'They nailed them up and left us with nothing,' Isabel told them. 'They took Mother's bed for FitzRanulf

315

and did not even leave us straw.'

When at last morning light came through the windows, Philippa and Magda crammed together to look down at the gateway. James and the nuns still stood their ground though FitzRanulf had his men arrayed against them, swords drawn.

'Leave now,' he bellowed. 'This moment. The Sheriff shall soon be at Langden. All those who do not leave shall be arrested. We serve the King.'

'Time for our signal,' said Philippa.

'Aye.' Marian caught up her bow and took careful aim from the window.

'Leave now,' FitzRanulf barked again. He snatched hold of Sister Rosamund roughly, hauling her away from James. 'I'll start with this sweet-faced nun.'

At that moment Marian loosed her arrow so that it fell with a thud before FitzRanulf's feet, startling the man.

James held up his hand as though he submitted. 'We shall go,' he said. 'We want no trouble from the Sheriff.'

The nuns and villagers stepped back from the gate, though James stubbornly held out his hand for Rosamund.

FitzRanulf released her with a shove. 'The King thinks poorly of meddling nuns,' he growled. 'He's still got bishops who will bring a charge of heresy. We like the smell of burning nuns – remember that!'

The three women at the window watched as their friends melted away into the village and woods. When at last they had gone they all sat down wearily.

'What now?' Magda asked.

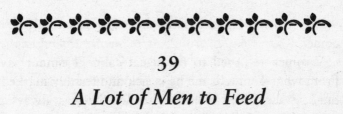

39

A Lot of Men to Feed

There was silence in the dark bare solar, then Philippa spoke up with her usual common sense. 'What now? We wait,' she said. 'We trust in James and set about making ourselves as comfortable and safe as we may. We must work out our rations; fresh food first and then the grain.'

'It's lack of water that I fear most,' said Isabel.

Philippa put out three large waterskins and the food they'd brought. 'We must sip carefully and eke it out as best we can.'

'If we're very careful we might last a se'nnight,' said Marian.

'Can there be any help for us?' Isabel asked.

Marian nodded. 'Our friends will not desert us.'

They told how John had gone off to find Robert and that James would rally all the aid he could get.

'Tom has gone off to find your Templar Knight,' Magda told Mother Veronica.

'What, sweetheart?' The old nun looked startled for a moment.

''Tis true,' Magda assured her. 'Do you think he'll come?'

Veronica returned to her usual calm. 'I cannot say. From what Tom tells me he is sick and terribly marked, but . . .' she added a little wistfully, 'he was always a brave man and did what he believed right.'

It was clear that Isabel and Veronica desperately needed rest, and Matilda careful feeding. Marian suggested that she and Philippa would act as lookout and nurse while the others slept.

Magda was trying to get comfortable beneath her cloak when it dawned on her that sleep was not at all what her body required.

She rolled over and got up. '*You* sleep, Marian,' she said firmly. 'I shall watch Lady Matilda; I know what to do. You did not sleep at all last night.'

Marian opened her mouth to argue, but somehow the calm sense of Magda's words made her close it again. Instead she kissed her and obeyed, falling quickly into a deep sleep of exhaustion.

When she woke, Philippa and Magda had quietly cleaned the solar and tidied their food and tools. They'd set a small fire burning on the hearthstone and tucked their discarded cloaks around Lady Matilda.

Marian woke with a start. 'How long have I slept?' she demanded. 'What has happened? What have they done?'

'Hush!' Philippa told her. 'They have ventured up the staircase and I believe they've set a guard out there, but naught else. Why should they do more? They've got us where they want us, haven't they? They do not know we've friends. They think they may sit tight and let us die without raising a weapon.'

'Do you think that's what's happened to Matilda de Braose?' Magda asked.

Philippa and Marian looked grimly at each other and nodded their heads.

'And her son too?'

Marian sighed. 'I fear so.'

'If my father knew that I was here, he'd come raging through the gates at them,' said Magda. 'He'd get himself killed.'

Marian smiled and nodded. 'But Robert is a wicked crafty fellow,' she said. 'He'll have other plans, and he and James will hold John back.'

'And what of Tom?'

'Who knows,' said Marian.

Three days passed and they took turns at keeping watch at the window. Lady Matilda gained strength from the careful feeding, but Magda was hungry. The bread and cheese and milk had gone; their kindling turned to ashes. Now they must crush the grain and mix the meal with a trickle of water to make a cold sticky porridge that did not satisfy.

'We must keep ourselves strong,' Marian insisted. 'We must be ready to run or fight.'

She made them bend and stretch in the confined space and practise drawing bows, though they did not let their arrows fly. Even poor weak Matilda had to stretch her fingers and toes and allow the others to rub her stiff shoulders and spine. Isabel was greatly cheered by their company and the hope they brought.

It was on the third day that the sound of horses arriving brought them to the window. Magda recognised the Sheriff at the head of a band of men, just as heavily armed as the wolfpack. FitzRanulf went out to meet him, and it was clear from the way they looked up towards the solar windows that the woman's fate was being discussed, though they could not hear what was said.

Magda shivered at the sight of them crowding into the courtyard. 'So many men and weapons,' she murmured.

Marian put an arm around her shoulders and hugged her tight. 'But remember, love, we do not only fight with weapons. We have different ways of doing things.'

They watched as the men pitched camp; some inside the house, others outside. Some of the kitchen servants lit a fire and set up a cooking pot out in the courtyard.

'It's a lot of men to be fed,' Magda said resentfully. 'And whatever they get to eat they'll be better fed than me.'

Marian smiled. 'Maybe not,' she whispered. 'I doubt the kitchen servants will relish this extra work. See who stirs broth for them?'

Magda glanced down, her mouth watering at the good smell that rose from the pot. 'Why, it's Margery.'

'Aye,' Marian nodded. 'Do you trust the lass?' she asked Isabel.

'Yes.' Isabel was definite. 'She's a bold lass, and I'd trust her with my life.'

Late that evening, when the soldiers had eaten and drunk, Magda was surprised to hear the sounds of quiet laughter. It was Marian, chuckling, as she stood at her watchplace by the window.

'What is it?' Magda asked, going to her side.

'Brave Margery!' she said with relish. 'Listen!'

'It sounds like someone being sick,' said Magda, puzzled.

'It's lots of people being sick,' Marian told her. 'You see, honey, they did *not* get better food than we.'

Magda understood. 'The forbidden herbs!'

The sounds of choking and retching came from the ditch at the side of the manor house. They could see the pale shapes of running men, dropping their breeches to the ground as they ran outside to squat, wherever they might.

Magda and her friends crowded at the window, stifling their laughter.

Philippa put her hand over Veronica's eyes. 'This is not a sight any nun should see,' she chuckled.

Mother Veronica laughed till the tears rolled down her cheeks. 'God bless Margery,' she said. 'Can you tell which herbs she used?'

'Oh yes,' said Marian. 'She's done very well.'

'Will the fellows die?'

Marian shook her head. 'No. They'll be weak and weary for a few days, but they'll not die from a good clear out. Still, Margery has other herbs than these in her care.'

One of the soldiers looked up at their narrow window and shook his fist. 'Barnsdale's Witch,' he shouted. 'We're cursed!'

The Best Right of All

The following day there was an outbreak of spots and
rashes amongst the mercenaries. The women watched
from the windows as men scratched themselves
against walls and fences, some rolling on the ground.
Despite their own hunger, the sights below brought
hope.

But again the soldiers gathered in groups in the courtyard, pointing up to the window and making signs
against the evil eye.

'Barnsdale's Witch! Barnsdale's Witch!' they chanted.
'She should burn!'

'I don't like it,' Magda whispered.

'Better they think it's my curse than Margery's stew-
pot,' said Marian.

They sat huddled together that evening, watching
their last scrap of candle burn.

'It must soon be All Hallows Eve,' Magda sighed. 'Oh,
how I long for soul cake and guisers and crackling
bonfires.'

'Why yes,' Veronica agreed. 'It must be soon. Can we have missed it?'

'You've not missed it,' Marian told them. 'It's All Hallows Eve tonight.'

'Oh no,' Veronica cried. 'I've been so muddled, I've lost track.' She bowed her head and started to murmur the special prayers for the dead.

Marian took Magda's hand. 'Don't worry,' she said. 'This little candle is our Samhain fire. We'll wish upon it, and whisper all our hopes for the coming year.'

Next day their hopes looked bleak, for the Sheriff and FitzRanulf marched out into the courtyard when the sun was high in the sky.

'Now!' they growled. 'Bring the slut out here, so her friends may see!'

'Oh no!' whispered Isabel. The women crowded at the windows.

Two men dragged Margery between them.

'How do they know?' Magda cried. 'What will they do?'

They watched in helpless silence as the men tied Margery to a post. The wolfpack gathered, pale and wretched after a sleepless night. Some clutched their stomachs, others still scratched; all were very angry.

'Poisoner!' they shouted. 'Stone her! Stone her!'

Marian quickly picked up her bow and took aim from the window.

Magda watched with horror. 'How can we save her, amongst so many?'

Marian shook her head desperately. 'We can't, but we can see she does not die alone.'

'Aye,' Magda agreed and snatched up her own bow.

The wolfpack set about collecting stones and dung from the yard, filling the air with foul threats.

'Look . . . look!' Marian cried, sudden hope in her voice.

From their viewpoint high above the courtyard they could see that a lone rider had emerged from behind Langden Church, cantering slowly towards the manor. The man wore fine chain mail and the white tunic of a Templar Knight. His shield was emblazoned with the red cross, but his face hidden by a huge white linen hood.

FitzRanulf stared open-mouthed as the knight in full battledress reached the manor, dipping his head to enter through the outer gate.

'Who the hell . . . ?' the Sheriff shouted.

'Saint Lazare,' FitzRanulf muttered, backing away. 'Leper knight – beware!'

The knight of Saint Lazarus brought his horse to a standstill behind Margery. His face was bandaged inside the hood, so that only his eyes could be seen. He raised his hand and spoke in a cracked and muffled voice, though he could be heard well enough in the shocked silence.

'Let the women go!'

The Sheriff and FitzRanulf looked at each other.

'What interest has the Temple in old women and witches?' the Sheriff asked. 'Here, help us burn the lot of them!'

The Templar drew his sword. 'Let them go!' he repeated.

Magda turned to Mother Veronica. 'Is it your man?' she whispered.

Silent tears poured down Veronica's cheeks. 'Aye, I believe it is he.'

'But what can he do, one man alone?' Magda asked.

Marian touched her shoulder and pointed. 'Not alone – not alone at all.'

Magda looked where she was bidden, out towards Langden village, and there she saw another Saint Lazarus knight riding out from behind the huts. His tunic was black with a red cross on the chest and a black hood shaded his face.

'See there,' hissed Philippa.

Yet another hooded knight in black came from behind the forge; a broad-built fellow, this one. Beside his horse bounded a limping dog.

'Fetcher!' Magda cried with delight. 'And see that horse behind . . . I know it. It's Rambler! But where is Tom? Who are these knights?'

'They are the guisers you wished for!' Marian's face was full of joy.

They watched then as more appeared, until a company of ten leper knights came cantering slowly and silently towards the manor house.

The Sheriff was pop-eyed with astonishment. Slowly a huge multitude gathered behind the Templars. They came flooding out from the quiet huts of Langden; villagers carrying forks and sickles, coal diggers with spades and charcoal burners with great quarterstaffs.

The women laughed out loud as the numbers grew.

'Where have so many people come from?' Isabel cried. 'They are not all our people!'

Veronica stood beside her frowning, then she suddenly snorted with laughter. 'That's no villager,' she cried. 'That's Sister Rosamund in lad's breeches!'

FitzRanulf swung round frantically as the ten leper knights headed steadily towards the low stockade. He turned to his men in panic. 'Fools!' he shouted. 'To your weapons!'

All hell was let loose as the men dropped their stones and snatched up swords and lances. FitzRanulf pulled a blazing brand from the cooking fire and threw it into the open doorway of the house.

'At least the witch shall burn!' he cried.

Then Magda watched appalled as FitzRanulf raised his sword – not to one of the advancing fighting men, but to poor helpless Margery. Without stopping to think she bent her bow and aimed between his shoulders. Her arrow sang through the air and buried itself deep into his back. FitzRanulf staggered, then turned back towards the house, a ridiculous expression of surprise written clear on his face. His sword clattered uselessly on to the ground at Margery's feet, then he crumpled and fell, disappearing amongst the dust and fighting that now surrounded him.

Utter chaos reigned. Some of the mercenaries made a good fight of it but most ran off into the woods, still sick and fearful, clutching their stomachs. The leper knights fought bitterly and Marian rained down arrows from the window, taking careful aim and making sure she hit the right targets. Magda could not stop trembling; tears poured down her face.

'I have killed a man,' she whispered to Mother Veronica.

The old woman gently took away the bow and hugged her tightly. 'You have saved Margery,' she said.

The Knights of Saint Lazarus, supported by the villagers, soon found themselves in charge of the courtyard. One black-hooded knight bent quickly to untie Margery. She wrapped her arms about his neck and clung to him. The man flung back his hood and the women cheered to see Robert's scarred, excited face. The big man beside him ripped back his hood and Magda saw that it was her father. Behind him came James and beside him on Rambler was Tom. But the bandaged knight with the husky voice did not remove his hood, nor did six more who gathered beside him.

There was no time for rejoicing, for thick black smoke began to puther out from the hall. The men saw the danger and looked about desperately for help.

'No water!' Robert bellowed. 'Can't save the house!'

'Just get *them* out,' John roared.

Robert leapt from his horse and ran to Isabel's low wooden stockade.

'John! John!' he cried, starting to tear up the wooden fencing. John understood and went to help. Soon all the villagers were tearing up the low fence of palings. They carried it to the manor house and propped it up beneath the window. One by one, the women climbed out precariously on to the rough wooden fencing. They slithered down it, picking up grazes and splinters, but they did not feel them much or even care.

Getting Lady Matilda out was more awkward, but the villagers brought ropes and, as the flames of her home crackled behind her, the old lady was safely lowered to the ground.

Robert snatched up Marian into his arms and swung her round until she shouted at him to stop. Magda flung her arms around Tom. Mother Veronica walked boldly towards the seven leper knights. Walter of Stainthorpe held up his gloved hand to halt her. She stopped obediently by his horse's head. Tears filled her eyes as she bent to kiss his stirrup.

Magda saw her father stamping out flames on the wooden fencing. She ran to him, but stumbled and fell over FitzRanulf's body. John bent at once to help his daughter to her feet, glaring down at the remains of his enemy. FitzRanulf's white, dead face still carried that surprised expression.

'Evil man!' John spat. 'I should have been the one to kill him, not Marian.'

Marian turned as she heard his words. 'I did not fire that shot from my bow,' she said.

'Who then?' John cried.

'The one who had the best right of us all,' she told him, gently touching Magda's shoulder.

John turned to his daughter. 'You?'

Magda nodded. He hugged her tight. 'Child of the May, my Child of the May,' he whispered.

41

The Fires of Samhain

The villagers watched helplessly as Langden Manor burned. But Isabel did not fret. 'We'll build another,' she said. 'It was damp and cold. Not all our memories are happy ones.'

Marian took her arm. 'Let's turn this misery to good,' she said.

Isabel smiled at her, puzzled.

'Did we not wish for guisers and Samhain fires?'

'Aye,' Isabel began to understand. 'We can turn our fire to celebration.'

And suddenly she was rushing about, ordering fowls to be slaughtered and food prepared.

'Is there grain left for soul cakes?' she asked.

'There certainly is,' Margery told her. 'I dragged three grain sacks from the kitchen and hid them in my mother's hut. There's honey too. I wasn't going to feed *them* honey!'

Isabel flung her arms about the girl.

James and Tom came pushing through the crowd to

find Robert. 'You'll like this!' they told him. They could not stop laughing and slapping each other.

'Whatever can you find so funny?' Philippa asked.

'The Sheriff,' cried James. 'The villagers have got him bound and gagged in one of their huts. They wish to hang him.'

'No!' Philippa chuckled. 'Hanging's too good. We should roast him alive!'

As darkness fell, the villagers fetched out trestles and stools and set them up around the still-burning ruins of the manor house. They brought trenchers of fresh-baked bread, piled high with nuts and fruit and little honey-sweetened soul cakes. Small cooking fires were lit around the main blaze and children set to turn the spits. Soon Langden was full of delicious smells as roasting fowls were slowly cooked. Jugs of good barley ale were brought from the cottages and Isabel gathered her friends for a strange feast.

The Knights of Saint Lazarus were given the seats of honour. They accepted politely but remained in their own small group, keeping a distance from the crowd.

Tom, with Alan at his side, went hesitantly towards the quiet, hooded fighting men. Walter of Stainthorpe turned and saw their approach. He held up his hand to stop them.

'Show tha clapper,' Tom told Alan.

The boy snatched up the clapper that swung at his belt and sent it clacking. There was sudden quiet as all turned to see what was happening. The leper knights looked at each other for a moment, but then Walter of

Stainthorpe pulled up a stool and beckoned the boy to sit with them.

Robert sat with Marian, deep in thought, his face mottled in the flickering light and shadows. He was silent despite the celebration all about him.

'What is it?' Marian shook his hand. 'Why are you so miserable, when we are celebrating? Never have guisers been so welcome at a feast. You saved us!'

'Aye, but for how long, sweetheart?' he asked.

Marian frowned too then, and sighed. She could see that he was right. How long would it be before the Sheriff's men came hunting them, their numbers swelled and weapons sharp.

'But just a moment!' said Robert. 'I think I have an idea.' A slow smile touched the corner of his mouth.

'What is it now?' Marian demanded.

Robert cracked out laughing. 'I have it!' he said. 'John, bring the Sheriff here!'

John looked a little surprised but did as his friend asked and dragged the terrified man from the hut towards the fire.

'Aye,' said Philippa. 'I said we should roast him!'

The Sheriff buckled at the knees with fright and Philippa burst out laughing.

'Untie his hands!' said Robert. There were gasps of surprise from all around, but Tom quickly cut the Sheriff's bonds.

'Where's Magda?' Robert cried. 'Come here, honey! Do you remember our feast in Nottingham Castle?'

'Aye,' she cried.

'Now we shall return the compliment. The Sheriff's lady made us guests and showed us a little kindness too.'

'Yes,' Isabel agreed. 'The Sheriff's lady let me bring my mother safe home.'

Robert picked up a stool and courteously invited the Sheriff to sit and eat. The man was white-faced and petrified, but sat as he was bidden.

Quiet fell as the villagers stared. Then resentful muttering rose all around.

'Has the Hooded One gone mad?'

'Drunk?'

'Stupid?'

But Marian put fresh roast meat on to a trencher and passed it to the Sheriff. 'It's plain but wholesome,' she told him. 'Eat up!'

Warily the Sheriff began to nibble at his food.

'When we have feasted,' Robert bellowed, 'we shall see our Sheriff dance around our Samhain fire.'

There was laughter then and protests faded. Soon everyone was eating and drinking again.

It was noon the next day by the time they all woke. They'd slept late on the floors of Langden's huts, now they yawned and stretched and wearily prepared to return to their homes.

But before they went, Isabel gathered visitors and villagers alike around the still-smoking mound of the manor house. Lady Matilda was carried out on a litter and gently lowered to the ground. Then John led forward the Sheriff and his horse. The man was pale, clearly still fearful that they'd kill him.

Once more Robert ordered the man's hands untied. James and Mother Veronica unrolled two carefully written sheets of parchment that they'd been working on. James read them out loud, so that all the assembled villagers could hear.

'I, Gilbert de Gorre, High Sheriff of Nottinghamshire, Yorkshire and Derbyshire, do solemnly declare that the Lady Matilda of Langden shall dispose of her daughter Isabel in marriage where she will. This I assert in the name of His Majesty King John, who as Shire Reeve I represent. To be witnessed by Veronica, Prioress of Saint Mary Magdalen's nuns, and Sir Walter of Stainthorpe, Knight of the Order of Saint Lazarus.'

A ripple of surprise and agreement went around the gathering as at last the villagers began to see some sense in Robert's madness. The Sheriff was given pen and ink and he glumly signed both papers.

'Now,' cried Robert, 'fasten him to his horse.'

The Sheriff's face was red with shame as he was roughly tied on to his horse, wrong way round. Robert rolled up one of the parchments and thrust it into the Sheriff's jerkin. Walter of Stainthorpe took up the other, handling it carefully in his gloved gauntlets.

'This copy shall be kept in the preceptory of Bitterwood,' he said. 'Should the agreement be broken, I shall call upon my Templar brethren to bring about the execution of justice.'

The Sheriff nodded, sick at the very thought. Robert

bent forward and spoke low to him.

'Thank your lady wife for your life!' he hissed.

Then he slapped the horse's backside and Tom led the miserable man away from Langden towards the bounds of Clipstone.

Later that day the Knights of Saint Lazarus saddled their horses and packed the armour and weapons that had provided disguise. Walter of Stainthorpe strode close to where Alan stood with Tom.

'Boy?' he called in his husky voice. 'We have need of one strong fellow to come with us and help us with our steeds and goods.'

'Me?' cried Alan, his face lighting up.

'Who better?' Walter asked.

Alan took a step forwards eagerly. 'I'll come, sir, willingly, but might I not stay with you? I'd serve you, sir in any way I could.'

'Aye? Indeed!' Walter cried. 'Would you learn to be my squire?'

Doubt and delight showed clear on Alan's face. 'You'll have me?'

'Certainly! You shall be my squire, and if you train hard to fight and pray, maybe in time you shall be knight!'

Then as Alan went with Tom to collect his few belongings, Walter of Stainthorpe went down on one knee before Mother Veronica. He took her hand in his great gauntlet.

'Madam, I am still your knight,' he said.

*　*　*

When at last it was time for them to go, Magda went to Alan hesitantly. She took his hand and pressed it to her face. Tears spilled down her cheeks.

'Don't cry,' he whispered. 'I am happier than I ever thought to be. Some day I'll come back and spar with thee.'

The Forestwife and her friends gathered at Langden for the Christmas feasts. The sturdy new manor house had been built with great effort before the coldest weather came. New Langden Manor was smaller and cosier, and Matilda and Isabel insisted that Christmas there was better than ever, with their friends all gathered about them.

There was sudden anxiety when in the middle of the meal, a red-faced kitchen lad announced the arrival of men and horses in the Sheriff's livery. Everyone got up from the table fearfully and ran to the door. Worries were soon turned to delight. It was not an armed guard, but a packhorse train, loaded with warm rugs and fine worked wallhangings. A present to Lady Matilda from the Sheriff's wife.

Winter passed and Langden and Barnsdale knew peace. The simple Christmas gifts had done much to calm nagging doubts, and as spring returned the forest folk planned their May Day revels once more.

It was May Day morning and inside the Forestwife's cottage, the fire was crackling.

'Hold still!' Marian cried.

Magda found it hard not to wriggle as Marian fastened the laces on the fine white linen gown that Isabel had brought for her. This year Marian had insisted right from the start that she was far too ancient to be the Green Lady.

The old one nodded mysteriously. 'It should be Magda,' she said. 'Best she learns soon what she must do.'

Magda frowned. 'What do you mean? Can you see what my life shall be?'

Eleanor shook her head. 'I cannot see it all, sweetheart, but this I know. That fine worked girdle round Marian's waist shall one day be yours.'

Magda caught her breath. 'I shall be Forestwife?'

Suddenly loving and fearful, she went and put her arms around Marian's neck.

Eleanor smiled. 'Not for a long time yet, but some day.'

'But if Robert is old or gone, there'll be no Hooded One to help me.'

Marian and Eleanor both laughed and Eleanor spoke firmly. 'There will always be a Forestwife and there will always be a Hooded One.'

In the distance they heard faint voices singing sweetly, but Magda was not satisfied.

'Who will he be?' she insisted.

Eleanor shook her head. 'Look to the Green Man,' she said.

'I thought that would be Father or Robert.'

Magda was uncertain about dancing with the Green Man if she didn't know who it was hidden inside all those leaves, but there was no time left to worry. The singers were at the door, demanding to crown her. Marian kissed her.

'Don't be afraid,' she said. 'You will enjoy being May Queen.'

Eleanor flung the door open and the hut was filled with children. They crowned Magda with sweet-smelling hawthorn and dragged her out to the maypole by the trysting tree. Robert and John were waiting there for them. Marian went to hug them both, while the children ran off into the woods.

'Who can he be?' Magda whispered, her heart thumping wildly.

At last the children were returning, dragging the strange leaf-clad figure out from the shadows into the sunlight.

Magda bit her lip and twisted her fingers together. The Green Man came dancing towards her . . . then suddenly she caught her breath and smiled with understanding. The Green Man was tall and beautiful, but as he danced and twirled, he dragged his right leg just a little. Magda held out her arms and ran towards him – the magical Green Man.

❧

Part III

THE PATH OF THE SHE-WOLF

42

Brig's Night

Some five years later on a bright chill morning early in December, Marian strode through Barnsdale Woods carrying bundles of herbs on her back. She was exhausted and saddened for she'd spent the night nursing a sick man, only to see him die as dawn came. She slowed her steps and looked about her seeking consolation from the woodlands that she loved.

Great swathes of grass were blanched with frost. A few small patches stood out bright green, where sun came spiking starlike through the trees. Those glorious patches steamed with mist. Marian's spirits lifted and she stretched out her fingers to touch the stiff white fur of frost that coated branches and twigs. The brown bones of last summer's bracken glistened in the sharp sun.

A distant regular thud told her that the coal diggers had started their work, and a tiny weasel shot across her feet into the cover of dried ferns. Suddenly Marian stopped.

Instinctively, she stood as still and rooted as the trees that surrounded her while a dark shape emerged from the undergrowth. It was a she-wolf. The creature leapt silently across her path; passing in an instant.

Marian was not afraid, for the wolf had no interest in a tired, middle-aged wisewoman. But long after it had gone she still stood there, seeing again the sleek brown, grey coat, the floating tail, the ripple of powerful muscles beneath the fur. The she-wolf travelled through the wintry woods at speed, calmly going about her business.

Marian set off again, her step a little lighter; knowing that she too must go her own way, follow her own path.

It was the first night of February. Magda crept away from the Forestwife's cottage into the woods, after dusk. She was now a strong young woman of twenty years. Once out of sight of the circling grove of yew trees, she leapt lightly through the familiar undergrowth, picking her way through the woods to the little woven bower of willow wands that she had made secretly during the day.

She took off her woollen girdle and wove it in and out, back and forth, until it became part of the bower, then from inside her kirtle she pulled a tiny straw plaited doll. She pushed it between one of the loops that her twisted girdle formed, so that it was held there firmly and bobbed up and down in the breeze. Then she sat back on her heels and solemnly chanted:

> *'Brig, Brig, bring us a bairn.*
> *Bonny as flowers.*
> *Bright as the day.*
> *Brave as a wolf.'*

Magda sat there for a while, watching the Biddy doll bounce up and down, and she sighed. Many a woman, both young and old, would be doing the same thing this night, warm by their hearths. But Magda felt that she must do it shamefully in secret. She could not explain to Marian the great wish she had for a child. The Forestwife would be full of sensible, practical objections.

'You're too young! We're so busy! Haven't you got enough to do, helping me with all the suffering folk that come here to the clearing? Anyway, wishes never do come true in the way you want them to!'

Magda pushed these nagging doubts away as she pulled her girdle carefully out of the bower and fastened it around her waist once more. However foolish Marian might think her still the young woman's spirits rose, for the woods were full of sweet scents and magical mists. On Brig's Night the year was young and fresh, and on such a night Magda could believe that her wish might be granted.

When Magda got back to the cottage Marian was outside, holding up a lantern and talking in a low urgent voice to two strangers. The chickens and geese fussed and honked at the interruption to their sleep. Cats circled about the newcomers, waving their tails, greeting them with curiosity and suspicion. The smoking lantern gave enough flickering light to show a poor woman, her face contorted with pain, far gone in labour, a pale girl-child beside her, trembling with fear.

'Ah Magda,' Marian spoke with relief at her return. 'I need you. These two met a giant of a man whilst wandering in the woods, so they say. They were very fearful, but instead of harming them, he sent them here.'

Magda laughed. 'Aye. That would be John, my father,' she said.

Marian smiled for a moment, but she was too concerned for the plight of the woman to spend more time teasing. 'Here Magda, take this bairn will you and feed her. Take her through to the lean-to and find bedding.'

Magda nodded. She reached up to the shelf for the stone pitcher that they saved the goats milk in, and took a hunk of grainy bread from beside the hearth stone. This was a common enough situation and Magda was well used to sorting out frightened children.

She lit a rush-light from Marian's lantern. 'Follow me!' she told the girl, then headed through to the lean-to. They were greeted by much friendly bleating from the few goats that had been spared for the winter and now slept warm in amongst the straw.

Though the girl's hands still shook she ate hungrily, dipping sops of bread into the warm goat's milk. Magda scraped together a pile of straw and made a sleeping place with the rugs that they kept there.

'Now, settle down for the night,' Magda told her when she'd finished eating. 'Your mother will be well taken care of.'

The girl lay down obediently, but though exhausted, she lay on the bundled straw restless and wide-eyed.

'Can't you sleep?' Magda asked, after a while.

The girl shook her head.

'I'll sleep here with you,' Magda said, thinking practically that she might as well stay there for the night as her own pallet by the hearthstone must surely be taken by the labouring mother. She made another straw pile and sank down onto it with a sigh.

'Don't fear,' she said to the girl. 'All will be well.' Magda lay back and smiled to herself. It seemed to her almost as though Brig had answered her prayer immediately, but as Marian always said not quite in the way that she'd hoped for. 'Ah Brig,' she muttered to herself. 'I asked for a bairn and you sent me a strange little lass and a babe arriving soon.' Then she spoke more loudly to the girl. 'What do they call you, honey?'

The child stared up at her with large, dark, fearful eyes. Then suddenly she seemed to muster her courage and spoke with dignity. 'My name is Brigit,' she said.

'Oh!' Magda gasped, her heart thundering, for a moment. 'How strange! You are Brigit, and you come here to us on Brig's Night.' Then she told herself not to be stupid. There were many young girls named Brigit for the popular Christian Saint who'd once lived in Ireland and whose feast day came at the beginning of February. But others whispered that Brig's Night was much older than Christianity and brought a magic more ancient, belonging to the fierce goddess Brigantia whose people had lived here, long ago.

Magda blew out the rush-light but senses that Brigit, though still now and silent beside her, lay wide awake. 'What a strange lass,' she told herself. 'Why cannot I be content with things as they are? What have I brought here? What have I wished for now?'

The next morning found Magda hard at work in the clearing, bending and pegging down the tips of the lowest branches on one of the great yews. She hammered the pegs firmly into dry ground, making a meagre hut that would shelter the poor mother and her two children for a little while once the ordeal of birth was safely over.

Brigit dragged spindly willow branches towards her from the woods, while animal-like bellows came from the hut. The girl looked anxiously up at Magda but said nothing.

'Don't fear,' Magda told her cheerfully. 'The bairn will soon be born, and then you shall have a new brother or sister. Marian, the Forestwife is the best midwife in Barnsdale.'

Magda spoke with a confidence she did not quite feel. It was true that nobody knew more about birthing than Marian, but this labour was going on for a long time, far too long. The mother must be growing exhausted.

The girl's eyes suddenly swam with tears. 'Aye,' she whispered at last. 'But I think the bairn should have been born by now, and . . . my father should be here.'

'Aye. So he should,' Magda agreed. 'Where is the man?'

The girl hiccuped, and swallowed hard. 'In

Nottingham Gaol. He's sent there for breaking the Forest Laws. We fear he'll die before they try him.' Once released, tears now flowed fast down her cheeks, as she sobbed out her worst fears. 'And . . . and when they do try him, well, we cannot pay the fine. There is nowt for him but to lose fingers, or maybe an eye, and I cannot bear to think of my father blinded.'

Magda dropped the branch that she held and went to fling her arms about the child. She spoke through gritted teeth, with quiet anger. 'There's not many that can pay the Forest Court's high fines! This new Sheriff puts them up every month.'

'All Father did was take a hare!' Brigit cried.

'Damn this evil king and his Forest Laws,' Magda growled. 'We hear now that he's taken another stretch of waste, north of Langden, and turned it into Royal Hunting Forest. He gets rid of the old Sheriff, who was nought but a buffoon and brings in this new man, de Rue, who's utterly ruthless in his duty and carries not a drop of compassion in his blood.'

'Aye, they all fear him,' Brigit agreed.

Now Magda was in full spate there was no stopping her. 'The king turns the very food in our mouths and the earth beneath our feet to money for his wars!' She spat on the ground, then spoke more gently seeing that her anger did nought to help the child's misery. 'But we are your friends Brigit, and we will not let you or your mother starve. Your father is not the only one to go hunting in Sherwood. If my father had a pound for every hare he'd taken, he'd be a rich man.'

'Your father breaks the Forest Laws too?' Brigit gasped.

'Every day of his life, honey,' Magda laughed.

Despite her fears, the girl could not hold back her curiosity about these strange woodland folk. 'Is the Forestwife your mother?' she asked.

Brigit and her mother had struggled fearfully through the wastes, knowing only the frightening stories that they'd heard of a witchlike woman who lived hidden magically away in the deepest part of Barnsdale with the wild Hooded One, the wolf-man, who was her companion.

Magda smiled at the question. 'The Forestwife is not the mother I was born to,' she said. 'My mother died when I was a babe. Marian has mothered me ever since, but my father is that giant fellow John. The one who sent you here from Sherwood.'

Brigit's eyes opened wide. 'They say that he walks with the Hooded One, along with the rebel monk whose fierce hound catches arrows and snaps them in its mouth!'

Magda laughed. 'Aye, all that is true, but believe me, you've nowt to fear from them. Now you forget about those wicked outlaw fellows for a while, for we must get this shelter made. We'll weave the willow in and out of the yew branches and lay turfs of grass on the top. Then there'll be a dry, sweet-smelling hut, all ready when your mother comes from the Forestwife's cottage with a fine new babe in her arms.'

More grunts and moans could be heard, but Magda

ignored the sounds of pain and made Brigit work even harder. They were almost finished and laying rushes on the floor of the makeshift shelter when the sound of a galloping horse frightened the girl.

Magda stopped to listen, a warning finger to her lips. The thundering of the hooves ceased and a peculiar stamping rhythm followed. Magda's stern face broke into a smile.

'Don't fear,' she shook her head. 'It's my sweetheart Tom on his fine horse Rambler. I swear he loves that horse as much as me! He's slowed up now and he's finding his way through the secret maze of paths that keeps our clearing safe and hidden.'

They came out from the new shelter as a grey stallion entered the clearing. Tom rode as though he'd been born on horseback. Hanging over the horse's rump was a large, dead stag, a fallow deer from the Royal Hunting Forest of Sherwood.

'You see,' Magda told Brigit, pointing to the beast. 'I told you your father was not alone in breaking the laws.'

43

The Bishop of Hereford

Tom swung down from the saddle and hugged Magda. Brigit smiled shyly while they kissed passionately. As Tom led his horse towards the Forestwife's cottage, Magda questioned him.

'What is it? Why do you look so pleased?'

'His Grace the Bishop of Hereford comes visiting!'

'What here? Visiting us?'

'Aye. Robert and John are bringing him, and his men. They follow close behind with Brother James.'

Magda was shocked. 'Here to our secret place?'

Tom laughed. 'That's why I fetch this beast. We shall dine on roast venison.'

'You must be mad to feed a bishop on the King's deer?'

Tom shook his head. 'The bishop will not blink at it. He will delight in it.'

Suddenly Magda remembered the birthing. She grabbed Tom's arm and pulled him back, away from the cottage. 'Stop! We must wait! Marian will not thank us for bothering her just now. There's a child coming into its life.' She nodded at the watchful girl behind her.

Tom stopped obediently but the eager look would not leave his face. 'This is the Bishop of Hereford,' he began. 'He's no supporter of the king.'

But Magda would not listen.

'Since when do we feast with bishops?' she cried. 'What does Robert think he's doing?'

Tom laughed and kissed her nose. 'We meant to rob him; you know how Robert teases these rich travellers. He found great bags of gold on the pack-mules in the bishop's train, and swore he'd invite the bishop to dine, then make him pay for it. But then we discovered the man's name, and reason he rides south with such a great store of gold!'

Brigit tugged at Magda's arm. 'More horses,' she cried, excitement overcoming her fear. 'Your father the giant, a hooded man and the monk—'

Then into the clearing strode Robert and John; Brother James followed them, his dog Fetcher leaping at his heels. Magda ran to hug her father. Robert led a huge fine-decked stallion, a tall man with white close-cropped hair astride. The visitor was clad in good leather riding breeks and boots, and a fine purple cloak, a gold cross hung about his neck; they were followed by twenty men at arms, more pack-horses and a wagon.

'Grand visitors for you daughter,' cried John, stooping low to give Magda a kiss.

'Marian!' Robert bellowed, pleased as could be. 'Come out and see who I've brought. Here's His Grace the Bishop of Hereford wishes to meet the Forestwife.'

'She's busy,' Magda hissed.

But the woven curtain that covered the doorway to the cottage was thrown aside. Marian came from the shadows into the light, her face pale, grey flecked hair ruffled, her apron soaked with fresh blood. In her arms she carried a tiny newly born child. She blinked at Robert stupidly, then looked past him to the bishop who still sat astride his horse.

'Forgive us Your Grace,' she spoke quietly. 'It's not the best time for visitors. This babe has had a struggle to be born, and his mother has just lost her life.'

There was a moment of silence then a small hiccuping sob came from Brigit. 'You said . . . y-you said the Forestwife would save her.'

'I did believe she would.' Magda turned slowly, her face full of sorrow, and went to gather the distressed child into her arms.

Wearily Marian set about cleaning herself and organising a feast. She sent Tom to beg help from their friends. Philippa and Isabel came from Langden Manor. With them came Will Stoutley, Robert's friend, who'd gone to work as Langden's reeve when the old Lady Matilda died and Isabel became Lady of the Manor in her own right. They also brought a strong young mother who was willing to feed the newly born babe along with her own.

Mother Veronica and Sister Rosamund came and Gerta the old besom-maker, who lived close by with her three young grandsons. They all brought food and drink to swell the feast and soon the clearing was thronging with bustle and work.

John and Brother James butchered the deer, fixed up a spit and got fires going for roasting. A trestle table was set close to the fire as the evening turned chill. They worked fast together, for Robert was in the habit of bringing unexpected visitors to dine. Though never before had he brought anyone as rich and powerful as the Bishop of Hereford; Robert usually had quite a different way of dealing with bishops!

Magda took no part in the preparations but sat in the small shelter with Brigit, trying to give what little comfort she could, talking and soothing until the child at last fell exhausted to sleep. Marian busied herself with washing and wrapping the new babe, and then with food preparations, ignoring Robert and the bishop. Indeed the two men were soon so deep in conversation that no courteous words of ceremony or welcome seemed needed. They spoke together in low urgent voices and Marian recognised the note of quiet excitement in Robert. She knew it only too well.

'What does this mean?' she asked herself. 'What wild scheme are we in for now?'

It was only when the meat was cooked and served with trenchers of fresh baked bread that Marian sat down and spoke to their guest.

'Humble food, Your Grace,' she said. 'But fresh and wholesome.'

The Bishop shook his head dismissing her worries. 'I eat very little,' he said.

Marian could believe that; the man was thin as a willow wand. At least he was no pampered overfed lover of luxury as so many of the bishops seemed to be.

'Marian,' Robert stood up formally and bowed to the Bishop. 'Let me present to you His Grace the Bishop of Hereford, Giles de Braose.'

Marian gasped and stared at the Bishop with new interest. 'De Braose? Did you say de Braose?'

Brother James laughed at her surprise. 'We thought that would interest you.'

'Are you . . . ?' Marian faltered. 'Are you?'

An expression of pain touched the Bishop's face, and he nodded. 'I am the brother of William who died an exile in France. Matilda de Braose was my very dear sister-in-law, and well—' the Bishop clenched his jaw. 'You know what happened to her, and my poor nephew.'

There was a moment of quiet. All the forest folk knew only too well how the King had taken Matilda prisoner along with her son and it was whispered fearfully throughout the country that he'd starved them to death.

'Did the King's quarrel touch you . . . er, Your Grace?' Philippa asked, curiosity getting the better of courtesy.

Giles de Braose swallowed hard, looking round at all their serious faces. He seemed touched by their concern but Marian got the impression of a man who rarely let his feelings show.

'Me? I fled to France, but the king has invited me back

and reinstated me. The fool thinks that I have forgiven him.' A wry smile touched the corners of his mouth. 'Now I travel the Great North Road from Helmsley Castle, where Robert de Ros gathers together an army of northerners. The gold I carry will buy weapons and fighting men for those who support us in the South. We shall bring out our charter, the one that is true to the laws King Henry made, and demand that the King reinstate his father's rule, and begin to deal justly with this country. If he will not, then believe me, his days are numbered, and at last my family shall be revenged.'

Marian nodded her head. Now it all became clear. There had been many whispers from those who passed through Barnsdale that even the most powerful northern barons were tired of King John's constant demands. He invented new fines and taxes every day, funding battles on foreign soil that were meaningless to all but him. So now, at last, rebellion was truly in the air.

The Bishop's men ate heartily of the King's deer, but the Bishop took little food. The outlaws ate quietly, with restraint, thoughtful at the Bishop's news.

Robert was fired with excitement. 'We could muster a hundred archers,' he suggested. 'Poor men, ill-fed and ragged, but greatly skilled with the bow and they are full of bitter resentment and hungry for change.'

The Bishop looked stunned for a moment but then he accepted this offer of support, though it came from so strange a quarter. 'Such men would be of value. I shall send word to you,' he promised. 'As soon as we are ready to move.'

'We'll come at once,' Robert assured him. 'We'll march to join you, travelling day and night.'

Marian looked from the Bishop to the outlaw, uneasy at this willingness for battle. Though so different in their stations in life, yet still they were two of a kind. The same fanatical gleam was there in the eyes.

As the evening air turned cold Marian got up and taking a flaming brand from the fire she went to the newly built hut. Magda was sitting shivering on the floor with her arms wrapped about Brigit. The girl's face was puffy and tearstained, but she slept.

'I think we should bring her out to the fire now,' Marian told her. 'Even though it means waking her, we must warm you both and make her eat and drink.'

Magda moved gently so that the child began to wake. 'Come, wake up now, sleepy one,' she spoke softly. Then her tone changed and she asked angrily, nodding at the Bishop. 'What is he doing here?'

Marian sighed. 'He is Giles de Braose, brother-in-law to the great Matilda that the King starved to death.'

Magda's eyes opened very wide. 'The one who was locked up with her son and neither of them seen again?'

Marian nodded. 'This man fled to France, but now he's back and, believe me, he is bent on vengeance. Now do you understand?'

'Oh yes,' said Magda. 'Yes, I do.' Then she turned to Brigit, who was stirring, and starting to shiver. 'Come on, poor lass,' she whispered. 'Time to warm you up and fill your belly.'

At last the girl woke properly. 'My mother?' she murmured.

'I fear that is true sweetheart. Your mother has gone, but now you must eat and drink and warm yourself, for you must go on living.' Magda pulled her to her feet and led her firmly towards the fire.

Brigit was made to eat. She was too tired and miserable to argue and sat quietly nibbling at the food and warming her hands. Magda left her in Marian's care and went to sit between her father and Tom. He rubbed her back and shoulders. 'You're freezing Magda,' he said.

The Bishop watched Marian as she fed the young girl who shivered and wept, but obediently accepted the food. 'This child,' he asked. 'She is the daughter of the poor woman who died and sister to that new-born child?'

Marian nodded.

'Has she no father?' he asked.

'Aye, she has, but . . .' Marian explained the man's plight. 'There is no money to pay his fine, and like so many he rots in Nottingham gaol.'

'That is one thing that the barons will demand of the King,' the Bishop said. 'We shall put this wicked ruler into a state of fear and demand removal of the Forest Laws.'

Marian looked across at Robert, and stopped feeding Brigit for a moment, spoon in hand. Everyone turned quiet at the sound of the Bishop's words. An expression of hope was there, just for an instant, on every face gathered about the flickering firelight.

'Now that,' said Marian quietly, 'would really mean something to us. That would truly be something worth fighting for.'

The Bishop waved one of his men forward and whispered in his ear. The man at once took a purse from his belt and gave it to his master. 'The barons can spare a little of their gold to pay one man's fine,' he said. 'Who will take this purse to Nottingham and fetch the child her father back?'

Everyone smiled and some clapped. 'I will take it Your Grace,' said Tom willingly.

Brigit looked up puzzled as the purse was passed from hand to hand.

'What are they doing?' she asked.

Marian took her hand. 'I believe they are going to get your father back for you,' she said.

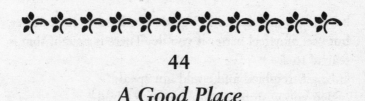

44

A Good Place

The Bishop and his men rode out of the clearing early next morning with Robert, and James to set them on their way. Tom went along with them on Rambler, travelling as far as Nottingham, the Bishop's purse hidden in his jerkin.

Magda was soon at her most hated job, digging a rubbish pit, for the Bishop's overnight stay had left the clearing littered with chewed bones and soiled rushes. She insisted that Brigit should help her. 'It'll take her mind off the waiting,' she said.

Marian agreed, but towards noon she came to take Brigit to one side. 'How old are you, honey?' she asked.

'I'm twelve,' Brigit told her solemnly.

Marian sighed. 'Old enough for sorrow,' she said. 'Old enough to know your mind. Come with me.'

She led Brigit towards the cottage, but when the girl understood where they were going she pulled back, knowing that her mother's body still lay inside. Marian put her arm around the girl's shoulders. 'You do not have to go in,' she said. 'You do not have to look at her, but you may feel better if you do. There is naught that is fearful to see.'

Brigit trembled and could not speak.

'Do you wish to see your mother, child?'

'Yes,' she whispered.

'Come then.' Marian took her by the hand and led her inside.

What the Forestwife had said was true. There was nothing to fear. Old Gerta had washed the mother's body and combed her hair. She'd covered her with a clean soft woollen cloak and set a small, sweet scented posy of snowdrops in the work-roughened hands. The careworn face was smoothed into an expression of peaceful rest.

Brigit knelt down and gently stroked her mother's hair.

Marian looked across at Gerta and tears filled both the women's eyes to see the young girl's touching gesture. Though they were constantly faced with pain and suffering, it never ceased to hurt. Marian dashed away the tears and forced herself to be practical. 'We cannot leave your mother unburied. We do not know how many days it will be before Tom can bring your father back. We could carry her to the Sisters of the Magdalen. They would give her a Christian burial in their churchyard, or we may bury her here at the top of the clearing where past Forestwives sleep beneath the yew trees. You must tell us what you want.'

Brigit shook her head. 'I cannot think,' she said.

Gerta got up and put her arm about the girl's shoulders. 'Would you like Marian to show you the place?'

'Aye,' Brigit allowed herself to be led back outside.

At the top of the clearing between two ancient yews there lay a row of unmarked graves, humps in the ground.

'It's very quiet here,' the girl whispered.

Marian nodded. 'We believe this clearing to be an ancient place of healing, with its circle of yews and magical warm spring. We do not know how old it is, but for as long as any of us can remember there has been a Forestwife living here; someone who will give help to any who come seeking it and do her best to heal.'

'We thought you a witch,' Brigit said, shamed at their foolishness. 'And we were fearful, but I am not feared of you now.'

Marian smiled. 'I am but a woman. I sometimes wish I were a witch, if such magic would give me better skills. I would have given anything to have saved your mother for you.'

'I know that you tried.' Brigit spoke with surprising maturity. 'I know that you did your best. Are these the graves of the ancient Forestwives?'

'Yes, but not only them. This one was Agnes, the old Forestwife and my dear nurse; she was also Robert's mother. This was Emma, my sweetest friend and Magda's mother. This one with still fresh earth is my own mother, Eleanor. The forest folk called her the Old

One. It's just two months since I came home to find she'd died.'

'Did you feel all dull and tight inside you?' Brigit touched her chest.

'Aye,' Marian said. 'I did feel that, but it's slowly getting better. That morning, before I knew she'd died, I saw a she-wolf out in the woods. When I got back and found my mother gone, I thought the she-wolf had been my mother's spirit and I was so glad that I'd seen her going bravely on her way.'

Brigit nodded. 'This is a good place,' she said. 'My mother used to make herb medicines for the village folk – she'd like this place. Will you bury my mother here?'

Robert and James returned, noisy and energetic with their plans. 'We'll send word to all our friends. We'll muster every man we know,' Robert told Marian. 'Philippa's blacksmith husband is willing, and Rowan, too. Philippa says she is going, for she's determined not to lose her youngest son, and she says they'll need someone sensible to keep an eye on them! Isabel agrees that Will may go though she says she doesn't know how she'll manage without him. What about you, sweetheart? We'll be in desperate need of a healer. You were never far behind when it came to a fight!'

But Marian shook her head. 'I have bad feelings about it all,' she said. 'Though Giles de Braose seems to be an honourable man, I do not trust the other barons. Since when have they helped such as us? Besides, there must be a Forestwife here.'

As soon as Magda finished filling in the rubbish pit, Marian asked her to start digging the grave.

'Am I the only one around here who can wield a shovel?' she complained. 'Ask my father, he that is so big and strong. He's getting fat, he needs the exercise!'

John came to her laughing. They wrestled over the shovel. 'Give it to me then daughter. I'll show you how it's done.' Then suddenly their laughter died as they saw Brigit watching them.

'I should like to dig my mother's grave,' she said solemnly.

'Come little one,' said John quietly taking her hand. 'We'll all help, and do the job together.'

They assembled to bury the poor mother as dusk fell. The young wet-nurse came over from Langden to join them at the graveside, her own big babe on one hip and the tiny child cradled in her other arm. The older child wriggled about and the new-born babe began to cry. Both Magda and Marian moved to help, but then stood back as Brigit strode over to the woman and took her brother into her arms. She rocked the child gently and stuck her little finger into his mouth. The child was instantly soothed.

Magda and Marian looked at each other. 'How old is she?' Magda whispered.

'Older than her years,' Marian quietly replied.

'Sorrow can do that to young folk,' Gerta agreed.

Magda went to stand beside Brigit. 'Your new brother

should be named,' she said. 'You are his sister. You should be the one to name him.'

Brigit looked uncertain for a moment but then smiled down at the baby's soft patch of hair. 'My father is called Peter,' she said. 'I shall call my brother Peterkin for him.'

'Peterkin is a fine name,' Magda touched the baby's cheek.

The days that followed were full of bustle, and the Forestwife's clearing was filled with the smell of hot metal poured to make arrowheads. The scrape of knife on wood could be heard as they worked hard to finish new strong bows. Arrows went whistling towards their targets, for Robert had all who presented themselves willing at bow practice each day.

Gerta's three grandsons begged to join the older men but the old woman was adamant that they were far too young and she marched them away, back to their small home in the woods, so that they shouldn't be tempted further by watching the preparations. Philippa and her husband were to go with Isabel's blessing, for their skills as blacksmiths would be needed as much as those willing to fight.

'Promise me you'll stay out of the battle?' Marian begged her friend.

Philippa had sighed. 'Oh aye,' she said. 'There'll be plenty to do without fighting. I dare say they'll have me hammering the dints from their swords and straightening crumpled arrowheads. They'll want their wounds tending, and they'll all need feeding. Trust me, I won't be joining any battle.'

'I don't trust you, any more than I trust Robert,' said Marian, hugging her tightly. 'Just make sure you come back safely to us.'

Magda was excited by all the plans and action that surrounded her home. She spoke of going with the men but John would not agree to it. A happy relief from the warlike plans came when Tom brought back Brigit's father safe and well from Nottingham Jail. Brigit was overjoyed to see him but her happiness did not last long for the man was determined to join the rebels.

'But father we need you, me and little Peterkin,' she told him.

'Do you feel safe here with the Forestwife?' he asked.

'Yes,' she agreed.

'Please try to understand. I must go to fight against these wicked Forest Laws. They make our lives a misery.'

Brigit just stared at him, deep sadness in her eyes.

When Magda spoke again of going to fight, Tom silenced her by pointing to Brigit. 'She needs you my love,' he said. 'More than ever now that her father insists on coming.'

Soon after Easter one of the Bishop of Hereford's men rode into the clearing with news that the barons were gathering at Northampton. Brigit's father was amongst those that set off, prepared for battle, all following the Hooded One.

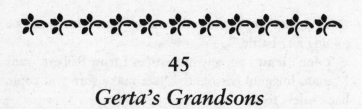

45

Gerta's Grandsons

Though the clearing felt quiet after the army of rebel northerners had gone, there was plenty to do as always. The May Day celebrations were meagre compared with the usual wild feast and dancing that went on, but they didn't let the day go by in silence.

'Who can be our Green Man this year?' Magda wondered. ' 'Tis quite a problem, now that all our men are gone.'

''Twould be good to make young Brigit our May Queen,' Marian, suggested. 'The child is so solemn and forlorn.'

'Ah yes!' Magda agreed. 'The honour would do her good and maybe cheer her and that gives me an idea; a very young Green Man would be just right to dance with Brigit.'

She persuaded Davy, the youngest of Gerta's grandson's, to allow them to paint his cheeks with green woodland dyes and cover his hair and clothes in fresh green leaves. When the misty May morning arrived,

Davy came dancing out from the woodland as the Green Man, bringing the summer in as the sun rose high in the sky. He enjoyed his part and delighted in crowning the surprised Brigit with a garland of sweet hawthorn blossom to make her his Green Lady, and the beautiful May Queen. The older women clapped and sang with determined cheerfulness as the children danced around the maypole by the trysting tree.

As the weather grew warmer, small scraps of news from the rebels reached the Forestwife's clearing and they were grateful for the messages brought by Isabel, whose Manor of Langden lay closer to the Great North Road. Within weeks they heard that the rebels had attacked the King's stronghold at Northampton, while the King stayed near to Oxford, gathering his wolfpack about him. Then the northerners marched on to London, climbing the walls and opening the city gates on a Sunday while the good townsfolk were at mass. They set about besieging the Tower of London.

'Sounds like Robert,' said Magda. 'If it's not his idea, he'll certainly be enjoying himself.'

'Aye,' Marian agreed with a sigh.

'There's some still loyal to the crown,' Isabel told them. 'Nichola la Haye holds Lincoln Castle for the King.'

Marian's mouth dropped open in surprise. 'Nichola . . . the constable's wife. Isn't she a frail old woman? What of her husband?'

Isabel laughed. 'She's old, but I doubt you'd call her

367

frail! Her husband was from home when rebels surrounded Lincoln. They thought they'd take it with ease, but they were wrong. It seems Nichola set about defending the place like a veteran warrior, and they've not moved her.'

'I can't help thinking, good for her!' cried Magda. 'But she's on the wrong side!'

'Yes,' Isabel agreed. 'We should have such a woman organising *our* men!'

Marian shook her head. 'I fear for our men,' she said. 'I don't trust these bishops and barons; I'm sure they're after their own gains. There are no clear sides to this struggle.'

As the weather grew warm and the June buds burst filling the woodland with lush green leaves they heard the most wonderful news. The King was asking for peace and agreeing to meet the rebels at Runnymede, promising he'd give them their charter. While the barons and bishops swore fealty once more to King John, the rebel army feasted.

A smaller celebration took place deep in Barnsdale Woods. The nuns brought bread and ale, Isabel ordered some of her geese slaughtered, and Marian cut down the haunch of venison that had been smoking above her cooking fire for weeks. Magda took young Brigit out into the woods and taught her how to snare rabbits.

The meal they produced was magnificent by their standards. The woodland folk sang, danced and drank, toasting the hoped-for lifting of the Forest Laws. Some of the young boys got a little too bold with drink and staggered off in the direction of Sherwood, swearing that they'd tear the fences down, and let out the deer.

Their mothers were fearful at the idea, but Magda was scornful. 'They'll be in no fit state to tear anything down. They'll end up snoring in a ditch.'

The Forestwife and her friends slept late the next morning. As they rose and began to set everything to rights, some of the lads came stumbling back through the clearing, weak-legged, sick and dazed. Marian made them drink a mug of steaming herb tea, sweetened with honey, while Magda gave them a good telling off.

'Serves you right,' she snapped. 'Puking up like little pigs! What a waste of good barley ale! I hope you have thudding heads all day!'

'We all have to learn,' Marian told them, smiling. 'I seem to remember a little lass that performed a wild dance one May Day feast. Then fell over and had to be carried sick and weeping to her pallet.'

'Hmm!' Magda frowned. 'It was the dancing that made me sick not the drink!'

Brigit swept up dutifully around their feet, saying nothing, but listening and watching, taking everything in.

When the sun was high in the sky, the lads were sent home to stop their mothers from worrying. 'Fresh air and a good fast walk through the woods!' Magda told them. 'That's what you lot need!'

Dusk was falling when Gerta came back into the clearing, her face all creased with worry.

'What is it Gerta?' Magda asked. 'Have those grand-sons of yours still got thick heads?'

'Thick heads or not, I don't know. I've not seen them all day,' said Gerta angrily. 'Our Jack swore he'd mend the fencing on our close, for my grey gander keeps escaping. When those lads get back I'll wring their necks. I wondered if you'd seen them?'

Magda shook her head. 'No, I've not seen your lads, but I shouldn't fret,' she soothed. 'They'll be sleeping it off under some hedge. We've had some of their barley-brained comrades here. Marian dosed them for their pains, but we've not seen your three.'

Gerta folded her arms and shook her head. She looked exhausted. 'I've asked all their friends,' she insisted. 'I've been walking round the woods since noon. All they can tell me is that my lads *did* go off towards Sherwood with axes stuck in their belts.'

Magda began to feel uneasy. Gerta was much loved in Barnsdale, for despite being old and poor, she'd taken her three young grandsons to live with her when their parents both died of the fever. She'd struggled to raise them on her pitiful earnings in her small hut close to Langden. Gerta loved the three boys fiercely and, though she was getting bent and thin with age, she usually kept them well disciplined with the sheer force of her temper.

'Axes in their belts?' Magda muttered. The picture that came into her mind of the three lads marching towards Sherwood brought a chilling touch of anxiety. 'I'll fetch Marian and see what she thinks,' she said.

Marian came out from the cottage followed by Brigit;

she was immediately concerned. 'Towards Sherwood?' she confirmed. 'With axes?'

They made Gerta sit down and without being told, Brigit brought out a warm drink for the old woman. Marian bent and sniffed the brew. 'Camomile,' she said. 'Well chosen, lass.'

'Soothes anxiety,' the girl told her solemnly. 'So mother always said.'

They stood quietly, watching the old woman sip the brew. Marian did not want to make Gerta more fearful, but she was filled with foreboding. The sound of a horse clopping through the darkening woods made them even more worried, but it was Isabel who rode into the clearing. She swung down from her sturdy grey mare and they saw from her face that she had something bad to tell them.

'What now?' whispered Marian.

Isabel would not speak straight out. She sat down beside Gerta and took hold of her hand, then began speaking gently, hating the news that she brought. 'There's three young lads been caught chopping down palings on the edge of Sherwood.'

'No!' Gerta cried.

Isabel nodded. 'I fear so. Hundreds of deer are loosed, and the verderers furious. The new Sheriff de Rue has sent word, they're to be hanged.'

'Ah no!' Gerta cried again.

Magda gasped. Brigit's hands shook as she took the cup back from Gerta; only Marian was stony-faced.

'Not my lads?' Gerta whispered. The old woman stared rocking backwards and forwards while Magda sat down on her other side and tried to comfort her.

Isabel's face twisted with pity. 'There's more, but I don't know whether to say it!'

Gerta stopped rocking at once. 'Tell me!' she demanded. 'I have to know!'

'The three will not give their names, but the oldest is a tall dark haired lad and the youngest fair and nowt but a child.'

'My Davy! They cannot hang my Davy. He's only eleven years old!'

'If my father and Robert were here,' Magda growled. 'If only Tom were here.'

'Well, they are not,' said Marian angrily. 'They have gone off on a wild goose chase. What fools we've all been! How could we think the King would end the Forest Laws just like that?' She snapped her fingers hard. Then she took a deep breath and sighed. 'Well, our men are not here, so we must take action ourselves.'

'Aye,' Isabel agreed. 'We must do something, but what? We must think hard and fast. The lads are due to hang tomorrow at noon at Ollerton Crossroads. The Sheriff himself will ride there to see it done.'

Marian frowned, tapping her head, racking her brains for an idea. Then she suddenly looked up. 'I'm asking myself, what would Robert do if he were here? And I think I know.'

'Huh!' Magda snorted. 'He'd disguise himself in filthy rags. He'd dress himself as a potter, or a priest, or a tinker, and he'd go marching right up to the gibbet!'

'Exactly!' Marian agreed. 'And that is what we will

do! We'll disguise ourselves and we shall go marching right up to the gibbet. But, I do not fancy filthy rags; I have a much more respectable idea. The boys live close to Langden, do they not? The Sisters of the Magdalen are Langden's nuns. Couldn't they insist on seeing them; to pray for their souls? Surely any man who refused such a request would fear his own soul damned!'

'Aye,' whispered Gerta, faintly hopeful. 'My hut's within the bounds of Langden Parish. The sisters would have the right to beg such a favour! But even if you managed to get them away, then the sisters would be followed and punished. We'd all be punished!'

'Yes,' said Isabel. 'But if we disguised ourselves as nuns and called ourselves by another name, not the Sisters of the Magdalen, then perhaps it could just work! It seems your brave lads will not admit they are from Langden, so the Sheriff doesn't know where they really come from. I think they mean to save us from trouble by keeping quiet. It might be just that courage that brings us the means to save them!'

'You could call yourself St Bridget's Nuns,' Brigit suggested, her voice shrill with sudden excitement. 'There were St Bridget's nuns who lived near Goldwell when I was a babe. Mother named me after them. But the last old nun died three years ago and now the convent stands a ruin in the woods.'

Marian hugged her. 'Clever lass!' she cried. 'It would sound real and even familiar, but if the Sheriff should send his men to hunt St Bridget's nuns, they'd find nothing, but a deserted convent.'

Magda laughed. 'It seems we have our plan.'

'Yes, but we must speak with Mother Veronica,' said Isabel. 'I know she'll help.

'I'll take my bow and arrow,' Magda cried. 'Though I never thought to see myself as a nun.'

'Yes,' Marian agreed, her cheeks flushed and eyes bright with anger. 'And I must go to Ollerton too. I do not like to leave the clearing without a Forestwife, but my shooting skills will be needed.'

'Shall I come with you?' Brigit whispered.

Magda shook her head smiling, touched by the offer. This quiet child was certainly no coward. 'She really is as brave as a wolf,' she murmured.

The hopes raised by their plan made Gerta calm and strong once more. 'No honey,' she told Brigit. 'You and I, little lass, we shall be Forestwife while Marian is away. I dare say we can manage well enough together, just for a while.'

Marian nodded. 'That is a good plan Gerta.' She

unfastened the beautiful woven girdle that she wore, the girdle of the Forestwife, retying it carefully around the old woman's thin waist. 'Take care of it,' she said. 'And any who come seeking help.' She kissed them both, then reached to take down her bow from the nail above the small window.

'Get mine too,' Magda was eager to be off. 'I shall fetch the new made arrows from the lean-to.'

'No,' Marian told her. 'There is something important for you to do first. Ride with Isabel and fetch Mother Veronica and Sister Rosamund? We need some real nuns, if we are to be convincing and ask if we may borrow extra veils and habits. Oh, and Isabel, I think we are going to need more horses. Can you find us some?'

Magda and Isabel rode through the woods, obedient to Marian's orders. 'I love her when she is like this,' Magda cried. 'Suddenly she throws aside all her carefulness and hurls herself into a wild adventure, all fired up.'

'Yes!' Isabel agreed, her face drawn with anxiety. 'But what we plan is fraught with danger, Magda?' she said, touching the young woman's arm. 'I do not forget how you came with Marian to rescue me when the wolfpack walled me up, leaving my mother and me to die. You risked your lives to save us then, and now we all risk our lives again for Gerta's lads. This is just as desperate and fearful a thing to attempt!'

Three new-made gibbets stood on the old platform outside the lock-up at Ollerton Crossroads. The Sheriff of

Nottingham's men were busy stringing up nooses. The news that there was to be a hanging had caused quite a stir so that the worn grass around the lock-up thronged with people. Some cheerfully elbowed their way through the crowd to get a good view of the spectacle, but many were moved to pity.

A skinny washerwoman pushing a handcart piled with dirty linen and small children spoke with sorrow. 'So young I hear. Nobbut bairns!'

'Does not this new charter change the law?' asked a stooped and aged alewife who carried her wares in buckets, fixed onto a wooden yoke across her shoulders. 'A hanging's good for business, but I thought the laws were to be changed.'

'Who knows what it does? Can laws change over night like that?'

'They say the Sheriff is making an example of them, won't let it go unpunished. He fears to have every young ruffian in the wastes ripping down palings if he shows mercy.'

'That man hasn't got a drop of mercy in his veins,' came the reply.

Others saw humour in the tragedy. 'Good on the lads,' an old man chuckled. 'They don't die for nowt. The King's deer run wild through Barnsdale and there's plenty with a full belly for once.'

'Aye,' the washerwoman laughed and dug him in the ribs. 'The scent of stewed venison reeks from every hut.'

Shortly before noon a plump, elderly nun came pushing

through the crowd towards the lock-up, followed by six of her sisters.

'Make way, make way! St Bridget's nuns from Goldwell,' Mother Veronica cried. 'These children live close to Goldwell Priory. We have travelled all morning, coming as soon as we heard. We must pray with them.'

The captain hesitated, uncertain as to whether he should allow this seemingly holy intrusion.

'Let us see the young sinners,' the Prioress begged. 'We must be sure that they repent. Should you deny this, why man, you'd risk your own immortal soul.'

The captain argued for a while, but his men shuffled anxiously and crossed themselves. At last he gave way and unlocked the door.

'Only for a moment,' he barked. 'The Sheriff will be here at noon!'

Mother Veronica marched into the darkness of the cramped room, her equally plump sisters crowding close behind her. There was a moment of confusion and hubbub, then the deep clear voice of Sister Rosamund could be heard chanting prayers for the dying.

Mother Veronica appeared again. 'Bless you for your mercy,' she cried making the sign of the cross.

The guards bowed their heads as nine nuns followed their prioress out, one of them very small and stumbling a little on the trailing skirt of the habit. In the pressing crowd it was difficult for the men to see that more nuns came out than had ever gone in. As the Captain turned to lock the heavy door, onlookers pressed close behind him trying to get a glimpse of the ill-fated lads.

Once they were out and through the crowd, the nuns walked fast towards a group of horses sheltering beneath a great oak nearby. Isabel of Langden, already mounted on her own grey mare, held the reins.

A sudden shout of anger was heard above the muttering crowd. 'Empty! Get after them. Unholy bitches! They've got the prisoners! They've taken them!'

The nuns picked up their skirts and ran towards Isabel. People milled about, arguing and pushing, unsure of what was happening, and uncertain as to whose side they should take. This unexpected turn of events was providing nearly as good a show for them as a hanging. The guards roared with fury, shoving folk aside, trying to follow their prisoners, swords drawn. The nuns leapt up onto their waiting horses with wonderful agility. Only aged Mother Veronica had to be hauled onto her mount. They set off galloping north, but two of the tallest nuns held their horses back, snatching up bows from their saddles. They pulled arrows from full quivers hidden beneath their long skirted habits and sent a hail of them flying towards the guards.

The men leapt back, too surprised to answer the attack with speed. Then Marian shouted as she wheeled her horse about. 'Tell your Sheriff this – he shall not hang children! So says the Hooded One.'

The whispered name of the Hooded One flew through the crowd and at once the soldiers found themselves impeded. Buckets of overturned ale made the ground slip beneath their feet, while old men on sticks and small children stumbled against the guards. They roared with anger, as they seemed to trip and tread in piles of soiled linen and clothing whichever way they turned.

The rescuers and rescued got back to Barnsdale exhausted but elated with their success. The nuns returned quickly to their convent and their prayers, cleaning the mud stained habits thoroughly, so that no sign or evidence remained. Gerta's grandsons clung to her as she hugged and berated them in turn.

'This calls for another celebration,' Magda suggested.

'No,' Marian told her dryly. ''Twas too much celebration that brought them close to death. We'll have no more for the moment.'

The boys swore tearfully they'd never drink again.

Later that night, when everyone had gone to their homes, Marian and Magda sat by the fire, quiet and weary. Brigit pounded roots in a wooden bowl, talking excitedly for once. 'I boiled up purslane for a sick baby who'd eaten green apples, and pennyroyal for Freda's birth pains. Then after Gerta had cut the cord, I gave her a warm brew of century to sip. Did I do right?'

Marian smiled. 'I couldn't have done better myself.'

Magda chuckled. 'A great deal better than I could have done.'

Then she lifted her head, suddenly alert at the sound of a horse moving slowly towards them, winding its way through the secret paths. All at once it turned into the familiar stamping rhythm of Rambler's hooves. They jumped up, snatching the lantern, all tiredness forgotten, and ran outside. Tom came riding into the clearing with Brother James mounted behind him. John strode at their side, the faithful Fetcher lolloping after them.

'Now we've got to have a celebration,' Magda cried.

'We'll have a small one,' Marian agreed. Then she sighed. 'Where's Robert?'

The men were tired and dusty from their journey. They sported a good crop of cuts and bruises but were otherwise unharmed.

'You're solemn for men who've just won a charter from their King!' Magda cried.

'Aye,' Tom hugged her tightly, but still would not smile. 'We've got good reason to be solemn. There was little in the charter for the likes of us, most of it favoured the barons – no real changing of the Forest Laws. All the King did was to grudgingly consent to give back the newest stretches of land that he'd put under the Forest Laws. We didn't think much of that! But even that small gain didn't last. Now the King says that he revokes the whole agreement!'

'What?' Magda cried.

'I knew it,' Marian shook her head.

'The King has gone straight back on his word,' James told them, grimly fondling Fetcher's rough ears. 'First he says he will, then he says he won't. He claims that he was forced to grant it, and that makes the charter unlawful. The man can wriggle out of any hole.'

'Aye,' John agreed. 'He's sent abroad for more mercenaries and the rebel barons look for men and arms once more. They'll be fighting again soon enough, you can bet on it, but we'll not be with them. It's clear to us now, the barons care nowt for Forest Laws or common-folk, they just want power for themselves.'

Marian pressed her lips tightly together, to stop herself from spitting out, I told you so.

The men brought news of Philippa's husband, who'd stayed in London working at his blacksmith trade for the rebel lords. 'They promise great wealth in payment,' said Tom. 'Rowan has stayed to help his father, but we doubt they'll ever see their money.'

Marian waited until they were fed and warmed by the fire before she asked again. 'And where is Robert?'

John shook his head. 'He was with us this morning, but there was hell to pay as we passed near Ollerton. Great gangs of the Sheriff's men marched everywhere, armed to the teeth. A guard picked me out as fellow to the Hooded One, so we had to split and run. Will insisted that he go straight back to Langden, he's anxious to see that all is well with Isabel. Why do you all smile so slyly?' John touched his daughter's cheek.

The women told of the day's events.

The men laughed and applauded them, but Marian thought she caught an anxious glance passing between John and Brother James.

'What is it?' she demanded. 'I know there is something! Is he hurt?'

There was a moment of hesitation.

'He is hurt!' she said.

'He took a bash on the head from a huge rock,' James said at last. 'The king's men drag about these powerful new stone-throwing machines that they call the *trebuchet*. There's many of our fellows have been stunned and many dead for they hurl great rocks with such a power.'

Magda shuddered at his words.

'They can bring down walls, and towers with the things,' John added. 'And if you are in the wrong place . . . ? Well Robert was in the wrong place as usual, but Philippa's looking after him. She won't leave his side. Better bodyguard than a bear, is Philippa. We thought it best to draw the guards away from them.'

Marian frowned. This was so unlike Robert, who was always in the thick of things. 'He can walk?' she asked.

'Oh aye,' John agreed. 'Your man walks, talks, eats and drinks, but sometimes what he says is rubbish.'

'Huh!' Marian cried. 'He always did talk rubbish.'

John smiled and nodded but he added solemnly. 'He goes wandering off in the wrong direction, if you do not keep a tight hold of him.'

That really alarmed her. 'I don't like the sound of it,' she whispered.

After the others had fallen asleep, Marian lit her lantern from the embers and went out into the darkness of the woods.

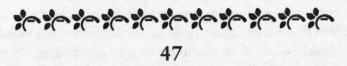

47

'Who is it that you think you've caught?'

Marian's search was fruitless and just as dawn light filtered through the trees, she returned to the cottage and fell asleep, exhausted. By the time she eventually woke again Magda had made oatcakes and the men had cleaned themselves in the warm waters of the Forestwife's spring. James and Tom started cutting yew staves for new boys.

'Robert's still not here?' Marian asked. 'Nor Philippa?'

John shook his head. 'Don't fret. I'm going off to look for them. We hadn't time to make plans and I don't know which way they'll come. Philippa might head for her home in Langden.'

'I'll come too,' Marian insisted.

But before they had a chance to set off Brigit, who'd been fetching firewood, came running and pointing. 'Gerta's coming!' she cried. 'Gerta's coming with an old woman who can't walk properly. She leads her by the arm.'

Marian went towards them, ready to give aid as ever,

but a shiver of doubt touched her as they came closer. Was this not Philippa's dark red kirtle and worn hooded cloak? But the bent, stumbling soul who leaned on Gerta could not be Philippa, who still strode tall and straight-backed through the woods, although she had aged. 'Who is this, Gerta?' she asked.

'Prepare yourself,' Gerta whispered. 'I fear you'll be shocked.' Then she reached over and pulled back her companion's hood.

Marian was indeed deeply shocked. It was Robert, but a Robert she had never known. He trembled and clung to Gerta's arm, his skin grey and sweaty. He stared up at Marian as though she were a stranger, mumbling words that made no sense.

Marian's stomach churned. Robert had been hurt many times before, indeed he was covered with scars that she had cleaned and healed, but no stinking wound or rotting flesh had ever seemed as terrible to her as this clinging weakness or the blankness in his eyes.

'I knew you'd be fearful,' Gerta reached out to touch her arm. 'But believe me, I've seen this before from a blow to the head, and still they may recover.'

'Aye,' Marian forced herself to be sensible. 'I've seen it too and you are right, some do get better. Rest and good feeding may do a world of good. Let us get him inside by the fire. Have you seen Philippa?'

'I have,' Gerta agreed, miserably.

They steered Robert into the cottage and settled him onto a straw pallet. As Marian fed him sips of a calming fever mixture, Gerta told them what had happened.

'There's much to tell and no time to waste,' the old woman was very agitated. 'I was alone, for Isabel has given my lads work up at Langden. Your friend Philippa came knocking at my door early this morning with the Hooded One at her side. She almost carried the man. Oh, I pray I have done right!'

'Tell us,' John spoke gently.

Gerta told them how Philippa and Robert had been tracked by some of the Sheriff's men, right through Barnsdale. It seemed they'd recognised the much-wanted Hooded One and were bent on getting themselves a rich reward.

'As soon as I let them in, Philippa started tearing off her clothes,' Gerta told them. 'I thought she'd gone mad, but then I came to understand and I helped her. I couldn't think what else to do. We stripped off Robert's clothes and exchanged them with Philippa's, so that he looked like this, and Philippa, she's so tall and upright, she looked like the Hooded One.'

'She's mad!' Magda gasped, starting to understand.

'Trust her,' Marian agreed. 'She's put herself in terrible danger.'

'She told me to bring him to you,' Gerta cried. 'She swore the men would ignore two old women, if they thought they'd got the Hooded One holed up. And she was right. They took no notice, letting us pass. All they did was to creep a little closer to my hut.'

'We've got to go,' Marian cried.

'Aye,' John leapt to his feet, lifting down the bows from the nail that they hung on.

Magda stuck her head out of the door and shouted for Tom and James, who were still unaware of this latest trouble.

'You stay!' John told Marian. 'Leave it to us!'

'But Philippa?' she cried, torn between concern for her sick lover and her dearest friend. 'I can't stay here by the fire, when she's in such danger.'

'I can look after the man,' a small voice spoke up. They turned to Brigit uncertainly.

'And I can stay with the lass,' Gerta told them. 'We played Forestwife together yesterday, now we can do it again. You get off as fast as you can and see that brave and crazy woman safe.'

They did not argue any more, but turned and ran, Tom leaping onto Rambler and leading the way.

Though they went fast through the woodland paths they slowed as they neared Gerta's hut, knowing that it wouldn't do to charge straight in. Tom got down from his horse and led Rambler quietly towards the small hut. Though at first all seemed quiet, the faint snorting and champing of bits and restless brush of hooves in the undergrowth told them what they needed to know.

There were six of the Sheriff's men creeping slowly towards Gerta's doorway, swords drawn. Two crouched down beneath Gerta's small window hole, though it was scarcely big enough for a child to escape through. The band of men were small in number, but well armed and excited at the prize they thought within their grasp. The reward offered for Robert the Wolveshead, also known as the Hooded One, went up at every court-leet. The new Sheriff would be grateful indeed, to any man who brought him back to Nottingham, dead or alive.

Marian and her friends had no sooner taken stock of the situation than they heard a low cough, followed by a sharp bang that sent clouds of rooks shooting from their nests. Then came the thumping sounds of a struggle and angry shouts. As Marian moved forwards she saw that they'd ripped aside the woven curtain and kicked over the low wattle hurdles that formed a close to keep in Gerta's geese. Now they hauled out a tall struggling figure dressed in Robert's forest-dyed hood and short kirtle. Their impulse was to rush forwards and snatch Philippa, but experience held them back, telling them that acting at the right moment was imperative. Meanwhile Gerta's grey gander made a good job of flying at the men's eyes, while his companions honked and flapped in panic.

'We've got him!' the men crowed, warding off the beating wings. Philippa continued to fight.

'Ah! Damned fellow's kicked my shins.'

'Dead or alive?' another shouted. 'Hang him! Run him through! Less trouble dead.'

'Aye, but will Sheriff pay more if he's alive?'

'Aye, maybe. Get him on a horse, and get him trussed.'

Philippa was bundled onto the nearest waiting horse.

'Now,' John whispered. 'Before they get moving.'

Without further discussion, Marian and her friends took up their bows, each notching an arrow. They crept silently forwards, forming a half-circle about the

Sheriff's men. Tom quietly mounted Rambler and urged him slowly on behind them. So quietly did they move and so close in colour to their surroundings were the woodland dyes of their clothing that they had their targets well lined up before one of the men noticed them. The man was so shocked that he couldn't speak, only croak and point his sword.

'Give us back our friend,' John's voice rang out. 'Give us our friend and you shall keep your lives.'

'Give up the Hooded One?' one of the men growled. 'You must be mad!'

'Fools!' It was Philippa who spoke, her voice full of mocking laughter. 'Who is it that you think you've caught?' Suddenly she pulled up Robert's short kirtle, exposing a pair of very female breasts.

The men gaped; their mouths open, eyes wide with astonishment. Marian and Magda could not suppress small snorts of laughter, but Philippa did not waste her moment. She was down from the horse and racing towards her friends in an instant. Tom hauled her up onto Rambler, then turned to gallop fast away, leaving the others to deal with the sheriff's men.

It was hard to aim carefully whilst holding back laughter, but they somehow managed to send a hail of arrows flying towards the still stunned soldiers. The four who'd pulled Philippa from the hut were killed outright, while the two by the window shot off in the direction of their horses. Magda and John moved to follow them, but could not keep up once the men were mounted and away.

'Don't worry,' Marian called. 'They'll not return here in a hurry.' She chuckled for a moment, then suddenly her laughter fled. She snatched the nearest deserted horse by the reins. 'I must get back to Robert,' she cried.

48

A Fine Little Herbwife

While Marian rode back to the clearing on the stolen horse, Magda, John and James took Gerta's digging tools and buried the four men secretly in the woods. They set about mending the smashed wattle hurdles, then caught the still squawking geese and returned them to the safety of their close once more. Then when all was neat and secure, they set off with three strong new horses for the Forestwife's clearing.

Philippa and Tom were just ahead of her when Marian arrived back at the cottage. The two women jumped down from their mounts and hugged each other fiercely.

'How could you? Marian cried. 'Trust you to save yourself so rudely.'

'Well . . . it worked didn't it?' Philippa laughed shamelessly. 'There was no need for you to go rushing out there. I could have sorted out those fools myself!'

'I swear that's true,' said Tom, shaking his head and smiling. 'Philippa and the grey gander might have managed very well! But now, what of Robert?'

The joy fell from both women's faces, and they turned towards the cottage.

'How long has he been like this?' Marian asked.

'Almost a se'nnight,' Philippa told her. 'He seemed to be improving, then slipped back worse than ever. I thought it best to bring him home to you.'

Marian stopped, smiling sadly. 'Aye, this is his home, though he never spends much time here. It is as much a home as he has ever known. Robert was born here in this clearing. Did you know?'

'Aye,' Philippa thrust her arm through her friend's. 'I remember his mother Agnes telling me. They have the blessing of the ancient yews, those born in the Forestwife's clearing, and I have to agree that your Robert is a very remarkable fellow. Something or someone has certainly blessed him!'

As they entered the hut they breathed in the woody scent of fresh marjoram. A sense of calm filled the small room; Robert seemed to be resting quietly, propped up on the straw pallet. He looked a lot cleaner, his cheeks flushed slightly pink.

Marian crouched down at his side and put her hand on his forehead. 'Much better,' she sighed with relief. 'So much better. What have you done?'

Brigit and Gerta sat by the fire, smiling and pleased with themselves. 'It's the little lass,' Gerta insisted. 'I helped and I did as she told me, but it was the lass's idea, not mine. We dragged him round to the spring and bathed him – dunked him right in the water. It seemed to soothe him, so we let him have a right good soaking.

Then we hauled him out and rubbed him down well with dried lavender and soft lamb's wool.'

'It seems you've done right.' Philippa laughed. 'He looks better than he has since that rock smashed down on his head.'

Marian sniffed at the drained wooden mug that stood on the rushes. 'Marjoram tea?' she asked.

Brigit nodded. 'Mother always said it was good for the head and it was you that told me that the warm spring was magical!'

'I don't know that I'd have had the courage to just dunk him in,' said Marian. 'Your mother taught you well, Brigit. You are turning into a fine little herbwife.'

Robert slept soundly, all through the afternoon and the next night. He woke the following morning still weak, but recognising them. Marian made him rest and fed him well, full of joy and confidence in his recovery. Though she'd feared him lost beyond hope, her man had returned to her yet again.

As the last days of July came, the charcoal burners and coal-diggers set aside their spades and stacks and gathered at Langden, ready to help with the harvest work. Lammastide celebrated the start of the cutting of the wheat, oats and barley.

Magda loved this time of year, for the first job to be done was not the cutting of the crops, but the clearing out of all the stale stinking rushes that covered the floor of each cottage and hut. The gathering and bringing home of fresh rushes brought the sweet smells of woodland and strewing herbs into every dwelling.

'We must have a feast now,' she told Marian. 'Asking for blessings on the harvest is important. You have always said so.'

'You and your feasts,' Marian laughed. But then a shadow of anxiety seemed to touch her face. 'But, yes,' she said solemnly. 'You are right! We must ask blessings on our harvest, before we cut and then be sure to give thanks afterwards. The harvest is always precious, but this year it shall be most precious indeed. And the gleaning. The gleaning must be done so carefully. Not an ear of corn, not a flake of oat must be left behind.'

Magda was pleased to have her feast and she did not notice the anxiety that lay hidden behind Marian's words. Lammastide brought a fine moonlit night and the clearing was filled with the smells of fresh rushes and roast venison, and they sang and danced until it was late.

Though the harvest made everyone work desperately hard, still a great joyfulness seemed to fill the clearing. So often the women had worked alone, but this year was different. Marian had expected Robert to proclaim himself fit, and go marching off to join some rebel baron, but this time even he spoke of staying to help with the work. If Robert was happy to stay, then so were Tom and James and many more.

As Robert's strength returned he even busied himself about the clearing, cutting firewood, reeds and rushes, and mending the leaking thatch. He left the wild safety of Barnsdale Woods only to make the occasional foray into Sherwood, returning with welcome fresh meat, venison or sometimes wild boar. The only ones who seemed unsettled were John and James. They spent much time together deep in conversation, and John, who had always loved the company of his friends, often wandered off without saying a word or telling anyone where he was going.

Marian had never been so happy. Since his bang on the head Robert seemed more gentle and loving than ever before. 'I swear that flying stone did me a favour,' she teased as they sat on the doorsill in the late afternoon sun. 'I could have done with it giving you a good thump on the head twenty years ago.'

Robert chuckled. 'Put down those stinking herbs and come here, sweetheart,' he begged.

Marian hesitated. 'There is much to do,' she told him.

'Aye,' he agreed. 'But who knows what tomorrow may bring us? This scarred old wolf thinks himself very lucky to have fought so many battles and still be here with his mate, sitting in the sun.'

Marian sighed, but she stopped her work and went to him. Tom and Magda returned with James from Isabel's fields at dusk and found them fast asleep, propping each other up, while herbs blew about in the dust and chickens pecked at their feet.

The Forestwife's cottage became very cramped with so many people and through many a warm night they ended up sleeping outside beneath the stars. Then one evening as they sat by the fire, exhausted and aching, Tom put his arm around Magda and told them that he had something to say.

Marian looked up in surprise, for Magda was usually the one that did any telling there was to be done. The younger woman had been somewhat quiet of late, though she and Tom seemed closer than they had ever been.

'We are going to build another hut, Magda and I,' said Tom. 'There are too many of us to cramp together in Marian's cottage when the cool of autumn comes.'

Marian raised her eyebrows and smiled. So, they planned to stay through the winter months too, did they?

'Aye,' John agreed. 'You're right, but where will you build it?'

'Close by,' Magda told him, though she glanced worriedly at Marian.

'Then we'll all help,' Robert said cheerfully. 'As soon as the harvesting is done, we'll set to work. It must be done before the weather turns. 'Tis better by far to spend our time building homes than fighting battles we can never win.'

John and James looked up at each other surprised but not displeased.

'Aye,' said James. 'My old bones would enjoy spending a winter by a warm fire for once.'

Marian was pleased at the plans but, as she looked at Magda's troubled face, a suspicion came to her. Brigit said nothing, but listened to it all a touch anxiously.

The following morning Magda moved to join the harvesting team, but Marian called her back. 'Robert goes with them,' she said. 'You stay here with me today. I think there is something else to be told. Don't forget, I know you very well my girl.' She set about scouring her cooking pots with a handful of sand. 'Come, sit down here beside me while I work,' she said. 'Now . . . tell me.'

Magda looked miserable, but did as she was told. 'You'll be angry,' she said.

'Huh!' Marian laughed. 'Since when have you feared my anger?'

Magda smiled, but her brow still creased with concern. 'I did not do what you taught me,' she said quietly. 'You told me many ways to stop a bairn from starting to grow, but I did not use them.'

'As I thought,' Marian nodded.

'More than that,' Magda gasped. 'I went out on Brig's night and made a bower and a Biddy doll. I begged for a bairn and Brig has sent me one. I thought it was Brigit that she'd sent at first, but now I have my own bairn coming too.'

Marian stared at her, surprised. 'You should have told me.'

'There is still more.' Now that she had started telling, it all came tumbling out in a rush. 'I want to marry Tom and be his wife. I want everyone to wish us joy and to know that he is my man, but you told me that the Forestwife should never marry. You always refused Robert, whenever he wished to be wed to you.'

'Aye,' said Marian. 'That is what I told you, isn't it?'

49

Under the Trysting Tree

They were both silent then, and all that could be heard was the crackle of the fire and the harsh scouring sound as Marian worked grains of sand around the pot.

'You chose never to have a child,' Magda whispered at last. 'You told me that being Forestwife was too important . . . and that I should be Forestwife after you. But I do not think that I am the right one. Little Brigit would make a better Forestwife; she has more knowledge of herbs and potions than I will ever have. She does not even need to be taught, she just knows. I think now that Brig sent her here to take my place.'

Marian stopped her scouring and dropped the bowl; she moved to Magda and put her arms around her. 'You must have wanted this bairn very much,' she said.

Magda nodded and buried her face in Marian's shoulder. They rocked together gently, both of them turning tearful.

'All will be well, all will be well,' Marian soothed. Then she heaved a great sigh. 'Of late I seem to look back on my life and wonder why I made such decisions. It's true that Robert wished us to be wed, and I refused him again and again. I was so young, and so desperate to play my part, wishing to right all wrongs. I charged into every battle that came our way, fighting for those who could not fight.'

'And you have done it,' Magda told her. 'You have saved many and made life bearable for those who would have suffered terribly. Every struggling peasant in Barnsdale has faith in the Forestwife and the Hooded One.'

'Aye,' Marian nodded. 'And I believed that I could not do it and be tied to a man. Now I come to think that I was too hard on myself, and also on those around me. I regret it much of late. I have learned that no matter how hard you fight, however much you sacrifice, still you can never win.'

'No,' Magda agreed smiling. 'But it is still better to fight.'

'Yes. You have learned that, so much younger than I did. It is just . . . keeping up the struggle that really matters, and there is one more thing that's important for you to know. I have never wanted to bear a child for I had you to mother. I never wanted another child but you.'

Magda smiled at that and kissed her, then doubt crossed her face again. 'The Forestwife? The sacred trust?'

Marian shook her head. 'You shall be Forestwife, I am sure of it, but maybe Brig did sent Brigit to us. Perhaps you need not do the work alone. Brigit is a wonderful healer, that's true, but there is more to being Forestwife than that. How many times have I put aside my potions and taken up my bow and gone running through the woods ready to fight? Can Brigit do that? I know that you can!'

Magda nodded. 'It's true, the work is not all healing wounds; you have done some fierce and terrible things.'

'And you have always been there at my side, spurring me on, giving me courage. That is the work of the Forestwife just as much as tending the sick. I grow a little tired these days; and come to think that we three might share the work; Brigit the maiden, you the mother, and I the Old One.'

'You are not the Old One yet!' Magda insisted, and Marian was glad to see the happiness back in her eyes.

'No,' Marian agreed. 'And if you wish to marry your Tom, go and do so. Go and tell Tom that you will marry him.'

Magda laughed. 'I haven't even spoken of it to him yet!'

Tom was willing enough, and as the harvest work went on they planned to have a late August wedding beneath the trysting tree. They'd celebrate the young couple's wedding, along with the cutting of the last sheaf of corn.

Every harvest was the same; Isabel always brought the last sheaf from Langden through the woods to the Forestwife's clearing. They'd twist and plait the stook until it took on the shape of a woman that they called the Corn Goddess; then they'd crown it with a wreath of flowers, and feast and dance around it, giving thanks and praise for the harvest brought safely in.

When the last few days of corn cutting came Marian insisted on going to Langden to make sure the gleaning was done thoroughly, but the rest of her friends stayed in the clearing and started work on Magda's new home. The woods rang with the sounds of hammering and the crack of splitting wood. Orders were shouted by Magda and ignored by most as their hands, already toughened with harvest work, grew strong as leather. They wove wattle panels that they stuffed with goats' hair and chicken feathers, then coated them with mud and left them to dry in the sun. With everyone helping the work was swiftly done.

Once the panels were dried out in the late Autumn sun, they fixed them onto a small but sturdy timber frame and set a hearth stone in the middle. They thatched the roof beams, leaving a small hole for smoke to come through. Magda was filled with excitement as the first wisps of smoke rose upward from the fire that she'd lit, drifting out through the hole 'Where is Tom, where is Brigit?' she cried. 'Fetch the rugs and bedding in!'

Brigit who'd helped quietly throughout the building work looked stunned. She stood there open mouthed. 'Am I . . . ?'

'Why yes,' Magda cried, hugging her tightly. 'Did I not make it clear? You are to come and live here with us and be my family.'

'Oh,' Brigit's face glowed. 'I didn't know. I thought you'd like to be alone with Tom.'

'Believe me,' said Magda, hands on hips. 'When Tom goes off adventuring with Robert in the spring, as I know he will, and I have a tiny babe to rear, then I am going to need you very much.'

So Magda ruled her new home with bossy pleasure, while John and James settled themselves in the lean-to with Fetcher to keep them warm, and Robert and Marian were left alone happy in the cottage like any old husband and wife.

The day of Magda's wedding dawned bright and sunny. 'See,' Marian pointed out. 'Brig is smiling on you still.'

Isabel arrived from Langden with the last cut sheaf and Philippa in the back of her wagon. Will Stoutley drove them, and they were all dressed in fine new clothes of scarlet cloth, and somehow looking very pleased with themselves.

Marian dressed in her only gown, a patched and worn green kirtle, suddenly felt old and tired. 'You look as though you are thriving, all of you,' she told them.

'Oh we are thriving as never before, especially some of us,' Philippa said, laughing and nodding towards Isabel and Will. 'This has been a fine harvest,' she told Marian. 'We've little to fear this winter.'

Marian pressed her lips together, biting back words of doubt, but then she smiled. 'I pray that's true,' she said.

The Sisters of the Magdalen arrived with little posies fastened to their veils, excited and chattering, for Magda wished them to take part in her celebrations. Then a great gang of ragged children from the woodland cottages came skipping and dancing into the clearing, carrying more small posies. They surrounded Magda's new home, chanting:

> 'Here we bring our posies,
> Our garlands, and our roses.
> Bring her out! Bring her out!
> So we can greet the harvest bride.'

Then to cheers and clapping the newly woven door curtain was thrown aside and out came Magda and Tom, both wearing new green dyed kirtles and crowned with flowers.

John took up his pipe, James beat a deerskin drum, while Fetcher pranced about his master and a happy procession formed behind the young couple. They led the dance around the clearing, pausing for a while beside the beautiful, bubbling warm spring that gave so much aid and comfort to Marian's most sickly visitors.

The children danced around the spring, singing:

> 'Blessings on the water,
> Blessings on the sea,
> Blessings on the woodland streams,
> And blessings on me.'

Then they threw their small posies into its clear waters where they bobbed up and down.

Suddenly the procession was moving on and round to the trysting tree. The Sisters of Magdalen waited there, standing in a half-circle around the last cut sheaf of corn that Isabel and Philippa had plaited and twisted cleverly into the shape of the goddess. It stood in the middle of them, shoulder high and crowned with a beautiful wreath of ears of corn and flowers.

Magda and Tom exchanged their vows beneath the trysting tree, and the nuns and brother James spoke their blessings. Then, as they kissed, everyone clapped and cheered. Magda turned to lead the dance back past the goddess towards the cottage, where a long trestle table stood, bearing bread, fruit, cheese and ale, but much to everyone's surprise Philippa strode out from the watching crowd and announced that another happy event was to take place.

'Come on,' she ordered, and Isabel came forward blushing and smiling. Will Stoutley at her side.

'I thought never to marry,' Isabel announced. 'As you all know, I fought bitterly against it, and many of you paid a heavy price for my freedom. Now, at last I have found a man that I can trust, and truly love. Will Stoutley is the man I freely choose to be my husband, and I beg you all bear witness to our vows?'

'Aye! Aye!' everyone bellowed with approval.

So there and then, both dressed in fine new scarlet, Isabel married Will beneath the trysting tree.

'Now to dance around the goddess,' Magda cried.

'No . . . not yet,' another voice rang out.

Everyone turned and this time it was Robert who

came forward, and he held up his hand for quiet. A sudden hush fell. When Robert decided to speak, there was no knowing what was coming next; a sudden joy; or a snatching up of weapons and a mad scheme that would leave the woodland half empty, and women and children alone and struggling.

But this time Robert had a wicked and cheerful gleam in his eye. He prowled around the Corn Goddess, and nobody moved or spoke; even the children were quiet. He stopped before Marian. 'There is so much joy and happiness here today,' he said. 'That I too dare once more to beg a favour that I have had refused so many times before. Marian, I beg you . . . marry me now, at last, here in this loving circle of friends.'

Everyone turned quiet again, shocked and surprised, straining to hear the reply. This was a joyful day, but the Forestwife belonged to the people of the woods, and not to any man. For a moment Marian looked lost and unsure, but then she pressed her lips tightly together, shaking her head.

'Nay,' she told him firmly. 'Though I love you better than life itself, we have chosen a different way – you and I. There will be no wedding for the Forestwife and the Hooded One.'

Robert flinched staring down at the straw-strewn earth beneath their feet, his thin scarred face grim. His friends watched in silence, dreading his anger, seeing his humiliation. But they needn't have feared for suddenly he smiled broadly, and swung back to being his usual teasing self. 'Maybe you are right, my Green Lady –

perhaps I'd have been shocked if you'd agreed. Will you still dance with me?'

'I will always dance with you,' she whispered. 'But I am no Green Lady – not any more.'

Robert turned and snatched up the beautiful flower-woven garland from the Corn Goddess, and placed it on Marian's head. 'No. You've become the Corn Goddess,' he cried. 'Beautiful and golden, touched with sorrow and sun. Now dance with me!'

'Yes,' she whispered.

'Now can we all dance?' Magda cried at last.

Though the feast was small, everyone was joyful at the day's events, and the singing and dancing went on till dawn.

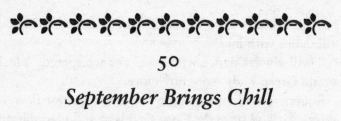

50

September Brings Chill

After the excitement of the woodland weddings it was hard to settle down to the autumn work that must be done. But as the weather turned cooler Marian returned to her usual practical preparations for the winter ahead. Nobody was allowed to sit and dream, and each day they went out into the woods returning with baskets and sacks full of mushrooms, berries, nuts and herbs.

Magda was so busy with her new home that she did not at first notice the strange restlessness that seemed to surround her father. John would wake early in the mornings and be off without telling anyone where he was going, then appear again late at night, quiet and tired with a bag half filled with firewood or a handful of yew staves. The only one he really spoke to was James. Despite her distraction even Magda noticed at last. She was puzzled. Robert was usually the unsettled one and John the calmer, more contented of the two men.

'Father's gone off again this morning,' she told Tom.

'Gone off without saying a word. I don't know what it is with him! Half the time I feel as though his mind is somewhere else.'

Tom did not look as surprised as she'd expected, but he sighed and then began to speak gently. 'Aye, I think his mind is often somewhere else, and I believe I know what it is that disturbs the man's peace.'

'Then tell me!' Magda demanded.

'Well,' said Tom. 'It all started when we marched down to Northampton to join the Bishop. We fell in with a gang of men sent down from Derbyshire. They were sent down to fight for their rebel lord, the constable of Peveril Castle, in the land they call The Peak.'

'Aye, and so?' Magda was impatient.

'Well, there was a fellow who knew John, the moment he clapped eyes on him. He came from the village of Hathersage.'

'Ah!' Magda began to understand. 'Hathersage where my father was born and raised?'

Tom nodded. 'The two of them marched side by side for days and whispered by the fire all night. They'd watched over sheep on the hillsides together when they were lads and believe me I have never known John to take such delight in talking as he did with that fellow.'

Magda frowned, unsure that she liked the sound of it. She herself had never known this distant Derbyshire village. She'd been born in the Forestwife's clearing, and that had been the centre of all her life.

'What did they talk about?' she asked.

'People, places, names they both knew. Wild

adventures of their youth! The old ones who'd died, and some young ones too.' Tom sighed. 'It brought John great pleasure,' he said. 'But I think it brought him sadness too.'

'And so this man, this old friend of my father's returned to Hathersage?'

Tom shook his head. 'That is the greatest sadness of it all. He was caught like Robert by one of the great stone-throwing machines. He was not as lucky as Robert was, for he died. So you see, there was no returning to Hathersage, not for him. Now,' Tom asked gently. 'Do you understand John's restlessness a bit better?'

Magda heaved a great sigh. 'Oh yes,' she said. 'I understand it very well, though I do not much like the answer that comes into my mind.'

'No,' Tom shook his head sadly. 'No, I thought you would not. That is why I never spoke of it before.'

Magda smiled at him, and patted her stomach that was beginning to swell quite noticeably. 'Ah well,' she said determinedly. 'I have got my wish. Father shall have his wish too, whether he thinks he should or not. Would you travel with him to see him safely there?'

Tom smiled at her. 'Of course I will.'

She went out into the woods, following the path her father had taken. Two days later, John set out for Hathersage, riding behind Tom on Rambler's strong back. John was reluctant to leave his daughter, but the quiet joy in his eyes at the thought of returning to his childhood home was there for all to see.

'You go with my blessing,' Magda told him, sounding

stronger than she felt. 'All I ask is that you come back to us at Christmas, for my child should be born soon after that.'

No sooner had John and Tom set out for Derbyshire than Philippa's blacksmith husband returned to Langden with Rowan her son. Philippa walked through the woodland paths to pass their news on to the Forestwife and her friends. She gently touched Brigit's head as she passed the child, sitting out in the autumn sunshine, steadily pounding dandelion roots.

'Are they inside?' she asked.

'Yes,' Brigit sighed. 'They do nothing but talk of the barons and the King.'

Philippa went inside and joined them by the fireside. She told of her husband's return. 'I feared he'd never get paid for all his work, and if the barons had had their way, he never would.'

'Who has paid him?' Robert asked.

Philippa smiled. 'Your friend, the Bishop of Hereford.'

Robert looked up, interested. 'I knew that man was different. The other bishops went running to side with the King as soon as they heard the pope had denounced the charter. Not Giles de Braose, even though we distrust them, the Bishop of Hereford still stands by the rebel barons.'

'Ah well,' Philippa cleared her throat. 'I'm not so sure. The King has tried to buy the man's loyalty back again. He's offered him the de Braose property fully restored, and all his dead brother's land, but the Bishop must swear fealty once more.'

'And what does the man reply?' Robert leant forward.

Philippa shrugged her shoulders. 'We don't know yet, and I have sadder news,' she sighed. 'News that will bring great sorrow to that little lass out there, who pounds roots as though her life depends on it.'

'Oh no,' Magda cried. 'Not Brigit's father!'

Philippa nodded. 'The man is dead. The King sent his wolfpack to take back the Tower of London. The barons had given way and agreed that it should be held in the Archbishop of Canterbury's name, but some of those who'd been defending it resisted. Brigit's father was one of them.'

Magda got up, her face all creased with pity. 'I'll tell her,' she said. 'I don't want to, but I will.'

Brigit took the news of her father's death quietly, but during the next few days she wandered aimlessly about the clearing as though she'd lost all purpose in life. Marian praised her herb skills and begged her help with the potions and simples, but the young girl refused politely. Magda followed her at a distance, feeling useless and somehow responsible. 'I wished for a bairn, Brig,' she murmured. 'And you sent Brigit that very night. Now she has nobody else but me.'

Concern for Brigit's sadness reached as far as Langden and one afternoon towards the end of September, Isabel arrived from Langden driving a small grain cart, with Philippa seated in the back.

Marian went to greet them, smiling; this visit was not entirely unexpected. Brigit looked up listlessly from the new doorsill. Magda marched over and mercilessly hauled the young girl to her feet. 'You have to come and see what Isabel has brought,' she ordered.

'Why?' Brigit cried, surprised and hurt by her friend's rough treatment.

'Come and see,' Magda insisted, pulling her round to the back of the cart.

'But I . . . oh!' Brigit's mouth dropped open in surprise. For there in Philippa's lap rolled a plump, well-fed, baby boy, dressed in a soft lamb's wool smock. His thatch of curly hair was the same golden brown as Brigit's, his cheeks pink as a wild rose.

'Is . . . is he?'

'Yes,' Isabel told her. 'He is your brother Peterkin, that you named for your father. His foster mother has fed and cared for him well, but now he's weaned from the breast and drinking goats' milk. He's a lively lad and his foster mother has her own children to see to.'

'Do you mean? Should I . . . ?'

'We thought that Peterkin might like to be with his sister,' said Isabel.

'But . . .' said Brigit, hesitating. 'But, I am very busy here. I don't know whether I can look after him, and still fetch the wood and pick the herbs and crush the roots.'

The women laughed and Magda put her arms around Brigit. 'If you want him here, then I should like to help look after him. We might share the job but only if you want that.'

Brigit took a step towards the cart and the wriggling baby. Philippa scooped him up and handed him to his sister. The girl put his chin gently to rest against her shoulder. She sniffed his soft hair and rubbed her cheek against it. Warm dribble tickled her neck, making her giggle. 'Oh yes,' she said, patting him gently on the back. 'Yes. Please let Peterkin stay.'

51

The Pannage Month

Through October and November the weather turned damp and chilly. Everyone wrapped up well and worked on, building up their stocks of nuts and meat for the very cold weather still to come. Sherwood and the surrounding wastes and woodlands were full of pigs, allowed to wander and forage freely for a short period of time in the pannage month so that they could gorge themselves on acorns and beech mast, fattening themselves up for the coming harsh months. Tom returned from Hathersage with news of the warm welcome that John had received.

'He is famous there!' Tom told them. 'They all know John of Hathersage who walks with the Hooded One. They treat him like a king and regale him with the stories of his doings. Some are true, but half of them are rubbish. John laughs and puts them straight but still they tell the tales. I shall go back to Derbyshire and fetch him home for you in time for Christmas,' he promised Magda.

'Will he be safe there?' Robert asked with unusual concern.

'I believe that they'd defend him with their lives,' Tom told him.

Now that Tom was back, more hunting trips were made to Sherwood and Marian salted and smoked the meat that they brought. The woodlanders always gathered and picked feverishly at this time of year, for the result meant the difference between eating and starving, life or death, but this year Marian worked more tirelessly than ever. Philippa often came over from Langden to help them.

'Even acorns,' she insisted. 'What's good for pigs is good for us! However bitter they may taste, ground-up acorns can keep body and soul together, and we must fetch nettles to dry and crumble and blackthorn berries and juniper too.'

'Haven't we got enough?' Magda complained. 'You'll wear yourself away to nothing if you don't stop. You'll have us gathering up the dust beneath our feet and storing it away for the snows.'

Philippa gave one of her sharp and humorous looks. 'If Marian says "gather" I'd advise you to take notice, my lass!'

Marian hesitated, her brow creased. 'It's just that I have a terrible sense of urgency come upon me. Almost like . . . like my mother, Eleanor. You remember how she knew when things were going to go wrong.'

Philippa nodded. She remembered well.

'Aye?' Magda was suddenly attentive.

'And somehow I know that we must gather and

gather, and not let one precious grain go to waste. I have other fears too; last week I thought I saw Robert's mother, Agnes, down by the spring washing clothes.'

'You saw her spirit?' Magda gasped.

'I believe I did, but it wasn't fearful. I could never fear Agnes for she loved me well, but as she scrubbed and washed I thought the water swam with blood. Then I blinked and she had vanished.'

Magda shivered and pressed her hands to her swelling stomach. 'Your mother did have the sight,' she agreed seriously. 'And she always saw true.'

Marian quickly understood the younger woman's anxiety and went to place her own hand on Magda's stomach. ''Tis not for this growing child that I see trouble. I think Agnes was giving warning for myself or maybe Robert.'

'Aye,' Philippa spoke to reassure her. 'Robert would be the one.'

'Yes,' said Marian. 'But do not speak of it to him, and certainly do not fear for this little one; I see nothing but happiness there.'

Magda was soothed a little. 'Don't you worry about Robert either,' she said. 'He's safer here than anywhere and he doesn't seem at all inclined to go off to join either Robert de Ros or another northern Lord.'

'Aye,' Marian agreed. 'As they grow older they seem less ready for the fight, and I for one am very glad of it.'

'My Tom's not old,' Magda insisted.

'No he is not,' Marian agreed. 'But then your Tom has never been one for rushing into the attack; he has more sense. But still, he's no coward; when there's something desperately needs doing, he's the one that's always there, quietly risking himself.'

'I know it,' Magda murmured.

'It's strange,' Marian sighed. 'I do not want Robert to go away adventuring,' she whispered, her eyes suddenly swimming with tears, 'but I cannot see him staying close by my side forever. How can I keep a wild wolf-man such as he, tamed like a tabby cat to sit by my fireside?'

Various well-armed expeditions were made by the sheriff and his men to the outskirts of the woods. These fruitless searches gave much amusement to those who lived outside the law and wild new rumours spread.

'Can you believe it?' Gerta told Marian and Philippa as they sifted through the crackling leaves beneath a chestnut tree. 'It's whispered that the Sheriff has this strange idea that the Hooded One might be a woman!'

Gerta continued digging her foot into the ground to drag aside the mushy green skins, leaving shining brown nuts exposed.

'No!' Marian looked up smiling, her hands full of the prickly fruit.

'Oh yes! Any woman caught running wild through the woods is to be searched for weapons! Though it seems his soldiers do not often venture very far into the woods, for they fear the Forestwife's curse on them!'

Marian clapped her hand to her mouth, choking with laughter.

Philippa hugged her, snorting at the joke. 'I can't think why the Sheriff could think such a thing! What could poor women such as us do? Pelt his men with sweet chestnuts?'

'No!' Marian howled, slapping Philippa's large backside. 'Now why should the silly man think that the Hooded One could be a woman?'

Gerta smiled, understanding their mirth, but still her expression was troubled. 'Even nuns are to be stopped and searched,' she said. 'For the Sheriff declares that no respectable nun should be out walking through the woods either alone or with her sisters.'

Marian turned solemn when she heard that and she looked at Philippa with concern. 'Have we put the Sisters of the Magdalen in danger?'

The taller woman shrugged her shoulders. 'We did what we thought best. We have always done that.'

Marian's fears that Robert might turn into a tabby cat were soon put to flight for one morning in mid November Brother James and Philippa came riding fast through the woods from Langden with frightening news.

'You must get up off your backside,' the plump monk told his friend as he burst into the cottage, his face all red and shaking. 'They've got Will and taken him off to Clipston. The Sheriff is there and arranging a hanging!'

Robert was on his feet in a moment. 'How have they got Will? And why hang him?'

'Did they ever need a good reason? A gang of the Sheriff's men turned up at Langden. Isabel got a little warning for some of the coal-diggers saw the gang of mercenaries heading towards the manor.'

'Why Langden?' Marian asked.

'It seems the Lady of Langden has been recognised and reported as one of the women who helped to rescue Gerta's grandsons.'

'I feared something like that!' Marian said quietly.

'Will insisted that Isabel took to the woods,' Philippa told them hurriedly. 'But then he stayed to see all the servants safely away and out of the hall. He did not manage to escape in time himself.'

'What do they want with Will?' Robert asked.

'I fear they may think they've got you,' Brother James cried. 'They bellowed and shouted that they'd got the Hooded One, and Will killed two of their men, before they could get hold of him.'

'Aye,' Philippa added. 'It's either that, or the Sheriff tries his hand at a different, more crafty way of getting at thee! But we must not stand here asking why! We must do something and fast. Tom has gone riding off after them on Rambler, but what can Tom do on his own? Rowan and Isabel are gathering together the servants, but they are just a tiny handful and they are farmers, none of them are fighting men!'

'Damnation,' Robert growled. 'Where can we get help from quickly? All those who fought with us for the charter have returned to their homes. It would take days to get them together.'

'I know,' cried Magda. 'The answer's there right in front of our noses. The woods are crowded out with pig-herders. The pannage finishes tomorrow, but they're still there today, getting every last scrap they can for their beasts.'

Robert stared at her, puzzled. 'But they are children and old folk!'

Marian quickly picked up the way that Magda was thinking. 'Yes,' she said. 'But there are so many of them. If we start marching towards Clipston, and beg the pig-herders to join us, we shall pass hundreds of them.'

Robert hesitated. 'But . . . will they be willing?'

'Yes,' Marian spoke with confidence. 'They'll be very angry and willing once they know that it is Isabel's new husband that is at risk! How many of them received gifts of grain from Langden in the harshest days last winter? How many of them wear a warm cloak, woven with wool from Isabel's sheep? The news of Isabel's marriage has spread far and wide and brought much happiness with it!'

Suddenly Robert laughed, and kissed Magda on the nose. 'You are a clever lass! It is mad, but it just might save the man!'

So though he felt a little unsure that they'd got the strength for this fight, Robert threw himself into action, gathering together all the bows and weapons that they could. They left the clearing soon after noon. Marian marched with them, insisting that Magda stay behind with Gerta and Brigit, the Forestwife's girdle fastened carefully around her stomach.

❧

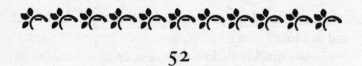

52

Peasant, Fool or Rebel Lord

Though Clipston was small compared to the great castle of Nottingham, the walls were solid and sturdy, built of strong, sandy-coloured local stone. The place was a hunting lodge, built to house the King comfortably when he chose to go chasing the fine Sherwood deer.

Sheriff de Rue went out to meet the gang of returning soldiers. They were delighted with the prisoner that they'd found, though still uncertain exactly who he was. Will rode amongst them in silence, with his head held high, even though they'd bound his arms behind his back and fastened his legs to the saddle.

'Who is this?' the Sheriff demanded. 'Haven't you got the woman?'

The men shook their heads and shuffled their feet. 'No sign of her,' they said. 'Just this fellow, defending the place alone. We think we've maybe got the Hooded One for you.'

'What makes you think that?'

'The fellow killed two of our men before we managed

to get him.'

The Sheriff looked at Will with uncertainty. 'Who are you?' he asked quietly.

Will smiled proudly. ''Tis as they say,' he agreed. 'I be the Hooded One.'

The Sheriff was puzzled. The man bore himself with great dignity and wore a fine scarlet mantle but spoke like a peasant. 'Who the devil is this Hooded One?' he muttered to himself. 'Is he peasant, fool, or rebel lord?'

'Put him in the lock-up,' at last he snarled. 'Whoever he is, he'll hang before the sun goes down.'

Will did not flinch or tremble as they led him away.

A gibbet was fast erected outside the walls of Clipston and a short while before the sun began to set, the great wooden gates opened and Will Stoutley was escorted outside, his hands still tied. The Sheriff came down from the ornate stateroom that he used himself while the king was not in residence. De Rue was still uncertain exactly who this prisoner was; but the man had killed two guards and that was a grievous enough offence to hang him without hesitation.

As Will was led out towards the gibbet, a fair-haired man emerged from the sheltering trees, and dismounted quietly from his horse. He moved slowly towards the raised platform, limping slightly and gripping the handle of a dagger that was stuck into his belt. His other hand, apparently, rested carelessly on the hilt of his sword.

The scarlet-coated figure of Will strode up the new-made steps. He glanced at the small crowd of foresters and soldiers and saw the face of a friend down there below him. No sign of recognition crossed his face; instead he turned to speak to the Sheriff. 'Let me die an honourable death,' he cried. 'Let me die as befits the Hooded One with a sword in my hand.'

A sneer touched the Sheriff's thin lips. He laughed: then spat into Will's face. 'Hang the fool,' he cried. 'Get on with it! Shut his stupid mouth up! Shut it forever!'

As the hangman moved to lift the noose, suddenly Tom was swinging himself up onto the platform with agility, despite his damaged leg, sword and dagger in his hands. He sliced through Will's bonds in a moment.

Will laughed, delighted.

'Here's your sword,' Tom cried. 'Don't die with honour; fight instead! Help shall come – I'm sure of it!'

Then the two men swung about back to back as they'd so often done in their practising. Will with a sword and Tom with his dagger were both ready to fight to the death any and all of the Sheriff's men.

The Sheriff howled with anger. 'Kill them! Kill them both!' he screamed.

But the guards hesitated to charge at them, for the gleam that was there in the outlaws' eyes told them that they would not die without taking others with them.

Then all at once an arrow went whistling over the heads of the soldiers, just grazing the Sheriff's cheek. The Sheriff swung round in fury as more arrows flew out from the edge of the woodland bringing down two more soldiers.

Then there started up strange distant thudding sounds that grew and grew, at last becoming thunderously loud.

'Look out! Look out!' one of the soldiers cried, pointing towards the woods. Everybody turned to see that the bushes and branches on the edge of the forest were trembling and shaking. Even tall trees twisted and turned, waving wildly about. All at once hundreds of squealing, grunting pigs came bursting out from the shadows of the trees, charging at speed towards the platform and the crowd of fighting men. There was sudden wild panic, every man shouting at his companions, nobody able to hear or make any sense.

'Ya! Ya!' came the cries of the herders as they still drove the pigs on. The gibbet was surrounded by fat, heaving, snorting bodies. More arrows whistled overhead and the Sheriff was grazed again in the elbow. He did not wait to see what next might come flying out from the forest, but fought his way through the charging beasts, slicing his sword in all directions, heading for the gates of Clipston. At last he reached the safety of the courtyard, his men streaming after him.

'Get back and fight them,' he cried, 'I order you back!'

The Sheriff tried to close the gates and make his men stay and fight, but they'd had enough of nasty surprises for one day and only when the last guard was eventually safe inside did they swing the gates closed.

There was just a moment of laughter and rejoicing, then the outlaws took action once again knowing that they must not hang about. Isabel rode straight at the collapsing gibbet and hauled Will up behind her onto her strong grey mare. Tom whistled for Rambler and in a moment the horse was by his side. There were a few more shouts and sharp bursts of laughter as the pigs were quickly rounded up and driven back into the woods. When the Sheriff dared to open the gates once more there was nothing left but a smashed gibbet and a great expanse of trampled ground and pig-muck.

'Get into the woods,' the Sheriff cried. 'Kill every pig-herder you can find. Kill every pig!'

But as the night grew darker, the pigs and their owners left the woodlands, slipping away to their homes along the secret paths that they knew so well. A thin mist rose from the sodden mossy grass, growing thicker in patches, sending the soldiers stumbling about, lost and weary. They fell into bogs and streams, cursing the pigs and their herders, cursing each other but cursing the Sheriff most of all.

There was much joy as Will and his rescuers returned to Langden, but Marian marched ahead of the others towards the Forestwife's clearing, her face grim.

'Do not look so anxious,' Robert begged, running after her. 'It was a mad idea, that you and Magda thought up, but it worked!'

'Aye. It worked,' she agreed. 'But the Sheriff will not forget Langden now! This will not be the end of it. We have made a fool of him, but this man's no buffoon like the last Sheriff was! He will not forgive or forget this night's work.'

Robert frowned and nodded but still his smile returned and he took hold of her hand. 'You are right as ever, but I tell you this. I would not have missed the look on de Rue's face when all the pigs charged out from the trees . . . I would not have missed it for the world! And I do not think this Sheriff will return to Langden in a hurry!'

'No, maybe not,' Marian relented and smiled at last. She moved closer to Robert and they marched along together, arms about each other's waists, their pace matching perfectly, step for step.

Though the soldiers spent a few more days scouring Sherwood for pigs and herders, there were none to be found. The pannage month was over and they'd all gone back to their villages. Robert once more took up his quiet fireside job of whittling arrow shafts and gathering goose feathers to make the flights.

53

King John's Revenue

In early December Tom set off for Hathersage, while Isabel and Philippa brought news that they'd picked up from travellers passing through Langden. King John had destroyed Rochester Castle by tunnelling beneath the ground and blowing up one of the towers with a huge explosion of fire and pig fat. He'd then marched on to Winchester and was said to be gathering together more arms and even more mercenaries.

'He's setting out from St Albans now, heading for Northampton,' Isabel told them.

Robert exchanged uneasy glances with James. 'I don't like the sound of him marching north. The farther he is from us the better,' he muttered.

'There's sad news of the rebellious Bishop of Hereford,' Isabel added. 'He agreed at last to swear fealty again, but the deed was never done. The man has died.'

'Indeed?' Robert growled. 'Then he never forgave the King. I cannot say I'm sorry! Let's hope this brings an end to that family's suffering.'

Everyone murmured agreement to that.

'There's a stranger story going about,' said Isabel. 'I can't believe it's true, but they say that the rebel barons have sent envoys to the King of France, begging him to send his son Prince Louis at the head of an army.'

'Why should the French come to England's aid?' Robert asked.

'They promise that if he support the rebel barons in their fight and help them get rid of King John, then in return they shall make Prince Louis our king.'

There were gasps from them all.

'What? It doesn't make sense,' Robert insisted. 'What good would it do to have another foreign king brought here? What does Prince Louis know of us?'

'Huh! It doesn't surprise me,' Marian told them. 'The barons simply seek another way to snatch power for themselves.'

'You best tell them about Robert de Ros,' Philippa prompted.

'Yes,' Isabel agreed. 'The great northerner lord returned to his castle at Helmsley, as soon as he heard that the King's army travels north. He's setting about building up his defences as though he expects a siege.'

'Aye,' Philippa added. 'And he is not the only baron who does that. They all seem to expect the worst and where does it leave us?'

'Defenceless! And right in the middle of it all, as usual!' Marian spoke with anger.

'We are not defenceless,' Magda cried. 'We must do what we've always done. We'll fight!'

'Aye, Magda,' Philippa smiled. 'But you will not be doing the fighting this time. You'll leave that to us.'

Marian expected Robert to agree angrily and speak of rallying men to defend them, but he stayed silent, staring moodily into the fire.

With a still growing sense of foreboding, Marian ordered the digging of deep keeping-pits to hide away their stocks of grain, oats, nuts and beans. Though Christmas came they did not organise the usual festivities, and the feast day itself was marred by the news that King John had arrived to spend Christmas with the Sheriff of Nottingham. Magda grew rounder and more restless every day and still Tom did not return from Derbyshire with her father. They heard that every pallet in Nottingham, every scrap of floor space in the city was taken up with a vast army of foreign soldiers who'd arrived armed to the teeth.

Marian grew tense watching and waiting for Robert's anger to explode, but instead he grew silent and grim, sitting hunched by the fireside, whittling knife handles until late at night. It was not the first time that he'd been like this. Marian knew the signs and worried herself to a shadow. When Robert had been in such a mood as this before, it had often ended with him going off without telling anyone and not reappearing for months. She wished very much that John and Tom would return; even Brother James who was so patient and good humoured could not lift the gloom.

'I don't know what bothers me most,' she confided to

Philippa. 'This terrible silence or his wild reckless courage.'

'Oh, I'd say he's much better charging madly about than only half alive like this,' came Philippa's quick reply.

'Yes, you are right,' Marian agreed with certainty.

The first day of January dawned, with heavy rain. As the wintry sun rose, the rain ceased and a damp cold mist drifted up from the earth. It was then that the real trouble broke. The first sign of it came as Gerta staggered into the clearing, her kirtle ripped and torn, young Davy in her arms, his head streaming with blood. Magda saw them from the doorway of her new home and ran to help, Brigit following close behind. The old woman panted and gasped, unable to get her breath.

'What is it?' Magda asked, trying to take the young boy into her own arms.

'Terrible . . . terrible things!' Gerta struggled to speak. 'The King . . . he rides north, with his new found wolfpack.'

'They've done this?' Magda cried.

'Aye. It's punishment! My hut's a smoking heap, my geese scattered in the wastes. Everyone who rebelled . . . everyone whose manor lord rebelled, anyone who gets in their way!'

'What? What are they doing to them?'

'Killing them!' the old woman sobbed. 'Killing, burning. Burning the crops! Setting fire to stores of grain! My big lads have fled to warn Langden, for that is where they're heading. And my lad . . . my little Davy . . .'

'He's gone white,' Brigit pointed out.

'Get him inside!' Magda spoke with urgency, frightened by his sudden pallor.

Between them they carried Davy into the cottage and gently put him down on the pallet by the fire. Marian at once snatched up her water pot and a compress of clean lamb's wool. She set about staunching the terrible wound, but the child's face stayed deathly white, and her actions slowed. She stopped. The blood had ceased to flow, and the child who'd been so desperately rescued from the gallows died quietly there by the hearth.

'He's gone,' she whispered.

'No,' Brigit cried out, 'Not Davy!' She stumbled backwards outside into the clearing.

Gerta didn't make a sound but went to crouch beside her grandson's body. She wrapped her arms about his small shoulders, rocking him gently back and forth as though he were a sleeping babe. Robert looked on, his own face very pale. 'Who has done this?' he asked through gritted teeth.

'It's King John's punishment,' Magda told him. 'Punishment for rebelling, for supporting the charter.'

Robert moved swiftly to his feet, his cheeks still ashen.

'They are heading for Langden now,' Magda cried.

Robert snatched his bow from the nail and strode from the hut. 'James!' he shouted. 'Fetch every weapon you can lay hands on! Bring the horses! We ride for Langden . . . at once!'

Marian looked up at Magda, a grim smile on her face.

'Whatever comes to us now,' she whispered, 'at least it will not be cowardice or shame.'

Magda went to lift down her own bow from its nail by the hearthstone, but Marian glanced out into the clearing and stopped her. 'No, not this time,' she said, her face determined. 'There is other work for us to do. See Brigit is at it already.'

'What?' Magda demanded.

'Come and look,' she spoke solemnly.

Magda went to stand beside her. The sight she saw was terrible, beyond belief. Though they had seen great sickness and sorrow there before in their clearing, nothing had ever been quite as fearful as the stream of poor folk who now wandered towards them dazed and desperate. Mothers carried wounded children, young folk supported the old, strong men wept helplessly. Everywhere she looked, they stumbled through the mud and wet grass with burnt hair, burnt hands and faces, all of them bruised and bleeding and as they watched the numbers grew.

Robert strode about, listening to their stories stony-faced. Young Brigit, despite her grief for Davy, already moved amongst them, giving help and comfort. James brought the horses round from the lean-to, stacked with every weapon that they had. 'Who will come with us to defend Langden?' Robert cried.

There was a great surge towards him and everyone who was able snatched bows and sticks and knives. Men, women, young and old shouting till their throats were sore.

Robert went to Marian and kissed her. 'Whatever comes!' he said.

'Aye,' she agreed. 'Whatever comes!'

Then they streamed out of the clearing behind Robert and James, ill-prepared and ragged but filled with bitterness, a great swarm of angry woodlanders.

Suddenly the clearing was quieter, but now the gentler whimpering of those who were badly hurt could be heard. 'Right,' said Marian rolling up her sleeves. 'Get that pot boiling, Magda, and Brigit, can you fetch buckets from the spring? We shall have to work as we've never worked before.'

Over the next few days they struggled tirelessly to give aid. Philippa came from Langden and told them that King John's wolfpack had set the barns and haystacks alight, but then moved on north with Robert and his gang hard on their heels. Isabel and Will had valiantly organised their people to beat out the fires and save whatever grain and food they could. In that, the damp weather was on their side. The Sisters of the Magdalen had taken all they possessed in food and medicine and left their convent, following in the wake of the trail of destruction. Now they tramped from village to village giving what help they could.

Magda was for once excused her hated task of grave digging as Philippa insisted on staying and making that hard job her own. Gerta buried little Davy, then resolutely set about comforting others who had lost family and friends. At last, on the third day, the flood of suffering newcomers ceased and some of those who had survived started to return to what was left of their homes.

'Today is calmer,' Magda said, stretching and rubbing her aching back. 'But this strange quiet that they've left behind bothers me.'

'Aye,' Marian agreed. 'We might have a few days' respite but then I fear the worst will come. They may live for a few days on rotting turnips but that will not last them long.'

Magda sank down on the doorsill, hugging her stomach. 'You knew,' she said. 'All that gathering and pit-digging, all that gleaning and fuss. I thought you'd gone mad, but you were right. You knew.'

Marian sighed. 'I could not see clear, as my mother used to say, but yes, now I understand why. I doubt we can feed them all, but we have good stocks hidden away and at least we may save some of them.'

Magda spoke bitterly, her eyes full of angry tears. 'They mete out the fast death first, then the slow death follows. Those who are left must starve.'

Brigit and Gerta who'd worked so tirelessly together came wandering over to the cottage leading a young girl who clutched a small rough-woven bag in her hands.

'Mother says have you a bit of grain to spare, or oats or turnips, or anything? For all our food is burnt and gone and father is hurt and cannot hunt.'

Magda smiled at Marian and struggled to her feet. 'Aye. Come on in. We shall find you something to eat.'

54

Creswell Caves

Even though Marian knew that they would come she could not have imagined how many there would be. The clearing was soon strewn with homemade shelters and smoking fires, for the weather turned against them once again bringing sleet and snow. Now they must struggle, not just to feed the wretched people who came to them, but somehow to clothe and keep them warm. Each day Philippa spent hours shifting snow and mud and digging up bucketfuls of grain from Marian's secret keeping-pits. Other women set up pots over cooking fires and produced huge quantities of wholesome bubbling stew, made tasty with nettles and garlic leaves, and carefully cut slivers of smoked venison and boar.

News came from Langden that the wolfpack had done their worst in Barnsdale, but not lingered to enjoy their spoils. Now they headed further north.

'They did not stay here for long,' Isabel told them, 'for wherever they set about destruction, they found themselves hounded by a strange Hooded Man and his gang of fierce wild wolves.'

Magda and Marian smiled. 'I'm proud of them,' said Magda.

'Yes,' Marian agreed. 'Though the members of this new wolfpack may be mystified, the woodlanders know that Hooded Man well enough.'

One cold January morning, Magda wandered around the clearing very early, for the wriggling of her babe inside her stomach would not let her sleep. Her ears picked up the clopping sound of a horse. She looked up with joy as the hooves beat out the familiar rhythm of Rambler's signal. She strode towards the entrance to the secret pathways, her happiness a little diminished as she greeted her new husband but no sign of her father.

'He's taken refuge in a cave near Creswell village,' Tom told her. 'It was hard to get him away from Derbyshire, for the people were setting about building up the defences of Peveril Castle, determined to withstand the King's revenge. They begged John's help and he could not be stopped from joining in and so I thought I'd best help too.'

Magda sighed, but smiled folding her arms. 'Aye,' she said. 'I can see it all.'

'Then the wolfpack came and went, and John is wounded,' Tom spoke with concern. 'Not fearfully I think, but he has an arrowhead in his thigh that I can't get out, and a sudden fever has come upon him. We travelled to Creswell, but I left him there, wrapped well and hidden away in the big cave that Robert often makes his refuge. He could not go further and I thought perhaps Marian would come to him.'

'I shall come,' Magda told him.

'No, not you.' Tom looked anxious. 'You should stay close to home at this time.'

'Oh yes, I shall come,' she spoke determinedly. 'It is not far to go, and Rambler can carry me as smooth and steady as a boat. Marian has too much to do here, as you will see. John is my father and I will go to him.'

Magda would not have any arguments about it and when Tom entered the clearing and saw the desperate people who filled it with their shelters and their misery, he understood that Marian was indeed needed there. So with many instructions and warnings from the Forestwife, they set off just before noon, Magda perched sideways on Rambler's back, supported all about with rugs, food, medicine and ointment pots.

Tom insisted that he lead Rambler at a steady walking pace through the secret paths. The sheltering caves of Creswell, that had often saved the outlaws from freezing overnight, were not far to the west so that they reached the place by dusk.

The cave was one of many, set into the steep rugged valley sides known as Creswell Crags. A dark shadow slipped away from the cave mouth and into the surrounding bushes as they arrived.

'What was that!' Magda cried. 'Was it a wolf? Has it harmed my father?'

'Hush!' Tom said. 'Wolves have never attacked us yet, though I did feel that someone was watching us when I was here before. This is a very strange and ancient place.'

'And still you left my Father alone?'

'I had no choice, love, and though there may be others taking refuge in the caves, I felt sure that they would be more fearful than us. They certainly kept themselves well hidden.'

'I hope you're right.'

They found John shivering and talking to himself, half-awake and half-asleep, but he seemed to be unharmed. He did not recognise them, ignoring their presence and continuing to shake. 'I saw her,' he muttered. 'Grey . . . eyes like fire! Wouldn't go!'

Tom quickly got a fire going and brought water from the lake that filled the valley bottom, setting it to boil. Magda found it difficult to remember Marian's instructions and hard to stay calm.

'Where to start, where to start?' she muttered.

'Clean the wound first,' Tom reminded her.

'All right!' she snapped.

She bathed and poulticed her father's wounded leg, though it had swollen badly and turned dark purple. She fed him sips of the Forestwife's famous fever mixture, but the big man continued to shiver and shake.

'Wrap him up.' Tom suggested.

It was only when they had piled rugs on him to sweat the sickness away that at last Magda took breath herself and lay back to rest, leaning against Tom.

No sooner had she relaxed and got herself warm and

comfortable than her body stiffened with a sudden tightness that pulled at her stomach. 'What was that, sweetheart?' Tom asked.

Magda stared up at him, wide-eyed and alarmed. 'Perhaps, after all, I should not have come,' she whispered. Then her stomach cramped again, so that she could do nothing but gasp at the power of it.

'Is it the child?' Tom asked.

'Aye,' she growled. 'Think so! Must be!'

Tom hesitated for a moment, but then he carefully moved aside and propped her up against a rug, protecting her back from the wall of the cave. Calmly he rolled up his sleeves and set the pot to boil once again, feeding small sticks into the glowing embers of their fire. Magda opened her mouth to ask him what he thought he was doing, but another cramp made her shut it tight and grunt instead.

Tom threw his small meat knife into the pot, then pulled loose one of the bindings that tied the breeks about his legs. He threw that into the pot along with the knife.

Magda gasped again as her belly cramped. Then as it subsided once more, she groaned. 'Not here! I'm not having my birthing here without Marian! You must take me back! You must go and fetch her.'

'I'm not leaving you and here will be fine,' Tom told her.

'But father . . . he needs looking after?'

'We have done all we can for him for the moment. What he needs now is rest.'

'Yes, but you cannot . . .'

'Oh yes I can,' Tom told her, smiling. 'It would not be the first time that I have acted as midwife. When you were a little babe and I lived with Marian, I helped with many a birthing. 'Twas long ago, but I do not forget. I know exactly what to do.'

Another birth pang came and prevented her from arguing more. Tom piled heaps of straw at her back, then he settled himself behind her, soothing and supporting her so that she could almost crouch upright. ''Twill not be long I'd guess,' he whispered. 'The cramps are coming fast. You are lucky!'

'I should blasted well hope it won't be long!' Magda snarled at him. 'And I don't call it lucky! You can damned well think you're lucky, to be sitting there behind and not growling here in front! You are lucky that I can't get up and thump you one!'

'Hush!' he told her firmly. 'Save your breath for getting the child out!'

'I'll save my breath for spitting in your face!' she cried. Then the sharpness of the pain took her by surprise, and an urgent downward movement made her want to start to push the child out. 'Coming . . . it's coming! Can't stop it!'

'I knew it would not take long,' he said.

Magda bellowed noisily, but the child slipped smoothly out into the world. Tom was so busy, tying the cord and cutting it, then cleaning and wrapping the child to keep it warm that he did not know that he was watched. The wild sounds of Magda's growls and groans had brought them small and nervous visitors, curiosity overcoming fear. At last Tom handed the struggling bundle to Magda.

'A beautiful strong girl,' he told her.

They both looked up startled as light pattering laughter and clapping came from the cave mouth. Magda clutched her baby to her fearfully for a moment. 'Who's there?' she cried.

There was silence for a moment, but then they saw a small face with eyes that glistened in the light of their fire. Another face came into view, and another. Six small ragged children crept towards the warmth and glow.

Tom and Magda looked at each other. 'Were you there all the time?' Tom asked.

The children nodded. 'Aye, we were.'

'Did you see my baby born?' Magda demanded.

The children nodded again and though they were clearly still frightened they pushed each other forwards, holding out thin hands towards the fire's warmth. They were bare-footed, their flesh blue with cold and terribly skinny.

'Where are your mothers?' Magda asked.

'King's men . . . got her,' was the tremulous reply.

'And your father?'

'Got him too!'

'Have you been living in the caves alone?' Tom asked.

The children shivered and nodded. 'Frightened of the big man!'

'He talks and shouts to nobody!'

'He's my father, you needn't be frightened of him. Give

them bread,' Magda said as she rocked her child. Tom searched in the baggage that they'd brought from Barnsdale and found some of Marian's fresh-baked, grainy bread. The children tore it apart, devouring it, whimpering with delight.

Magda leant back against the cave wall, exhausted, watching the children eating so hungrily. 'Well,' she sighed. 'If you saw my baby born, then that makes you her new brothers and sisters, don't you think?'

'Aye. Brothers and sisters,' they answered, smiling at last.

Tom sat down beside his wife and child, putting his arms about them both. 'You wanted children,' he said. 'Have you got enough now?'

Magda kissed him. 'I think I have,' she said smiling. Then suddenly a great bubble of mirth welled up in her chest and she clutched at her sore stomach as they both leant back against the cold cave wall and laughed.

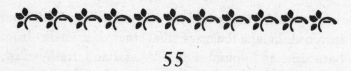

55

The Gift of Making People Happy

When the first rays of sharp winter sunlight crept into the cave, John opened his eyes. He was warm and calm, the feverish shaking gone. He looked about him and thought he must be dreaming for there was Tom slumped in the curving back corner of the cave, his arms wrapped about Magda. They both slept deeply, but beside Magda lay a small bundle of soft woven lamb's-wool, that moved and wriggled.

John raised himself onto his elbow, gritting his teeth for his leg was still stiff and swollen. He stared about him at the six children, now warmly wrapped in Marian's rugs, sleeping soundly in a gently snoring heap, beside the dying embers of the fire. He turned smiling back to Magda, then laughed out loud; from the small bundle came a tiny tightly clenched fist that seemed to salute him cheerily. A small hungry cry followed.

Magda opened her eyes and stirred. She pulled herself up, a little awkwardly. 'Well father,' she said. 'You look a lot better now.'

'And it seems that your family has grown, daughter. It has grown quite a lot.'

Magda bent to pick up the small wailing bundle with the flailing fists as Tom stirred. 'You'd best meet your new granddaughter,' she said. 'We're calling her Eleanor after Marian's mother.'

John laughed again, delighted. 'Listen to her howl! Look at the strength of her little punching fists. Something tells me we have a future Forestwife here.'

The happy parents smiled down at Eleanor.

John turned, looking out towards the round shape of the cave mouth, lightening now as the sun rose. 'I must have been dreaming,' he said, 'but I thought I saw an aged she-wolf, here in the cave with me.'

Magda gasped. 'I knew we saw a wolf,' she said. 'I saw it slip away as we came.'

'Don't look so fearful, daughter,' said John. 'Perhaps I did see it. The creature looked straight at me with eyes golden and bright as fire but then turned her back on me, settling down by the cave mouth. I must have been crazy with the sickness but I swear it seemed for all the world as though she were guarding me.'

Magda fell silent and wondering, remembering Marian's story of her mother's wolf spirit in the woods. She hugged the new little Eleanor tightly in her arms, rocking her gently back and forth. 'Thank you Old One,' she whispered.

Back in the Forestwife's clearing the weather had turned so bitterly cold that each morning brought new deaths, not from wounds or starvation but simply from cold. It troubled Marian greatly that these people should be losing their lives for the need of warmth.

The day after Magda had gone Marian took Brigit and Gerta with her to raid the empty convent of the Magdalen. Brigit did not like the idea much. 'The sisters are our friends,' she protested.

Marian smiled as she strode through the icy paths. 'You do not know Mother Veronica as well as I,' she said. 'If they were here they'd give us their last scrap of food, their last warm rug. And I know where they keep their cloaks and the warm woollen habits that they weave and stitch so carefully.'

'Are we going to steal nuns' clothes?' Brigit was still worried.

Gerta put her arm about her. 'Believe me, honey. This is what the nuns would want, if they could see the ragged folk who shelter with the Forestwife. Their cloaks and habits will save many lives and without them there'll be more frozen corpses to bury in the morning.'

Marian knew the small convent building well and it was easy to remove the neat stack of woven nuns' clothing that had been prepared for next winter's use. Gerta had been right, for the following morning brought no deaths and for once Philippa did not have to get out her spade. The strange sight of old men and little children wrapped in nun's veils and habits made everyone smile.

Robert and James returned to Barnsdale in the middle of January with others who'd fought with them. They found the clearing quiet and organised.

'You have done well,' Robert stared about him at the orderly queues for food, the careful, industrious stacking of firewood. 'I dreaded to find it a smoking ruin like so many that we've seen.'

'Have they punished the people enough?' Marian asked. 'Have they given up their murderous task yet?'

Robert shook his head, his face grim. 'They head up north towards the borderlands, too fast and too many of them for us to follow. We have lost many friends. We are weary and bruised. Mother Veronica is returning to the convent; the sisters are badly in need of a rest. We wonder now what will happen when they return south, as they must eventually do.'

'Do the rebel barons fight back?' Marian asked.

Robert put his arm about her. 'Some do, some give in at the first sight of so many mercenaries, all well-armed. Pontefract's lord has surrendered to the king, and York and Richmond. They say Robert de Ros still holds out at Helmsley.'

'His serfs and peasants will suffer whichever way,' Marian said bitterly.

The men stayed in the clearing, licking their wounds, resting and feeding, though Marian's hard won stocks of food were beginning to dwindle. In the dark evenings they sat about the fires talking and fretting and making plans. Marian clung to Robert in the long nights, knowing this momentary peace could not last for long. A terrible quiet and sense of misery seemed to settle about the place, even though the deaths grew fewer. It was only the happy return of Magda and Tom towards the end of the month that broke through the gloom. Everyone was amazed and cheered that she should come back with not one child, but seven. John's leg still troubled him and Marian did her best, but even she could not remove the arrowhead.

Magda insisted that little Eleanor must have a naming feast and no sooner was she back than she sent the men off to make a swift raid on Sherwood. They returned with a cart piled high with deer carcasses.

'The wardens run in all directions,' Tom told them. 'Starvation makes the most law abiding reckless. The deer vanish from beneath their very noses.'

'Aye,' said Robert, smiling grimly. 'But we hear that the Sheriff has sent messengers to the King, begging him send a gang of his best trained men to put a stop to it.'

'And do you think the King will do it?' Magda asked.

Robert shrugged his shoulders. 'The Sheriff is no rebel baron, that's for sure. He's supported the King throughout. He'll find out soon if the King is loyal to him or not!'

'And we hope not!' chuckled John.

'Brig's Night can be my little Eleanor's name feast,' Magda told them. 'And Peterkin is one year old, he must have his birthday celebration. Brig more than answered my prayers for a child, and we've had no Christmas, no mumming, no dancing. We must not let Brig's Night pass in silence.'

Marian hesitated. 'Well, we have plenty of venison to roast, but little ale to drink.'

Magda was in full spate and there was no stopping her. 'We don't need drink to make ourselves a feast. There's plenty of wood stacked and charcoal. We can celebrate with fire and dancing. Father can play his pipe and James can make a new drum from deer hide.'

Marian could not help but smile. 'What do you think, John? Is this giddy daughter of yours right? She's got it all worked out!'

Suddenly everyone was roused and laughing and fetching wood to build a big bonfire. They built it in the open space before the great oak: the trysting tree.

So Magda got her Brig's Night celebration, and they had a fine bonfire and ate and danced and sang until they were all warm and cheerful. Brigit sat quietly on the doorsill of the new hut watching them with little Peterkin wriggling in her lap.

Tom saw the sadness in her and remembered that Brig's Night had brought her mother's death as well as Peterkin's birth. 'Will you not dance with me?' he begged, sitting down beside her. 'Magda will look after Peterkin for a while.'

Brigit smiled sadly, but shook her head.

'Your mother would not want to see you sad on your brother's birthday. Now tell me? Would she want that?'

Brigit gave a great sigh and shook her head again.

'Magda!' Tom called. 'Come take the birthday boy while I dance with his sister.'

'I've been making something for him,' Magda cried, as she came over to them, little Eleanor tucked into one arm. 'We've nowt to give but love and kisses and . . .' she brought out from behind her back, a little wreath of mistletoe. She crowned his curly head with it. 'Come on, all of you,' she cried. 'All the brothers and sisters. We'll do a special birthday dance for Peterkin.'

Then the cave children followed her, snatching up each other's hands, while Magda took the birthday boy up into her other arm and jogged gently around the fire, her arms full of babies, singing:

> 'Mistletoe for happiness,
> Mistletoe for luck,
> Mistletoe for a fine little man,
> The sweetest little duck!'

Peterkin laughed and chortled, his cheeks rosy in the fire-glow. His sister danced happily with Tom, keeping a watchful eye on her brother in case he tired.

Marian danced with James and then John, though she was saddened to see him limping awkwardly. It was only later when the fire was beginning to burn down that she went to Robert. The brief happiness that was all around was so bittersweet, once she'd wrapped her arms around Robert's neck she wanted desperately to keep him locked there, chained to her forever.

At last, as their feet slowed, and they began to wander exhausted to their beds, a strange distant honking started up in the woodland nearby. For a moment the revellers grew quiet and fearful but then Gerta roused herself from dozing by the Forestwife's doorsill, crying out, 'I know that sound! I know it well!'

She struggled to her feet crying 'Chuck! Chuck! Chuck!' and clapping her hands. To everyone's delight her old grey gander came waddling out from the bushes, still flapping and honking, a neat procession of geese following meekly behind. Everyone cheered and that made him flap and honk more than ever.

Marian went to hug Magda as they returned to their huts. 'This was all your doing,' she said. 'It's done us more good than the most precious medicine money could buy. You'll make a fine Forestwife, Magda. You have a very special gift; the gift of making people happy.'

'It's been a fine night indeed,' Robert agreed quietly. 'But tomorrow we return to shooting practice and sharpening our knives.'

56

The King Rides South

In the third week of February the news they'd dreaded arrived. Will Stoutley galloped through the woods from Langden with Isabel and Philippa following, driving a cart. It was crammed full of the very youngest and oldest Langden folk and two mothers with tiny babies in their arms.

'They're coming back again,' Will told them. 'The King rides south from Scarborough, but his men swarm all over the north in murderous gangs. Can you take care of those who cannot fight?'

'Yes,' Marian agreed. 'They'll have to camp out in the cold but at least they should be safe here.'

'I must hurry back,' Isabel insisted. 'We mean to be ready for them this time. Philippa's man has worked like a slave to produce arrow heads and knives.'

'Aye, and you'll not be alone,' Robert vowed. At once he was a bundle of energy, striding about the clearing, barking out orders and gathering weapons together.

The men left for Langden in twos and threes, as soon

as they were ready. At dusk Marian looked up from settling the newcomers and making them as comfortable as she could. 'Where are the men?' she asked Magda, looking about the clearing.

'Gone to Langden! Did you not know?'

'Has Robert gone?' she asked.

Magda nodded.

'He never said goodbye!' Marian whispered, suddenly weepy.

'It is only to Langden that they've gone,' said Magda, surprised at her distress.

'Aye,' Marian frowned, pulling herself together and laughing. 'Only to Langden, and anyway when did he ever say goodbye?'

The numbers of those who took refuge in the Forestwife's clearing grew over the next few days, and once again the women had to treat burns and wounds and dig more graves beyond the yew tree grove. Just as mercilessly as before, the wolfpack harried the villages and hamlets of Barnsdale, leaving death and ruin in their path. Sister Rosamund and the younger nuns took to the road again, giving what comfort they could, but this time Mother Veronica stayed behind with two of the other oldest nuns who were just too sick to leave their beds.

Marian's days were so frantically full of bandaging, poulticing, cauterising wounds and mixing herbs that she scarce knew what day it was and fell exhausted to sleep for a few hours each night. She was up at dawn one morning, wrapped in one of the nun's warm cloaks, taking round drinks and checking who had survived the cold night when she heard the familiar stamping rhythm of Rambler's hooves.

'I love to hear that sound!' she murmured, remembering how Tom had first come to her as a desperate, fearful child. And here he was now, husband to Magda and a brave and resourceful man that they all depended on.

Marian went out to meet him, smiling and hoping for better news but Tom's face was grim.

'What now?' she whispered.

'You must come with me!' Tom gasped.

'Why?' she cried.

'Get your bundles and herbs. Robert's wounded.'

'Where is he?'

'At the convent,' Tom was impatient with her questions and she saw that his eyes were wet with tears. 'John and I carried him there. We've had a great fight for Langden and chased the wolfpack off towards Nottingham. But Robert's got a sword slash, and we've taken him to the convent.'

'Why there?'

'We dare not stay at Langden. Though the wolfpack may be puzzled, the Sheriff will surely guess who the Hooded Man is who's defended Langden so fiercely.'

'But why did you not bring him here?'

Tom shook his head with sorrow. 'I doubt he'd have made it. There's no time to waste. Mother Veronica does her best, but says you must come at once and bring your herbs . . . she says bring all your herbs!'

Marian dropped the jug that she carried, her stomach

lurched, then turned to the heaviness of lead as the picture came into her mind of Agnes scrubbing washing at the blood red spring.

'All the herbs! All the herbs!' she muttered as she turned and ran back to the cottage, Tom following close behind. She snatched up her bundles and medicines, hesitating only for a moment before reaching up to the high shelf to take down the forbidden herbs. Tom spoke quickly to Magda, blowing her and the babe a kiss, then, without further ado, he pulled Marian up behind him onto Rambler's wide saddle and turned to leave. As he urged his horse to a canter Marian twisted around seeing Magda's white worried face in the misty morning. She stood by the doorsill with Eleanor in her arms and Brigit clinging to her side; little Peterkin pulling himself up onto wobbly legs.

'I should have given her the girdle,' she muttered pulling the stolen nun's cloak that she still wore tightly about her.

John was looking out anxiously for them as they galloped up to the quiet woodland convent. Marian leapt down from the horse and ran to him.

'How is he?'

John shook his head and looked away. Another wave of sickness swam through Marian's belly at the misery she saw in his eyes. But John himself was bleeding once again for the old wound in his thigh had opened up. Through force of habit she put her fingers gently down to touch the place.

John pushed her gently away. 'Nay! Go to him!' he insisted. 'Tom and I stand guard!'

Robert had been put to rest in the Prioress's own bed. The old nun was kneeling beside him, stoop-backed, her lips moving in silent prayer.

'Robert!' Marian marched in full of a sudden, senseless, bitter anger. 'You went off to Langden, and you never said goodbye.'

The wounded man stirred slightly and Mother Veronica pulled herself upright, reaching to kiss Marian's cheek. 'I'm sorry Marian, so sorry,' she whispered. 'I fear that now is truly your time to say goodbye.'

'No! I have brought my herbs and all my medicines!' Marian cried.

Mother Veronica bent down slowly and pulled back the blood-soaked covering, revealing a deep and gaping wound in Robert's chest. 'Your herbs cannot mend that, honey,' she said gently. 'No Forestwife, however skilled, however devoted, could mend that dreadful hurt.'

'I must, I must mend him,' Marian cried, dropping down on her knees beside him.

Robert stirred again and groaned. His face was grey and his mouth tightened into a terrible grimace.

'Not this time, sweetheart,' he hissed. 'Not this time. Just hold me tight?'

Tears would not come, though Marian wished that they would. She could feel them there inside her, filling up a deep, tight well of burning anger in her chest. She took hold of Robert's hand and held it for a moment, then put her face down onto the pillow beside him so that she could stroke his scarred cheek.

'I can ease the pain,' she whispered.

Robert nodded. Marian got up and started sorting through her bundles. Mother Veronica brought a cup and poured water from a jug, so that Marian could mix a sleeping potion. As she started to feed it carefully to Robert there came thuds and the sounds of shouting outside. Then all at once came the thunder of a horse, galloping away fast.

'You stay here with him,' the old nun told Marian. She hobbled through the passage and Marian could hear her speaking fast and low with John. She returned grim faced and breathless.

'What?' Marian asked.

'The blasted Sheriff',' she told them, crossing herself as she swore. 'The Sheriff and a gang of King John's men. They've surrounded our convent and Tom has dashed away on Rambler to try to bring us help from Langden.'

'Do they attack?' Marian asked.

Mother Veronica laughed bitterly. 'They seem to be hesitating. I believe they're afraid to rush fully armed into a holy place. They're more afraid for their souls than of the Sheriff's wrath, but they will not leave us in peace— not if they think they've got the Hooded One in their sights! John takes aim at them through the window and he's killed two men who moved towards the door. His stock of arrows is small but he has shown that he will not miss his target.'

57

The Last Arrow

It was clear that Robert could hear and understand for he groaned, making as though to get up but Marian pushed him down. 'Keep still!' she hissed, none too gently. Her mind was racing and her heart pounding like a hunted rabbit. Sharp cracks came as the Sheriff's men kicked down the low wooden close that kept the sisters' poultry safe.

'Sweetheart,' Robert muttered, groping for her hand. 'Give me your special herbs . . . the forbidden ones.'

Marian shook her head. 'No,' she cried, her voice hoarse and choked.

'Yes,' he insisted, struggling to make his words clear. 'It's time. The time has come. Don't let them take me! Death . . . it does not frighten me . . . not half as much, as to be made their prisoner.'

Marian looked despairingly up at the old nun. Mother Veronica turned away, her face full of pity, tears rolling steadily down her wrinkled cheeks. 'There is naught else that you can do for him, honey,' she shook her head.

With trembling hands Marian fumbled through her bundles, until she found the one that she sought; deadly nightshade, all carefully tied in purple cloth. With trembling resolution she untied the bundle and tipped the dark powder into the cup, swirling it about.

'It might taste bitter, sweetheart,' she spoke through gritted teeth, supporting Robert's head and lifting the cup to his lips.

Though he shuddered at the taste, he drank deeply, then lay back. 'Hold me,' he whispered.

Mother Veronica turned away and left them alone, she went stumbling down the passage towards John. Marian climbed up onto the bed beside Robert, and wrapped her arms about him gently stroking his head.

'I hear the sweetest sound,' he murmured. 'I hear the rush and lap of the sea.'

Marian tried to smile, but a deep sigh came instead that turned into a sob. 'Do you remember Baytown, sweetheart?' she whispered, her eyes spilling over with tears at last. 'Do you remember how we lived together on the cliff tops there, high above the sea.'

'How could I forget it?' Robert answered, his face relaxed and smiling now. 'For it was there by the sea that the beautiful Green Lady first came to sleep with me.'

'We were happy in that strange, storm-battered place.' Marian made her mouth work, though her lips were stiff and unwilling. 'We should have stayed there and lived quietly together.'

'I would not have had it different, my love,' he whispered. 'I am happy now. All pain has gone. It is only the bitterness of leaving you that makes me sad.'

Suddenly Marian was sitting up and reaching for the cup. 'It will not be goodbye,' she said. 'We shall not be parted.'

She gripped the wooden cup that was still half full of the deadly powdered berries and raised it to her lips, but Robert saw and understood. He lurched upright and smashed it out of her grasp. 'No!' he shouted, then slumped back onto the bed, as dark liquid splashed over her kirtle and down onto the floor.

Mother Veronica came hurrying back at the shout and quickly understanding what had happened, bent to take Marian into her arms. 'No!' she told her firmly. 'Not you too! He has gone and you cannot help him any more. You've got to save yourself!'

But Marian pushed her away and struggled to her feet. She looked down at the motionless figure on the bed and saw that the old nun was right. Robert had gone, all breathing ceased, his face grey-blue and still contorted from the angry shout.

A thunderclap of furious rage exploded in Marian's head and she stared wildly around her at the sparsely furnished convent room with its crucifix and bare scrubbed floor. There at the bottom of the bed was Robert's bow and an almost empty quiver thrown carelessly down beside it, just one arrow left.

'No,' Mother Veronica cried. Seeing where she looked and fearing the madness in her eyes.

'Oh yes!' Marian snarled. 'Oh yes!' She swooped down upon the weapon and snatched up the arrow.

She strode down the passageway and before John could understand or do anything to stop her she was out in the bright sunlight of the woodland. She marched, arrow notched, bow drawn, out into the middle of the broken close.

The men were hidden amongst the trees, for fear of John's sharp aim, but they were shocked at the sight of the furious tear-stained woman wrapped in a nun's cloak, her clothes marked with blood and a weapon in her hands.

A horse moved forwards, its rider so amazed and stunned that he forget to control his beast. 'Can it be true?' he murmured. 'The Hooded One a woman?'

Marian caught the glint of sunlight on his golden chain and laughed. She knew that gold chain, it bore the badge of office of the Sheriff of Nottingham. Though her hands still shook Marian took aim.

'One last arrow for the Sheriff,' she cried and let it fly.

'No!' John shouted.

'Yes!' Marian howled with delight, as the arrow sank deep into the Sheriff's chest. The man lurched forwards, the surprised look on his face turning to horror.

Then Marian dropped the bow and staggered back-wards. She neither saw nor cared where the answering arrows came from but John leapt up with a bellow of despair as six arrows thudded into her body. She sank quietly down to the ground.

Though arrows rained all around him, John burst out from the convent doorway like an angry bear, his face white with rage and wet with tears. He did not hear the distant sound of galloping horses but whisked arrows out fast from his quiver and sent them flying like bolts of lightning. At each movement of a branch, at each glint of a weapon, at each gasp of fright, he sent an arrow whistling in that direction.

'Come on, come on,' he cried. 'Take me as well! You have taken my best and dearest friends. You can have me too!'

The sound of hooves grew louder and the air was filled with shouts. Still John moved steadily on towards the spot where Marian lay until at last he threw his weapon down and bent to gather her body up into his arms.

He expected arrows to thud into his own great frame but they did not come. At last he looked up and saw that the mercenaries had fled, leaving the Sheriff's body lying beneath the trampling feet of his frightened horse. Out from the bushes came Tom leading Rambler, followed by Isabel, Will, Philippa, James and Sister Rosamund. They stood there grim and silent as John wept.

Philippa moved forwards and sank down onto her knees beside her friend's body.

'Agnes was right,' she murmured. 'Agnes was always right!'

Bending over Marian, she reached out and carefully broke off the arrow shafts.

Mother Veronica came slowly from the convent, clinging for support to the frame of the door. 'Bring her inside,' she said quietly. 'Put her down beside Robert, that is where she wanted to be.'

* * *

They buried the Sheriff in an unmarked grave, in the convent's sacred ground. Though John complained, Mother Veronica insisted that it was done. 'I doubt that it will bring us trouble,' she said. 'Those with him will go running back to their pay master, the King, understanding naught of what has happened here. We nuns are Christians,' she said. 'And we are decent folk! We are not like them!'

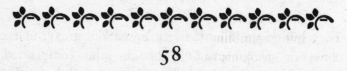

58

Those who Light Up the Dark Woods

It was at dusk that a small procession set out from the convent. John, James, Tom and Philippa carefully carried the bodies of their friends, lying together in a new-made litter. Isabel walked ahead with Will, carrying flaming torches to light the way. Mother Veronica and the nuns followed behind. They set off walking slowly through the woods, heading for the Forestwife's clearing in the gathering gloom. As they passed the coal-diggers' huts close to the convent, some of the ragged, dusty children stood silently by a glowing wood fire, watching out for them. There came the sounds of their soft voices whispering, hushed and reverent.

'They come, mother, they come.'

'The Hooded One is here and the Forestwife.'

Then out from the crumbling hovels came the coal-diggers and their wives with babies strapped to their backs. Old men and women hobbled out on sticks and each of them, both young and old, carried a rush-light that they lit at their fire.

John was moved to tears once more and stopped, his huge frame trembling. 'It is too much, too much to bear.'

Philippa took his hand in hers. 'We are not alone,' she told him. 'You see, they tell us that we are not alone. It is not just us who have lost our dearest friends.'

John's wounded thigh bled slowly.

'You do not need to help us carry them,' Tom whispered. 'There are plenty of us to do the work.'

John shook his head and moved forwards. 'Nay, I must do it,' he insisted. 'This night shall never come again.'

The procession moved on, and the coal-diggers quietly followed behind. As they passed beneath the trees shadows lengthened and the woodlands grew darker with every step they took. But though the night sky turned to black above them, a new, flickering source of light began to grow and spread all about.

Out from the charcoal burners' huts came more ragged workers. Mothers with children in their arms and on their backs; strong men with scarred, disfigured faces, missing fingers, maimed hands; hooded lepers stumbling behind, keeping their distance; each and every one of them carrying a starlike rush-light. Their numbers grew and grew.

The word had gone ahead and by the time they reached the Forestwife's clearing, the darkest night was lit by thousands of rush-lights. The circling yew tree grove thronged with silent crowds that moved respectfully back as the procession arrived and went towards the burial ground.

Philippa and Tom set about digging the grave at once,

for they feared angry retribution when the remainder of the wolfpack returned to the King. Such retribution could be terrible and desecration of an outlaw's body might serve as dire warning to those who thought they might rebel too.

Clouds cleared and a bright moon at last lit the clearing. There were many to help with the work. They made John sit with Magda, who refused to stay inside, insisting on sitting out there, beside the grave, her child wrapped in her arms. So father and daughter sat close together, tears coursing down their cheeks. They watched as they saw a deep pit grow that was wide enough for two.

'Agnes gave warning,' Magda sobbed. 'Agnes gave warning and I feared for myself, not them.'

'Nothing we could have done would have prevented it,' John told her.

Then suddenly Magda was anxious that all should be done well and properly. 'Primroses,' she cried. 'Fetch leaves to put beneath them,' she sobbed. 'And primroses to sprinkle on top.'

The distant sound of howling wolves could be heard as Gerta and Brigit organised a gang of young folk who rushed to obey Magda's wish. A great hunt took place in the moonlight and children emerged from the shadowy foliage with bundles of fresh picked primroses in their hands.

At last they prepared to gently lay Robert and Marian side by side to rest.

'Wait,' said John. 'There is something we must do.'

He bent with trembling hands to loosen the beautiful woven girdle from Marian's waist: the symbol of the Forestwife. He wept afresh for as he lifted it the girdle fell apart where the arrows had cut through the intricately woven bands.

Tears poured down his face. 'All is wrong!' he cried. 'This was meant for you, daughter.'

Magda stared. She put out her hand, still cradling baby Eleanor, and took hold of the three separate strands. She looked puzzled for a moment, but then she smiled through her tears. 'No,' she said. 'I understand. I think I understand. This is right. Marian knew it should be like this. There is not to be one Forestwife, but three.'

The people all around them gasped when they heard her, but Magda went on, growing in conviction. She turned to Brigit, who stood at her side, calm and helpful as ever, Peterkin sleeping on her back. 'One is for you,' she said and quickly fastened the still beautiful loose strand about the girl's slim waist.

Brigit opened her mouth to protest but then closed it as Magda solemnly kissed her brow. Then Magda turned to Gerta who stood there on her other side.

'What?' the old woman protested. 'For me? You want to give it to me?'

'Yes,' said Magda. 'Your kindness and wisdom has helped us through so much and now we stand in greater need of it than ever. Will you stay here with us in the clearing, and comfort all those who are full of sorrow as you have been doing?'

A ripple of approval ran through the watching crowd

as the old woman fastened the strand about her waist with shaking fingers.

'Now it's your turn,' Gerta said. 'Come help me, Brigit, and together we three shall try to be as good a Forestwife as she who we have lost this day.'

So they tied the third strand around Magda's still slightly thickened waist and little Eleanor's foot somehow got tied up in it too. There were smiles and whispers went flying through the crowd as they released her.

'That little one shall be Forestwife too, some day.'

Then more murmurs of approval came. 'Look at them. It must be right.'

'The Old One, the Mother and the Maid.'

'It is meant to be!'

Then John stooped once more and took from Robert's lifeless body, the worn and faded hood that he had always worn. He held it up, like a crown, so that everyone could see.

'We called him the Green Man,' he said. 'He was young and strong and fearless when he danced at our May Day Feast. But then, when bitter trouble came to us, he led our fight and we called him the Hooded One. His spirit and his fight for justice must not be allowed to die.'

He swung round and held out the hood to Tom.

'But you . . . you should take his place, if any *can*,' Tom protested.

John shook his head. 'I am old and sick and weary of it all. You are the one. This wound of mine troubles me sore. It is too late for me.'

'No!' Magda cried out. 'We will nurse you and make you strong again. Brigit shall mix up potions and I shall make you live for my child.'

'Dearest daughter,' he said, taking her into his arms. 'There is naught that you can do to heal this slow and aching wound. I am so happy to have seen this strong child of yours, but you must let me go now. I wish to return to the mist-filled valley of Hathersage, the place where I was born.'

Magda thought she could not bear so much sorrow all at once, but Gerta spoke softly to her. 'You must be strong and let him go. You must let a bird fly free,' she said. 'That is the only way that it can be happy.'

Magda sighed and gritted her teeth. She looked up from her father to Tom. 'Yes. You must take Robert's hood, my husband,' she told him. 'You must now be the Hooded One.'

'Yes, yes,' agreement came from all around.

Tom kissed Magda, then bowed his head and allowed John to fasten the hood around his neck.

The children came forwards and threw their flowers into the grave, covering the two who lay there together. Magda clung to John, while Tom and Philippa took up their spades and filled the primrose-scented space with earth, and piled it high.

As the first light fingers of dawn touched the dark woods, a lithe shape emerged from the undergrowth. A male wolf stretched and yawned, then shook himself so that small droplets of dew sprayed the grey stones and bracken all about him. He turned, giving a deep-throated cry. It was answered by a sharp, yipping sound, and out from the shadows of the undergrowth came a she-wolf.

The rays of the sun grew in strength, reaching in amongst the bushes and branches. The purple greys of night lifted, patterning dull clumps of grass with bright green and yellow streaks. Wood pigeons started their gentle cooing, greeting each other and greeting the morning. The she-wolf nuzzled at the roots, snuffing the earth and the damp air, her ears twitching as she picked up the faint gurgling sounds of water. She turned to her companion and licked his face, then gave him a playful nip, leaping high over his shoulders and past him, leading the way towards the plashing of a fast-running stream.

Water rushed over the rocks and poured down between two stones, making a waterfall that filled a sparkling, mossy-edged pool. The two wolves ran fast towards it, splashing into its swirling waters, drinking deeply.

As they drank, the light lifted further, turning the budding primroses that grew all around the pool to gleaming gold, and when they'd drunk their fill they climbed out of the water and shook themselves again sniffing the faintly flower-scented air. Then yapping joyfully, they raced ahead, leaping over dew-laden grass and foliage, following their own path through the awakening spring woods.

Author's Note

From an early age I have been fascinated by myths and legends. Stories of King Arthur, Merlin and Morgan le Fay were full of romance and magic, but Robin Hood, champion of the common folk, was my favourite. I lived close to places associated with him, and the image of this ordinary man who fought against injustice appealed to me enormously. He was a hero that I could almost identify with, but it was natural as a girl to see myself more as Maid Marian: and she was usually locked up in a castle and needing to be rescued – being terribly brave about it, of course. What I really wanted was to imagine myself running through the forest, ready to do the rescuing.

My obsession with the People's Hero was revived when my youngest son became addicted to making bows and arrows, and the film 'Robin Hood Prince of Thieves' brought new interest in the stories. I was pleased that the film gave us a tougher version of Marian – and introduced a wonderful new character in Fannie – Little

John's wife. I felt that the idea of whole families living in the woods could be taken much further. Gradually an idea emerged for a book that would be much more of a Maid Marian story. I began to research the subject, visiting places linked with Robin Hood: Little John's Grave at Hathersage, the Major Oak in Sherwood Forest, Nottingham Castle, and Robin Hood's Bay in North Yorkshire, close to where I lived as a child.

One of the references to Robin Hood as a real man (Dodsworth, 1620) stated that he came from Bradfield Parish in Hallamshire (now Sheffield, where I live). This version told how he was accused of killing his stepfather, and fled to the woods, where he was helped by his mother, until he was discovered and outlawed.

I discovered, to my disappointment, that the earliest ballads contained no references to Marian; she seemed to have joined the merry men, along with Friar Tuck, in the sixteenth century. Although I had found a satisfying female character in Robin Hood's mother, Marian was central to my story idea and at one point I almost gave up the whole project.

However, I decided to turn my attention to more general women's history in England at the time of Richard I and then King John. This cheered me – I discovered that while many lords were going off to the crusades, taking their menservants and skilled craftsmen with them, the women left at home were taking charge of castles, manors, crafts and businesses. I was delighted to find that there were records of female outlaws. For example, Agnes, wife of John Sadeler of the village of Ramsley, was outlawed in 1386 for leading a rebellion against the manor. (See *Women in Medieval Life*, by Margaret Wade Labarge, published by Hamish Hamilton Ltd). This information gave me the idea for the character of Philippa and put my story back on course. I discovered Matilda de Braose and her family. Matilda was a real women who rebelled against King John and her story could not be left out.

Marian had become so important a part of the legend that she must remain the central character, but I felt that her story should represent the real lives of medieval women. I became interested in the rebellion that led to the charter that King John agreed and then revoked in 1215, later to become known as Magna Carta. I thought, if Robin Hood had been around at that time, how could he not have been involved?

Then a very different aspect came into question: in 1846 Thomas Wright put forward a theory that there was never a real Robin Hood, but that the stories represented a pre-Christian nature spirit and the human desire to be one with nature. Some writers have seen Robin Hood as a representation of the Green Man, an archetypal figure depicted in ancient carvings, with the face surrounded by leaves and vegetation. (See William Anderson and Clive Hick's book *Green Man* published by HarperCollins). Ancient Green Woman carvings do exist and they seemed to me to be the female equivalent of this ancient archetype. I discovered that others were thinking along the same lines. (See Chesca Potter's Afterword to *Robin Hood: Green Lord of the*

Wildwood, by John Matthews, Gothic Images Publications). Though I saw Marian and Robert very much as real people, I felt that this theme could add something of a magical atmosphere to the story.

I have taken from my research whatever interested me and ignored whatever I disliked. For example, I love the traditional theme of disguise, but the contest for the silver arrow leaves me yawning! The end result is a strange mixture of ideas from the very earliest Robin Hood stories, women's history and legends from my own locality.

Detailed reviews and an interview with me can be found on the website 'Robin Hood Bold Outlaw of Barnsdale and Sherwood', along with more information about Robin Hood and the legends. www.geocities.com/puckrobin/rh/

Theresa Tomlinson
February 2003-01-30
www.theresatomlinson.com